Praise for
GEIST

"Absorbing adventure that revels in both the creepy and the courageous."
—Gail Carriger, *New York Times* bestselling author of *Heartless*

"With its richly detailed world and wonderfully realized characters, *Geist* is one of the most vividly original books I've read this year." —Nalini Singh,
New York Times bestselling author of *Kiss of Snow*

"An incredibly rich story . . . rich in high action, rich in mystery, rich in characters, rich in ghosts. Absolutely not to be missed." —Barb Hendee, national bestselling coauthor of
Of Truth and Beasts

"Part of the entertainment in this novel is putting the pieces together to get a picture of the complicated political situation, the period (they have magical airships!) and the nature of the geists . . . Plenty of magic-blasting action keeps things lively for a rousing start to this new series." —*Locus*

"Philippa Ballantine has crafted a unique and engrossing tale with *Geist*. Memorable characters, multiple subplots and spot-on dialogue combined with some dramatic action scenes create a vivid and satisfying read . . . a promising start to a unique series." —*Fresh Fiction*

"In the tradition of greats like Margaret Weis and Robin Hobb, Philippa Ballantine has woven an excellent tale of fantasy, paranormal, black powder, steampunk goodness."
—*Geek Life*

"An intriguing blend of fantasy, paranormal and history."
—*Night Owl Paranormal*

Ace Books by Philippa Ballantine

GEIST
SPECTYR

SPECTYR

P H I L I P P A B A L L A N T I N E

ACE BOOKS, NEW YORK

THE BERKLEY PUBLISHING GROUP
Published by the Penguin Group
Penguin Group (USA) Inc.
375 Hudson Street, New York, New York 10014, USA
Penguin Group (Canada), 90 Eglinton Avenue East, Suite 700, Toronto, Ontario M4P 2Y3, Canada
(a division of Pearson Penguin Canada Inc.)
Penguin Books Ltd., 80 Strand, London WC2R 0RL, England
Penguin Group Ireland, 25 St. Stephen's Green, Dublin 2, Ireland (a division of Penguin Books Ltd.)
Penguin Group (Australia), 250 Camberwell Road, Camberwell, Victoria 3124, Australia
(a division of Pearson Australia Group Pty. Ltd.)
Penguin Books India Pvt. Ltd., 11 Community Centre, Panchsheel Park, New Delhi—110 017, India
Penguin Group (NZ), 67 Apollo Drive, Rosedale, Auckland 0632, New Zealand
(a division of Pearson New Zealand Ltd.)
Penguin Books (South Africa) (Pty.) Ltd., 24 Sturdee Avenue, Rosebank, Johannesburg 2196,
South Africa

Penguin Books Ltd., Registered Offices: 80 Strand, London WC2R 0RL, England

This is a work of fiction. Names, characters, places, and incidents either are the product of the author's imagination or are used fictitiously, and any resemblance to actual persons, living or dead, business establishments, events, or locales is entirely coincidental. The publisher does not have any control over and does not assume any responsibility for author or third-party websites or their content.

SPECTYR

An Ace Book / published by arrangement with the author

PRINTING HISTORY
Ace mass-market edition / July 2011

Copyright © 2011 by Philippa Ballantine.
Cover art by Jason Chan.
Cover design by Lesley Worrell.
Interior text design by Tiffany Estreicher.

ISBN: 978-0-441-02051-5

ACE
Ace Books are published by The Berkley Publishing Group,
a division of Penguin Group (USA) Inc.,
375 Hudson Street, New York, New York 10014.
ACE and the "A" design are trademarks of Penguin Group (USA) Inc.

PRINTED IN THE UNITED STATES OF AMERICA

10 9 8 7 6 5 4 3 2 1

For Dad and Mum.
You lit the fire and kept it burning.
Words of thanks are barely enough,
but they are all I have to give in return.

ACKNOWLEDGMENTS

Like Raed, I have many people on my ship without whom I would be stuck in port:

My navigator and agent, Laurie McLean, who is not only a fantastic business partner but also a brilliant mentor and friend. You told me this would happen, and I really should have believed you.

My quartermaster and editor, Danielle Stockley of Ace Books. She knows how to make sure things are where they should be, and what I really need on a journey.

The head of the press-gang, Brady McReynolds, one of Ace's marketing whizzes. Thanks for helping people find *Geist* in the sea of books.

My redoubtable first mate, Cathy, who has listened to my complaints and fears for nearly fifteen years. Though we are on different shores right now, I know the tides will soon bring us together again.

My captain, who provides advice, support and motivation. Also, you make me laugh when I really need it. You set sail with me, and I am looking forward to discovering what lies out there.

My marines on this ship, who are all my new friends and family in America: Jen, Elena, Linc, Mary-Ann, David and the card-night ladies.

My crew on the ship, who are, of course, my podcast listeners. Thank you for helping me row out from the shallows into deeper waters.

ONE

A Thing of Beauty

In the Imperial Palace Grand Duchess Zofiya slept on sheets of polished white satin in a grand bed painted and carved like a sailing ship. Around her gleamed the treasures of her brother's and father's dominions.

These, however, did not guarantee her a night of peaceful slumber. Her long black hair lay in a sweaty tangle, while her tawny limbs were twisted in the covers. Nightmares crashed through her head, breaking her famous calm in ways that would have surprised any of her Imperial Guard had they been privileged enough to witness it.

Finally Zofiya jerked awake, lurching upright in her bed with a half-swallowed scream. Her hand instinctively went to the medallion around her neck as she tried to control her rapid breathing.

The bedroom was nearly silent; there were only the fine curtains blowing in the wind, and far off in the corridor the sounds of the many clocks ticking away to themselves. That noise was familiar and calming; her brother had inherited a love of machinery from their father. Still, what she was not used to were nightmares. In this one a person had been killing Kal, and she had been unable to reach him in time.

Her brother the Emperor was a great man, but his sense of

personal safety was limited. He firmly believed that he had tamed this continent and the worst was behind them. Zofiya knew better.

Slipping from her elaborate bed, the Grand Duchess padded to the window and looked out over the sleeping city—not realizing that she had failed to let go of the medallion. Thousands of lights twinkled all over the lagoon. The bridges were reduced to a string of bright pearls. Even the slum areas of the Edge were smoothed to attractiveness by darkness and the occasional gleam of a streetlight. Directly below she could make out not only her own Imperial Guard at their posts but also the swathed forms of the soldiers from Chioma.

The delegation had been in the capital for a month, testing the waters for a marriage between the Emperor and Ezefia, daughter of the Prince of that distant principality. No promises had been made, but she knew Kal was entertaining the idea. The throne had to be secured quickly, and Onika, the Prince of Chioma, was fabulously wealthy.

Her brother, she knew, would have preferred the group marriage practiced in their homeland, Delmaire, but he was wise enough not to try to push that custom on the citizens of Arkaym. Change came slowly here, but it did occur. Take the city, for example. It was not as majestic as Toth, her father's capital, but it was pulling itself out of generations of misery and torment. All of which was her brother's doing. Yet there were plenty who wanted to stop him.

Zofiya clenched her fist on the curved edge of the medallion until it hurt. She had lost the one she brought from Delmaire a week before in the training ground. No amount of sifting the sand—which she had gotten the servants to do—had located it.

However, when she had come in that evening, this new one was lying on her pillow. It was not the same; there were five diamonds set in the snaking curve of stone that represented Hatipai's constantly moving nature, and it was larger than the one she had lost. Some aristocrat had probably had it made to curry favor.

In Court her faith was an open secret. The little gods were not persecuted, but they were figures of amusement and derision. Nearly a thousand years was a long time to hold on to faith in the face of derisive public opinion, but the sect of Hatipai that the Grand Duchess subscribed to had managed it. Though she kept her medallion tucked inside her clothes during daylight hours, she would not deny her goddess. If the people around Zofiya wanted to gossip, then she had no way of stopping them.

Kal knew of his sister's beliefs—though he dismissed them as superstitious nonsense. When the geists had come and the Otherside had poured in, most of the population had lost faith—including the royal family of Delmaire. Zofiya was made of sterner stuff.

Yet, now as she looked out over the city, her mind turned to the dark realities of the world—and most especially the events that had occurred under the ossuary.

"The Murashev." Zofiya shivered under her spider-silk nightdress, as if even mentioning the geistlord's name would bring its arrival. Only a month before, the creature had almost been brought forth into the heart of Vermillion—an event the city would not have survived. She had been at the secret briefing from the new Arch Abbot and had shared her brother's shock. "Hatipai, give us strength," she murmured.

That was when she heard it: a clatter of pure notes, like those from the bells of the Temple in Delmaire. She recalled them clearly, because even as a child she had spent much time there. The bells had been strung in long skeins across the doors so that each penitent who went in made them ring, high and sweet.

She heard the cluster of notes again. It was not the sound of one of the clocks in the hall. The Grand Duchess slipped on her coat, took her belt and scabbard from the chair close to her bed, strapped it on and went out to investigate. She had already dismissed her personal guards for the night. If trouble was going to come to one of the Imperial siblings, she wanted it to be her and not her brother.

Growing up in Delmaire, she had been used to the fact that she would always be the surplus child. Kal had wanted her to come to Arkaym, and their father had not protested. He had daughters enough to fill a royal barge—all of them far more compliant than her.

She stepped into a hallway lined with lush carpets woven

in red and yellow, the Imperial colors. The sound came again, and this time it could be clearly heard over the numerous clocks ticking gently to themselves on this floor. With one hand on her sword hilt, Zofiya went down the back stairs and out into the courtyard. The ringing had come from the garden. The warmth radiating from the goddess symbol spurred her on, through the mist-shrouded topiaries and flower beds. Finally she reached the walls of the palace. The bells rang a third time, so she found herself sneaking out of the postern gate and into the city itself.

The Grand Duchess was not frightened, even if she was only wearing her greatcoat and her nightclothes. She had her goddess with her. The warmth of the medallion and the sound of distant bells led her on. In bare feet she crossed over the Bridge of Gilt and into the Tinkers' Quarter. Under her brother's patronage, the Guild had grown in power, and many of the houses here were nearly as grand as those on the Imperial Island. Yet, Zofiya took no notice of fine architecture or well-tended gardens. Instead, she followed as bidden, until she reached a house at the end of Piston Street. The sound of bells now led her around the rear of the property to an open door. She paused for a moment, for the first time noticing the deep shadows that surrounded her. She almost had the impression that there were eyes moving within them. For an instant she considered how vulnerable she was, but then the tide of her faith washed back. She entered, walked confidently down the stairs and into the basement. Let the contents of the shadows look to themselves.

It smelled very strange here, musty and dank, but she stepped over the piles of soil, barely noticing her grubby feet, and toward a magnificent brass door. That such a thing would exist in the home of a Tinker Zofiya didn't question.

Inside she did pause, though. The corridor she was in was unlike any tradesman's house she'd ever seen. It was covered in frescos that rivaled decorations in her brother's palace. Neither did the theme of the artwork slip past her notice; it was something not often depicted. The Break—the arrival of the geists and the revelation of the Otherside. The Grand Duchess tilted her head and let one of her fingers trace the outline of the design.

Here was the population screaming and cowering as shapes stepped through the gap. Padding on a little farther, Zofiya found the rising of the dead and the arrival of the spirits to haunt their loved ones. Circles of rei led the innocent to their deaths. Spectyrs brought retribution on those who had wronged them.

A little gasp escaped her when she reached the final frame in the frieze. Here was displayed the Season of Supplication— the final nail in the coffin of faith. Believers of all religions were shown gathered around a central point, blood pouring from knees they had been on for weeks, while they raised their hands to the gods.

No salvation had come. And those that had been revered and trusted were ever after referred to as little gods. Zofiya felt tears well up, and she couldn't remember when that had last happened. Her goddess' Temple had at least survived. Many others had fallen into ruin when their followers abandoned them altogether.

Yet she had faith, she had belief, and she would never give up. The thought was warm and comforting. As she leaned against the frieze, she smiled softly. Something moved behind her hand, like the shift of a snake, smooth and sinuous under her palm.

Taking a step back, Zofiya watched as the ancient artwork flexed and twisted. The supplicants' self-inflicted wounds oozed blood, while fresh tears streamed from their eyes, rolled down the wall, and pattered on the floor. Above, the symbols of the gods boiled, gray and thick like thunderclouds, yet among them she recognized one. Hatipai. Her goddess' symbol gleamed gold and bright among the others.

The Grand Duchess' smile broadened as she reached out and touched it. Instantly she was filled with glory. Her head snapped back, and she let out a groan of pleasure that went right to her core. All physical delights paled in comparison to this one. No aristocrat or Prince could make her feel like this. The goddess was with her, and she was pleased that her daughter had held her faith when so many others faltered.

The symbol moved again, and Zofiya followed it, barely aware of the steps passing under her feet. Her deity whispered into her soul.

Together they went down deeper into the earth, two more flights of stairs, and then the frieze stopped at a blank wall of stone. Zofiya leaned forward and touched it. When the medallion grew hotter on her skin, the Grand Duchess was not surprised.

The walls were smooth white stone, fitted so tightly together she could not have slipped even her narrowest blade between them. Though she had no torch, Zofiya did not fear stumbling, for tiny weirstones embedded in the walls let off a cool blue light. She should have been afraid at this flagrant use of those dangerous power receptacles, but she knew the goddess would not let her acolyte fall. Beneath her fingers the gold symbol traveled on, and the Grand Duchess followed in her wake—feeling more content and calm than she ever had in her life.

The frieze had changed though. Now it showed only abstract forms, shapes of birds and animals—but nothing human. She would have stopped to examine them if she had been alone, but the goddess still held her dazzled.

She went on until she came to a small side room. Here the stone was polished to such a high sheen that Zofiya had to avert her eyes, while under her fingertips the symbol of Hatipai faded. The removal of the goddess was painful, but she did not cry.

Hatipai must have brought her here for a good reason. Shielding her eyes from the glare, Zofiya looked around. The chamber was bare of any furniture; the blank piece of stone that gleamed so brightly was the sole focus of the space. Something inside the Grand Duchess told her that to go forward armed and proud was not the thing to do. This was the goddess' place.

Taking off her sword belt and laying it by the door, Zofiya dropped to her knees and shuffled forward, mimicking the gestures of those long-ago penitents. Reaching the gleaming stone, she laid her fingers against it and bowed her head.

The light bloomed around her, so bright that even through closed eyelids it burned. When it faded, Zofiya risked opening them again.

The stone was transformed into the finest sheet of rock

crystal. Beyond was something that made her sit back on her heels and gape like a child who had just seen her first dirigible.

An angel waited on the other side. Its form was wreathed in light, so that it was hard to discern much beyond the humanoid shape—but behind trailed wings, fine as silk, fluttering in ethereal winds.

It was a sight so beautiful that Zofiya felt fresh, hot tears coursing down her cheeks, and yet she sensed something else. For as the light dimmed a fraction more, she was able to see a dark sword in the creature's white hand. Now when she glanced up, its eyes were staring back into hers. They were beautiful but pitiless. In them Zofiya could feel herself being judged, weighed, measured and held to account.

Suddenly she questioned every action in her life, every misstep, every harsh word, for this angel was no creature of kindness.

Kindness leads to weakness, child.

The voice in her head was a whisper, a murmur in the night.

You, of all people in this city, are a creature of faith. We have searched long for one of your kind.

"I'm not worthy of your attentions." Zofiya bowed her head and meant every word of it. Daughter of Kings, with a lineage stretching back to the beginning of civilization, she might be, yet in the presence of this angel she felt as common as a pig farmer.

Be that as it may—but you have been chosen.

The angel pressed against the crystal sheet, though its form was still indistinct.

Only you can bring me through. Only one child of faith and blood is required.

In Zofiya's heart belief burned, but Hatipai's texts warned of creatures of ill intent that could lead even the most devout followers astray.

"Give me your name?" she whispered, though she trembled at her daring.

Those dark eyes, full of condemnation and strength, bored into hers, but Zofiya did not flinch.

I cannot—I am Hatipai's angel and have none of my own, it whispered, laying its empty hand flat against the surface, a mirror of hers on the other side.

"What is your purpose?"

To kill the Young Pretender.

Zofiya's jaw tightened before she could voice a protest. Raed Syndar Rossin, only son of the deposed Emperor. He had saved her life at the fountain. Someone had shot at her, planning to end her existence in front of a crowd of people. He'd tackled her to the ground, taking the bullet for himself when her own bodyguard had failed to see the danger.

He'd been willing to sacrifice himself for the sister of his enemy. A mob had tried to kill Raed, and Kal had him imprisoned for his own safety. The Emperor had hoped to buy some time to decide what to do with the Pretender to his throne. Yet Raed had escaped. Zofiya knew she still owed him.

His death is necessary.

The angel's face was now so close that Zofiya could begin to make out details. The skin was faintly blue and marked with lines that were Hatipai's secret sigils, known only to her most ardent followers.

He will bring geists, and they will dance on the cinders of your world. The smooth, dark eyes never flinched from hers.

Yet the Grand Duchess was not so far lost in awe that she did not consider the possibility that this was an agent of evil. So she leaned forward. "Forgive me, bright angel. But speak the words on the inner Temple of Hatipai—the secrets only the acolytes of her divinity know."

For a moment, the angel glared at her with so much wrath boiling behind its eyes that even the fearless sister of the Emperor trembled. Then it tilted its head, a sliver of a smile on its full lips.

Truly, you are a wise creature, Zofiya of the Empire.

Zofiya's heart remembered to beat again. And then the angel whispered to her the words that had been passed down in great secrecy to the Grand Duchess by the most holy sisters of Hatipai. These incantations were the heart of the goddess.

As the angel's words reached her ear, Zofiya began to smile. When the angel had finished, it looked down at her with an almost maternal pleasure. *Now, child, let me out to begin the goddess' work.*

The Grand Duchess leaned forward again, placing her lips against the cool slab of mysterious stone. Her warmth traveled into the stone, and a sound like a distant bell rolled from the earth.

The wall shook once and then crumbled like a theatrical curtain being dropped. Zofiya looked up to see the angel step delicately over the rubble. The wings of light trailed behind, and the shifting face beneath reminded her of her long-dead mother—though it was hard to sure under the veils of light and mist.

"You have done your world proud, Zofiya, child of Kings." The sound of her voice, here in the real world, was sharper—like bright knives in the Grand Duchess' ears. A cold hand touched her shoulder—it burned. "I will hunt the scourge of your world. The Rossin will die."

Then the angel wrapped her wings about herself, dissolved into light, and blew from the room. Zofiya was left kneeling on the floor, sobbing frantically with joy.

↠ TWO ↞

Whispered Messages

"When you've buried your husband three months past, you don't expect to come home and find him rattling around in your attic!"

The old woman stood there, an ancient blunderbuss cradled in her arms, looking ready to go upstairs and blast her undead spouse for his temerity. However, her real ire was directed at Deacons Sorcha Faris and Merrick Chambers—as if the Order of the Eye and the Fist was solely responsible for this awkward situation.

Sorcha, who had managed to perch herself on the low wall outside the lady Tinker's shop, watched with amusement as her partner tried to negotiate his way in. Perhaps she was enjoying the situation a little too much, but these days she savored any excuse to leave the grounds of the Mother Abbey. Her cigar was already half-smoked, evidence of just how much the owner did not want them to go inside the shop.

Merrick, who had always been the more diplomatic of their partnership, posed the same question he had when they'd first arrived: "What is the deceased's name?" He had to raise his voice because Widow Vashill was impossibly deaf—which only served to increase Sorcha's enjoyment of the situation.

The old woman's eyes narrowed as if she suspected it was some sort of trick. "Joshem Vashill—and I was never more happy to see a person in the ground."

"Doesn't sound like he had much reason to come back," Merrick muttered softly over his shoulder to Sorcha. This was why she liked working with the younger man; when she'd been partnered with her husband, Kolya, he had not been nearly as amusing.

"You are sure it is Joshem?" Sorcha shouted, then blew out a smoke ring and tried to keep her hopes in check. The Order had been plagued with a spate of false alarms recently, and though she appreciated getting out of the Mother Abbey, she wasn't about to crawl around in a dusty attic chasing a figment of this Master Tinker's imagination.

"I know my own husband!" Widow Vashill snapped. "Now you just yank him down out of there, and I can go about my business."

"'Yank'?" Sorcha managed not to roll her eyes. People so quickly forgot the nature of things. Her Order had only been here in Arkaym a scant few years, and yet the population seemed incapable of remembering the plague of geists they had suffered from before the Order's arrival. "We have to go up there and deal with him," she replied in what she thought was a perfectly reasonable tone, "because we don't just 'yank' geists. It's more like wrestling."

"What?" The Widow Vashill bellowed.

Sorcha gestured up to the top story. "We're going to have to go up there!"

The woman's face went abruptly pale. "Oh no—I must have been mistaken. I'm just a silly old woman seeing things in the shadows. No need to—"

"Madam"—Merrick pushed his dark curls out of his eyes with something that looked awfully like exasperation—"if you will just let us up into the attic, we can assess the situation and take care of things for you." His earnest youth usually moved even the most elderly of women to compliance—this one, though, hesitated.

Tinkers' Row had grown under the patronage of the forward-thinking Emperor Kaleva: ramshackle houses had been transformed into impressive new brick buildings, the open drains decently covered, and sweeps employed to keep the street clear of filth. Carriages and pedestrians bustled up and down the Row, which had become one of the busiest in Vermillion. The sign above this particular door said VASHILL—MASTER TINKER TO THE PALACE, but then most of them on this street did. The Emperor had become the patron to nearly all the Tinkers in Vermillion.

Sorcha sighed, knocked the top off her cigar and pulled her Gauntlets out from her belt. Usually these symbols of her rune powers tended to grab people's attention. She was sharply aware of this as she fixed the old woman with a cold blue stare. "So, what's really up there, apart from your dead husband?"

Widow Vashill's lips pressed together in a pale line, and she leaned forward. "Things. Secret things."

Every guild had their mysteries, but the Tinkers, thanks to their close working kin, the airshipwrights, were especially paranoid since the Emperor wanted full control of the new technology. Merrick stood to his full height. "Madam, as long as the devices you are working on are regulation, then you have our assurance that we will never reveal anything to another soul."

If Sorcha had tried to sound so officious, people would have taken fright, but out of that earnest young mouth it was so much more reassuring. The old woman smiled, revealing a broken expanse of teeth. "Never doubted it, lad; it's just that many of the devices in the attic contain weirstones."

Sorcha clenched her teeth on an explicative. The Order had long ago limited the ownership of those things to Deacons and members of the Imperial armed forces—but the Emperor had extended that in recent years to include Master Tinkers.

At her side, Merrick shifted—well aware of her particular bugbear with the stones. Along the Bond they shared he tried sending out waves of calm, but it didn't make any difference. She didn't want to be calm. She'd had far too much of being calm lately. Time to let some of that frustration out.

"Then we will just have to manage," she growled. "Now let us get about our business." Sorcha stepped around the Tinker and strode into the shop, leaving protestations and excuses in her wake.

The inside of the building was dim simply because of the

very few windows. A single lamp burned on the back wall, illuminating the devices of brass that the Tinkers had lately become specialists in. The constant rattle of clocks, all slightly at a different tempo, put Sorcha's nerves on edge. Perhaps the Widow Vashill's deafness was an advantage.

Merrick, standing in the doorway, had the look of a child on the threshold of a candy merchant. Sorcha knew her partner fancied himself an amateur Tinker, but she held hope that he would snap out of it soon. Undoubtedly the smells of linseed oil and the whiff of sulphur were exciting her partner a little too much to be healthy.

While Merrick crept in, casting covetous eyes over the goods displayed in the shop, Sorcha stalked over to the lifting pallet at the back of the room, stepped aboard it, and kicked the crank handle with one foot. The machinery whirred and clanked, its staccato rattle occupying her mind, while the mechanism carried her up three stories into the storage attic. Her partner would just have to take the stairs.

Whatever else was true of Widow Vashill, she looked to be in demand as a Tinker. The storage area was stacked with many crates and other more mysterious sheet-covered items. The Deacon examined them curiously. From the labels she could see many were waiting to be shipped all over the Empire.

"Sorcha, wait!" Merrick, in the way of the young, did not sound at all puffed after three quick flights in pursuit. Her partner caught up and looked at her from under his curly hair with something close to reproach. "You shouldn't get upset over people's disrespect for the Order"—he adjusted his emerald cloak and tilted his head—"especially after what happened at the ossuary this winter."

Sorcha's stomach tightened, and she felt herself flush. "Actually"—she pursed her lips—"after what happened at the White Palace, the people of this city should trust us *more* not less. They treat us more like ratcatchers than protectors."

"We'll earn back their respect and trust," he replied with a certainty she did not possess. "Anyway"—Merrick touched her arm—"she is probably just jumping at shadows—most people are these days."

Sorcha smiled bitterly. "You're right—it's not like Rictun

would ever knowingly send us anywhere that actually has a geist." She did not give him his proper title; to her there had only been one Arch Abbot. Despite his treachery, the now-dead Hastler had earned her respect. Rictun, who currently sat on the Council in that position, was worse than a fool—and he had always despised her, for reasons she could not deduce.

A cruel fool.

"Yes, yes, he is." Merrick probably didn't even realize he had picked unspoken words from her head. Their Bond was not supposed to work that way. A topic they were both avoiding. "However, that doesn't mean we shouldn't be cautious all the same."

"I think we can handle one little shade, Merrick. We can't possibly be that out of practice." Still, she did turn and regard the attic with some caution.

The world bloomed to life as her partner's Sight enveloped her; it heightened her awareness and gave her own powers direction. As an Active, Sorcha was only too well aware that her life relied on her partner. Without him she would be a raging fireball with no direction that was more likely to hurt herself than a geist.

Sorcha's breath coalesced in front of her eyes. Outside it was summer, but the chill on her skin was as if the depths of winter had come again. It was a sign every human in the Empire could read.

Her heart raced, and her skin ran with goose pimples, yet a slow smile spread on her lips. It had been far too long since she had done the job she'd trained for all her remembered life.

Suddenly Merrick was at her shoulder, the only warmth in the room, and she was very grateful for it.

Caution. Watch. Danger.

His Sight meshed with hers again, and now she began to realize she should have stopped to question the widow a little more thoroughly. Their Sight was compromised in the attic—a low-level gray light flooded the space. It came from the number of weirstones used by the Tinker.

Their shared Sight dipped and swayed as Merrick tried to compensate for the staining of the ether. A scuttling sound made his mouth snap shut. Rats were running from every corner, scrambling through the walls, and skittering down the drainpipe. Animals were more sensitive than humans and always fled in the face of the undead. The noise was unnerving—even to the trained.

Leaving her partner to hold his position at the rear, Sorcha crept forward. Until recently the very idea of an unliving incursion into Vermillion would have been unthinkable; however, everything had changed since the battle in the ossuary. It had taken the Order back to the bad old days when they had first arrived on this continent. Now once again they were flooded with alerts of geist activity—both real and imagined. The new Arch Abbot Rictun had made sure his Presbyter Secondo gave only the latter kind to Deacons Chambers and Faris. So whatever chance had brought them here to an actual geist she was not going to question.

They were bitter thoughts to keep Sorcha company as she scanned between crates, her hands steady in her Gauntlets. They were the holder of her magic and her only protection against the geists.

Something flickered between the rows, a suggestion of shadow darting away from the Deacons and deeper into the attic. So it was not a brave geist—surely only a shade and nothing as dangerous as a ghast or a poltern. Still, after a long dry spell, she would take whatever she could get.

Yet, by the time she had reached the far end of the attic space, Deacon Faris had the sinking feeling that it was she who was imagining things. Her shared sight detected nothing. Perhaps she had been too hopeful, and her eyes had seen only what she wanted to see. After so long she was practically conjuring geists from the woodwork. Her hands clenched in the smooth leather of her Gauntlets.

Sorcha turned back to Merrick with a sigh. "I think you were right. The woman was just jumping at shadows. There's nothing here." She couldn't contain the disappointment in her voice.

Her partner shrugged. "Maybe she saw what—"

And that was when she felt every hair on her body stand on end. The rush of intense cold flooded down her spine, and in the corner something metallic rattled. Sorcha spun around and jerked the drop cloth off a six-foot structure. It was a calendar, with the phases of the moon and the date inscribed on a huge dial—probably meant to stand in a warehouse. On cue it began to tick loudly, almost in time with the rhythm of her heart.

Sorcha! Merrick's voice blared in her skull, just as their shared Sight cleared. Something was wrapped around the base of the clock, spinning and shifting like a bundle of snakes. Her eyes widened. She took a shocked step back and raised her Gauntlets. Shades were the remains of a recently dead person—spectyrs were their evil cousins. Twisted by the Otherside, they were human souls who sought revenge. However, they usually manifested alone—what she was faced with now was entirely different. A shade haunting was usually more irritating than terrifying. These spectyrs were not.

The rattle of irritated spectyrs grew louder, as the spinning knot of them flew apart to darken the ceiling and every corner of the attic. Sorcha knew that she had received far more than she wanted.

"Stay still," she bellowed at Merrick, as she ducked away from the swooping shards of darkness that were beginning to shape themselves into skeletal forms.

A nest of spectyrs was particularly dangerous, a fact that Sorcha became aware of as the contents of the attic began flying at her head. Ducking and diving was making it rather hard to concentrate. What appeared to be a lighthouse lens tipped over, knocking her off her feet and exploding glass all across the floor.

With one hand Sorcha called on Shayst, the Sixth Rune of Dominion, and the attic flared green. Shayst sucked away the spectyrs' power, at least those she was lucky enough to hit with the rune. That power became hers, enough that she could lever the lens mechanism off her and crawl out.

Out of the corner of one eye she saw Merrick step toward her, his hands reaching for his Strop, the talisman of the Sensitives.

Sorcha could taste his fear. "Don't you dare go Active!"

Though every Deacon had both talents in them, a Sensitive using their Active power was ridiculously dangerous and ultimately pointless. He made a face at her. "I think I have something better." He called on Masa, the Third Rune of Sight, and their shared Center blurred, deepened, and now Sorcha saw double. As the contents of the attic tumbled, as the spectyrs wheeled, hissed, and threw them at her—she was able to see everything before it happened.

The Active ducked and rolled as a tall machine with long lines of cogs and wheels toppled from the wall. It was hard to imagine what the widow Vashill was thinking outside. It couldn't be good.

A twisting cluster of spectyrs dived at her, their skulls screaming for vengeance, ready to burrow into her body and take it for their own. Sorcha dropped onto her back, raised her Gauntlets; one lit with the blue fire of Aydien, holding off the larger mass of spectyrs, while she concentrated Shayst on the immediate attackers.

A line of sweat broke out on her lip as she drained them of their strength, and in the back of her mind was the joyous hum of delight.

Take it. Take it all. Take everything. The insidious, tempting call yammered in her head, because it felt so very, very *good.*

Sorcha was so busy draining the spectyrs swarming on the ceiling, she almost missed the stragglers that were darting and blundering through the crates in the attic.

Sorcha! Merrick, still standing motionless in the corner, howled, but she had only two hands and two Gauntlets. Though she dropped Shayst and reached for Chityre, she wasn't quite fast enough. The spectyr came barreling out of the shadows, its jaws wide and snapping.

She heard Merrick yell—this time physically, but she saw nothing else, because they were on her then. The nest turned everything black, and her throat became abruptly unable to utter anything at all. Sorcha scrabbled at her neck, choking. Despite everything she had learned, primitive physical reactions were impossible to deny.

As she rolled across the floor, unable to use her Gauntlets to get more air into her lungs or summon a rune, the screaming of the damned wailed in her ears. It was the sound of the unliving calling her to them, and she was aching to go.

Then dimly, on the edge of consciousness, she felt Merrick. He slid across the floor to her, throwing himself into the middle of the snarling, vengeful geists. A Sensitive was supposed to stay out of the melee, out of harm's way. But her partner broke through the swarm and put his hands on her.

The Bond flared, suddenly stronger and more important than anything hidden in shadow. Merrick was in her head, she was in his, in ways that no Deacon Bond should allow.

Yet Sorcha didn't care about that, because up against their surge of power the nest backed away. She could breathe. Gasping, with Merrick wrapped around her, she released the rune Pyet.

The attic was full of flame, blessed cleansing fire that flickered and danced in the polished brass of the Tinker's craft. The spectyrs wailed loud enough to rupture normal human eardrums, shriveling as the geist power that held them captive was burned away.

Together, she and Merrick got all of them—all bar one.

"Wait!" Her partner called, but she was already up and chasing the fleeing geist. This one was not going to hang about and be sent back to the black embrace of the Otherside. It flashed away from her, phasing out and passing through the crates, before heading for the far brick wall.

"Sorcha!" Her partner's voice chased after her, but she refused to acknowledge him as she dashed after the spectyr. Damn it, after weeks of inactivity, she wasn't about to let any of the undead get away from her.

Sorcha raised her right hand, spread her Gauntleted fingers, and called Voishem. The air bent around her, twisting, breaking into the space between things. Brick, stone or wood could not stop her now.

On the heels of the geist, Sorcha slipped through the wall and into the adjoining attic. The Bond, though, held tight, and she still shared Merrick's sight. In fact, once through the wall, the influence of those cursed weirstones was mercifully dampened.

This second attic was completely empty except for two crates by the far window. It was full of enough dust that Sorcha was surrounded by dancing motes, and for an instant she was confused by the flicker of light. The spectyr she half expected to have moved on was in fact huddled at the far end of the new room, crouching in shadow. All of her training as a Deacon told her this was very strange behavior for this kind of geist.

Though her heart was pounding, this was the one remaining problem from the whole vicious nest. She wasn't afraid of it. Still, she kept her Gauntlets raised as she approached the cloaked form. Stopping two feet from the spectyr, Sorcha waited. It had been a long time since she had tried to communicate with a geist—usually the mistake of a newly minted Deacon—but she opened her mouth and said the first thing that came to mind. "Why are you here?"

Slowly the spectyr pivoted toward her, like a circus ringmaster revealing the final act in his show. Despite all her power, all her training, Sorcha swallowed hard.

In the dim light of the attic the transparent skull in a gray shroud flickered, a reminder of every humans' fate. Suddenly Sorcha was no longer thinking of it as a simple, single geist. It was a part of the great void that waited for them all: the Otherside. She had danced there for a while the previous season—but her memory of that time had faded. Now, as the geist faced her, flashes of it returned. Sorcha wanted desperately to smoke a cigar in that moment—remind herself that she was still among the living.

She cocked her head, Gauntlets half raised, waiting to ignite a rune and send the apparition tumbling back to the Otherside. The spectyr mimicked the gesture, and then its bone white jaw creaked open.

"Sorcha!" The voice was like the wheezing cry of a dying man, stretched out and desperate in the silent warehouse attic. The Deacon could not have been more surprised than if the geist had started a song and dance routine.

"Sorcha?" Merrick's voice came from below and was an eerie echo. She heard her partner's boots on the stairs and was reassured that soon he would be here.

"Sorcha," the geist repeated, raising a shimmering hand and reaching out to her. "You must save him, Sorcha."

In many of the religions it was said three repetitions of a name were required for a binding. As a Deacon she didn't believe in such foolish nonsense—but, oddly, a chill still ran up her spine. She smothered the rune that she had been meaning to cast—because she guessed who the apparition meant—and now she had to know.

Sorcha remained stock-still as the spectyr's hand touched

her face. She let it—something that went against every ounce of her training. Beyond reality and time, the Otherside held knowledge that no human could ever possess, so the greatest Deacons of the Order had often taken chances to snatch what they could from the void. This was her moment.

Slowly her eyes drooped, heavy with the cold of the undead. As Sorcha trembled on the edge of death itself, she accepted its vision.

Raed Syndar Rossin, Young Pretender to the throne, fugitive, and the man she had not stopped thinking of since she met him. Sorcha could see him, like looking through water: as if she was below, and he was above.

A girl who she couldn't quite make out was screaming while men carried her away—then her face changed to a terrifying smirk. Raed was there trying to save her, yet dark hands reached out and took him. Lured into a trap under a circle of spinning stars, he and the Beast within were devoured by a creature of snapping, snarling gold and scarlet. It was awful, terrible, and as she watched, Sorcha was sure it had not yet happened. However, it would—this was Raed's fate.

A sense of peace stole over her, and for an instant the voice of the spectyr was familiar: light, womanly, one that had given her life for them all. Nynnia, the creature from the Otherside, was whispering into the mind of the Deacon. The words were far off, but Sorcha caught "angel," "son," "trap" and "stars."

The Deacon strained to hear the rest, but then Merrick was screaming her name more forcibly: standing on the top stair and shouting to her. Her concentration was broken, and Nynnia's voice melted away into the still air.

Merrick's yells were not without reason. Sorcha shook her head and looked up. The shrouded skull now loomed forward, and its eyes caught fire. A cloud of freezing air blasted into her face and knocked Sorcha back a step.

The burning skull under the hooded cloak snarled, its teeth snapping as its hand of bone reached for her. Sorcha spun away and summoned Yevah from her Gauntlet. The shield of fire leapt between them, giving her a moment to breathe.

Raising her Gauntlets, she next called the rune Tryrei. Opening up a tiny pinhole to the Otherside would draw away the power of the geist and send it back where it belonged.

Opening even a tiny crack to that place hurt. The sound of the hungry void was like a thousand screaming voices, calling for love, friends, life. It was a noise that would have driven a normal human insane, but a Deacon was trained and honed to not bend in the face of the undead. Sorcha stood before it, hands spread, directing the anger of the Otherside toward the spectyr.

Yet, it did not succumb but rather elongated. It came at her still, stretched and spinning, the white bones of its fingers reaching for her. However, the Otherside continued to exert its pull, and the vengeful geist had nothing to hold it in the human world. It scrambled, it fought, but then the terrible void took it.

Sorcha closed her fist on Tryrei, and the crack was sealed. Just as suddenly as it had come, the terrible noise and fury was gone. The two Deacons stood in the silent warehouse and stared at each other, not even panting.

"Nynnia was here." Sorcha took a deep breath. "She used that last spectyr to send us a message."

Her partner's deep brown eyes studied her for a minute. The Bond between them was stronger than any normal Deacon pairing—she had no doubt Merrick had seen a portion of what she had.

Carefully Sorcha removed her Gauntlets, folded them up, and took out the remains of her cigar. The sole window in the warehouse attic looked over the mercantile quarter and toward the Imperial Palace.

Merrick stood beside her, by now used to her smoking and her silences. For a young man he was very good at being still. He was well aware of his partner's feelings for the Young Pretender but also of the bind they were in. Even in the best of times no Deacon was a free agent. And these were not the best of times, for Arch Abbot Rictun had them under close observation. He would never let them leave Vermillion.

Sorcha inhaled the smoke, letting it sit heavy in her mouth for a moment before exhaling it toward the window. She was trying to logically assess the situation, but each time she did, she saw Raed's dying gasp. "He's not dead yet," she said calmly, "or we would have felt it." An attempt to control the Beast inside the Young Pretender had also ended up binding the two Deacons to the fugitive—a triple Bond.

"It could be a trap," Merrick replied softly, pulling his cloak around him.

"Yes." She blew a smoke ring. "It very well could be. Yet—"

"—apparently we have allies on the Otherside." Her partner glanced up and then away. Nynnia had undoubtedly been more than human, but neither of them had expected to hear from her after death.

Sorcha examined the glowing tip of her cigar. "But we don't know what her nature really is. Quite a bit to hang our future on, don't you think?"

"Raed is our friend . . . more than that." Merrick's mind reached out, tugging on the Bond like a boy might pull on a fence wire to test its strength. The part between them sang, and there was a distant whisper of the one between them and the Young Pretender.

Sorcha had made the Bond in haste, but none of them had been able to cut it. Wordlessly, both Deacons reached out for the Young Pretender, searching for the connection they had spent the last three months denying. He was out there somewhere—they could tell that—but too far for them to sense very much else.

"I saw them kill him, Merrick." Sorcha turned to her partner, her blue eyes gleaming in the half-light. "We can't let that happen—even if it is a trap."

He sighed, looked up at the ceiling as if searching for answers from some uncaring little god. But when he looked back, on his lips was a wry smile. "No—you're right—we can't. The trick of it though will be getting the Arch Abbot to agree to us leaving."

Sorcha's expression was amused as she knocked the end off her cigar to save for another occasion. "We've spent long enough playing by Rictun's rules. There's no fun in it anymore."

Her partner's reaction was a slightly nervous laugh—but he didn't for one second try to stop her. Sorcha knew it was another reason she liked the boy.

→ THREE ←

The Bonds of Duty

The instant a drunk sailor grabbed the quartermaster's behind and then pulled her into his lap, Raed knew there would be trouble. Laython was a kindly sort of woman, but she only liked to be manhandled by those she knew.

Her scarred hand grabbed up the nearest object, in this case a full mug of ale, and smashed it against the offending sailor's head. The crew of the *Dominion* leapt from their chairs and rushed to the aid of their companion.

Raed, who had long been without a decent brawl, joined them. He might be the Young Pretender to the throne, with a royal lineage going back to before the Break, but he was not the sort to put himself above his crew.

The wharf-side bar was packed with more than three ships' complements, and since night had fallen they'd all been waiting for a moment to get some trouble started. Before he knew it, Raed was in among the swinging, swearing mass of sailors, giving just as much he got. He was splashed with a goodly amount of ale but found he was grinning.

Looking almost haughty, his very tall first mate pulled a red-faced man off Raed. It had crossed the Young Pretender's mind more than once that Aachon should have been born the Prince—not he.

"Is this not, perhaps, an inappropriate pastime for you, my—" The first mate paused and managed to stop himself before his said "Prince." "My captain?"

Raed took the offered hand and let himself be pulled to his feet. "We're in a rough, isolated little port town—what else is there to do?"

He caught a glimpse of Aachon's dark eyebrows drawing together into a dire expression but then found himself whirled away by another opponent. Raed grappled with him, getting in a few good punches, before the larger man tossed him through the pub's window.

Luckily, this particular establishment was not exclusive enough to afford glass, and Raed sailed through where it would have been, only catching his shoulder against the shutters. He landed on the ground, had the breath knocked out of him, and lay there for a second. Slightly dazed, he contemplated when he'd last felt this unfettered.

Before he had met the Deacons Sorcha Faris and Merrick Chambers, he had spent very little time on dry land. The Beast inside him was triggered by the nearness of other geists, and so he had spent his life on the open sea. Until that safety too was denied him. So, indeed, it had been a very long time.

When Aachon flew through the window and nearly landed atop him, Raed couldn't help bursting into real laughter. It must have taken at least three men to sling the first mate in such a way. As Raed pushed him off his chest, he was reminded of his friend's considerable weight.

He was just about to commiserate with Aachon, when he realized that a pair of fine boots were standing only a few inches from their heads. Cautiously he rolled onto his side and looked up at their owner.

And there she was. Captain Tangyre Greene looked down at him with an odd sort of smile tugging the corner of her lips. She was older than the last time they had talked, though her hair had always been gray, and the long scar on the right side of her face earned in the service of the Unsung was as deep as ever.

"Tang!" Raed bounded to his feet. "You remember my first mate, Aachon?"

The brawl inside was reaching some kind of crescendo,

and another body was tossed through the window. Laython landed nearby, cursing through her split lip.

"Oh, and my quartermaster."

"Still the same old Raed." Tangyre dusted off Raed's shoulders. "But I am surprised with you, Aachon—how can you let your captain get into such antics?"

"Even I cannot perform miracles, Captain Greene." The first mate rolled to his feet. Behind them the noise in the pub had died down, and all that could be heard were the cheers of the *Dominion* crew. Now they would be spending their hard-earned coin on buying drinks for their opponents. Laython shot a glance between her captain and this newcomer and then strode back into the pub. A fresh chorus from the sailors revealed they fully expected her to buy them all a round.

Raed and Aachon did not join them. Instead, the Young Pretender clapped Tangyre in a tight embrace. She had been one of the few officers in the Unsung's forces who had treated a young Prince like a friend rather than a royal. "Wonderful to see you again, Tang. What brings you from the Isles?"

She pulled back, and the hint of a smile on her lips faded. Suddenly Raed knew that her arrival was more than coincidence. "My Prince"—she seldom called him that, and his stomach lurched appropriately—"if only I could come on the wings of better news." From her belt she produced a folded missive and held it out to him like it was poisoned.

Raed took the piece of vellum with his father's seal on it from her extended fingers. That piece of wax said the Unsung was still alive—so there could be only one other person who could bring Tangyre so far.

His hands were sweating as he snapped the seal and read what was written there. Even in panic and loss, his father wrote long and florid passages. His son found himself scanning down the letter to get to the real story as quickly as possible.

The raiders came in the middle of a storm—they took Fraine. You have brought attention to our family after so many years of peace. This is all your fault.

"I am sorry, Raed." Tangyre touched his shoulder and squeezed.

A wave of numbness passed through him as he recalled his sister's curls and deep blue eyes. She was fifteen years younger than he—a product of their parents' reunion after years of separation. He remembered carrying her on his shoulders when he'd been home between sea battles.

All this was naturally before the Rossin's Curse came to fruition and their mother was killed under its claws. Fraine had been so sweet, yet with a streak of genuine stubbornness that was required of anyone bearing the name of Rossin.

His sister's existence was the one reason Raed had not taken his own life in the terrible dark times after their mother had been slain by the geistlord inside him. Like he, his sister had been born outside of Vermillion, and therefore if he were to die, the Curse that plagued their family would fall on her next.

Now Raed feared that his father was right. He had opened the door when he'd gone into Vermillion. Their enemies had almost forgotten that the Rossin line still existed. Even the Emperor.

Tangyre's hand tightened on his shoulder. She smelled of sea salt and leather armor.

"How hard did the old bastard try to get her back?" Raed was fully aware his voice cracked with anger and guilt.

Tangyre stiffened. "It wasn't his fault; there was a storm and—"

"He should have sailed through it!" he snapped, yanking his shoulder back out of her grip. "He should have chased them to the Otherside if necessary!"

"Your father is far too sick to take to ship," Tangyre replied, "but he sent all those at his disposal to get your sister back. We lost four in the storm, and the scum still outdistanced us. Once they reached Imperial waters they went up the Saal River—and that was as far as we could go without frigates." She looked him in the eye defiantly. "Having our ships blown out of the water by the Imperial fleet would not get Fraine back."

For an instant Raed wanted to scream that she'd been a coward, that they should have followed his sister down to the last man—but then logic washed over him. He nodded stiffly. "So how did you find me?"

The corner of Tang's lips twisted in an ironic smile. "I still have plenty of contacts on the mainland. I took a guess that reports of a Pretender to the throne along the coast of Gallion pertained to you."

Though she was a friend, Raed did not like the idea of anyone being able to track him so easily. To mask it he replied swiftly, "So you brought *Gullwing*?"

Captain Greene turned and pointed toward the ships moored at the jetty, bobbing under the light of a full moon. *Dominion* was as identifiable as his own hand, but also now he could make out another familiar shape tied next to it.

He had many fond memories of running the deck of this sloop as a child. She might be one of the older ships left to them, but she was also light, fast, and often carried the word of the Unsung from the Coronet Isles. In the last few decades, though, there had been precious use for that to be transmitted anywhere.

"She is my ship now," Tangyre replied, "and one of only three others to survive the storm."

The two captains, trailed by the still-wary Aachon, walked back toward the jetty. Tangyre ran her eye over the *Dominion*. "However, you look in good order."

"Not good enough to take on the whole Empire"—Raed stroked his short beard—"so you best tell me what you know."

"Our informants tell us only that the ship sailed up the Saal—but from there, the trail runs cold." Tangyre tucked her thumbs into her belt. "Your father asks you to follow."

Had the Unsung really thought he wouldn't? Raed managed not to take his anger out on Tangyre; she was but the messenger. "You may tell him I will find her."

"My Prince," Aachon finally rumbled, "unlike his father, is not afraid to go against the edicts of the Assembly of Princes and the Usurper."

Raed was shocked and surprised. He had never heard a bad word from Aachon's mouth about the Unsung, let alone the suggestion that his choice to remain safely in exile was some kind of cowardice. It was not an uncommon view.

Captain Greene tilted her head but chose to completely ignore Aachon's comment. "My *ship* shall return to the Coronet Isles, my Prince. I will remain and help you."

Looking into those flinty gray eyes, Raed knew there would be no argument. Tangyre would cling to the outside of the *Dominion* even if he gave her a direct order; she had taken the kidnapping of Fraine as a personal affront.

"Very well, then," Raed said, tucking his father's missive into his pocket. "Luckily Aachon and I have discussed this before. We have a way to both get us back into the Empire and strike at an abomination."

Tangyre's eyebrows shot up. "That sounds most impressive."

"My Prince always is." Aachon folded his arms so they bulged. He could not have looked more imposing even if he'd been made of stone.

Raed rolled his eyes. "Forgive my first mate, Tang. He hates slavers almost as much as I do."

"Perfectly understandable"—Captain Greene pressed her lips together—"a pet peeve of mine as well. I already suspect that this is going to be a most satisfactory outing."

→ FOUR ←

A Warning from Beyond

"Your husband is now properly dead." Merrick found it amusing how unaware his partner was that her tone was far from reassuring. She sounded so merry that the widow had to be wondering if something dire had happened inside.

The younger Deacon could understand Sorcha's mood, though; he too had been glad to come face-to-face with a genuine geist. The strange message it bore, however, was unnerving. The three months of quiet were well and truly over—he didn't need to be Deacon Reeceson, with his wild talent of prescience, to know that.

The Arch Abbot had kept them occupied with as many menial tasks as he could find since the incident in the ossuary. They had guarded endless empty corridors, escorted wagon trains of porcelain, and entertained every vapid courtier in the palace. With Rictun's eye so firmly set on them, leaving Vermillion was going to be as problematic as getting in had been when they had been hunted fugitives.

"So what's the situation, then?" The light, firm voice at his side made Merrick wince.

Turning, he saw that Deacon Kolya Petav had once again followed them on assignment. Though still pale and thin after months of recovery from the geist attack outside the Imperial

Palace, Sorcha's husband was stubbornly sticking to his rights as a partner. Kolya, as in all the other times, had not an ounce of guilt on his face.

Merrick blinked, unable to quite believe it. He knew if he was in Kolya's place he would not dare Sorcha's rage; instead he probably would have been curled up somewhere sucking his thumb like an infant in swaddling clothes.

Two months ago Sorcha had gone to the Civic Court, spoken the ritual words three times, and signed the writ before the worthies as required. The final death knell for her and Kolya's marriage would be accepted in another full spin of the seasons. By comparison, breaking the Bond of partnership was almost impossible—at least when one of the party would not accept it.

Deacon Petav was definitely not giving up on that particular side of his relationship with Sorcha. Instead of accepting his soon to be former wife's petition, he had gone before the Presbyterial Council and put up a strong argument for his rights. Why he had done that was still a mystery.

This was the second time he had turned up while Merrick and Sorcha were on duty. Now he stood before them like a statue wrapped in the emerald cloak of the Sensitive. Previously his wife had ignored him, but Merrick wondered if this time, after recent revelations, she would be so restrained. Deacon Chambers feared a scene—something the Order could well do without these days. As Sorcha finished her discussion with the widow, Merrick scrambled to try to prevent that possibility.

"Deacon Petav"—he dared to put a hand under his fellow Sensitive's elbow—"we have dealt with the geist, so there is no real call for you to be here." He thought his voice was both deferential and low.

Kolya looked down at Merrick, the only sign of any emotion being a slight hardening around his eyes. "Are you trying to hurry me along?" He might not have said the word "boy," but it was implied. "I have the same right to be here as you."

Merrick could feel himself beginning to bristle and remembered Sorcha's description of why her marriage had died. *It was like struggling against a void, looking for love and affec-*

tion but finding none. He had nothing but admiration for Deacon Petav as a Sensitive, yet as a man Merrick thought he was a fool.

"But Sorcha . . ." he hissed to Kolya.

"Sorcha is confused," his fellow Sensitive replied mildly. "She imagines life is a fairy story. When she realizes that it's not, she'll come round."

This was so contrary to what Merrick knew of his partner that he stood there for a moment, completely unable to come up with an answer.

Kolya took his silence for something it was not. "She is such a child—sneaking out of the Abbey to avoid me."

Now Merrick could feel his awkwardness turning into anger. He was searching for words that would not communicate that when Sorcha turned.

Merrick knew her natural inclination was to rage, but even Deacon Faris realized how precarious the public's faith in the Order was at the moment. Her brow darkened like a storm front, and her mouth opened to let something fly. Then, in a display of control, her jaw snapped shut. So as the Merchant Quarter continued on its business, she stalked away past the two Sensitives—not acknowledging either of their presences.

Unfortunately for her, Kolya was taller and easily kept pace. "You should keep me informed when you go out like this, Sorcha." His voice remained low, and it was not tinged with anything like accusation. He said it as conversationally as if he were asking her to pass the salt.

Merrick had already been caught in the middle of several of these "discussions," and now, as then, he felt as useful as . . .

"Tits on a bull?" Sorcha shot a grim look at him over her shoulder, before turning back to her original partner. "Can't you see you're not wanted here, Kolya? Be a man, and let it go."

Her old partner shrugged. "Arch Abbot Rictun has not decided what will happen in our . . . unique position. I have primacy over Deacon Chambers, after all."

Sorcha's back stiffened. Rictun was an old adversary of hers—though Merrick was not certain of the reason for it. If the younger Deacon had been given a choice, he would have picked a partner without these issues, but in his own way he was just as stubborn as Kolya. The Bond and the history between Merrick and Sorcha were strong, and he would struggle for them as his partner did.

"This is not the place," Sorcha hissed, "but I can tell you that I only wish you had fought for our marriage as you are fighting for our partnership."

With an outraged snort, Sorcha set a cracking pace through the city and soon got them out of the Quarter. Merrick trailed behind as they climbed over the gleaming Bridge of Gilt, which as its name suggested had been gilded by a rich trader seeking favor. It was the most impressive and, Merrick thought, most ridiculous of Vermillion's many bridges. Tall gold cupids cavorted on a series of plinths along its length, and even the oak boards under their feet were decorated with insets of brass. The broad deck was also lined with many small shops that stood cheek by jowl right up to the very end where it landed on the Imperial Island. By law there was no trade in this part of the city, but the merchants played it as close as they could. The three passed through the granite gates and into the gleaming center of the Empire, walking briskly past the homes of the aristocracy, up the hill toward the Mother Abbey. Only the Imperial Palace stood higher on the man-made mount in the middle of the lagoon. Merrick's wide-eyed view of the beauty of the place had changed—he now knew that not everything was as it seemed. He loved the Order, believed in the good work it did, but Arch Abbot Hastler's failed attempt to bring the Murashev into the world had revealed a hidden side to it that he had never imagined.

As he contemplated that, Merrick had been left behind by Sorcha and Kolya, who were striding along at great speed. Deacon Petav's soft voice was hard to make out over the rumble of carriages passing them—Sorcha's was not.

"—don't try to sell me that, Kolya! I know the Otherside ebbs and flows, but this is *not* part of that natural cycle. And if Hastler—" Sorcha stopped, catching herself using the dead Arch Abbot's name rather than that of his successor. She growled in irritation and walked even faster up the hill.

Kolya shrugged at Merrick as if they were part of some club of Sensitives confused by Sorcha. The older Deacon cultivated an aura of passive acceptance, but Merrick knew he could turn that around suddenly, making it seem as though it was the other person in the wrong. It was quite a talent.

Luckily they reached the Abbey, and never had he been so grateful to see the high, white walls that surrounded it. They went in the postern gate, past the lay Brother guards, and into the courtyard. To the right: the infirmary, the gardens, and the stables. To the left: the dormitory, the refectory, and the novitiate house. Ahead were the lines of cloisters with Deacons strolling through them, talking or just quietly contemplating.

As Sorcha lowered her head and made her way there, Deacon Petav stopped and called her name. She completely ignored him, pulled her cloak around her shoulders and stalked off. Now it was Kolya who caught at Merrick's arm. "She has to talk to me!" He appeared genuinely bemused by his nearly former wife.

The other Sensitive stopped and stared at him. "You must know she is resolute in her decision, Deacon Petav, so tell me, why do you persist?"

His tall form bent then, just a fraction. "This is all that remains." He spoke the words quietly before walking away toward the dormitory. Merrick watched him, wondering at the man who had let Sorcha go without complaint yet now regretted it so bitterly.

However, Deacon Petev had made his own bed—his inaction had consequences that he must now deal with. Merrick turned and ran to catch up with Sorcha, who he suddenly realized was making her way through the cloisters directly toward the receiving chambers of the Arch Abbot. Going toe-to-toe with Rictun was in no one's best interests. Merrick called her name. It echoed in the ceiling of the cloisters, and several of their fellow Deacons glanced up. Surprisingly, she did stop.

"Not there—please, Sorcha!" He didn't care who heard, because they were already the talk of the Abbey.

Their eyes locked, and it was she who flinched. Her hands clenched the edge of her cloak. Instead, she stalked into the Devotional. Before the arrival of the geists this had been a church—a place to worship the gods. Now it hosted gatherings, meetings and training to fight the unliving. Still, as they entered the heart of the Abbey, the great soaring ceiling, the beautiful stained glass windows, even the statues of the

Deacons of the Old Order stirred Merrick's heart. He loved the services they had here, the words of wisdom passed on by others of the Order, stories of the past—all those things. It gave him peace, and he hoped it did the same for his partner.

It was a sign of Sorcha's bewilderment that she let herself be hauled into one of the chapels that ran the length of the great vaulted space that was the Devotional. Merrick could read her confusion in the tight line of her jaw and the way she would not meet his eyes.

"I saw him die." She whispered, so that the vast space would not catch her words. Sorcha looked up at him then, her blue eyes uncertain—frightened, perhaps, of her partner's response.

"I saw it too!" Merrick touched her shoulder, and for a second she did not move.

Then, sliding away from his touch, she leaned against the gray stone wall and looked through the stained glass window at the lay Brothers. Out in the garden they were bustling to harvest late-summer crops. "But I suppose you think it means nothing?"

"Actually"—Merrick leaned on the wall opposite and tucked his hands inside his cloak—"I believe it would be foolish to ignore this message."

She looked at him askance. "It was Nynnia who delivered it."

Merrick shook his head, terrified and hopeful. "I don't know if that is even possible—we still don't understand what she was."

"But what if it is true?" Sorcha returned. "What if Nynnia is on the Otherside, and she wants us to stop Raed's murder?"

Outside, the bells began to ring, summoning the Initiates to their classes. Merrick had very recently been among their number, and yet now he was preparing to go against all those years of training. Again. Still, he too was bound to Raed and knew him for a good man.

So, pushing off from the wall, he smiled at his partner. "Then let us do just that."

The brightness of Sorcha's smile could have melted winter ice.

Merrick held up his hand. "On one condition—we do not go haring off without preparing properly."

Sorcha's lips twitched, but she sketched a bow in front of him. "Whatever you say, my lord Chambers."

That one gesture brought up long-forgotten memories, which he struggled to stuff down. With a cough he turned away. "Let's adjourn to my cell and see if we can find out what that message of yours really meant."

The dormitory was quiet at this time of day, with most Deacons being on duty, but a few retired to their cells to study or mediate with the talismans of their art. Sorcha had moved from a large cell shared with Deacon Petav to a smaller one next to Merrick's. It was a significant sign that he knew had caused the birth of many rumors.

Despite being serious people dedicated to protecting the world, Deacons were just as prone to foibles as the rest of humanity, and gossip could be as rampant in the dormitory as at any boarding school. Though Merrick had gotten over his fear of his partner, he was not going to reach out to her in that intimate way. They already had enough complications in their lives.

His cell was just like every other one in the dormitory: whitewashed, narrow, containing a bed and a set of camphor wood drawers. A Deacon was only supposed to have enough possessions that could be carried in saddlebags—a throwback to their history of wandering the land serving the people. It was all very different from his childhood as a young aristocrat.

Merrick rolled the meditation rug out on the floor. It was a fine piece of tapestry with the Ten Runes of Dominion and the Seven Runes of Sight on it. It was woven by the lay Brothers with fine Frigyian wool and was the only splash of color to be found in the room. The runes themselves, unlike cantrips, held no particular power—only when carved on the Gauntlets or Strop by a Deacon were they given potency—but they did serve the purpose to concentrate a Deacon's mind. In the days before the Break of the Otherside, the ancient days when the Order had been a religious one, it would have been called a prayer rug.

Sorcha knelt on it, her fingertips brushing the Runes of

Dominion, while Merrick took up a mirror place next to those of Sight. He did not need to work hard to find the rune Sielu, the First. Activating this old friend did not require the Strop over his eyes.

"Think of the spectyr," he said in a soft undertone. "Think of what it showed you."

Sorcha sighed, sounding exasperated, as if she would rather be running to the stable for their horses. The Bond suggested that was exactly her immediate instincts.

"Sorcha," Merrick snapped, closing his eyes, "concentrate!"

Sinking back on her heels, he was surprised when she didn't reply. Against his eyes the images she had been fed by the spectyr danced. They were quick, like a flicker of cards in the hands of a master player.

Merrick invoked the rune: capturing the images, holding them, and then seamlessly playing them back through the Bond. Sorcha hissed over her teeth, and that was the only admission of admiration his partner would give.

Indeed, there was a lot of blood in the imagery—and a lot of it was flowing from Raed. The Rossin was also there—dying. It was a great red room, but the details were obscured. The flicker passed on, and he saw something that he immediately recognized. It was not anywhere that he had been, but as an avid student, Merrick had no trouble identifying the Hive City.

"Orinthal." It sat on his tongue like a foreign fruit, full of mystery and promise. His great-grandmother had come from there, bringing wealth to his great-grandfather's meager estate—and adding a little dark coffee to their skin tone. He recalled the heavily wrought gold chain nestling against his mother's collarbone as she told him bedtime stories that, to his childish imagination, had smelled of spices.

"Never heard of it." Sorcha eased herself off the rug. "Damn it, I think my bones are getting older."

Merrick refrained from making any jokes about his partner's not so really advanced years. She had a good ten on him but was still a handsome woman.

"The capital of Chioma. I will need to do some research, but I am sure that is what you saw."

Sorcha leaned across to touch Merrick's shoulder. "I know

this sounds ridiculous . . . I admit we didn't know Raed long,
but—"

"I share the Bond with both of you," he reminded her
somewhat awkwardly. "I don't want him to die either."

"We'll make sure that doesn't happen," Sorcha said,
stretching her back.

"To Orinthal, then," he replied, and despite everything, he
felt his own excitement rise.

Up there on the dais everything probably looked very simple.
Sorcha, standing below on the mosaic floor of the Chapter
House, tilted her head skyward and tried not to feel intimi-
dated. She also tried not to glance to her right and see Kolya.
Much as she'd hoped that her soon to be former husband
would not be present at this hearing, he had found out. It was
easy to guess who had given the game away.

Arch Abbot Rictun, wrapped in his cloak that was both
blue and emerald green, sat on his newly carved chair and
smiled down at her. Two chairs on his left and two chairs on
his right held the rest of the Presbyterial Council. The only
one Sorcha did not know well was Thorine Bolzak, the new
Presbyter of the Actives. She was young and had been chosen
by Rictun from one of the outlying Abbeys. When Zathra Trelaine had been promoted to Presbyter Secondo, Bolzak had
been brought in to take his place. She was remarkably quiet
for an Active, but maybe that was merely the shock of such a
sudden elevation to power. And now she was one of the five
people who held Sorcha's future in her hands.

Merrick had not been included in this hearing. Having just
finished her defense of the decision to stay with the younger
Deacon rather than return to Kolya, she was feeling confident.
That was until she locked her gaze with Rictun. Multicolored
light from the windows gleamed on his golden hair, but there
was no reflection in his eyes. With an inclination of his head,
he let his words fall on her like little sharp stones. "We have
still to decide on this issue, Deacon Faris."

Kolya shifted beside her. Once, his attention was the only
thing she wanted, and she had dreamed of her husband fighting for her. However, he had let those times pass by, and now

he couldn't seem to understand that she no longer cared. Sorcha carefully tucked her hands under her blue cloak, behind her back, and squeezed them so tightly her knuckles cracked. She counted her breathing, one, two, before opening her mouth.

Melisande Troupe spoke before any words could escape Sorcha. The Presbyter of the Young brushed her white gold hair from her eyes and spoke in a gentle tone. "You must not think us unmoved by your plight, Deacon Faris and Deacon Petav."

Yvril Mournling, the Presbyter of the Sensitives, fixed Sorcha with a hard gray gaze. "We are still looking for precedent for your . . . peculiar situation." He gestured to the stack of leather-bound books piled by his chair. "The partnership between Active and Sensitive is sacred—even if you think of it a tad more lightly than we do."

"Thank you, Your Grace," Kolya broke in, his voice calm and dispassionate. "While our marriage vows may be broken with ease, the Bond we made within the Order should not be so lightly abandoned."

"The Bond can be broken by death or madness—lack of love should be another reason." Sorcha cleared her throat. "With respect, while you wait to test our case, neither of us can move on. Do you not think this a waste of our talents?"

Rictun snorted, but when Presbyter Secondo Zathra Trelaine spoke, he was abruptly silent. The old man's voice was cracked like a piece of sun-dried leather, but it had the weight of authority and wisdom. "She does have a point. Deacon Faris is the most powerful Active we have—having her sit idle goes against good sense."

Sorcha caught a breeze of a chance. She dipped her head so that the Arch Abbot would not see how much she needed this. "I would like to get out of Vermillion for a while, Presbyters. Just for a time, to let the dust settle and while you decide. Having Deacon Chambers, Petav, and me in the confines of Vermillion has become untenable."

"I am sorry you find this situation awkward"—Kolya stepped forward into her field of vision—"but this has never happened before—and I think—"

"Having both you and Deacon Petav in the same place is

rather disturbing," Presbyter Troupe broke in. The corners of her beautiful lips lifted. "Especially to my charges." She directed her brown eyes on their very new Arch Abbot. "At the moment we all need stability. Time to heal."

Sorcha could swear that her breath was choking her throat. Presbyters were nominated for their skills but elected by all of the Order. The Arch Abbot was chosen by the Presbyterial Council—but people in that position had been unceremoniously removed before. Rictun was still very green and undoubtedly anxious not to be the shortest reigning Arch Abbot in the history of the Order of the Eye and the Fist.

A little muscle in his jaw began to twitch. "Very well, perhaps a small break from this tension will be good for everyone in the Mother Abbey."

Kolya's shoulders slumped a little, but he dared not challenge the Arch Abbot—that would have been supremely out of character. He glanced over at Sorcha, his look pleading, but any power he had to move her had been washed away through years of disappointment. She would not show an ounce of sympathy for him; she knew how he turned that always to his advantage.

"I have just the role for Deacons Faris and Chambers." Yvril Mournling's eyes fixed Sorcha to the spot. She recalled how he had covered up the wild talent Merrick had used to save Raed. It was still uncertain why exactly he had done that. The Presbyter flicked his cloak aside with his great sinewy hands. "The delegation from Chioma needs two Deacons as escort home."

Presbyter Bolzak was looking nervously between her colleagues, feeling the tension but not knowing what to do about it. She shifted in her carved wooden chair uncomfortably. "You mean the delegation dealing with the Emperor's marriage negotiations?"

It was the talk of Vermillion and had been for weeks. The Principality of Chioma was far to the south, a kingdom that had stuck firmly to its traditions. Yet it was also rich with gold, spices and gems. The delegation had come to negotiate for one of its princesses to marry the Emperor.

Rictun's smile was thin, and Sorcha could almost hear him

thinking. Chioma in summer would be hot, dusty and damn uncomfortable. The Arch Abbot nodded. "Indeed—a fine idea, Presbyter Mournling. The journey will give Deacon Faris here time to think and decide if this is what she truly wants."

"And carry messages to the Hive City," the Presbyter of the Sensitives agreed.

"The . . . Hive City?" Sorcha dared a question.

Mournling nodded, his eyes drifting to a point somehow past her. "The city of Orinthal is made of the mud of the land, baked hard, like the homes certain insects of that place build."

Deacon Faris had to swallow hard while the image of a tall earthen building, made of ocher earth, rose against a flawless blue sky. It was the city the spectyr had shown her. Risking a glance at the Presbyter, she caught a flicker of something that might have been the slightest inclination of the head. Mournling was among the greatest Sensitives of his age—and she shouldn't have been surprised he had gleaned something from her thoughts.

Presbyter Trelaine leaned back in his chair. "I concur; let us have some more time and send our best Active to guard the Ambassador. It seems a good choice to me, and it will please the Emperor."

Rictun waved Sorcha away. "Go, make your arrangements. The Presbyter Secondo will give you details later."

Sorcha tried not to show her joy as she left. Despite everything, she did not want to rub Kolya's face in her little victories. She had no idea what Mournling was doing—why he was helping them—but one thing was sure: she had more allies than she ever guessed.

The Hive City of Orinthal awaited, as did Raed Rossin, the one man she wanted to see above all others in the world. It was almost enough to make her start believing in fate. Almost.

FIVE

Prayers Answered

Winds blew over Arkaym, but Hatipai flew against the prevailing currents. She had been forced to lie to that royal nothing. It would not do to have her believers see that she could be so restrained, so she had claimed to be an angel. Soon enough she would reclaim her power, and then the time for deception would be over.

The hunger inside her burned white-hot; if she had been human, she might have called it pain. This fragile form was not yet physical, and only faith would improve it.

Finding that was far more difficult than Hatipai had anticipated. Before the Break and the arrival of more of her kind, she and a select few had this world all to themselves. They had been the strongest, able to cross between worlds before there was a rift. Competition was the way of things on the Otherside—and if she was forced to compete here, then she would. Hard.

As Hatipai floated high among the clouds, her perception was spread wide, a net seeking faith. She could not linger long in Vermillion—not with the Mother Abbey in control of the city. If she took blood, bone and skin from there, the consequences could be fatal.

Finally, Hatipai felt a tug from below. It was faint, oh so

very faint, but there it was. Faith. Wrapping her golden wings around her, the angel fell. Four tiny lives were below, looking up, praying to the Bright One. They could not know what a visitation from their goddess truly meant. They would learn.

Walls, doors and locks made no difference to Hatipai—for at this moment she had no body. A family prayed in the close confines of the cabin on their tiny ship tied to a city dock: mother, father and two teenage boys on the edge of manhood. Ripe and sweet to her senses.

On their knees, they whispered the secret names of Hatipai to a small statue of her. The goddess of wisdom and strength, depicted as a full-breasted woman with spread wings and a beatific smile. She felt not a flicker of compassion; these mortals only existed to supply her with what she needed.

Hatipai began to glow, and the family looked up as the tiny cabin filled with light. Their simple meaty faces spread in delight.

"Great lady," the mother whispered, and her eyes began to water, "all these years we have prayed—our mothers and fathers, their mothers and fathers, and nothing . . ." Now her tears were pouring over her cheeks, stricken by the joy of having her faith finally confirmed.

It was a common reaction. The family groveled before her as was just. Hatipai remembered vast churches full to bursting with penitents, the songs, the sacrifices and the heavy smell of incense. She had been truly mighty then, the greatest of all her kin. Now she was reduced to this. Yet, if her plans succeeded, that would change.

She looked down at them through blazing eyes, weighing the value of their meat for her needs.

"Oh, Bright One"—the husband, still on his knees, put an arm around each of his sons—"bless my children with your healing light."

That was it. They were young, strong, full of faith and fervor. They were just what Hatipai needed. She spread her frail, ethereal limbs wide, her wings swinging up to take in all of the cabin space. "I shall indeed." Her voice rang like bells around them.

The younger boy's smile was awestruck when she reached

down to touch him. Hatipai's ethereal body pierced him through, and immediately the boy screamed. It was a pure, musical sound that did not last. Hatipai took his bones, drawing the ingredients that made them into herself, while he collapsed to the floor, a bag of flesh robbed of structure.

The remaining three made guttural sounds of panic, like cattle that finally smell the butcher's purpose. Yet familial bonds stopped them from rushing away from her immediately. As the mother dashed to the remains of her child, Hatipai stepped forward to wrap her now more structured arms around the other boy. He tried to run. His eyes widened, bright blue and panicked. He burst away from the protective hold of his father and leapt for the door.

She was faster. When her wings curled around him, he howled, feeling the sharpness of her power puncture every muscle and sinew. Hatipai sucked them down greedily, pulling his form into her with a sound that would have been disgusting if she had possessed any mortal sensibilities.

When their second child's form splattered to the ground, a dry mass of skin and bone, the two parents didn't scream. Nor did they try to run. The mother's eyes darted to the remains of her sons as if she thought it some magic trick in very poor taste. Then she looked at Hatipai. The geist was used to worshippers admiring her beauty, so she felt the nakedness of her brand-new body especially sharply. It needed covering.

The man was closest. His skin came free with a sound like ripping velvet, while his screams erupted from a mouth now devoid of lips. The woman wailed with him. It was only bare moments, heartbeats, since she had been pleased to see the gleaming angel in her home.

Mortals were such fickle creatures. They called into the dark, demanded answers and attention from forces they could not comprehend, and yet when they had that attention and those answers, they complained about them.

The skin settled around her form, and now Hatipai could feel the warmth of the room and smell the tang of blood and fear. It was a scent she remembered well. The man staggered, blood pouring from his body like a squeezed sponge, and then shock took him. He crashed into the small altar the family had been praying at, sending food offerings and incense sticks clattering into the gore. Then he was on the floor spasming like a gutted fish.

Hatipai was no longer interested in the man. She was already appreciating his gift.

Looking down, she saw that the body had also shuffled into a familiar pattern; it was modeled on a princess of Delmaire—one that Hatipai had devoured from within in the earliest years of her arrival in this world. In her opinion, this use of bone, flesh and skin was much better than any their original owners could ever have put them to. As she was admiring what she had made, the woman came at her with a knife.

It was certainly not the first time a mortal had attempted such a thing, but it was quite possibly the most pathetic. Hatipai caught her arm before it had even completed its downward descent.

While a knife blow could not have killed her, it would be a shame to mar this fine new form. It might not be enough to contain her for long, but she still enjoyed it. Holding the woman in place, she looked down. Her eyes still blazed gold; for some reason, the human eye was something her magic could not replicate. Her first instinct was to kill the pathetic creature, but when she looked deeper, she realized that would have been a kindness.

Hatipai was not prone to kindnesses—so instead she smiled, working her lips around teeth made from the woman's child. That was when the new widow broke down. Sobbing, she slumped to the floor.

"What . . . what are you? What are you?" Her questions were squeezed out of a chest that appeared to be having trouble breathing.

Hatipai raised an eyebrow—an expression she had always been fond of. Her voice was sweeter than honey, more vicious than grief. "I am the goddess you called for. You did call, didn't you?"

Through her pain the woman nodded, unable to deny their prayers and offerings.

Hatipai smiled again. "So for your faith and your offerings, I thank you." And then, naked, she walked from the room, her tiny, perfect human feet trailing patterns of blood and gore after her. The music for her progress was the wretched lamentations of the woman.

As he stood on the quarterdeck of the *Dominion* and looked toward the shambling hulk of the ship on the horizon, the Young Pretender's stomach clenched in anger.

Many people, Raed among them, acknowledged that the new Empire had brought with it advantages: warfare was a thing largely of the past, commerce was flourishing and the people were no longer plagued as frequently by geist activity.

One of the terrible things that remained, however, was a rotten, stinking carcass at a fine feast: slavery.

His grandfather had often been tyrannical—holding an Empire together was not an easy task—but the issue that had haunted his reign most of all had been slavery. His crusade against it had been one of the reasons the Assembly of Princes had turned on him. At least a half dozen of them claimed their kingdoms could not manage without it.

The new Emperor, the one who the Princes had imported from over the ocean, had proven far more compliant to their wishes. He looked the other way while islands off the coast were raided for their inhabitants, who were set to work in distant parts of the Empire. Perhaps he didn't want to test the loyalty of his benefactors so soon. Perhaps he felt he needed to wait and find his feet. Whatever his reasoning, Raed had none of those concerns.

Slave ships were his natural prey. His hunting earned his father much kudos among the ramshackle towns of the scattering of small islands between Arkaym and Delmaire. Today he would free more slaves and then use the stinking remains of the ship for his own purposes. Two birds had never been more efficiently killed with one stone.

With nod of his head, Aachon called for the topsail to be unfurled, and the *Dominion* leapt through the water to her purpose. Her crew meanwhile sharpened cutlasses and prepared for battle. No slave ship, low in the water and with the blunt scow features, could ever hope to match the brigantine's speed.

At his left shoulder, Tangyre drew her sword. "I find I am rather growing to like your plan, my Prince."

"This is the easy bit," Aachon observed in a low undertone.

"But also the most satisfactory," Raed replied, as the *Dominion* bore down on the slave ship. This close, the grubby lettering on its hull could be made out.

Sweet Moon might be a very unlikely name for a ship of this ilk—slavers often had a curious sense of humor. On the deck, several of them could be seen, also preparing for battle.

Raed called out, and Aleck quickly raised their flag. The Rossin's mer-shape flapped free and loose, spilling out into the breeze with a sharp snap. The Young Pretender felt his throat constrict at the sight of his tormentor. Yet it was not just he who feared the image. A cry arose from the slavers. They now knew whom they faced.

Skimming across the waves, the *Dominion* came on fast like retribution. Aachon steered them skillfully, until they were stealing the wind right out of the *Sweet Moon*'s sails.

"Heave to," Aachon bellowed, "or we will blow your sorry arse out of the water!"

Perhaps the Rossin flag had been the wrong choice, because the slavers did the exact opposite. As the sailors of the *Dominion* scrambled to navigate their ship up within grappling range, the slavers on the *Sweet Moon* began throwing struggling forms off the stern.

"By the Blood," Raed roared, standing on the rigging. "Filthy murderers!" He knew there was no time for grappling hooks.

"My Prince—" Aachon surged forward, but it was too late. The Young Pretender wrapped one arm around a portion of the running rigging and kicked out hard from his ship. The ocean raced by under his feet, but years of sailing made Raed very adept at judging distance. Behind him a half dozen of his crew followed in his wake.

He landed on the swaying deck, dropped down lightly from the rope and grappled a swarthy shape that was about to thrust a manacled woman into the heaving sea. The slaver howled as Raed buried his knife into his neck. Blood poured onto the deck, while the woman screamed like it had been her who had been cut.

More of his crew landed next to him, and suddenly the slavers found their mettle was being tested by people who could fight back, sailors and soldiers trained in combat, and not shackled villagers.

The crew of the *Dominion* set to their work with relish, and for a little while the deck heaved with grunts and groans. Blood made the deck slippery, but Raed barely noticed—caught as he was in the delight of good, honest combat.

It didn't last long, however. Raed wiped his blade clean on the cloak of a fallen slaver. In truth he was glad they had put up a fight. He had no mercy for their kind, and yet he couldn't have brought himself to act as they had. As his crew brought the *Sweet Moon* to a dead halt in the water, Raed found the ring of keys on the chief slaver's body.

Gently he touched the woman on the shoulder. She looked up, tears streaking a face that was twisted with fear. "Please," she whispered through a strained throat, "make it quick."

Raed bent and unlocked her shackles. "We are your rescuers, not your killers, my lady."

The look she leveled at him was not just filled with gratitude—it also contained a fair amount of anger—not at him but at a world in which people could be sold like cattle, a world in which you could be tending your fields in the morning and find yourself shackled in the bowels of a slave ship in the evening. Outlying islands were treated like farms by certain principalities.

Raed didn't know what he could do to dampen that rage. With a gesture but not a touch, he indicated she should go forward to where the crew of the *Dominion* were flinging open the hatches.

The slaves clambered out, reeking of sweat, urine and terror, unable to even move to have their shackles struck loose. This was a small consignment on a ship designed to stick to the coast and bring slaves right into the Empire via the river systems. They must have spent weeks in a holding pen before being shipped out on this vessel.

Aachon strode up to his captain and looked down at the pitiful scene without uttering a word.

"With everything we suffer, why do they have to add to this?" Raed muttered. "How is it that I thought the geists were the worst affliction of the Empire?"

His first mate sighed. "It is not a perfect world, my Prince."

Wiping her blade on a portion of fallen slaver's coat, Tangyre joined them. Her expression was one of distaste. "I had forgotten that such filth had returned to Arkaym."

It was not his friend's fault, but Raed knew that in his father's sphere of influence many things about those left behind had been forgotten. In the Coronet Isles it was easy to forget the world beyond their shores. "Unfortunately, I cannot fix the ills of the Empire, Tang."

As they had planned, they shepherded the slaves—who flinched from even the kindest hand—over to the *Dominion*. Aachon stood on the gunwales and looked between the crew and those ten men chosen to remain with Raed.

The Young Pretender stepped closer to his friend. "You are to return these people to their homes and then take shelter in the islands off the Bay of Winds, Aachon. Plenty of places to hide there, just in case the Emperor decides to raise the price on my head. We will look for you there when we have Fraine safely back."

"My Prince"—the first mate put up one final protest—"there is still time to reconsider this."

Raed also felt the wrench, but this was the only sensible thing to do. "You swore to protect me, old friend, but you also have a duty to the crew. I will not sacrifice their lives for mine, and I cannot take all of them into Chioma. You're the only one I would trust to keep the *Dominion* safe."

Aachon sighed. They had argued long the previous day, and it had taken a direct order from Raed to finally get him to obey.

"Look"—the Young Pretender clapped Aachon on the shoulder—"Tang is here, and you have always been my friend, not my bodyguard—despite what my father said to you. You know we cannot abandon the crew out here."

The first mate thought for a moment and finally gave a curt nod. "I only do this because Captain Greene is, like I, ordered to protect the royal bloodline." He gave an elaborate Court bow. "Remember who you are, my Prince, and bring your sister and yourself back safe."

With that, he stepped across to the *Dominion*, and in his great booming bass voice ordered the crew to cast off. He did not stand on the deck and watch the *Sweet Moon* fall away. Raed smiled. No, his friend would never do that.

So, taking a leaf from his book, the Young Pretender would not look after his ship like a love-struck fool, wondering if he'd ever see her again. He had plenty enough of that in his life.

Raed turned his mind away from his ship and toward Fraine. He took stock of those he had chosen in this mission; five of his most reliable fighters from the *Dominion*. They included Laython, the dour little quartermaster; Snook, the best navigator of river or sea; and Captain Tangyre Greene. These were three women he would stake his life on. It felt like he was always placing his life into the hands of women.

His thoughts were getting away on him again. *Sorcha.* He pushed that memory away as best he could—as he had for the last season.

Snook, the rail-thin navigator, took the wheel in her hands and looked straight at him. "Where to, Captain?"

It was said so lightly that they might have been going out for a Sunday stroll rather than proceeding into the heart of the Empire. It made Raed smile as he strode over to stand at her shoulder.

"Your best speed to Londis, Mistress Snook. We need to get our papers to travel farther upriver."

"Your sister will be so proud," Tangyre whispered into his ear.

"I hope she lives to tell me that," Raed replied as the *Sweet Moon* swung to the south, into the night and toward the danger of Chioma.

SIX

Watched Clocks

Everything was taking a damned long time. Sorcha stood in the shade of the portico, smoked her cigar and watched the baggage train being loaded with all the patience of a child waiting for a treat. So far, preparations had eaten up the entire morning, and the oxen had not even been secured. Her mood was not helped by Kolya's presence. He was smart enough to stay out of her way on the far side of the courtyard, but his eyes never left her.

Despite the Council's ruling, part of her was nervous he would jump aboard the dirigible at the last moment. She'd thought him so predictable when they were married, but everything was different now. His sudden streak of determination had her worried.

In her pocket, under the cover of her blue cloak where he could not see, her hand was clenched on the mysterious badge she had found on the dead body of Arch Abbot Hastler. On one side was embroidered a picture of a snake eating its own tail, but it had been the image on the reverse that had caused her far more concern.

The shape of a circle of five stars impressed itself on her palm as her fist tightened. She had needed no research to tell her what it was. That symbol could still be found on pieces of the Abbey—those that were out of reach of the ancient vandals, that was. It was the sign of the Native Order, the one that had been obliterated long before her own had come over with the Emperor scant years before.

For three months Sorcha had kept the badge behind a loose brick in her chamber, but this morning she had fished it out. The spectyr had shown her a circle of stars, and she would have been a fool not to spot the connection.

"Still at it, are they?" Merrick, the master of silent arrivals, made her jump. He was chewing on a bit of white bread smeared with a great yellow gob of butter, while holding another in his left hand.

"Thought you were just going for a breath of air?" Sorcha slid her fist out of her pocket, ground out the stub of her cigar and calmed her thoughts as best she could. She was not yet prepared to share her concerns with him—not until they proved more solid.

Her partner shrugged. "I happened to pass by the Imperial kitchens—their food is so much better than even the Mother Abbey's." He held out a portion of the still-warm bread. "Tell me I am wrong."

Taking his offering, Sorcha perched herself on the railing and bit into the bread. The food at the Abbey was perfectly fine, if plain—this was another matter. The taste of spices filled her mouth as the crisp crust broke into the soft fluffy center—it needed neither butter or cheese to make it delicious.

Her eyebrows shot up. "I can see why the aristocrats always have a difficulty with their girth."

Merrick, who was more of a stickler for the politenesses of society, finished his mouthful before replying. "The spices are the baker experimenting—apparently they brought boxes and boxes of them." He jerked his head to where the silk-clad Chiomese were adjusting packs on a line of donkeys. Then his eyes alighted on Kolya. "Quite persistent, isn't he."

It was not a question. Sorcha decided this particular bull needed his horns taken hold of. Kolya straightened as she came his way, a genuine smile on his face, and for an instant she actually caught a glimpse of the man she'd married. That only irritated her more. She had pleaded with him time after time to show her his feelings, let her in, but it was only once she had left him that he had done anything about it.

"Just come to see you off." Kolya gave her a somewhat stilted bow.

It was incredibly awkward, and Sorcha's irritation withered away. She'd spent so many years with this man, trusted her life to him, but now they were caught between intimacy and coldness. Yet she knew if she reached out, he would take it as good sign and expect something she could no longer give him. So she kept herself still. "You shouldn't have," she said, finally meeting his eyes. "Really . . . you shouldn't have." He winced at the sadness in her face.

Kolya's jaw clenched. "I still care, Sorcha."

Sorcha bit back her reply that she did too. It would only hurt and confuse him, so she replied, "I am afraid that some things you can't fix once the time has passed." She folded her hands to stop them from doing anything that might be misconstrued. Instead she turned away and returned to Merrick.

"So"—she leaned next to her partner and deliberately did not watch Kolya leave the courtyard—"educate me on this Kingdom of Chioma."

He glanced at her but was wise enough not to ask about what had transpired. Besides, he was younger than she and enjoyed, perhaps a little too much, any chance to show his skills. Unlike Kolya, who had always talked down to her when imparting information, Merrick oozed almost puppy-like enthusiasm. She knew which she preferred.

Pulling up a chair, he sat down and propped his feet on the low wall. "As a boy I read as much as I could about it—not that there was much to find. It is the only principality that has never been invaded and never had its Prince deposed."

"Impressive." Sorcha glanced over her shoulder with new appreciation. The Empire's history was rife with conflict, invasions and atrocities. She knew of no Prince of Arkaym whose dominion went back more than a few generations. It was what made her own Emperor nervous of Raed and his distant father. One day, when Kaleva was more secure on his throne, she was sure that the Coronet Isles would no longer be far enough away to protect the Unsung. Even the Emperor was not immune to arranging accidents for his opponents.

"They also have kept hold of their state religion"—Merrick

grinned—"so remember not to call the little gods that there. It could be . . . awkward."

Sorcha rolled her eyes. As someone who had looked into the bleak face of the Otherside, she had no time for such foolishness. "It's like that, is it? Very well, I will hold my tongue."

The corner of Merrick's mouth twitched, but he made no comment. "Actually, they are so firm in their beliefs that the Prince of Chioma had to give special dispensation for the Imperial Dirigible to even approach Orinthal."

"What?"

Her partner flicked crumbs off his cloak and chuckled. "They don't much hold with new inventions. In fact, they believe flying through the air an affront to their goddess Hatipai."

"Sounds like a wonderful place." Sorcha didn't care if her voice was dripping with sarcasm.

Merrick cleared his throat. "Perhaps not in all things. They still cling to very"—he stopped and pressed his lips together before going on,—"regional ways. Only men are allowed to rule there—just as the place I was born."

It was the first time he had ever spoken of his home, but he looked dreadfully uncomfortable about it, so Sorcha held back her sharp reply. The Emperor still had much work to do, and she was not so blind to think the world a perfect place. Slavery and ignorance, like stubborn weeds, still clung here and there.

"Yet it is the place we will find Raed," she said finally.

Sorcha closed her eyes for a second and tried to gain control of her emotions. She and the Young Pretender had shared a passionate few days, but whatever else she might feel for him was unclear. The desperate loneliness she'd suffered in her marriage had left her uncertain of her own feelings for the first time. It almost made her afraid to see Raed again—and yet she was not about to let him go to his death.

Sorcha swallowed hard. "Is this a mistake, Merrick?"

He chose his words carefully. "Perhaps. But we owe Raed a great debt and a Bond." His mind tugged on the connection lightly, sending a shiver down Sorcha's back. "It is not something to be lightly cast aside."

She'd had enough of that sort of talk from the Council, but

if that was what he believed, and it would get them out of the
city, she was willing to go along with it.

Beyond the portico the servants pulled the oxen into the
traces, so Sorcha stood up, finally convinced that they might
be moving soon.

"What is that?" Merrick leaned forward and yanked her
sleeve back from her wrist. On her hand she had slipped the one
other thing she kept hidden in the Abbey. It was Raed's ring,
embossed with the rampant Rossin of his house, the item he had
given her before leaving Vermillion. It had felt right to put it on.

Sorcha jerked back, unable to find words that would not
reveal how embarrassed she was. The damn Bond meant he
probably knew anyway, but she was certainly not about to
wrench it off her thumb. Instead she stared at him, until eventually it was he who flushed and looked away.

Luckily at that moment chaos broke out. "Wait! Wait!
Don't forget this!" A burly Imperial servant came racing out
of the palace with a large painting tucked under one arm. It
was of the Emperor himself, in full dress uniform.

Relieved at the distraction, Sorcha got up and helped the
distraught servant find a place for the portrait on the last cart.
It was so handsome that perhaps the Princess Ezefia would
think it painted with too much appreciation for the Prince's
status. In fact, Sorcha knew it did not really capture her
Emperor—his handsomeness yes, but not the charisma and
charm he possessed as well.

Bandele, the ambassador from Chioma, finally appeared.
He was hard to miss: over six feet tall and wrapped in orange
and bright green silks that set his dark face in shocking contrast. When he smiled, which he did often, the flash of white
teeth was broad and startling. Apparently the Princess Ezefia's suit for the Emperor's hand had gone very well, because
her representative was in a fine mood. He nodded to the Deacons before taking his place at the head of the procession to
the Imperial Dirigible Station.

Merrick and Sorcha were just behind him.

"All ready, then?" Bandele asked, as if it had been the
sparsely equipped Deacons who had caused the delay.

Merrick stifled a grin while Sorcha was not nearly so
amused. "For hours, actually," she snapped.

It might as well have been water off a duck's back. "Excellent—then let's move out." He waved his hand, and the gates were finally opened. The whole wagon train, including the dozen guards, wrapped far more somberly in dark silks, moved out.

Sorcha let out a long breath that felt like she had been holding it all day. Glancing to her right, she was slightly disturbed by Merrick's broad grin—but then the younger Deacon had somehow managed to keep his boyish enthusiasm for most things.

If he stayed with her, Sorcha thought morosely, it would soon wear off.

Three days lingering in the port of Londis was driving Raed more than a little crazy.

Certainly the Saal River mouth was busy. The *Sweet Moon* was tied up among other ships, some fellow slavers, some carrying other cargo such as wheat, spice and oil. However, the delays in getting the proper forms from the Imperial Trade Office were ridiculous.

If the *Sweet Moon* had in fact been full of slaves, a goodly number of them would have died in the sweltering hold. Bureaucracy was something none of his crew was used to dealing with, and Raed chafed under it.

So for the third day in a row, Raed and Tangyre stood on the bustling quayside in the Imperial port town of Londis and breathed in the real heat of the south.

"I had forgotten how wonderful it is here," Tangyre said, flicking open a couple more buttons on her shirt.

"Watch yourself, Tang," Raed laughed. "We need to keep the illusion of respectable slavers."

If he did not think about his sister lost somewhere in the vast Empire, he might have enjoyed this. Since the confrontation under Vermillion, the Curse of his family, the geistlord Rossin had not stirred inside him. He had almost forgotten what it was like to live without fear of turning into the great cat and killing those he cared for.

As they strolled through the yelling, cursing traders and toward the Customhouse, Raed's mind drifted much farther. The space on his finger where his signet ring had been was still pale, the skin there not yet as tanned as the rest of his hand. He wondered what had happened to Sorcha. Her place in the Order had felt precarious, and smuggling him out of the city had without doubt endangered it further.

He had no idea what her feelings for him were, and he was still uncertain on his own. Yet he thought of her often. Raed had never wanted the eldritch connection of an Order Bond, but he liked knowing that they were still joined—even if he could not feel it.

"Shall we go in?" Tangyre, who naturally knew nothing of Sorcha, was standing at the impressive ironbound doors of the Customhouse and eyeing him curiously.

Tangyre had been his friend almost as long as Aachon, but she was considerably less demanding and far more relaxed about his princely duties.

"Sorry, Tang." Raed rubbed his beard. "I was miles away."

Inside were more accountants than Raed had ever had to deal with. His heart sank a little on seeing the rows of desks manned by sharply dressed clerks, all with their heads down, writing and stamping piles of paper. "By the Blood—more lines!"

His words echoed in the chamber. A couple of resigned-looking men standing before the desks turned and glanced over their shoulders. The looks said it all.

Tangyre laughed and guided them over to what appeared to be the shortest line. "My captain is in fine form today."

It was warm, stiflingly warm, and Raed shifted from foot to foot, holding in an exasperated sigh. The people ahead of them moved at a snail's pace, and all he could think was that every second wasted, Fraine traveled father away.

Eventually the line dwindled until only two men stood between them and the sweating paper shuffler. That was when the bells began to ring. Not the polite bells that stood on the table to summon a Customhouse manager—no, the great bells at the end of the pier. Everyone was suddenly on their feet, and the orderly room dissolved into scattering people. The clerks were folding up their books and disappearing behind sturdy office doors.

"Is it for us, do you think my P—" Tangyre caught herself in time. "—my captain?"

"Our reception would be guards, not ringing bells, I think." Raed muttered. "Come on, let's see what's going on."

They joined the general rush outside toward the piers. Harbor officials and wharf workers were trying to handle a distressed knot of people milling around a small ketch. Raed and Tangyre shouldered their way through the press. There on the pier sat a woman, screaming. In her crimson splattered arms, she held the pale, limp form of another woman. The second woman was drenched in blood; it covered her arms, soaked her dress and oozed from the strange bundle she clutched to her. Raed's practiced eye noted much of the blood was clotted and semidry. It looked like she had lain in it for some time.

"Sister," the first sobbed, rocking the comatose other, "let me have him."

This only made her tighten her grip on the thing she held. It looked more like the leavings from a butcher's shop than anything human. The Young Pretender's stomach turned. Flayed fingers peeked from the bundle. It had once been a person.

A whisper passed through the crowd, then a ripple of indrawn breath.

"She took them! She took them!" The woman soaked in blood began to scream. "They're all dead . . . all dead!" She waved her hands back toward the small ship, tethered there with all the other vessels of trade. Now beyond words, she began to wail like an animal caught in a trap, thrashing around in her sister's arms, her mouth stretched in a painful circle.

Raed and the rest of the crowd flinched as she went on and on. It took a while for words to become apparent. "Hatipai! Hatipai!"

He recognized it—as a young boy he had been forced to commit to memory the names of the little gods. So that explained it—she had to be mad. He watched as horrified as the rest of the gathered crowd, as she rocked the bundle of stripped flesh.

A couple of brave souls, wharf workers by their stature and dress, boarded the ship. When they emerged pale-faced, staggering and retching, Raed knew it had to be awful; tough port workers were not known for their sensitive dispositions. "Fetch the sheriff," one groaned. "It's a bloodbath in there!"

"Not the sheriff—the Deacons!" another bellowed. "Get the Deacons!"

Then the crowd's mood changed to panic. Raed, however, was thinking of the last bloodbath he'd seen on a boat: an Imperial warship scattered with bodies. One glance told him that Tangyre was thinking the very same thing.

"It is not the Rossin," Captain Greene whispered under her breath. "The woman went mad and killed her own family."

It made sense, yet something in the haunted woman's eyes told Raed she had seen too much. They were taking her away, though none of the workers could get her to relinquish her gruesome burden. Her sister looked down at her soiled apron and hands in blank dismay—as if she didn't know if she should head to a laundry or slump down on the pier.

Raed stepped forward, took her under the arm and guided her out of the way. People were in such a rush to follow after the deluded woman or crowd as close as possible to the scene of the crime that she was in danger of being trampled.

She appeared ready to tumble, so Raed sat her on a large crate and handed her his kerchief. For an instant she looked at the neat piece of silk.

"This is too fine to get blood on it," she whispered.

"Nonsense." Raed felt badly enough about what he was going to ask her that the loss of one of his few remaining fineries was trivial. "I am sorry to ask this, ma'am. But . . . was your sister well before this? Did she and her family fight often?"

She looked up at him, her face twisting while her fingers still squeezed the kerchief. "No, never! Joi's a good woman. She loved Yorse and the boys. They loved one another so much . . ." That was when weeping once again overcame her.

Tangyre took him by the elbow and pulled him away. "We must get back to the Customhouse." She leaned in and whispered, "Especially with Deacons coming."

Raed nodded, allowing himself to be guided away from the sobbing woman. Though it had ebbed away as far as it could, he could feel the supernatural tide from the Otherside now rushing back. Whatever respite he'd enjoyed these past months was over—and it couldn't have happened at a worse time—but there was no chance he would turn back. Fraine still had to be found. He could only hope the Rossin would remain somnolent and agreeable.

SEVEN

Fallen Dreams

In the dark of the third night of their voyage, Merrick woke. The Imperial Dirigible was silent around him—at least as silent as anything made of wood and silk could be. The tiny creaks were like that of a ship, but without the comforting slap of the ocean against the sides. It served as a constant reminder that they were flying hundreds of miles above solid ground.

He lay looking up at the beams for a moment. Only a few feet away, Sorcha slept, emitting a slight rumble that he wouldn't have dared called a snore. Usually a Deacon would have been afforded the comfort of a cabin, but the Chiomese delegation took priority, and he and Sorcha were far more comfortable bedded in the empty hold reserved for horses. They would have both loved to bring the Breed horses with them. Melochi and Shedryi would at least have been comfort on nights like this.

"Better we be mistaken for an honest beast than for a diplomat," had been Sorcha's comment as she'd unfurled her bedroll.

In three or four more days they would reach Orinthal. It should have been exciting to Merrick, since a journey into the heart of Chioma had been his boyhood dream, yet he could not shake the feeling of impending doom.

That Sorcha, Raed and he had been manipulated into nearly causing the destruction of Vermillion still rankled. A Sensitive was supposed to See clearly, if not all, then at least what was happening to him.

Merrick glanced to his right. Sorcha was lying curled on her side, her long red hair almost hiding her face. Despite her being the elder, it was his responsibility to look after her.

So he slipped out from under his regulation blanket, his Strop clasped in one hand. Here on the swaying deck of the dirigible, Merrick was able to let out a breath. The ship was running under a hunter's moon, overripe and ominous—if one believed in such things. His mother had remained a believer in the small gods, and those superstitions implanted at her knee had been hard to shake. A hunter's moon had been called that as it gave nighttime stalkers the best light to see by. After the Break it was found to be the most preferred time for geists to appear.

Sailing up here they were safe from geist activity—it was thought. As Merrick peered over the edge at the landscape sliding below them, he wondered what the folk down there were experiencing, but he had not ventured out into the chill night air merely to think dark thoughts.

Locating a space that was small and out of the way on the efficient deck was hard, but eventually he found a box tucked behind the main cabins that was part of the overflow from the delegation. Sitting himself cross-legged on it, Merrick took out the Strop.

The long, thick piece of leather was tooled with the Seven Runes of Sight, and its making had been his final achievement before becoming a Deacon. Under his fingers the runes were slightly warm.

Merrick slipped the Strop over his eyes, tied it into a knot at the back, closed his eyes and opened his Center. It was the calm place that all Deacons had: their seat of power, where all things passed away and only knowledge mattered. At least that was how it was experienced by Sensitives.

Masa, the Third rune of Sight, was always tricky to use. Seeing into the future was inexact. Whatever he would be able to squeeze from it would not be as accurate or obvious as anyone with a wild native talent, or even the Possibility Matrix, could find. That damned device that had provided their enemies prescience was gone—he was relieved about that, yet he could have done with its foresight at this moment.

Merrick's Center flew forward like an arrow. He saw the Hive City, though he only knew it from picture books, so it was indistinct and fluttered in the winds of his mind. Overhead the stars gleamed in a carpet of beauty, deeper and more magnificent than even the real night sky. Then as Merrick watched, the stars all dimmed, except for five. These grew brighter and pulled themselves from the sky. The young Deacon held out his hand, and they flew to him, twisting around his outstretched fingers to lie in a circle. They twinkled bright and lovely, yet somehow to look upon them made Merrick sick. Such a visceral sensation was something unexpected while wearing the Strop.

He was used to the signs and interpreting them—what he was not used to was the feeling of not being alone that now came over him.

Once, as a child, he had lost his mother in the bustling market. Wandering the streets alone, he had heard footsteps behind him, and he ran. But the shadow had given chase, and though his mother had eventually found him, that memory was still a powerful one. He felt that fear again—right into his bones. And so his spirit ran in a display of panic that his tutors at the Abbey would have despaired of. As his discipline crumbled in the face of such a primitive force, he heard it—words in a space where there should have been none.

Come back to us, Brother. Come back . . .

It was a voice of such yearning and familiarity that he turned. The young Deacon caught sight of a man, cloaked in darkness and circled by stars. Merrick only had time to make out his hawklike profile and the eyes that were focusing on him.

Then the real world called. Merrick gasped, feeling the Sight being ripped away from him deep down in his gut. When he yanked off his Strop it took a moment for his head to stop spinning enough to focus on the woman standing in front of him.

Captain Vyra Revele had her hand raised to her mouth in shock. "Damnation, I am sorry—"

"So you should be," Merrick snapped, caught unawares by his own annoyance. His heart still pumped fast, so that he was forced to wipe the sweat off his palms and onto his trouser leg. In Captain Revele's eyes he saw how he must look and was not pleased. The captain of the *Summer Hawk* had only shown them courtesy this trip, and on their previous encounter she had assisted them at risk of her own life and commission. "I am sorry, Captain." He unfolded his legs and slid down to the deck. "Using the runes sometimes makes me forget my manners."

In her smart Imperial air navy uniform, her short dark hair ruffling in the wind, she was very much part of her ship but completely clueless about the world he walked in. Her smile was hesitant. "I did not see it was you, Deacon Chambers. I thought it was one of my crew hiding from his duties."

He laughed at that, trying to dispel the final fears that still clung to his brain. "I wouldn't think any of your crew would dare such a thing."

She tilted her head, nodded slowly, but did not reply. For some reason, it seemed she was suddenly out of words, and Merrick found himself struggling for something to fill this mysterious gap.

"So, Captain Revele—"

"You may call me Vyra," she said as they walked the deck of the dirigible, heading forward where the clouds could be seen skidding around the airship's hull.

Merrick heard the tone in her voice, a slight intensity that made him feel uncomfortable. So he did what he had been trained to do—he faced it. "It is a wonderful coincidence that the *Summer Hawk* is the ship assigned to take us south."

Vyra leaned on the ropes. "I confess, Deacon Chambers—"

"You may call me Merrick."

"That would be inappropriate—and against regulations." She stood suddenly military straight, and then shot him another glance. "But thank you. I must confess that when the assignments were handed out, I volunteered *Summer Hawk* for this detail."

"Why would you do that? This delegation must be the dullest use of an Imperial Dirigible possible."

Vyra shrugged. "I have a feeling, Deacon Chambers, that wherever you and your partner go, it is never dull."

Merrick let out a breath. He had been worried that the

captain's interest was related to him—never thinking that it was just a desire for action. The Imperial Air Fleet was still new, and the Empire largely quiet—so much of what it did was act as a courier service for goods all over the continent.

"I am afraid that this is a mission that even Sorcha cannot make more than a civilized delegation."

The captain shrugged. "The marriage of Emperors is perhaps not as simple as you think."

The tone of her voice was enough to raise Merrick's curiosity. "Have you heard something?" It was one of the risks of being a Deacon; gossip and scuttlebutt tended to not be passed on to the Order.

Vyra's lips pursed as if she were considering the wisdom of doing that very thing. "Let us say that the jockeying for the position of Empress has not been . . . gentle."

A stray fact, one of the many he had learned of Chioma, suddenly emerged from the depths of Merrick's recollection; the principality was not only the home of every strange and exotic spice in the Empire but also some of the most powerful and hard-to-detect poisons. Suddenly their trip seemed to become far more complicated.

"It is good then to know you are our backup, Captain Revele."

Her smile was sudden and brilliant in the moonlight, but she did not reply. Instead she squeezed his arm in a most familiar manner before she turned and strode the rest of the way up the deck toward the wheelhouse.

Merrick was left looking over the night of tumultuous clouds and angry moon. He didn't need the Sight of Deacon Reeceson to know bad things awaited them in the rich principality of Chioma, but that was not what made him shiver.

It was instead the memory of the man that had chased him in his own sacred space. He would not sleep this night—and for many more, most likely—because of what he had felt. Merrick would be glad when they reached Orinthal and its Abbey. Maybe it was an illusion, but he felt sure he would at least be able to sleep there.

EIGHT

The Wakened Dark

After getting the appropriate paperwork, the *Sweet Moon* sailed up the Saal without much ceremony, but Raed couldn't shake the memory of the blood-soaked woman holding her kin in a dripping bundle and screaming to an impotent goddess. Tangyre had tried to distract him to little effect. The surroundings of a slaver ship, even an empty one, were not that conducive to laughter.

Only Raed and Tang were above deck on the third morning, while the crew breakfasted below. The Young Pretender had felt very little like eating since leaving Londis. Instead he watched the riverbank slide away from the ship.

Despite it being over a season since he had been tormented by the Rossin, Raed was still wary of being this close to land. The urge to turn about and head for the open ocean, as he had done for most of his adult life, was powerful. Only the thought of his sister Fraine somewhere out there kept him on course.

The land they were sailing deeper into was unfamiliar to him, hotter and more parched than any he had seen. Yet it was part of the Empire and by rights should have been ruled by him. His grandfather, he knew, had sailed this very river heading north to Orinthal. Naturally, it had been with consid-

erably more pomp and ceremony than their current circum-
stance called for.

Raed gripped the railing of the ship hard. "Life is never
quite how you imagine it."

"Indeed, my Prince"—Tang leaned on her elbows next to
him—"but how we overcome adversity is the ultimate test of
who we are."

Raed swallowed hard. "I just hoped—well . . . I hoped
that—" He stopped short, realizing the words he was about to
say were ridiculous. His hopes were ridiculous. This world
had to live with the geists, and more powerful men than he
had tried to change things to no effect. Instead of letting out
words that would make him sound like a petulant child,
Raed shrugged. "I just feel as if something is waiting for us.
For me."

She squeezed his shoulder. Neither of them mentioned the
Rossin and the fate of his mother, who had died beneath the
geistlord's claws.

"No one knows we are coming." Tangyre turned around
and said the next few words in an offhand manner that he did
not buy for an instant. "Perhaps you are merely thinking of
distant places—distant people?"

Raed arched an eyebrow, glad of the distraction from
thinking of his sister or the Rossin. "I did not realize that
Aachon had time to spill all my secrets to you."

Captain Greene grinned broadly. "You just have to know
which handle to crank to get everything out of him."

Raed laughed.

"You are still not very good at hiding your emotions,
Raed." Tang was relentless. She knew him far too well—
probably even better than Aachon, since she was not as lumbered with the first mate's belief in the royal hierarchy. She
fixed him with that hawklike stare. "This Deacon got under
your skin."

"In more ways than I can express," he replied, thinking of
their days on the Imperial Dirigible. "But the situation is
complicated."

"I can imagine. A Deacon, a married Deacon?" She laughed
and slapped him on the back. "Would a simple tavern wench
not have been a smarter choice?"

Raed grinned ruefully. "Everything else in my life as it is—I wouldn't know what to do with something simple."

Apparently just getting him to laugh had been her entire goal. "Then things are normal, my Prince." Her voice dipped into quite a wonderful mimic of Aachon. "I better go find myself a spot of breakfast before the crew devours all there is."

She left him alone on the deck but actually in a better mood. The scorched land looked less dire.

When the hatch to the slave quarters banged open, Raed did not move. Only when an unfamiliar voice spoke to him did he turn around. A strange woman stood on the deck, and apart from not knowing who she was, the Pretender was struck by one thing—she was impossibly beautiful.

It was not merely that her body was long and lithe, or even that her honey hair curled and gleamed down to her waist—she glowed. Even in the warm, sunny morning weather, she was the brightest thing about. Her lips spread in a smile that would have driven men mad, and her eyes were gold—a color never seen in a human skull. As Raed frowned and took a slight step backward, he noted something else strange. Her skin, gleaming and beautiful as it was, was also strangely patterned, almost like quilted-together remnants. Some pieces were pure white, others caramel colored. It was odd yet strangely compelling. A curl of displeasure filtered up from inside Raed, a flicker of awareness from the long-silent Rossin.

The woman's hand fluttered to her cheek. "Yes." She smiled, and it was like the grin of a wolf. "I am not as I once was. Perhaps I am not as practiced as I once was either—but I will remember eventually."

Her tone was light and almost pleasant, but Raed did not mistake this for kindness—for her eyes were those of a predator. "I am dreadfully sorry," he said, this time taking a step toward her, which also drew him closer to the hatch to the cabins, where his sword and gun were lying. "I don't think we have been introduced." Whatever this creature was, he was certain there was no way she could be a geist. They were on moving water. And yet, and yet—his mind slipped back to the destruction he had witnessed on the Imperial Navy ship earlier in the year. It was apparent that for every rule there was an exception.

Her head tilted, and her hands clenched at her side. "I was not talking to you—I was talking to him." Her chin lifted, and the contempt in her eyes froze Raed for a second.

No, she was not addressing the Young Pretender. She was addressing his Curse: the geistlord within. Fear flooded up through Raed, and his thoughts darted to those belowdecks. The danger to his crew was real, and he had to do something.

"Raed?" The hatch to the cabin popped open, and Tangyre emerged carrying a tray. For one frozen moment the three of them stood facing one another in an unlikely tableau.

Then the stranger moved. Raed wasn't sure what was going to happen, but what he certainly was not prepared for was the woman charging at him. He was suddenly caught in a tangle of arms and hair, and her strength was unexpected. Raed found himself tumbling over the gunwales with the woman clawing at his face.

They hit the water hard. It was warm, murky and choked with silt and weed. Raed inhaled in shock and drew an unfortunate draft of it into his lungs. The woman's hands were now on his throat, and there was nothing the Young Pretender could do. Her grip was like iron, and though his fingers scrambled at hers, he could not pry her loose. Raed caught a fractured glimpse of his attacker. She did not seem to worry about the water; instead, her gleaming eyes focused solely on him.

A peculiar lethargy stole over Raed. A long second passed where just giving up felt like the easiest course. But then he thought of them. Fraine, his little sister, lost somewhere in the Empire, abandoned to a bloody and cruel fate. Sorcha, the red-haired Deacon, who he had said good-bye to on a pier. Her words had been strong, but her blue eyes had been soft. He'd been certain they would see each other again.

For those two, he would not give up. Yet he was falling— spiraling into darkness. What other choice did he have but to call out to the Rossin? His Curse. His enemy. His only hope.

Down in the depths of blood and bone, the Rossin stirred as his host called. Life was fading around them both, smothered in dank river water and under the golden eyes of the woman.

It could stay quiet and let their attacker have her way. By

the time that twisted geistlord had crushed the Young Pretender, the Rossin would already be far away inside the body of Fraine—next in the bloodline.

Yet that powerful entity did not like to give in to another of his kind, and the royal line was not as large as it had once been. Hatipai may have been a shadow of her former power, but he was not. The Rossin called on his shape.

Raed's body was his material, and the geistlord stirred and molded it to his own purposes. Sinew and muscle snapped, twisting out of the woman's unnatural grip even as her hands clawed deeper. The Rossin's mer-shape, the one that was emblazoned on the flag that flew over the *Dominion*, sprang into being; the front a great pard, all claw and tooth, while the rear of it a coil of mighty scales and fins. The muscle-bound shape flicked its tail and dived deeper.

Hatipai's hand was wrapped around its fin, and she would not let go. The Rossin roared into the water and snapped at her with long teeth.

It was beginning to recall how it felt to have a real enemy. Those of its kind that had relied on the faith and worship of humans had faded and withered. He had never expected to face another.

Yet here she was, in a form stitched of stolen bodies, glaring at him with radiant hatred.

You helped them imprison me. You betrayed me to humans! After all these generations her voice was the same, as beautiful as broken stained glass.

You wanted to destroy my bloodline, my home, he replied as he swam deeper, all the time twisting and turning to shake her off, but not quite able to reach her with his teeth.

It didn't matter. She wore a human body. It could be a useful thing but also a liability—especially when stolen and stitched as hers was. It told the Rossin one important thing; she had to be on the very edge of nonexistence to form such a worthless vessel.

Yet, as the Rossin swam deeper and deeper, he realized something else—so was he. The battle with the Murashev had taken much of his power, and he had not been able to consume any more blood and flesh since then.

The Rossin could feel his enemy's grasp puncture his flesh.

He turned in ever decreasing circles, snapping with his teeth, but she was faster. She swapped her hands, yanking her body out of the way just in time. They were nearly at the bottom of the river, and both wrapped in slimy riverweed. Terrified fish and crocodiles swam away from their thrashing bodies, which churned the water.

Hatipai would take the remaining power for her own—thus had it always been between their kind—only the strong would survive and feed off the lesser. He spun and twisted, but now rocketed up toward the surface.

Hatipai laughed, triumphant. *Revenge is indeed as sweet as humanity says.*

Yet the Rossin was not as he had been when last they tangled. Deep down was the Bond, the connection that ran invisibly between the geistlord and the two most powerful Deacons in Arkaym. Just as his attacker pulled the Rossin down to take everything that remained, the Bond bloomed. The power of the Active and the Sensitive filled him—sweet and delicious. It fueled his depleted muscles, giving the Rossin enough strength to complete his last hope.

The great mer-cat leapt clear of the river's surface, a lion's roar breaking the quiet of the morning. This time Hatipai's human body did let her down. She slipped and lost her grip as he tumbled through the air.

The Rossin dived back in, turned savagely about, and fell on her like the beast it had chosen to be.

In an instant it ripped apart the flesh and bone she had taken such pains to construct. Though it felt very good to tear and rend, he had to be quick. If he could get to her core hidden in the soft meat and devour it, her power would instead become his.

Yet it was a long time since he had fought another geistlord, and Hatipai was unfortunately too fast. She gave up the rent shell of flesh, leaping away skyward, where he could not follow without great risk. Her voice floated down to him. *I know what you are doing, old friend. I am not as foolish as the humans.*

The Rossin was left bobbing in the river, his thick tail wrapped around the remains, while his eyes followed the trail of her flight. He knew that she would not give up so easily.

Geists, most especially geistlords, were creatures of infinite malice and infinite determination. Hatipai would come again—but first she would regroup and find more power.

Deep within the Rossin he felt Raed struggle, pitting his useless strength against a foe he had never won against. *First we must feed.* Discarding the now flavorless corpse, the Rossin ducked under the lapping waves of the river. This place was full of humanity, and he would not be caught unawares like that again. He would take blood and wreak havoc in the villages—only then would he surrender the reins of control back to his host.

Let him do his weeping and wailing once it was over. Grief and kindness were not emotions the Rossin knew. He did, however, have a sense of self-preservation—and Hatipai had been a fierce opponent in the Dark Time. He would not be this weak again.

With a snarl, the Rossin flexed his scaled tail and made for the shore. Blood and flesh would fill him. Let the humans of Chioma run screaming; it only added flavor to what he needed. Their laws and fears were of no concern to him.

→ NINE ←

Into the Hive

"Are you aware that no one actually knows how ancient the city of Orinthal is?" Sorcha had already noticed with some amusement that there were certain subjects that revealed Merrick's youth.

He certainly made her feel old, leaning over the edge of the airship with unmistakable glee—ready for whatever came his way. His curly dark hair was fluttering in the breeze, so that when he glanced back, he did indeed appear like a young boy. "Bandele says that I may find in the Prince's library many things that not even the Imperial Palace has."

Whatever he saw when he looked down at the jumbled array of red buildings, she did not. Sorcha wanted to be there now, not observing it from above.

She was well aware impatience was one of her faults. Her tutors in the Abbey as a young Initiate had repeatedly pointed that out to her—sometimes with willow lashes on her open palm. However, they never cured her, and neither had a little age.

Even though they had completed a journey that would have taken months riding, right across the Empire in a mere week—it still felt ridiculously slow. At least on horseback there were things to do; trapped in the dirigible she had spent the last week looking at miles of clouds.

So she tried to appreciate the city below. It was already far warmer than Vermillion. Spring was just giving way to summer in the north, but in Chioma it already had a warm, sticky grip on the country. Sorcha wiped a thin line of sweat from her forehead. They had not yet landed, but she could tell this kingdom was going to make her suffer.

Captain Revele was bringing them in slow to the port city, probably showing off for Merrick's benefit—or to keep him on the dirigible for just that little bit longer. Revele's feeling for Sorcha's partner apparently sailed right past her target, though. He could have spent a week having fun with the captain, at least at night—yet he had not availed himself of the opportunity. Sorcha found it curious.

Merrick had, like most Deacons, been in the Order from childhood, but he had somehow missed a vital part of growing up that was certainly available even in the confines of the Abbey. He was utterly unaware of his effect on women, and Vyra Revele could not say anything, because a Deacon was, strictly speaking, higher in the chain of command than she.

As if summoned by the wandering of Sorcha's thoughts, Captain Revele appeared out of the wheelhouse, adjusted her jacket in a sharp, telling little gesture and strode toward them.

"We'll be landing in a few moments." Her voice was almost as disciplined as a Deacon's. "The Navy only has a small tether port here, but we have been instructed to wait for your return."

Merrick didn't say a thing, still too entranced by what was below. Sorcha tapped his leg, and he jerked upright. "Thank you, Captain."

She gave him a tight smile and then returned to her post. The crew brought the *Summer Hawk* down with absolute precision—so much so that even Raed would have barely noticed when they finally landed. The recollection of the Young Pretender's nervousness around the airship was both amusing and painful. Sorcha was used to being her own person, and yet here she was chasing after a man. How Kolya would have laughed.

The ground crew scurried to secure the dirigible, while the sailors on board threw out ropes to them. Eventually the *Summer Hawk* was as tightly wound to the ground as a fly in a spider's web. Ramps were thrown out, and the passengers disembarked.

The Deacons got off first and waited for the deputation to organize itself. The relentless Bandele began shouting at his men as they moved grumpy donkeys and angry oxen out of the hold. Sorcha knew if she watched the whole painful process of reassembling the caravan she would probably chew her fingernails off. So instead she wandered away for a little, while Merrick stood talking to Captain Revele. His thoughts, however, were tightly locked away, so Sorcha concentrated on her surroundings.

At first Orinthal did not look that different from any other city in the Empire Sorcha had seen on her travels. The tether station was the only one in the principality and tacked onto the edge of the wharf area. Sail and rowing boats skidded around on the dark water of the Saal River like so many water insects.

Then as she turned west she saw what the city was known for: the towering cone-shaped mud structures that made up the place. They were constructed of the red earth from the hills, carved in outrageous detail, and the reason for the city's other name, the Hive. As the sun was setting, it appeared to glow like embers. It rarely rained in Orinthal, but on the occasion it did, Merrick had informed her, the artisans came out, remodeled the decorations, and repaired the roofs. Despite herself, the Deacon was impressed and curious to see what the interiors were like.

Sorcha turned around and wondered how much longer she would have to wait for the deputation to be ready. After a while she realized that she was not the only one watching. Two figures in mustard gold cloaks stood in the shadow of the outlying buildings—but were observing her rather than the charming river scene.

Sorcha put her hands on her hips and stared back at them. Most people would have quickly made themselves scarce when glared at by a Deacon, but she was mightily confused when the figures strode over toward her. Sorcha waited, fingering her Gauntlets.

It was only when the people, two tall, dark-skinned women, were within a few yards that she noticed with great surprise that they were wearing the Eye and the Fist badge of the Order pinned to their shoulders. A glance behind told her Merrick was nowhere in sight, having disappeared back into the *Summer Hawk*. She would just have to police herself.

"Greetings, Sisters." Yes, that felt like a safe beginning.

The older Deacon bowed slightly. She had a long streak of a scar pulling up her lip. "Welcome to Chioma, Sister. I am Delie and this is my Sensitive, Jey. We heard from Vermillion that you were onboard and have come to offer you the comforts of our Abbey."

Sorcha wondered what Rictun had told the Prior of Chioma about her via weirstone. He now had a very long reach.

"It is not as grand as the Mother Abbey," Jey said, her voice low and sweet, "but we have cool baths and comfortable beds. We hope you and your partner will enjoy it."

"As well as the royal caravan," Delie went on, pulling her strangely colored cloak around her. "Recently the gates to the palace are being closed to all after nightfall—no exceptions. You will all be safe in our Abbey."

Sorcha frowned at that odd statement. A caravan, especially one under the banner of both a Prince and an Emperor, should have been safe anywhere in a city. She cocked her head. "Safe from what exactly, Sister?"

The pair exchanged a glance before answering. "The upsurge in geist activity in the last two days," Jey murmured.

Sorcha's heart sank. "We have been in transit for a week—what has been happening?"

Delie's eyebrows drew together. "More attacks have been reported in the last two days than in the whole of the previous month—and the most deadly have been in the palace."

"The palace?" Sorcha cocked her head.

"Chioma has always been blessed." Jey's eyes darted in the direction of the palace. "We suffered far less geist predations than any other kingdom; however, it seems whatever may have protected us, no longer is."

"Yet we will not bend under this trial." Delie's voice contained a note of reproach for her younger partner.

"Indeed, the fortitude of the Chiomese is legendary." Merrick had walked up on their conversation. He bowed to their colleagues. "Deacon Merrick Chambers, at your and your Abbot's service."

Delie introduced herself and then Jey. Her smile was charming, even with the scar. "So you know something of Chioma, Brother?"

Sorcha laughed. "Oh, he is quite the scholar on the delights of your land."

"Then you will enjoy the city," Jey murmured. "Our Abbot will apprise you of the situation."

Merrick inclined his head and replied far more sweetly than she could have, "That would be wonderful."

The whole caravan lined up behind them, and they set off, the Chiomese Deacons leading the way.

Above the complaints of the oxen, Sorcha leaned over and asked her partner, "So what is with their cloaks? I've traveled most everywhere in the Empire and never seen Deacons wearing anything but the green or blue." She flicked her cloak, which was the blue of the Active, but lined with the traditional black.

"Chioma is different. Weren't you listening to me all the way here?

She laughed. "I didn't realize there was going to be a test at the end! I admit I stopped listening just after we got onboard the *Summer Hawk*."

"Well—" He looked dangerously as though he were about to give her another lecture on the principality.

"Please"—she held up her hand—"the short version."

The corner of Merrick's mouth twitched. "I suppose I have rather fallen into the schoolteacher mode."

"Honestly, I thought I was back in the novitiate."

"The brief answer, then." He gestured toward the tall forms of the Deacons ahead of them. "Chioma kept many of its beliefs in the little gods—"

"Aha!" Sorcha flicked him on the shoulder. "I do recall you said not to call them that here!"

"Nice to know you were listening sometimes," he retorted, "but indeed we should not. Yellow is the color of their goddess Hatipai, and the only way the Order could enter Chioma was to align themselves with her—hence the unique cloaks."

Sorcha rolled her eyes slightly. In Delmaire too there were pockets of religion.

"Chioma is the oldest kingdom in Arkaym." Jey turned and smiled, dropping back to walk between Merrick and Sorcha. "We are very proud of its history."

The narrow streets suddenly flared into a wide town square, and the caravan was now moving through a choked marketplace. The guards ran forward to clear a way, ringing bells and shouting, "Make way for the royal Ambassador. Make way!"

Sorcha looked about with interest, getting her first real glimpses of regular Chiomese. The markets of Vermillion were familiar, bringing produce from every kingdom to the capital city—and so she had smelled the spices of Chioma before—but not in such abundance, and not so fresh. Her nose was full of sharp smells, sweet smells and ones that made her almost choke. Sacks, bowls and containers of all sizes were piled high in the tiled marketplace.

The heat in the square packed with people was overwhelming. Sorcha felt a new line of sweat break out on her back, and suddenly the idea of a cool bath in the Abbey sounded absolutely essential. She noticed the citizens around her moved languidly, which made them seem both much more elegant and much more sensible. Vigorous action of any sort here would be punished for certain. Without warning, her mind leapt back to Raed and their time locked in the cabin on the *Summer Hawk*.

Suddenly the heat on her wasn't all the fault of Orinthal. Merrick glanced over his shoulder at her—the curse of their unusual Bond once again striking. Sorcha knew she blushed and hated it. In a vain attempt at recovery, she tried to examine the market more thoroughly.

The peoples around her were not as varied as those in Vermillion—faces were mostly dark, though there were shades of olive tones, much like Merrick's. It was easy to pick out the traders and travelers from farther north—most doing business with the spice merchants—and not just because of their paler skins. Their clothing was drab by comparison. Every one of the citizens of Orinthal was dressed in vibrant colors; intense purples clashed with greens the color of a butterfly's wing, while deep red sashes were worn about the waist of every woman she saw.

"In addition to poisons and spices," Merrick hissed in her ear, "Chioma has the most wonderful selection of ingredients for dyes. The Imperial Coronation robes were made here."

Her young partner was always such a wealth of information. Sorcha pursed her lips, holding back a comment as they left the market and headed up the hill toward the Abbey.

Buildings of the Order usually occupied high ground—much like temples or palaces. It made for not only the best scenery but also the best view of geist activity.

They were on the incline of the hill. The houses were beginning to dwindle and become more like shacks, when the familiar wailing of mourners reached them. They had come across a cemetery. That also was traditional. Burying the dead within sight of a Priory or an Abbey had become almost a necessity in the Dark Time and continued to be recommended. A burial was in progress.

Jey whispered in her partner's ear—rather bad manners Sorcha felt.

"We must stop here for a moment." Delie turned and addressed the Vermillion Deacons somewhat stiffly. "There were more deaths last night."

No further explanation was necessary. Sorcha waited by the gate, while Merrick went back to tell Bandele to go on ahead to the Abbey. They had Deacon business to take care of.

It felt good to be of some use to their hosts. The two sets of partners examined the scene with practiced eyes. The Sensitives sent their Centers out, while the Actives remained poised in case they found something.

The knot of mourners was streaming into the graveyard. The gate and fence were both made of bone-white wood and rattled in the light wind. The sound was mournful, disturbing and had to be deliberate. When it mixed with the cries of the bereaved, the effect was enough to raise goose pimples on Sorcha's arms, despite the heat.

Unlike in Vermillion, there was no coffin, just the body wrapped in brightly colored cotton carried on the shoulders of menfolk. Small medallions glittered and flashed in the sunlight where they hung from the body. Sorcha had studied enough to know they were symbols of little gods—indicating that this man was a believer. It mattered little to the geists.

"I see nothing suspicious," Merrick whispered. His eyes were closed, but as he was sharing his Sight with Sorcha, she could see what he meant. The grief of the funeral cortege was all that stained the ether.

"The spectyrs have been very cunning of late." Jey's eyelids flickered. "We should make absolutely sure."

Both Sensitives reached for their Strops by instinct. When Merrick secured the leather rune-carved strap over his eyes, Sorcha again shared his vision. The world was a beautiful place when her partner looked at it. They could see the movement of the wind, the sorrowful plumes of grief wafting from the mourners and the flicker of tiny insects over the flowers in the cemetery. Nothing escaped their gaze.

No shades followed in the wake of the dead. No spectyr wore the face of the lost one. Sorcha let out a held-in sigh of relief as her hand dropped away from her belt.

"Can you see this, Deacon Jey?" Merrick's voice was full of dread, but he was not looking at the cemetery any longer.

Sorcha shared his vision, and what he was looking at was far in the distance. Against the horizon, on the other side of the river Saal, were a line of low hills. She had already noted them as they climbed out of the port city. The day was cloudless and relentless in its heat. However, with the aid of the Strop the scene was quite different. On those hills a gray mass, which could have been mistaken for thunderclouds, was gathering. It was as if a stone had dropped into the pit of Sorcha's stomach.

"I can," the Chiomese Sensitive choked out, "but I have never witnessed the like before."

"Neither have I." Her partner's voice came out rough and shaken.

Naturally they would not. Both were too young to remember. Sorcha, however, had come across with the Emperor from Delmaire years before and seen many deadly things.

She had stood on a ship with Arch Abbot Hastler, the one who would later betray his Order, on one side, and Kolya on the other. Sharing his Sight and looking out toward the continent that would be her new home, she had seen the mass of clouds where there were actually none. She'd asked her Abbot what they signified, and his response had chilled her then as it did now.

"The geists are gathering, preparing for us, waiting for battle."

"By the Bones." Merrick took his Strop off with shaking hands. "We had better report this to the Prior."

Their simple trek to the Hive City was coinciding with something else—something far more momentous. Sorcha felt foolish that she had ever thought this journey would be simple—that it would ever be just about Raed. The maelstrom was focused once again around the Triple Bond.

→ TEN ←

Within a Welcome Embrace

Merrick's stomach rolled on seeing the cloud of geist activity on the horizon. It was always that way with a Sensitive; the body reacted against the undead. Sorcha might have witnessed such things before, but he had only read about them. As he fought down his nausea he realized that, despite his satisfaction at finally seeing Chioma, he would have been quite happy to never experience a geist storm firsthand.

Without a word passing between them, the four Deacons turned and very quickly passed the wagon train on the way to the Abbey. They all knew their duty to report what they had seen.

They were just going underneath the red archway of the building, into what Merrick might have termed safety, when the Bond sang. His Sight blurred, and he staggered back as the world that he knew dipped away. Inexplicably, his mouth tasted of dirty river water, and there was pain—so much that it felt as though his spine was being ripped out through his throat.

The sound of a savage growl echoed in his head—one that he knew very well. In the ossuary under Vermillion, Merrick and Sorcha had lost themselves, becoming part of a creature with Raed and the Rossin. It had been both terrifying and exhilarating—the kind of exhilaration that was full of danger. The kind you could easily get used to.

It didn't matter how far away the Deacons were from the Young Pretender and the geistlord he carried; they could still draw on magic from Merrick and Sorcha.

They drowned in the geistlord for a long moment, lost in his strength and bloodlust. Then, mercifully and just as suddenly, they were free.

Jey and Delie were staring at them, wide-eyed and concerned. Sorcha had collapsed back against the door of the Priory, while Merrick found himself kneeling on the floor like a penitent of ages past. He knew they could not say anything to their fellow Deacons. Not even their superiors back at the Mother Abbey knew about the Bond with the Young Pretender—and for good reason.

The penalty would most likely be death. The sentence for any Deacon who had dallied with the Otherside was to be cleansed in the rune Pyet and their Strop or Gauntlets thrown in after them. It had been a generation or more since such a punishment had been meted out—but it was a ceremony that could easily be revived.

"Are you all right?" Jey bent down to help Merrick to his feet, while Delie ran to assist Sorcha.

His partner thought faster than he did. "Your weather takes some getting used to." She mopped her brow and smiled shakily.

The look that passed between the two Chiomese Deacons said they were not entirely convinced that *both* of their Vermillion counterparts had been overtaken by the heat at the exact same time. Yet they were luckily too polite to challenge the explanation.

Bandele and the royal caravan passed under the mud brick arch last, and the gates were secured shut behind them. Merrick sidled up to Sorcha while the unloading went ahead. She must have felt what he had, but he still had to ask—to make sure he was not running mad.

Her face was white, her jaw set. Shoulder to shoulder, under the cover of their cloaks, he squeezed Sorcha's hand. "He's alive."

She gave a quick nod as if she could not quite bear to speak yet.

"And close," he added under his breath. The rest went unspoken. *And so is the Rossin.*

Sorcha flinched, but they dared not discuss this more,

because someone in a vibrant green and blue cloak topped with a mustard yellow hood was coming down to greet them. The color clash alone drew the eye, but he was also a tall, broad man with a flashing smile—the kind of solidly built figure that would have made a fine warrior in any army. "Welcome! Welcome, Brother and Sister!" He eschewed the traditional bow and instead clapped them around the shoulders, as if they were indeed long-lost kin. "I am Abbot Yohari."

Sorcha shot Merrick a surprised look, and he realized that she had not fully grasped how very different the Chiomese Deacons were. Such a greeting in any other kingdom's Abbey would have been unthinkable; this man was among those who chose the Presbyterial Council, after all!

Lay Brothers scampered to help unload the caravan for their short stay. Guest quarters would house the royal retinue, while the two Deacons from Vermillion would naturally stay in the dormitory. There was one place that Merrick was longing to be. Chioma had been the only principality not to fall during the Dark Time, and it was rumored to contain some of the oldest manuscripts anywhere. However, he had not forgotten the menacing line of shades lurking in the mountains.

He gave an awkward little bow to Yohari. "If we could talk to you in private, Abbot. We have some concerns about what is happening in Orinthal."

The smile faded on their superior's face. "You are not the only one, Brother." He gestured them in toward the cool interior of the building.

Once inside, Merrick could feel a little of his calm returning—enough to notice the architecture. Again he was reminded how very different Chioma was. All Abbeys, even the Mother one, were rather stark, removed of any decoration that harked back to the little gods. In this principality, however, the Order of the Eye and the Fist had to tread carefully, and the Priory held on to its religious roots in ways that would have shocked the Order back home.

The symbol of Hatipai was repeated on the tiny tiles that decorated the inside of the Abbot's receiving room, and they made Merrick deeply uncomfortable. So he took a seat in the sunny nook where he wouldn't have to look at them directly. A tall, clear window surrounded by panes of colored glass looked out over the city, and Sorcha remained standing before it. Her nerves would have been apparent even without the Bond.

"I too have seen the shades." Yohari's voice was now solemn; the act outside had been for the benefit of his Deacons. He gestured over to the desk where his Strop sat. "The gathering of them on the hills began two days ago along with an increase in general geist activity. So few of my Deacons are here in the Abbey—nearly every one fit for duty is out fighting the good fight."

He leaned back, steepled his fingers and looked at them sternly. "If you were not escorting the royal Ambassador, I might prevail on you to assist."

"Perhaps we could find some time . . ." Sorcha offered.

The Abbot inclined his head. "No, protecting the Ambassador is vitally important."

Now Merrick was curious. "I am sorry, but we were given this job merely as a courtesy. We weren't told to guard—"

"I think we can all agree circumstances have changed." Yohari gestured to the corner where a gleaming blue orb rested atop a brass stand. Merrick saw Sorcha flinch at the weirstone, but even she couldn't complain about the Abbot having one or their use in the Imperial air navy. They made many things possible, the most important of which being communication between far-flung Abbeys, Priories and cells.

"I am waiting on word from the Presbyterial Council," the Abbot rumbled, "though I certainly cannot mount an attack on them in the hills—not when the city needs protecting."

Merrick nodded. If it was beyond the Abbot's experience, then waiting was the wiser course. "Then may I ask permission to examine your library, Father Abbot?"

"The library?"

"If there is no service we can offer you, then I would very much like to view the treasures in it." Merrick tried to keep the hint of avarice out of his voice.

The Abbot dismissed them quickly—having ascertained that two more Deacons would not make those hovering shades disappear. They took their leave from Yohari, and Sorcha let out a long sigh of relief.

They stood in the quiet corridor as lay Brothers began to light candles around them against the drawing night. Even so,

Merrick could make out deep shadows beneath Sorcha's eyes. "Go get some rest."

She raised an eyebrow at his almost commanding tone. "I hope you are not going all mother hen on me. Remember, I am old enough to actually *be* your mother."

He laughed at that. "You're not that ancient." He chuckled somewhat forcibly. "I just think we need to be fresh tomorrow."

Even Sorcha, spoiling for a fight, couldn't argue with that. She rolled her shoulders and let her eyes close for a moment. "A cool bath and a warm cigar would be splendid. Are you really set on scouring the library?" He grinned, and she sighed theatrically. "I see you are."

"I managed to sleep on the *Summer Hawk*," he lied, knowing that thanks to their unusual Bond she wouldn't believe it anyway. It was a little game they played.

Sorcha clapped him on the shoulder and then, muttering to herself, left him to it.

The Abbey was silent around Merrick, but that was just fine. He was itching to see what the library might hold. After a few wrong turns he found it.

It was larger than he had expected and packed with books, scrolls and manuscripts that made his blood rush. He was hoping to find something in here that might account for the cloud of shades, yet his scholarly instincts made him just want to dive in.

The sun began to creep down behind the horizon, and still Merrick kept scouring the shelves. He knew if he looked out the window aimed toward the mountains he would get all the inspiration he needed. Yet the library was proving a disappointment. Most of the works here were about Hatipai, and there was only so much adulation to a goddess even he could take.

Finally Merrick slumped down at the broad table in the middle of the room and admitted defeat. With his head in his hands, exhaustion began to overcome him; the long hours of traveling finally catching up.

He was just about to stagger upright and go to find a place to give in to sleep—when a strange noise made him pause. It sounded like one of the eerie sounds made by the Chiomese nose flute—the kind of vibrating noise that had sent him as a child running for his mother's lap. It filled the long lines of shelves with a kind of tuneless vibration that he could feel in his bones.

Then the whispering began. A cool chill ran up his neck, as subvocal human noises echoed through the library. He was sure that there were words in there, but as much as he strained his ears, he could make none out. So he did the one thing that a trained Sensitive Deacon would always do; Merrick closed his eyes and flung out his Center.

His awareness spread wide over the whole building. He could count every Deacon in the Abbey and every animal too. Swallows were nesting under the building's roof, a colony of ants were harvesting leaves from the garden, and a hundred tiny pinpricks of awareness in his sight showed where earthworms were digging deep in the soil seeking whatever moistness remained there. He could sense all of these tiny things, yet apart from himself and a straying bee battering itself against the window, there was nothing else in the library. No hint of the Otherside was anywhere in the room.

Merrick told himself that, yet the ominous sounds continued around him. They ebbed away, seeming to move through the stacks of books, roll around in the corners and come back stronger.

Wrapped in confusion, he took a step back, banging into the table. All of his life in the Order he had been able to depend on his Sight—it was the one constant. And more than that, he was the best at what he did. His tutors had told him so. He had been partnered with Sorcha Faris because of it. It was the one thing he relied on.

His childhood had been ravaged. Every happy memory had been stained by seeing his father killed on the stairs of their castle by a terrifying, still unidentified geist. So he had run, taken another name, taken refuge in the Order—because that was what they offered—order. And now, in one instant, he was beginning to doubt all that.

The whispering continued, as if mocking his uncertainty. It sounded harsh and demanding now—like all his worst thoughts were bubbling to the surface. Merrick's head was spinning, and he had the horrible feeling that maybe he was going mad. No—he would not allow that. Surely madness was something that came on gradually, not as a sudden avalanche of half-heard voices. Perhaps the Bond that Sorcha had created with the Cursed Young Pretender was having consequences; maybe the Rossin power was finally corrupting him.

Then just as the whispers rose to the point where he could almost discern words—there was silence. Abrupt and total; the atmosphere went from tense to serene. Merrick stood very still and held his breath. His mind raced to find an explanation.

It had not been a geist. So what else could it have been? If only he were back in the Mother Abbey. He might have plundered their larger library or had a quiet word in Deacon Reeceson's ear, because one explanation remained: a wild talent.

Shaking, Merrick sat on the nearest chair. He'd tried to block out all memory of the incident outside the jail. Just after they had rescued Raed, the three of them had been nearly torn apart by an angry mob. He had no clue how he had brought all those people to their knees racked by sorrow—but he had.

The wild talents, not sanctioned by the Order, were dangerous things to admit to. Even Deacon Reeceson, an elderly and venerable member of the Order, kept his gift of prescience to himself—sharing it with very few. So when Merrick thought of what these whispers might mean, what wild talent they might be revealing, he shuddered.

He couldn't give in to fear though. Deacons had to face the darkness. So he got up from his chair and stumbled toward the shelves—to where the sounds had come from. Naturally it was in the darker recesses of the library. Back here everything was covered in cobwebs, and the smell of dust competed with the odor of old books for supremacy.

The faintest echo of the whispers drew him to the carved rear wall. *Follow. Follow.*

Merrick ran his hands over the wood while putting his Center forward into the darkness. *Hidden and secret.* It was very like when he sensed the living things around him, but it tasted strange in his mind; dry and musty. The little click under his right fingertip sounded so very loud, but when he slid the secret compartment aside, it was as silent as a lonely grave.

The compartment beyond was packed with books, ones that judging by the amount of dust on them had not been touched for a very long time. He knew before even lifting them what they were about. The round shape of stars on the cover told him, and the shiver down his spine confirmed that these were books on the Native Order. Books that should have been destroyed with the downfall of that organization.

Certainly there were plenty of folk tales about the past—how the people had risen against the old Order, how the ruling Emperors of that time had hunted them down—but their books were burned, and their history had been deliberately destroyed and none in the Order of the Eye and the Fist knew anything of them.

It was not the first time Merrick had discovered that all was not as it seemed within the Abbeys. He let out a long, deliberate breath and then reached for the book. It was the Chiomese Abbott's journal—but definitely not the current one.

As Merrick scanned down the entries, his blood began to run cold as he realized this was no record of geists destroyed or banished. Instead, he saw words like "captured," "resistant" and, most chillingly of all, "useful." It began to make sense. Unlike his Order, the native ones had taken a step down a darker path—a path that used geists for their own gain. It was, to put it mildly, terrifying: an idea that he knew his own superiors would not want even in the heads of their own Deacons. It was no wonder the voices said *Hidden and secret.*

"Merrick?" His partner's voice made him jump. Sorcha was standing in the shelves, her hair damp, her eyes half-lidded with sleep. Even when slumbering, the Bond alerted her to his fear and confusion. "Are you all right?" While she rubbed her hair briskly, her partner tucked the journal under his cloak and clicked shut the compartment. With so much dust, he knew these were long forgotten.

Merrick turned and smiled. "Yes . . . just tired."

"Well then, you should get some sleep." She sighed. "Silly boy." She said it with such affection that he couldn't really take offense.

For a moment he considered telling her about the journal, but she had so much to think about that ancient history seemed a silly thing to bring up now. Still, he wouldn't be sleeping well tonight, no matter what his partner said.

* * *

The crew of the *Sweet Moon* fished their naked captain out of the river the next morning. Raed lay gasping on the deck with the taste of blood and dirty water in his mouth. They stood around him in a somber circle. His fingers tightened into fists as he remembered other times like this. It had been many years, but the memories were still vivid and still cut.

"Captain?" Tangyre's voice was soft and her hand gentle on his shoulder.

Raed closed his eyes and tried to recover what remained of his humanity, piece together the shreds that the Rossin had left him. The geistlord was like a leech—only once he had taken his fill of blood would he drop away. Raed had lived in the shadow of this parasite for far too long, but it still became no easier.

Finally, gathering his remaining strength, he levered himself up with every muscle and sinew aching.

Tangyre draped a blanket over him, helped him up, but barked to the crew, "We still have to get to Orinthal. Jump to it!"

Leaning against Tangyre, his limbs heavy, Raed let himself be led into the small cabin and tucked into the captain's bed. Wordlessly, Tangyre washed him of the river water, examined the cuts and bruises and finally sat down to put salve on them. Her fingers were strong and sure, but her voice when she finally spoke was gentle. "One woman did all this?"

"I wish," the Young Pretender whispered. "She must have been possessed by a geist. This is all the Rossin's doing." To Raed the concerns of his body were very far away.

His friend knew better than to pursue further questioning—there were answers best left unknown.

Raed kept repeating Fraine's name in his head, conjuring up images of her face framed with curls and her wide blue eyes. They were hard to retain because as always the Rossin had left him with shattered images of the night before. It might not have been him who did the killing, but it had been his flesh—transformed, yes—but his all the same. Flashes of a woman, her white skirt gleaming in the darkness among the grass. Glimpses of a farmer standing before his house, sickle in hand, then nothing but frenzy and the feeling of thick blood in his mouth. Reflected emotions that were not his: hunger and delight.

Raed rolled to one side, heaving. Tangyre, who knew the way of things, had a pot ready. She rubbed his back while he vomited the contents of his stomach—but there was no blood to get rid of. The Rossin had taken that. It was only his own honest dinner from the night before that reappeared.

The Young Pretender slumped back on the bed.

"It was not you, Raed. Remember that." Tangyre tidied away the soiled pot and handed him a glass of water. "It was that creature, the Curse—not you."

He worked his mouth a few times before being able to speak. His throat felt raw, broken from too many Rossin snarls. "I know that, Tang . . . it doesn't make it any easier." He took a few gulps of the liquid, but the taste of blood was not removed.

Tangyre opened Raed's pack and fished out some fresh clothes. "If only you had been born in Vermillion as the Curse dictates. If only those worthless Princes had crowned your father instead of—"

"That's a lot of ifs." He closed his eyes again, trying to imagine how his life would have been different. "Perhaps if we could go back and change my grandfather to a kinder Emperor—but we have to live in this world, Tang. This reality." Raed, finding some little remaining strength, pulled himself upright and swung his legs over the side of the bed. He took several long gulps of air. "How far to Orinthal?"

"We should be there by nightfall."

Chioma was not one of the principalities that had slavery, but they allowed slaver ships to pass up the massive Saal River to places that were less enlightened. It meant they profited from the vile trade—yet remained aloof from it.

It was not just this aspect of Chioma that disturbed Raed. He had studied a lot as a young man: history of the Empire, family legends and all his ancestors. Something from that time was worrying at him.

"In the bottom of my pack," he croaked weakly to Tangyre. "My grandfather's journal."

Captain Greene frowned. "I don't think you—"

"By the Blood, Tang!" Raed growled and immediately

wished he had not. His head felt stuffed with snapping turtles. He waved his hand. "I can at least read. I promise not to get up immediately."

His friend let out a sigh, retrieved the journal and handed it to him. "Just promise to keep to that bed." Then she tucked a blanket over him and retreated out of the cabin.

With a ragged sigh Raed obeyed, even as he opened the book on his lap. The last Rossin Emperor's journal was not studded with gems or even terribly thick, and it was not the official record—that still remained in Vermillion Palace. Instead, this journal contained Valerian's personal writings; after his death it had been carried away by his few remaining supporters.

The Young Pretender had been born years after the last Rossin Emperor had died, but he had read enough of his writings to have a pretty good idea why the Assembly of Princes had chased his son out of Vermillion. It mattered little to them that the meek heir, who was branded the Unsung, was nothing like his father.

Raed shivered and pulled the blanket closer. He had no way of telling if his life would have been better if his father had retained the throne; he might have grown up as foolish as his grandfather and met just as untimely a death. But he would never have had to live with the Rossin.

Raed's jaw clenched, and he began to flick determinedly through the journal. Having already read the damn thing before, he was aware it was soaked in the arrogance and pride of the dead Emperor, yet there was still much of value to be found in its pages. As a young man Valerian had traveled with his father the length of Arkaym and visited every one of the principalities. Even with his many faults, the last Emperor had still been a shrewd observer of character.

After a few moments Raed found the section that dealt with Chioma, the spice land of the Empire. It remained a strange case among the principalities of Arkaym, skating at times perilously close to independence. Its history could be traced unbroken as far back as the written records went and, curiously, its royal family had never changed throughout the ages. No other principality could lay the same claim.

Raed frowned and read on. Valerian recorded his impression of the Hive City, the vast markets for spices and dyes, and the beauty of the women—even if he could have been only thirteen at the time.

However, it was the portion about the Prince of Chioma that caught Raed's attention.

The ruler of Chioma keeps himself in remarkable seclusion that no other Prince we have visited would dare. None have ever seen the heirs to the throne of Chioma—nor the face of their liege. Even in the presence of his servants, his nobility and his women, the Prince's form is covered in blue robes—scandalously close to Imperial purple! When my father and I were taken into his presence, it was like we were the penitents rather than he. I was horrified to find even then, when we were in his presence, a glittering wall of crystal beads obscured his face.

He bowed most politely, correct to the tiniest degree, yet he did not once offer to remove the covering before his face. I wanted to take my sword and smite him down for the offense given to my father—but he held me back with a stern look. After the audience I said to Father, "He should be whipped for his insolence." He only replied, "In Vermillion he would be, but in Chioma that would be dangerous," as if that were explanation enough!

Later that night I managed to corner some of the Imperial Guards, who told me the rumors surrounding this Prince. One told me that he was so hideously scarred none could look on his face and not go mad, while another fool suggested the Prince was immortal. The final one whispered the Prince had died years before, and it was his mother concealed behind the veil.

Raed scanned the pages further, until he found another mention of Chioma.

Only three years after taking power, Valerien had nearly lost his throne to a conspiracy of aristocrats in Vermillion. He had not been able to prove the involvement of any of the Princes—but he knew very well that some of them must have taken part.

Valerian wrote tirades against those he thought most likely—but one name caught his grandson's eye.

I have had reports that the poison meant to do me in may
have been traded in Orinthal—that serpent's den of thieves
and assassins. My spymaster was only able to get this
information with application of the rack, but then the trail
ran cold. I am sure that hidden viper in Chioma, our ancient enemy, is responsible.

Raed paused, his finger tracing the word with some confusion. This was the first he had ever heard of such a royal feud.
Flicking back through the pages, he passed another hour trying to find what that curious reference could be in relation to.
Finally, he had to admit defeat.

Closing the journal, he let out a sigh. His scholarly instincts
had been piqued, but unfortunately, trapped on the *Sweet
Moon*, he had no way of doing further research. Raed had
studied all the official accounts available—except for those
held in the palace library—and he had never heard of a feud
between the Imperial family and the Chiomese ruler.

"My Prince?" so engrossed in his study had he been that
Raed had failed to notice Tangyre's reappearance.

"I am all right." Raed sighed and pushed himself out of
bed. "We must put all efforts into finding Fraine so that I can
get back to open water. The tide of the Otherside has obviously turned against us."

Tangyre nodded but offered no comment on his Curse.
Instead, she stuck to what they could control. "We are nearly
to the port of Orinthal. Slavers do not stay here long; there are
no markets for their cargo. I hope you have a plan to explain
our presence there."

Raed ventured a smile. "I do indeed—and I think the crew
will enjoy it."

After getting dressed, he joined Tangyre and the circle of
sailors on the deck. They would not meet his gaze, and he
didn't blame them. Even those who had been with him since
the beginning had not seen him transform for a long time.

Raed cleared his throat and addressed the stocky crew
member closest to him. "Balis, go below with a hammer. See
what damage you can visit upon the *Sweet Moon* without
totally sinking her."

The sailor grinned. "It'd be a pleasure, Captain—though sinking this filthy tub would be a kindness."

"Not in the plan"—Raed gave him what little smile he could find—"but I very much agree."

By the banging and whooping that came from belowdecks a short while later, Balis was making the most of the opportunity to take out his frustrations on the slave clinker.

"Nice to know this ship won't be used again," Tangyre said as the river port appeared round a bend in the river.

Long piers, made out of the local red stone, extended out into the river, displaying to everyone its wealth, while ships of all sizes bobbed in the Saal.

Snook took the helm and slowly guided them into a free berth. The smell of rich spices combined with the more musky smell of camels, goats and sheep assailed the nose in a way that was pleasant and shocking.

The grinning Balis returned to the deck, just as Raed swallowed a knot of concern and addressed the sailors again.

"Please remember you are slave ship crew, so act accordingly. And by the Blood, do not call me anything but 'Captain.'"

"Good thing we did not bring Aachon, then." Balis chuckled, folding his arms around the sledgehammer.

The laughter took a little of the sharp edge from the moment.

An army of harbor officials were already scampering in their direction, forms and paperwork trailing in their wake. Raed and his crew dropped down onto the pier as the harbormaster's second homed in on them.

The captain handed over his paperwork and waited for the official to notice the rather impressive damage in *Sweet Moon*'s hull. The Deputy was examining the order in such minute detail he didn't even raise his head.

"Ahhh"—Raed cleared his throat and jerked his head toward the damaged vessel—"we had some trouble . . ."

"Trouble?" The official's gaze flicked up, and then his eyes widened on seeing the gaping holes. "What . . . what about your cargo?"

"They got loose in the night, put up a hell of a fight, then jumped right into the damned river." Raed let out what he thought was an exceedingly cruel laugh. "Hope the crocodiles ate the lot of them."

"Yes, well . . ." The Deputy Harbormaster didn't seem to get the joke. "You were supposed to move on tomorrow."

"How am I supposed to do that?" Raed leaned in close to the smaller man. "My ship is full of holes, and I ain't taking my men back on the water again until it is fixed."

The other looked down at his notes. "We can accommodate your vessel in one of our dry docks—but it will be at least a week until it can be worked on."

"Hear that, lads?" The Young Pretender shouted to his crew. "Rest and relaxation on the owner for a whole blessed week!"

The *Sweet Moon*'s crew did an admirable job of impersonating slavers looking forward to barmaids, brothels and beer. They whooped and hollered until everyone on the pier was looking in their direction.

Raed pressed his thumb in the inkpot of the Deputy Harbormaster and then to the form allowing the ship to be moved to the dry dock. Somewhere the owner of a slave ship would eventually get a terrible shock. Raed grinned at that satisfactory thought.

Finally all of them sauntered along the pier and into town.

"What now?" He asked Tangyre quietly over his shoulder.

"We make contact with our man here." Captain Greene also kept her voice low, while her eyes scanned the many dark alleyways that lined the approach to the port. "The pub should be nearby."

"I like the sound of that." Raed tucked his fingers in his belt with a lot more bravado than he felt. He could do with a beer to wash away the final taste of blood that the Rossin had left him. Once it was gone, perhaps he could live with what had happened the previous day—or at least file it away with the rest of the horrors the Curse had brought him. Ahead lay his sister, and that was the anchor his sanity clung to.

ELEVEN

Buried in Roses

After three beers at the Angry Trout, Raed was ready for action. Tangyre sat at his side, but he noticed she did not touch her pint of beer.

The interior of the pub was the same as every other one in the Empire: dark, smoky and filled with patrons intent on reaching the bottom of their mug as soon as possible. Orinthal was a great trading city, however, so there was a mixed selection of facial features and clothing in the Trout.

Crowds made Raed nervous, not just because of the possibility that Imperial spies might be about but also because he could not help but imagine the chaos the Rossin would create in such a place. The Young Pretender shuddered and took another healthy draft of his beer.

"He has eaten, Raed." Tangyre leaned close and whispered into his ear. "You are safe for now." She was well acquainted with the Curse as were all in the inner circle of his family.

He looked up at her serious face and thought to himself, *You don't know, Tang. Those rules that I lived by as a young man are gone. There are none. I can't say anything with certainty now.*

Yet he did not share those dark revelations, because the truth was they would do none of them any good.

Once the Rossin had only appeared when a geist triggered its awareness. Once being at sea had been protection. Now Raed did not trust any of those things. Something had happened in the ossuary when all three of them had fused with the geistlord. Not anything good.

"I know." He muttered the lie to his friend, scarcely caring if he sounded convincing or not. "We just need to find Fraine, and then—"

The door banged open, and a young man swathed in a dark brown cloak strode in. Raed felt Tang flinch at his side and guessed this was their man.

Together they rose and, via a slightly circuitous route, reached this newcomer's side. Raed's eyes darted about, but no one was taking particular interest in any of them.

Tangyre gave their contact a little nod, and the three of them wandered back through the door where straining ears could not hear. Outside in the sticky, warm darkness, she led the way around the corner of the pub. Alleyways were the traditional place to conduct covert activities.

When Captain Greene spoke, her voice was low as to suit the surroundings. "My Prince, may I present Isseriah, Earl of Wye."

It was a title about as useful as his own as heir to the Empire. The Earls of Wye had famously stuck by the Rossins and had paid the penalty—hence why they were meeting in a filthy alleyway now. Still, Raed greeted him as if they were in the Imperial Hall. "Well met, Wye. Your grandfather served mine admirably."

Isseriah stepped forward. "I remain your man—even in exile, my liege." He was taller than Raed by a head but bowed low enough for it not to show.

"Wye is far from Chioma," Raed said, uncomfortable with the admiration in the young man's eyes. It was clutching at straws in the saddest way.

The young would-be Earl smiled and shrugged. "And there is a price on my head if I ever return there. I have been making my way as a merchant since birth, just like my father."

"I hear you are doing well," Tangyre added.

"Not as well as I should." Isseriah turned his face and showed the long scar running down his left cheek. Wye had the tradition that its rulers had to be perfect in mind and body to rule. Obviously someone had made sure that this heir to the principality would never be able to contest his place, even if he should chose to.

"I am sorry." Raed found himself apologizing for something he had not done.

"My family does well enough for itself, but we can never be aristocrats or rule again, unless—"

Raed cut him off. "For now, Isseriah, we are only looking for my sister, Fraine."

"I am sorry, my Prince"—the other man dipped his head—"but if I had known she was your sister—"

Raed steeled himself, wondering if their trip would stop here. Had Fraine been killed and thrown into the river? His mind raced through a whole range of terrible possibilities.

"She has been taken to the Hive City itself."

The relief that washed over him made Raed actually take a step back. Though it was a terrible thing to hear, it was wonderful to know that she was still alive. "Tell me more."

"Many slavers pass through Orinthal, as they cannot be sold here." Isseriah was incapable of voicing the rest.

"Go on," Raed urged, though his stomach was in a tight knot.

"However, sometimes those seeking advancement in the Court of the Prince have been known to buy the prettiest and pass them off as their own kin."

"Into his harem, you mean?" Raed's hand went to his sword hilt. He was so used to thinking of Fraine as a little girl—yet when he calculated, he realized she had to be twenty years old. Then he thought about their mother: she had been the beauty of the Empire. He had almost forgotten that, because his last image of her had been anything but lovely. If he pushed past that, however, he could recall her thick waves of gold hair and brilliant blue eyes. If Fraine had grown up to look anything like their mother, then indeed she would be a striking woman.

"So, into the palace we must go," Raed replied firmly. When their informant exchanged a glance with Tangyre, he asked, "Is there some sort of problem with that?"

"The palace is, as you know, highly guarded." The young

Earl looked about as if he expected to be overheard. "Every caravan must have permission to enter—but since I am going there, it will be easy enough to swap your crew for my workers—it is not that . . ." He trailed off again.

"No need to mince your words, my lord." Tangyre let out a short laugh. "The price on the Prince's head has been reposted by the Impostor."

Like the reprieve from the Rossin, Raed had taken heart from the fact that the bounty on his head had not been increased nor found its way to market squares since before the fight in the ossuary. Obviously saving his sister's life had not wiped the slate clean in the Emperor's eyes.

"None of your usual contacts can be trusted," Isseriah whispered. "We must make sure none hear of your arrival in Orinthal."

His eyes locked with Raed's, making an accusation his lips would not. "My crew are reliable—down to the last one."

"Then how did the Emperor know you were coming to Chioma?" The Earl-apparent asked softly. "Excuse my boldness, sire—but Captain Greene said that you only got news of your sister's kidnapping a mere week ago . . ."

Raed stroked his beard but did not mention that Possibility Matrix that he, Sorcha and Merrick had found beneath the Mother Abbey. The Abbot was dead, that pit of conspiracy cleared out. Wasn't it? Sorcha had told him about the lengths the Order had gone to, but he could not recall if she had mentioned the eventual fate of the unholy creation. The idea that once again someone could be dogging his steps before he even made them was maddening.

He could not explain such horrors, such impossibilities to them. "There are fell things abroad in the world, things that would reveal our path before we walk it—yet walk it we must. I cannot have my sister disappearing into the harem of the Prince—or worse."

"Agreed," Tangyre murmured. "The Princess Royal must be recovered."

Raed's heart sank further because Isseriah still looked worried. "There is more, isn't there?"

"Only . . ." The youth stopped and cleared his throat.

"Only rumor, my liege—but I am sure you would hear it from others. They say there is a murderer on the loose in the Hive City. The guards of Orinthal are trying to keep things quiet, but there have been deaths among the aristocracy, which is harder to hush than if it were any unfortunate on the street."

So she begins.

Raed managed not to jump. It was the Rossin. The Pretender stood stock-still for a moment, feeling every twitch of his muscles, every slightly rapid breath—trying to ascertain if any of them meant that the Curse was about to surface. Finally, after a few heartbeats he realized it was not.

What the Beast might mean Raed did not know, and it did not elaborate further.

Isseriah kept talking, his words tumbling over one another as if he was somehow embarrassed to bring such bad news to his liege. "You may stay in my warehouse tonight; it is safe enough. I will tell my men that you are my cousin, and I am showing you the trade. I have enough of them to make that believable."

Raed looked at the young man and saw what had been in his own eyes once—hope. He was scared to let it show, but there it was. So the Young Pretender clapped him on the shoulder. "Your grandfather would be proud, Isseriah. You are taking great risks for my family and me."

"We all hope to see you restored." The tall young man ducked his head. "So whatever I can do for you is my pleasure and duty."

They had been a long time hugging the coast of the Empire, so Raed had in truth forgotten that the fire of rebellion did still burn among the lesser and dispossessed nobles. As much as he believed it was a wasted effort, he was not going to destroy this young man's kindly given allegiance.

"Thank you all the same," he murmured. Then with some embarrassment, Raed let Isseriah drop to one knee and press his forehead against the Young Pretender's hand—where the signet ring should have been. It had been many years since he'd let anyone do that, and it felt more than just awkward—it felt dishonest. The sooner they found Fraine and he got back to the *Dominion*, the better.

* * *

The Grand Duchess was fighting in the Long Hall in Vermillion Palace, but her mind was elsewhere. Her thick plait of dark hair was tied back, though some strands had come loose and were stuck in the corner of her mouth. Trails of sweat were running down her face. Zofiya was aware of all these minor irritations, but they were distant things—even the fight was some way off.

For today she had received several disturbing pieces of information that suggested the life of her brother was in danger.

It was no new thing. In Arkaym she had taken it on herself to be responsible for his continuing good health, and in all those years the number of assassination attempts were numerous. She knew because she kept meticulous records.

In the last year malcontents had gradually worked out that the punishment she inflicted was dire, and so the attempts had dwindled away. Zofiya had unroofed castles, turned aristocrats of many generations into peasants and generally caused as much fear as her brother would let her get away with.

Their father had this expression: "Always hammer the nails that stick up, down the hardest." Though the Grand Duchess disagreed with the King of Delmaire on many points, on this one they were in complete agreement.

Yet, despite all that she had done, she'd heard from a reliable source that something might well happen to her brother "in among the roses." It was probably just more rash talk from among the gentry who had not been hammered quite enough. Still, she ignored no threat. Just as a precaution, she'd informed his personal guard that the Emperor was to go nowhere in the gardens today.

Light from the large windows flickered from gray to white as the clouds outside raced through the sky. The change distracted her opponent for an instant, and deciding that this practice had gone on long enough, Zofiya took an aggressive lunge forward. The training foil in her hand flashed, and the unfortunate Imperial Guard who was her target tried to quickly step back. He couldn't get his own weapon up fast enough, and she rapped him hard against the mesh helmet.

The snap of the strike echoed down the marble hallway, bouncing off the rows of paintings and sculptures.

"Dearest Sister." The voice startled her, and she spun around to see the Emperor of Arkaym standing in the shadow of the archway. Kaleva, her elder brother, watched her with dark eyes and a smile.

For an Emperor he smiled far too often, but as always, what he was thinking was hidden. Zofiya took off her own helmet, tucked her foil under her arm and strode toward him.

Years of growing up in their father's Court had taught them one thing—knowledge was power. Yet she was afraid, afraid that as much as she did love her brother, she didn't really know him. She might adore and protect him, but he kept his true heart hidden from her.

That lonely thought made Zofiya abandon protocol momentarily. Despite the sweat and that they were, as ever, not alone, she grabbed Kaleva in a tight embrace. For that split second they were children again—the youngest, the most insignificant, yet still required to conform to the rules of their elders. Ignored by their mother and viewed as pawns by their father—no one could ever have expected them to be here now—the Emperor and the Grand Duchess of Arkaym.

Kaleva returned her hug for a moment but then pushed her back. "Sister, I fear you need to go easier on your guard, or they may request a transfer to the kitchens."

"You don't mind, do you, Hosh?" Zofiya shot the question over her shoulder.

The guard took off his helmet, revealing that his salt-and-pepper hair was wet with sweat, but he nonetheless sketched a very fine bow. "Not at all, Imperial Highness. It makes the rest of my day seem like a holiday by comparison."

Laughing, Kaleva drew his sister aside—as far away as an Emperor could, anyway. As always there were his guards, his personal secretary, his current favorites and two members of the Privy Council waiting in the wings. Zofiya missed the privacy they had shared as children.

Over at the window looking down the hill that the palace occupied, they stood for a moment, with their backs to the rest of the people in the room. It was a beautiful city, seen from a distance. The changing light alternately lit up the lagoon and the channels, making them look like mirrors for a short instant, before the clouds once again took over, hiding them in shadow.

Zofiya waited for her brother to speak, untying her hair and trying not to get curious as to what brought him to find her. Finally, Kaleva took out of his pocket three miniatures of three ladies and laid them out on the table in the flickering sunlight.

"So these are the final choices, are they?"

Kaleva nodded curtly. Youngest son of the King of Delmaire, he'd never been expected to rule anything, and now he was learning that there was more to being Emperor than merely dealing with bureaucrats and bickering Princes. An unmarried ruler was not acceptable in any shape or form, and yet picking a bride was loaded with layers of meaning and consequence that could freeze even the most intelligent, commanding man in his place.

"Yes." Her brother sighed, tucked his hands behind his back and looked down at the images. "One from Chioma, one from Seneqoth and one from Hatar—all beautiful, talented and from families deemed not strong enough to unbalance the Assembly of Princes."

"Poor Brother"—Zofiya chuckled—"to have to pick from such beauties. It is truly a cruel life you live." She kept her tone light, though she itched to fling away the images of the women from Seneqoth and Hatar, however she knew that doing so would draw unwanted attention from her brother. Always she had to take care not to remind him of her faith.

The Emperor pressed his lips together. "Perhaps I have been putting this off—but I am sure these ladies are not really pining for me." He couldn't help it—he looked over his shoulder. They were there, in the shadows: Otril and Eilse.

He was a minor Earl from Delmaire, and she a quiet beauty with no aristocratic blood in her veins at all. Yet it was well-known that Kaleva loved them.

The Emperor had taken care not to give them too much power in Imperial affairs, knowing from their father's Court that the influence of lovers could end with their death or that of the monarch. Yet their very closeness to him was beginning to spread more than a whisper in Vermillion.

Some talked of Otril and Eilse actively working against

the Emperor marrying—though Zofiya was sure they were not that foolish.

No, she sighed, it was her brother. Other royals were comfortable with mistresses, affairs, concubines, but not Kaleva. To marry was to deny his feelings—and it was not like the Emperor of Arkaym could act as the Prince of Chioma did—keeping a large harem of lovers. Tradition had it there was one Emperor and one Empress.

Eilse could not be that woman. Her low birth would have been an insult to the role.

"Brother"—Zofiya laid her hand on his arm, dropping her voice to a whisper that would remain just between the two of them—"Father was wrong about many things, but he was right in that the prime responsibility of a monarch is to continue the bloodline. We have a tenuous fingerhold on this continent as it is."

Kaleva turned his back to the magnificent view, leaned on the table and stared at his lovers. When he looked at his sister she saw him again: that little boy, the one she had perhaps read too many fairy tales to. Romanticism still clung to him miraculously, even after a war, assassination attempts and the machinations of a resentful Court.

Reaching behind him, he blindly picked one of the portraits; then, holding out his arm to Zofiya, he opened his hand.

Both of them looked down into the beautiful dark face of the Princess of Chioma.

Zofiya's heart skipped a beat. "Random chance, Brother?" The Grand Duchess tilted her head and smiled at him. "Is that really how you will choose the next Empress for Arkaym?" She knew it was anything but random.

Kaleva shrugged. "They are all equally worthy, equally beautiful—if their portraits are to be believed. I think this lady is a good choice. Her father has never—"

The rest of her brother's words faded from Zofiya's hearing, because just then the clouds parted. For an instant her eye caught movement in the tower opposite the Long Gallery.

It was an older portion of the palace, made of rough stone and not the smooth marble of more recent additions. What this particular spire did have was a great round stained glass window, the type called a rose window.

When light filtered through this particular rose window, Zofiya caught a glimpse of the figure behind it.

"Protect the Emperor!" she screamed, shoving her brother off the table, sending him flying to the floor just as a shot shattered first the rose window and then the one they were standing right in front of. It hit one of the portraits, exploding it into a thousand porcelain shards. Then everything was a whirl of movement, as Imperial Guards rushed forward, and the small huddle of courtiers scattered like chaff.

Zofiya didn't have time to notice any of that. Her brother was down, covered by those sworn to protect him, and now she had a job to do. The palace was a rabbit warren of rooms, passages and hidden entrances—the attacker could be away in an instant.

Zofiya flew down the Long Hall, skidding on the polished marble, but flinging open the latch in the wainscot in an instant. Down a set of stairs she ran, hearing the echo of the second shot dimly behind her. She made no effort to be quiet, but as she was wearing her practice slippers so as not to damage the floor of the Hall, she was considerably more silent than usual.

The Grand Duchess ran through the rough corridor, her arms pumping. In her mind's eye, the castle opened before her—every corridor, every archway, every staircase. Through the pounding of her heart and her feet against the castle floor, her breath came easily enough. Both Zofiya and Kaleva were studious about not letting Imperial food send them to the way of fat, and now all those laps around the gardens proved very useful.

She burst out of the secret door and into the room at the top of the Maiden Tower with barely a break in stride. The would-be assassin was turning, the length of his rifle only just pulled away from the hole in the window. He was dressed in the red of the Imperial Guard—an insult that Zofiya could not let go unpunished.

However, there could not have been a worse time for the Grand Duchess to go into battle. She wore light linen breeches with a similar shirt and carried nothing of greater length than her ceremonial dagger of Hatipai.

Zofiya was, however, of the blood of kings and beloved of

her goddess—she would triumph over some second-rate assassin naked from her bath if necessary.

She yelled, lunged and grabbed the barrel of the rifle with both hands. As the weapon came around, her forearms brushed against the barrel, pushing it up toward the ceiling. Once she felt the scalding metal sear her fingers, she pushed toward the assassin. Even over the sharp discharge of the weapon, she heard the crunch of the barrel slamming into the man's nose. His scream was a strained, muffled sound as he suddenly found it difficult to breathe. It was most satisfactory when droplets of his blood splattered onto her face—this man had come the closest to killing Kaleva in all their years here.

With a savage snarl, she grasped the butt of the rifle and yanked it toward her. Following its natural momentum, she brought it up, and then back down straight into his groin.

With a labored gasp, the assassin dropped to his knees. Apparently he was unable to choose which was the most painful: his nose or his genitals. Whatever pain he felt, however, was not enough as far as the Grand Duchess was concerned.

Burying her hands in his hair like a lover, she tugged his head forward viciously, directly onto her upraised knee. Now his scream was reduced to a gurgle. Yes, it was gratuitous. Yes, it was unnecessary. Yes, it felt delicious.

The Grand Duchess felt her own blood boil, a heady mix of terrible rage and savage joy. Her right hand wrapped around the hilt of Hatipai's dagger. Now her hand pulled his head back by his hair. Looking into his confused, pained eyes, Zofiya smiled.

"This isn't political," she hissed. "This is very, very personal."

She needed him to know that, even as she jerked the blade across his throat. The scarlet blood of the assassin was quite impressive on the pure linen of her white training uniform. Looking down at the silver dagger, Zofiya was abruptly entranced by the coating of blood it had now acquired.

Hatipai's dagger was meant only to show her willingness to sacrifice for the goddess—she had never heard of one that had been used to kill before. Yet, seeing it now, Zofiya realized it suited the blade well.

More than that—it felt warm in her grip. Through the

broken, glorious remains of the rose window, Zofiya saw
something moving that was not just the clouds. Not putting
away her knife, not even cleaning it as was proper, she walked
over to the view, broken glass crunching under her nearly bare
feet, and peered out.

The Grand Duchess did not look over to the Great Hall to
see if her brother was safe; instead she looked up. The clouds
were still skidding across the blue of the sky, but something
else was moving even faster among them: clusters of shadow,
balls of gray smoke were darting south, like a flock of supernatural birds heading for home before winter.

Yet it was not winter, and she should not be able to discern
geists. Zofiya glanced down again at her hands, still coated in
blood, and then up again, suddenly making the connection
between blood, knife and what she was seeing.

They were spirits, and if she concentrated hard enough,
she could hear their song. It was a hymn of adulation for
Hatipai, and she knew who they were—the dead worshippers
of her goddess. It was a revelation—a true goddess-given
revelation.

But what could it mean? Where were the true followers of
the goddess going so very quickly?

To me. They come to me.

The voice of Hatipai rang bell-clear in her head, and the
vision of the angel appeared among the broken remains of the
rose window. Suddenly Zofiya was glad of the assassin's
attempt on her brother's life. Without today's blood, she would
never have been granted this wonderful vision.

Tears began to roll out of her eyes and down her cheeks, as
if she were a child again. Her fingers grew numb, and the
knife fell from her fingers to rattle among the ruined glass. It
was unimportant. Nothing mattered now as much as the clear
voice of Hatipai in her mind.

You must come to me. It was the voice of her mother—or
rather the voice that she wished her mother had used. *Bring
me this.*

An image flashed in her mind. A grand Temple, with towering red walls, each one carved with scenes from the Holy
Book of Beauty—the sacred text of Hatipai. The light that
streamed in through the arched windows was yellow, bright

and strong in a way that no sun in the north could possibly be. Zofiya saw the font where water was sacrificed to the goddess, and in rare and important moments other liquids. Her mind's eye watched the font drain clear and a set of stairs grind into place—a marvel of ancient engineering. A cold dread formed in the pit of the Grand Duchess' stomach—though she had no idea why.

Go down into the earth and bring me what only you can—my royal blood in Chioma has failed me. You shall not. The goddess' tone grew harsh and angry, enough to make Zofiya quail.

As she trembled, the voice became soft again, bringing warmth to her suddenly cold limbs. *I believe in your strength—you will not fail me, blessed child.*

"Indeed, Bright One," Zofiya whispered, her eyes half-shut, "I will not fail you. Whatever you need done, will be done."

You must bring me what you find in the Temple. You will know it when you see it.

It was strange that the goddess would tell her no more—but it was not the place of even a Grand Duchess to question Hatipai.

Tell no one what you are doing—there are many in this forsaken kingdom that would try to prevent you going.

It disturbed her to hear her brother's Empire described thus, but she wouldn't question what any of it meant. A sword did not question the motives of its wielder. She would immediately take the swiftest Imperial Dirigible south. How many weirstones they broke getting her there was of no account.

When the Imperial Guard found Zofiya, she was kneeling in the broken glass, looking out the window and weeping. She heard them whispering that she was a true and brave sister to cry for the salvation of the Emperor—but Zofiya knew better than they. She was weeping for the gift of sight. Something wonderful was happening to the south, and she would soon be part of it.

TWELVE

The Bond Reborn

"Still no sign?" Sorcha hissed out of the corner of her mouth.

The rest of the petitioners in the room took no notice—or at least pretended not to. The heat in the domed red room was stifling, and the Deacon could feel sweat coating her neck. Her robes had never felt a more foolish fashion choice. She would have been content to wait for Raed in the city, but the Prince apparently had different ideas. He had requested the Deacons from Vermillion be formally introduced to him.

Merrick, who sat opposite her in the room, wiped his own beaded forehead. "Raed is in the city, Sorcha, but I am no more able than you to say exactly where"—he gestured vaguely—"only that he is close."

By the Bones, she needed a cigarillo, and it had to be now—etiquette be damned. Several of the other people in the room were already smoking; two beautifully carved pipes in the elegant fingertips of two merchants.

Obviously they were used to all this waiting, because they had the studied expressions of Sensitives at meditation. Actives were taught the very same lessons but were far less adept at it—Sorcha least of all.

Still, she had developed her own ways of coping. She lit her cigarillo, slumped back in her chair and contemplated seeing

Raed again. He would not be able to sense they were in Orinthal, so she'd get a chance to observe his reactions. Maybe from them she could decide on what her own would be.

Leaning her forearms on her thighs, Sorcha glared down at the space between her feet, studying the mosaic floor. The question of her feelings for Raed was something she had avoided until now. Sorcha couldn't decide which was worse: if she had been wrong about the giddy rush of desire, mistaking it for something deeper, or if she had been right.

In children's stories when the Princess found her Prince, things were simple; they got married and lived that way forever. Life had taught her such things were oversimplifications—wishes that seldom came true in the complicated realities of existence. Most people never got to ride into the sunset with their one true love.

And yet Sorcha could not deny that in their brief time together, as tumultuous as it had been, she had felt more alive than in all her years with Kolya.

The smoke curled out of her mouth slowly, spiraling past her eyes. Through it, she could see Merrick watching her as covertly as the young man was capable of. The Bond was so fickle that she could barely tell what was leaking across to him.

Further thoughts were disrupted when the waiting room door burst open, and Ambassador Bandele strode through with two courtiers following his wake. Though his mission to Vermillion was over, he was not done with the two Deacons.

As his sharp eyes descended on the other occupants of the room, they scurried to vacate it. Merrick rose to his feet, but Sorcha merely watched Bandele. He'd been of mild importance when they'd been protecting the deputation, but now in her opinion he was just another painful hanger-on.

The Ambassador looked Sorcha and Merrick up and down. His brown eyes flickered over their rather plain Deacon robes as if he somehow found them offensive. He gestured, and one of his followers darted forward with a scarlet robe draped over an arm.

"This will do the trick for you, Deacon Faris." He made to hold it in her general direction.

Sorcha knocked the top off her cigarillo and considered how on earth to reply without shouting.

"I am sorry"—Merrick stopped him, though he did look suspiciously as if he were about to burst into laughter—"but the Order specifically forbids us to wear anything but our robes. We are supposed to reject the perils of the material world, you see."

"But this is hardly a peril"—Bandele waved the outrageously colored length—"just enough to make you acceptable in the Prince's Court."

Sorcha swallowed her anger. "Are you saying we are not 'acceptable' here?"

Bandele opened his mouth, but Merrick was quicker. "It is just not possible, Ambassador. Thank you for your kind offer, though."

He glanced between the Deacons and then admitted defeat. Bandele waved away his helpers. "I can hardly believe"—he sighed—"that I am introducing such dull birds to the greatest Court of finery and beauty in the world."

That was quite a sweeping statement. "It is impossible," Sorcha replied sharply, "that the Court of your Prince can match that of the Emperor in Vermillion."

The Ambassador tilted his head and grinned. "Oh, the Emperor's Court is indeed most"—he pursed his lips—"civilized. But the beauty of it cannot compare to the silks and organzas of Chioma." He glanced over them one last time. "Are you sure you will at not least put on the more acceptable robes that our Order wear?"

"*Your* Order?" Sorcha's jaw clenched. "As far as I know, the Order belongs to itself and not—"

Merrick gave a hasty bow. "The ways of the Chiomese Deacons are for its citizens alone—and not for us, I am afraid."

The Ambassador sniffed, but seeing no flicker of compromise in either of them, he turned back to the door. "The Prince will see you now, then—as you are."

The inside of the palace was even more beautiful than the outside. Long galleries that somewhat resembled ones back at the Mother Abbey opened out onto many little gardens with intricate plantings and burbling fountains. Each one was a gulp of blessed cool in the heavy blanket of heat that existed outside of the thick walls of the palace. They passed under the red mud ceilings and, craning her neck as surreptitiously as she could, Sorcha saw how intricately they were carved. She was used to the Imperial Palace, but she still managed to be impressed with the Prince of Chioma's residence. Naturally she would not let a bit of it show to Bandele.

Merrick leaned over and murmured in her ear, "I think he already knows."

Sorcha shivered, thrusting up the mental shields that all Initiates learned to hold against geists—she hoped it would provide some protection from the leaking of thoughts across the Bond. Merrick was lifting more and more of them from her mind, and she was concerned that her partner was less and less aware that he was doing it.

As they passed through the palace corridors and drew closer to the throne room, she began to smell the thick odor of frankincense—it was beautiful and exotic.

They reached the waiting room directly outside the throne room where there were crowds of people. These were not aristocrats; these were the common folk: traders, penitents, the desperate and those looking for advancement. Women with eyes of ebony chatted in corners and watched them cautiously. Sorcha suddenly did feel underdressed—and realized Bandele had been right—she and Merrick were dull indeed. The riot of blazing purples, rich reds and eye-popping oranges were almost blinding. Sorcha had never before had cause to feel jealousy for another woman's dress, but she found that she did feel self-conscious.

As they trailed at the rear of the procession, surreptitiously eyeing the waiting crowds, a strange sensation began to build inside the Deacon. It was so warm and deep down that for a second she was almost embarrassed at its primitive nature. Sorcha dared not show her reaction, but she was confused by her body's odd reaction.

She glanced up at Merrick to ask him if he too felt it, perhaps offer some Sensitive insight. Instead, over his shoulder Sorcha glimpsed the face she had been looking for—but had not expected to find here.

Bandele, totally unaware, strode on toward the doors, while both Deacons stopped dead in their tracks.

Sorcha forgot to breathe. The world narrowed until there was only the three of them: her, Merrick and Raed, the Young

Pretender, the third in their Bond. Her eyes couldn't get wide enough to soak all of him in. Suddenly the worries and cares she'd held on to so tightly meant nothing.

He was wearing the traditional Chiomese head scarf and bright, loose clothing—so his face was partially concealed—but she would have recognized him anywhere. Raed, however, was talking to a tall young man and didn't notice them. He was so unreal in a real situation that she stood stock-still, examining him, feeling a ridiculous smile spread on her lips. She took half a step toward him, her mouth opening to say his name.

Wait, Sorcha! The words in her head were like a slap in the face, and then Merrick's hand clamped down on her arm, as if she was a little child who would run and throw herself on Raed.

He might not have been able to feel their Bond, but the Young Pretender heard her indrawn breath. He turned and saw them both. The Bond flared, releasing a rush of sensation that almost toppled her. Every memory, every sensation of their time together came racing forward. Sorcha had been trying not to think of them, tried to deny their power—under this new assault she had no defenses.

Raed's hazel eyes held hers. She noted the flex of his hands into fists and the tremble in his posture as if he too was holding back movement.

So many people stood around them, chattering, arguing, lost in their own world. Sorcha realized she was not free to simply walk over and throw herself into Raed's arms. They were in a foreign Prince's Court, with eyes everywhere watching them, observing, noting. She knew full well how the report of a Deacon flinging herself on a man in Orinthal would go. It could be even worse, if she drew attention to the fact that the Young Pretender was that man.

Deacon Sorcha Faris was frozen with indecision. She had so much to say to him—but dared not voice it.

"Honored Deacons?" Bandele had breezed right past the mass of people and was now standing before the massive cedar doors, his brow furrowed. The Chiomese guard, with their rifles on their shoulders and elaborate feather headdresses, were waiting to announce them. Gradually the heads of everyone in the hallway were turning toward the motionless Deacons.

"Walk on," Merrick whispered, his voice taut. When she did not, he hissed again, "Keep walking, Sorcha!"

By the Bones, she needed to smile, and with difficulty she managed it. "Coming, Ambassador," she called cheerily.

Walking past Raed felt deeply wrong, but as they did so, Sorcha flicked her head to the left and caught his eye; she hoped he could see or sense how much it hurt to turn her back on him.

"Wait here," she mouthed to him while her heart raced. *Please don't die before I can warn you.*

He stayed where he was, and then she saw him no more. Sorcha barely heard the seneschal announce them or saw the Court itself. It was only feeling Merrick at her shoulder that kept her moving.

"It'll be all right," he murmured to her. "He's here, but he's alive. We have time."

Sorcha took a breath, and it felt like the first. Her partner was correct. They were in foreign territory, and she had better take notice of the Court around them.

A subtle glance to her right told her that Merrick was already entranced. It was, she supposed, a feast for the eye. The people of Chioma, with their high cheekbones and gleaming dark skin, were even more impressive when dressed in Court attire. Servants stood in the corners, beating the air with fans of peacock feathers, while another played a curved flute, filling the room with a strangely melancholy tune. Upon the dais were a rank of beautiful woman—the most striking collection of slightly dressed women that Sorcha had ever seen.

The women of the Imperial Court were lovely too, but their charms were considerably more hidden. The Deacon suddenly made the connection; these exquisite women who peered down with somnolent assurance of their place in the world were members of the Prince's harem.

It took a moment for her to notice the man buried in among them. Seated at the top of the dais was a throne carved from dark wood, and on it was the most extraordinary man she had ever seen—or not seen.

He was totally cloaked in the deepest blue, swathed so completely that she could not have said if he was tall or short, thin or fat. The real strangeness was that she could not make out a single feature of his face. The Prince of Chioma wore an odd headdress with a bar of silver across his forehead from which hung rows upon rows of tiny white glass beads. They gleamed and danced and were very pretty—but they also denied anyone any chance of seeing his face.

Sorcha shot a glance across at Merrick—and he gave the slightest of shrugs. Apparently this scholar of all things Chioma was just as baffled. The Prince was an enigmatic figure, he'd told her that, but obviously he hadn't been expecting him to be *this* enigmatic.

Bandele was bending low in a bow that bordered on that which might be given to the Emperor. "Majesty, these are the Deacons from Vermillion who escorted us safely here. I present Deacons Faris and Chambers."

"Welcome to Orinthal." The voice that emerged from behind the beaded headdress was deep, smooth and remarkably young. "It has been a long time since any Deacon from the Mother Abbey has ventured this far south."

Sorcha and Merrick sketched a bow, but it was the Sensitive who replied. "Your Majesty, it has long been my dream to visit Chioma."

The Prince nodded, the only gesture that Sorcha could be sure of behind that strange mask. "I have long wished to see the Imperial City myself. But perhaps I can send my daughter in my stead." It was the most polite and gentle probe, delivered in a perfectly level tone of voice. "What do you think, Deacon Faris—shall my daughter see Vermillion?" The Prince shifted, and the crystals swayed as his head turned in her direction.

Sorcha, used to her partner's handling these subtle interactions, found herself caught unawares. "I . . . I truly cannot say, Your Majesty. I know he has received the suits of many ladies from all over the Empire."

The gasp that ran through the crowd implied that might not have been the best choice of words. Sorcha felt increasingly frustrated and irritated. She had stood before Princes before, even the Emperor, and yet this one was so hard to judge with the royal face obscured.

Merrick could not step in; to do so would imply weakness in his partner. Sorcha did, however, feel him stiffen at her side.

When Onika, Prince of Chioma, laughed, the pressure valve was let off a little. "Very true—I can only be grateful not to have to choose from so many." His voice was laced with amusement and irony—as it should be, considering the women of his harem stood not five feet from him.

While the Court tittered at their Prince's little joke, a small brass door opened behind the throne. A group of five young women with one older and heavily pregnant entered. These newcomers were far more demurely dressed, and Sorcha knew immediately that the youthful ones were his daughters. They whispered among themselves and moved to the other side of the throne, well away from the women of the harem. Among them was a tall, striking girl with such a look of confidence that the eye was immediately drawn to her. It was not a great stretch to guess that this had to be the Princess Ezefia who was suing for the Emperor's favor. Her eyes darted to the Ambassador, but seeing nothing, she quickly replaced the mask of boredom. So, she was an expert in the games of Court—she would have to be if she were to become the next Empress.

The older woman, swaying slightly with her swollen belly, still moved with the economy and grace that would put a dancer to shame. Her dark braid swung down her back, and she smiled beatifically at the Court—the smile of the truly happy. The Prince turned and held out his hand to her; however, it was impossible to tell if he smiled or not. Sorcha guessed that he did. He did not introduce the newcomer, but she slipped into a place just at the foot of his throne.

And then across the Bond Sorcha felt Merrick fall into a well of panic. It was so deep that she jerked around to look at her partner, wondering what in the Bones could be the cause. Nothing on his face could possibly have told her that he was close to bolting—his expression remained clear and calm.

Unaware of any change in the Deacons, the Prince fixed his gaze on them once more. "I will have many questions for you, Deacons." He paused. The Order stood apart from the usual machinations of the Princes: their rules, their squabbles. The only people whom Merrick and Sorcha had above them were the Priors and Abbots of the Order of the Eye and the Fist—and ultimately the Emperor.

Perhaps the Prince realized that he had pushed the line between Order and aristocracy a little too far, because his voice softened. "It would assist me, honored Deacons, if you could talk with me later about your Emperor. I would know his mind on some matters."

Sorcha's stomach clenched for two reasons: the way he said "your Emperor" as if he had no connection with the man and the idea that they were to be quizzed about politics. The Deacons could refuse, use the vaunted independence of the Order, but they were a long way from a Priory or Abbey—and even farther from the Mother Abbey itself.

However, it was the perfect chance to stay on in Chioma—the perfect chance to save Raed.

Sorcha reached out along the Bond, seeking Merrick's opinion. However, there was nothing. Somewhere during the confusion, he had slammed down his shields. Sensitives were always better than Actives at such things, but she would never have expected it from Merrick—especially right now.

She used another bow, perhaps one too many, to hide her confusion. "It would be our pleasure to offer assistance, Your Majesty," she said as graciously as possible.

They were swiftly dismissed by the Prince, but she made damn sure that they did not back out of his presence—there were some local customs she was determined not to adopt.

Outside, she scanned the petitioners, looking for Raed, but he was gone. When she turned for advice to Merrick, he held up his hand. "I really need to rest, Sorcha." His tone was clipped, rough and distant. "We can talk about this later."

He sounded like a different person—not her partner, not her friend. As Sorcha watched in shock, he turned on his heel and left her standing there with absolutely no explanation. Her frown was deep but robbed of a target.

Merrick and his mystery would have to wait; for now she had to hunt down Raed—and quickly—before the spectyr's vision came true.

THIRTEEN

Returning Home

Merrick was glad that, in the manner of the Chiomese, the male and female accommodation was separate. He didn't want to see Sorcha, didn't want to keep the shields up on her and most certainly did not want her questions. His thoughts needed to be his own.

She had recognized him. He had seen that in the flicker of a frown on her brow; a tiny gesture that no one else could have spotted. However, he had grown up watching her beautiful face.

Merrick sat on the bed, his hands clenched on the edge. So it was that simple, that easy, to throw him straight back into the tumult of his childhood. His training as a Deacon might never have even happened.

He was just a boy again.

The door creaked open, because he had not locked it. He didn't turn, but he heard her slip into the room.

The Deacon took a long breath and then faced her. He realized age had not dimmed the beauty of his mother; it had placed a few fine lines around her brown eyes but had left her thick, dark hair alone. His eyes drifted down to her swollen belly, and her hands strayed there as if protecting it.

"Ales." She whispered the name he had given up.

"No, Mother"—he tugged his cloak tighter around him, so that the badge of the Eye and the Fist gleamed in the candle-light—"I gave up that name when I entered the Order."

With a wince Japhne del Torne, once Baroness, still his mother, looked away. "We scoured the woods for you, then the city, but we just couldn't find you . . ."

"Merrick." He spoke his chosen name. The hardness in his voice was completely beyond his control.

"Merrick." Then she did the one thing that every mother held as a trump card—she cried.

He was ten again, standing in her chamber holding the broken remains of a delicate bowl her own dead mother had given her. He'd felt like a terrible human being when she'd burst into tears. Then as now, there was nothing to do but run to her and let the apologies flow.

It was different: her belly made any hug awkward, and now he towered above her. She still smelled the same, how-ever: roses and warmth. The scent hit him in a primitive way, and Merrick cried too. The memories of leaving, the burning vengeance in his heart that had driven him from home, were as fresh as the day that they had happened.

"Mother"—he held her back at arm's length—"what are you doing here? What of del Torne? Tell me what has happened!"

"Your half brother rules there," she said flatly. "Berne came of age, and suddenly his stepmother was surplus to requirement."

When her shoulders slumped, he guided her over to sit on the bed. Merrick dropped down to his knees and looked up at her. His elder half brother had been sent to be educated in the nearby Abbey when Ales had been just a toddler. He recalled that Berne looked very like their father, and he'd always assumed that the heir to the estate had a similar personality. Guilt washed over Merrick; blinded by his own pain and mis-ery, he'd never spared a thought for his mother.

"Tell me what happened." He squeezed her fingers.

Japhne brushed her tears. "I asked to move to the gate-house—I would have been happy to end my days there—but he would have none of it. I was forced to go back to my broth-er's home."

Merrick knew his uncle Edrien was a prickly bag of bones

and the main reason Japhne had married so very young. Returning to his care must have been galling for her. Da Nanth was in many respects a throwback to an earlier age—very like its neighbor Chioma. Women there did not hold property or title and were totally dependent on their male kin.

"That was where I received Onika's suit," she whispered. Her cheeks flushed red, and her hand rested on her ripe belly. "How he heard of me, I don't know."

The flower of Da Nanth—that was what they called her. Snatched up and married when she was but sixteen, even in the last days of her thirties she still deserved that title.

Although there was some part of Merrick that disliked that she had remarried, the logical part of him realized that she had few other choices. Japhne had been thrust into an untenable situation under her brother's constantly watching eye—no position, and no way to support herself. So Merrick choked back his first reaction in his throat before it had a chance to escape.

His second thought was to wonder if the Prince took his crystal mask off beyond the throne room—but then the images of where he might do that were far too disturbing for any son to contemplate. Her swollen belly loomed large in his vision.

Instead, Merrick choked out, "What . . . what is he like? Does he treat you well?"

Her smile was soft. "He is very kind. I do not understand why he bothered with me, though—and I am certainly on the verge of not being able to bear any more children. So this was a surprise." A gentle rub on her stomach communicated contentment and joy more succinctly than any words could. "I was just a wee slip of a girl when I married your father and had you. This feels very different—not bad—but different." She settled back on the bed. "Now I want to hear about your life. I would never have guessed you would choose the Order."

"I am sorry." Merrick clenched his hand on hers. Opening the deep well of grief and guilt was something he had avoided doing for years, yet under the gaze of her gentle brown eyes he had no chance.

Japhne's fingers ran lightly over his hair, her gaze distant. Merrick knew he looked very like his father.

"No need for sorrow—just tell me," she whispered. "Tell me what happened to my boy."

Merrick shrugged, feeling the weight of the cloak and the badge. "I wanted vengeance for Father. I wanted to help others. I wanted to be a better Deacon than those who came to save him." He smiled a little. "But Fate does have a funny way of turning things around. My partner is now Deacon Sorcha Faris."

"I thought I recognized her." His mother let out a long breath. "Hers is a face hard to forget."

"She has a certain"—Merrick paused and then looked up with a slight smile—"way of doing things."

"Just don't fall in love with her!" Japhne flicked the tip of his nose.

"Never!"

One of her hands cupped his face. "What I really want to know, my dearest son, are you happy?"

No one had asked him that—not in all his time in the Order—and it was easy for the unconsidered reply to slip out from his mouth. "Absolutely—this is what I always wanted."

"But you gave up your name—"

"If they knew who I was, Mother, who my father was and that he was possessed, they would never have taken me." Guilt, the kind of guilt he had first felt when he spoke his new name to the Presbyter of the Young, surged through him.

She bit her lip and nodded. "It seems we are both caught in a similar trap, then. The Court of Chioma is even more riddled with conspiracy than Da Nanth. If any of the other wives found out you were my son, they would use it to their advantage."

Her voice trailed off. For a moment mother and son sat there, aware how completely they were snared in their past. Finally, Japhne levered herself off the bed. "I must get back to the women's quarters—I cannot afford to be missed." Her hand described a circle on her belly. "The cantrips said this little one is a boy." Her smile was uncertain. "And heir."

Her son the Deacon squeezed her fingers. They both were perfectly aware of the consequences—both good and bad—of giving any Prince an heir.

Finally she bent and pressed her lips to Merrick's forehead. "I do appreciate your new name though, my son. I know

your grandmother would be very happy that you are carrying
it forward."

He pressed his eyelids closed, feeling the sharp prick of
tears against them. "Will I see you again?" He sounded just
like that boy in a run-down castle, with his parents the twin
pillars of his world.

"Of course." She stood at the door, shadow hiding her
round belly. "Onika has many questions for you and your
partner—I will try and get him to keep you here as long as I
can." Then she blew him a kiss, glanced once out the door and
slipped into the corridor.

Merrick stayed where he was, seated on the floor, uncertain what to make of this revelation. He would soon have a
half sibling in line for the throne of Chioma—but that was
nothing compared to the emotional stomach punch of his own
guilt. Tonight he feared would be a restless one.

Sorcha sat on the wide, luxurious bed and felt her nervousness
sink its teeth into her. Keeping her arms wrapped around her
knees, she couldn't help but wonder if she'd been rejected by
both men: the Bond was silent, and Raed was nowhere to be
seen.

She jerked her Gauntlets out from her belt and stared down
at them. Once she had thought all the answers lay in those
Runes—that the Order was the great protector. No longer. It
had been years since Deacon Sorcha Faris had cried with
despair, but now she was perilously close. She had never felt
so out of her depth, plunged into a principality that was unlike
any of the ones she knew. Floundering was not a sensation she
enjoyed in any capacity. And yet she was doing it twice over.
Raed—am I being a fool over Raed?

While Sorcha had not thrown herself into his arms, a portion of her was rather upset that he had not done the same to
her. Ridiculous, but she would have known what he was
thinking.

From her pocket she pulled out the ring he had given her.
It remained unknown if it were a promise or just a keepsake
that he had boxes of and cast to women who lay down with
him throughout all of Arkaym.

Not for the first time did Sorcha think that she was too old for so much turmoil.

With an aggravated groan, she stripped off her cloak and flung it over a chair. At least she could get some sleep tonight. This separate and guarded wing of rooms only for the women was a strange idea, but she would be grateful for an undisturbed rest. These thick mud walls ate up sound even more completely than they swallowed the heat.

Sorcha was just unbuckling her belt when she heard a scraping at the window. Snatching up her knife, the Deacon padded to the shutters. They were three stories up, but assassins were always a possibility in any Court.

The shutter moved a little, and as Sorcha slipped into the shadows, she saw the tip of a knife work its way between them to lift the latch. Then they were flung open, and only the flare of the Bond stopped her from plunging the knife into the back of Raed Syndar Rossin.

"Hello there." He swung his legs over the lip of the window and smiled as if he'd happened upon her in the street and not climbed three stories into a sealed harem.

A thousand possible answers to his jaunty greeting flashed across Sorcha's mind, but none of them mattered as much as the fact that he was there—in the room. Instead, she dropped the knife to the floor, stepped forward and grabbed him by the tunic. Her lips were on his immediately, and they were sweeter and better than she remembered. He tasted of leather, cigars and sex. All other concerns and fears evaporated.

Raed kissed her back and pulled her in tightly against him so she could feel his sudden rush of excitement. For a long, heady moment the Deacon indulged her pent-up frustrations and desires.

Then Sorcha shoved him back—though taking her lips from his felt incredibly wrong. Trapped in contrary emotions, she fell back on what she knew—outrage. "What are you doing here?"

Raed cocked his head with a grin on his bruised lips. "What am *I* doing here? What are you doing here?"

"*I* am escorting the Chiomese Ambassador back from Vermillion. *I* am not a wanted criminal with a bounty on my head in the middle of the Empire!" She was so vexed she wanted to throw something, but she also wanted to rip off both of their clothes and use the large bed for a better purpose than mere sleep.

He sighed. "I have no choice—I got word that my sister has been taken—and the trail led us here."

"To Orinthal?"

"To Orinthal." Raed picked up her hand and kissed her palm. The feel of his lips and the brush of his beard on her skin sent shudders running into Sorcha's core.

"I am sorry to hear it." The anger was melting out of her. "Can I help?"

"I am sure you can." Now Raed pressed her hand against his chest, so she could feel that his heart was racing. "But not tonight."

Sorcha could tell him about the spectyr, the visions and everything—but it would make no difference—not to this moment.

The Deacon ran her thumb over the line of his lips, feeling them curve upward under the delicate touch. Something about him was so beautiful to her.

"You make such a fool of me." It was the truth, but she was half laughing.

His smile, the secret smile she only saw when he was alone with her, struck her through. His hazel eyes gleamed in the candlelight.

"As you do me, Deacon Sorcha Faris." Then he kissed her again, slower this time, but full of the same hunger.

Raed was alive and so was she—there was nothing wrong with remembering that. Under her fingers his skin felt so exquisite that she wanted more. She wanted it all. They stumbled, fumbled with clothes; it had been so long, so many weeks, so many months. Sorcha was hungry, and she could feel that hunger in him too. Need would have to be satisfied before anything else.

"No swinging bed this time." Raed's laugh was low and throaty and set all the deep places inside her on fire.

"We'll make do," she replied before fastening her mouth on the warm, soft spot on his neck.

He groaned when she nipped him there. "I am glad these walls are thick," she went on, her hands tugging on his belt buckle. The jingle of it hitting the ground was deeply erotic.

Raed's hands buried in her hair, tugging her tightly against his mouth—the sting of it was sweet. In return, she raked her fingers down his back. The most basic part of her wanted to mark him, claim him, make him say that he was hers, just as he had taken all of her without so much as a by-your-leave.

The circular effect of want and desperation made their embrace into almost a tussle, until falling onto the bed, Raed began licking his way down her body. She wanted more, wanted him, but his strong arms held hers down, until his tongue drove all struggle from her. It was the ultimate indulgence, and Sorcha knew life seldom afforded her such moments. She was happy to voice her delight, so he knew what he drove her to.

When finally she spiraled into pleasure, only then did Raed slide up her body and enter her. Yet, when he began to stoke slow and deep inside her, Sorcha twisted under him, spilling him onto his back.

"Now," she laughed wickedly, "who is the prisoner?"

The Young Pretender chuckled in response, his hands falling back on the sheets. "I am yours once again, fierce Deacon—to do with me as you will."

"I will," Sorcha returned, rocking her hips upon him. "But there will be long hours of interrogation for you, I fear."

Raed tilted his head back on the pillow, closing his eyes as her hands clenched on his chest. For an instant—just a split second—Sorcha saw something else there too, the hint of something darker. The Rossin flickered across the face of the man she was so addicted to. It was a reminder of the Beast within.

Yet, Sorcha was too far gone to deny either of them pleasure. When Raed's eyes opened again, the hazel of them had gone dark green in the half-light of the candles, and his breath hissed over the perfect line of his teeth.

She had never thought to see him again, and so she would make the most of this moment—and make it last as long as possible. Sleep was, after all, highly overrated.

➤ FOURTEEN ➤

Alone with Consequence

When finally Merrick slept, it was not the deep rest he really needed.

Every Deacon knew there was one place where the barriers they trained so hard to create slipped. Sleep, which every mortal needed, was a perilous place. Luckily there were few geists that could penetrate that landscape—but it didn't mean that it was secure.

Merrick was on a great plain of sand, standing naked looking up at the stars. The air was cool, a breeze coming as if from some distant sea. He felt open to the world and to nature as he could not remember being since childhood. Even his nakedness did not disturb him.

Above the sky was a stretched silk of deepest blue, unmarked by any moon—all there was were stars. Merrick had studied long hours. He knew every constellation and formation in the night sky both north and south. The stars above him were in the constellations he recognized, but not a single one was in its correct place. It was as if some great hand had adjusted the parchment of the sky, and now many of the southern shapes were in the northern sky.

Where was he? The edges of fear trickled over him. On the horizon five stars detached themselves from the firmament and spun toward him. At first he was amazed, but then horror overcame him. The stars loomed bright and larger as they bore down on him.

Merrick turned to run with the stars burning and snapping at his heels. Under his feet the sand was fickle. It pulled him toward the stars, rushing past his toes. He stumbled many times, his breath rammed in his throat, his heart hammering in his chest. Yet he was unable to make any distance.

Our son—the voice in his head was not Sorcha's—*do not run, there is nothing to fear.*

Ahead a palace erupted from the sand, and suddenly the dreadful singing of the stars stopped. Now sand was blown against his face, stinging it like acid. Merrick stopped, panting, terrified, and craned his neck to look up at the building.

The white stone was carved with many seated figures, all of them the same, all of them wearing the crystal mask of the Prince of Chioma. When the crystals moved, it seemed as though he might be able to see beyond them and make out a face. Yet, whenever he leveled his gaze upon that space, all he beheld was a blindingly golden light that hurt his eyes more than the sand. Something beautiful and terrible was beyond.

With a grinding sound that made him clap his hands to his ears, the statues all stood, but as they did, they broke and shattered.

All must be broken. All must bow. All must be made anew.

The voice was female, seductive, and it surrounded Merrick. It was not his mother. It was not Sorcha. Yet he knew it. He knew it from childhood.

Somehow, though, the stars were gone. All of them. The sky above him now was totally blank. Instead, the golden light was spreading across the horizon, banishing the darkness.

The light was all around him, wrapping him in its embrace. Merrick bowed his head, accepting the light if it would have him. He fell to his knees—

And that was when the screaming woke him.

While Sorcha lay tucked in his arms, her breathing slow and deep, Raed found he could not do the same. Their sweat was drying slowly in the sheets, and yet he could not rest as his mind was troubled.

When he had turned to see her simply standing there, he'd felt as though he'd been hit between the eyes. Yet it was Sorcha, wearing the same unassuming clothes and blue cloak of the Deacon as when Raed had last seen her. Merrick, a little more muscular, a little more adult around the face, stood at her shoulder. In that instant, even Raed, without the training of the Order, felt it. The Bond they talked about. The one that Sorcha had formed so flippantly in a moment of danger.

If there were gods, they had an interesting sense of humor.

Raed trailed one hand down her cheek. She murmured and stirred under it, wriggling closer to his naked skin. He'd been afraid to see her—afraid that what they had shared in those moments on the dirigible had been merely a reaction to the danger. Now he didn't know what to think—or where to file away these sensations.

With him, women and relationships had always been short-lived things; his status as hunted criminal in the new Empire forced them to be. Dare he start thinking that these interludes with Sorcha could be strung together into something approaching a real relationship? It would mean she would have to surrender all of her current life.

Raed knew he certainly had nothing left to give up, or to offer her, for that matter. As a fugitive, the Young Pretender had to make do with moments of happiness, so he wasn't going to spoil this one thinking about what he could not have.

He also wouldn't tell her about the Rossin having broken free so recently; he knew what would happen after that. Sorcha would offer to find Fraine herself and send him back to the ocean and safety, and he feared that with the Bond she could force him to do just that. He couldn't risk it. His sister's life was at stake.

Gently blowing aside a strand of Sorcha's long red hair, Raed worked his way down to rest in behind her as close as he could: one hand wrapped around her waist, the other gently cupping her breast. He had just closed his eyes, when the scream rang out.

Both of them scrambled out of bed and reached for weapons before their clothes. With her hair curling down her back and around her breasts, Sorcha went to the window, inched open the shutters, and looked out. Raed waited.

"Something is happening in the garden." Sorcha slammed the shutter tight. "Lots of torches and guards."

Without further discussion they got back into their clothes, while outside they could hear a commotion growing. They were not the only ones to be disturbed.

Sorcha glanced at Raed. "You can't go out the way you came in. Here." She threw her cloak about him and pulled the hood up. "I think there is enough trouble out there that they won't notice you're not exactly female."

He grabbed a quick kiss. "By the Blood, you do know how to flatter a man."

She was right; out in the hallway there was much running and wailing as women woke to the chaos outside. They pushed through the panicked women and ran down the stairs.

"Is it a geist?" Raed spoke directly into Sorcha's ear—suddenly worried that whatever had attacked him on the boat had found him again.

She paused in the tumult, and her eyes unfocused as she concentrated on the world that only the Deacons could see. "It is hard for me to tell—I need Merrick." She sounded annoyed, then her head flicked around. For a second Raed thought he heard the younger Deacon's name repeating in his skull—a whisper that made his skin crawl.

Before he could wonder on the strangeness of that, Sorcha darted down the remaining stairs, pushing aside the women-folk as if they were not even of the same species as her. Raed wouldn't let her get out of his sight, however; he followed in her rather rude wake.

Outside, the courtyard garden was all lush tropical foliage and hanging exotic flowers. It was not laid out in the northern fashion with symmetrical design. This was a little slice of luxury from the jungles in the eastern part of Arkaym—where there was more rainfall. It did, however, have a white gravel path, so he and Sorcha dashed along it, following the universal call.

"Alarm! Alarm!" It was the hue and cry that every citizen of the Empire was called upon to answer. The palace guard would quickly come running.

They rounded a large ficus tree and found themselves at the scene of the disturbance. Three guards stood among this beauty and looked down at a scene of utter horror. This was the center of the pleasure garden, marked with a delicate marble fountain—and perfumed by exotic honey scents.

At least, that was how it should have been. At first glance it was hard to tell that the bodies lying there had been human. Blood was everywhere: splattered against the beautiful fountain, pooling in the white gravel and covering the bodies.

"I need those torches closer!" Sorcha's Deacon training brought so much command to her voice that these men did not question. They moved, but she had to snap, "But not *in* the blood, fools!"

The nearest guard, young and with barely a beard on his face, turned white.

Raed knew the look from green sailors, and apparently so did Sorcha. "And Unholy Bones, if you need to be sick—go do it elsewhere!"

Handing his torch to his colleague, he trotted off to do as bidden.

"Stay close," Sorcha whispered somewhat redundantly. As a Deacon she would not be questioned, whereas he, an unaccompanied male, would probably be killed on sight. He certainly wasn't going to just wander off.

"I'll do my best," Raed muttered, feeling utterly useless but somewhat relieved that at the moment the Rossin was silent.

After the guards lit the scene a little better by planting their torch spears in the gravel, Sorcha waved them back. Despite the difference in Chiomese and Vermillion Deacons, the guards did so—most likely they were grateful to have someone else to defer to.

Leaves on the other side of the garden rustled. The guards, naturally jumpy, nearly sliced Merrick in half as he stumbled out of the bushes.

He blinked at the pair of swords leveled at him before calmly brushing them aside with the tip of one finger. With all the situations they had been thrown into, Merrick had always shown the kind of center and focus that the Order specialized in—a graveness seldom seen in one so young.

The Deacon nodded to Raed, though his barely buttoned shirt and badly fixed cloak were evidence that he too had been caught unaware. "What do we have, Sorcha?" Merrick asked.

Crouched over the bodies, she glanced at him with dark humor. "I could be wrong—but I am fairly sure it is murder."

One old woman and one young lay spread in the white gravel of the garden, their blood staining it as red as spilled wine. Their throats had been ripped out with savagery—more than enough to kill them. And yet their murderer had gone much further. Their chests and bellies had been cut open. The final outrage in this bizarre display was that the killer had placed their organs between their legs. The smell was awful, even in the sweet-scented pleasure garden.

"No hearts." Sorcha poked delicately at the mound of organs. "The hearts are missing."

"And this blood is still very fresh." Merrick's eyes darted around the scene, with the slightly glazed look that signaled the use of Sight. Raed was impressed the young Deacon had managed to keep his dinner down. "And such ritual is usually the domain of someone possessed—it could even be an attempt to open a gateway to the Otherside."

The guards, already jumpy, spun around to peer into the shadowy corners of the jungle gardens. "Geists," one whispered, "like last time."

"Last time?" Sorcha's head jerked up, her blue eyes fixing on the slightly older guard.

Under such a concentrated gaze, stronger men had given in—and this poor old sergeant had no chance. "More deaths— last week—but in the city," he choked out.

The Young Pretender thought of the creature that had attacked him in the river—but that had been miles away. *And yet . . . and yet . . . by the Blood, let it not be so.*

"Wonderful." Sorcha's voice indicated it was anything but.

Raed considered himself as much an expert on geists as anyone outside the Order—having one living inside him had given him a unique insight. It did look like the work of someone possessed; since geists could not affect the world directly, they usually had to take on flesh already made to wreak ruin in the world. Even his own Curse, the Rossin, had been forced to link himself to a bloodline to both survive and make its presence felt.

"Merrick?" Sorcha looked up at her partner. The young Deacon's eyes continued to flick around the garden—even as a shadow of a frown began to darken his brow.

Finding Fraine would be so much easier with their power to aid him. The meaning of this double murder and how that fit with his sister's kidnapping, that was what frightened him. A pit of possibilities yawned before him.

Sorcha and got to her feet. Deacons were always so damned inscrutable that Raed was forced to ask the question that the spooked guards were all wondering. "So, is there any geist activity?"

"Not that we can see," she replied—though no further words had passed between her and her partner.

"Who are these ladies?" Merrick gestured down to the victims. Raed wasn't entirely sure of the fashions of the Court of Chioma, but one glance at the richness of their dress and the coils of jewels on their wrists and necks was answer enough. These were not some unlucky serving girls.

"Meilsi and her daughter Rani," one of the guards choked out, "from one of the best and oldest families in Chioma. Good, kind ladies—who would do such a thing to them?"

The Deacons had no answers; in their profession they must be often asked that question.

"I thought you could see everything?" Raed said to Merrick. "How can someone slay two women and then disappear without you noticing anything at all?"

The young Deacon let the accusation roll off him but closed his eyes one more time. "Still no geists, and I can feel every human in this palace, but none with blood on their hands or murder in their hearts."

It was exasperating—but it was the way of the Deacons. Raed, having learned to rely on non-magical senses, gestured to the guards. "Stay still."

The gravel in the center of the garden was churned up, covered in blood and gore and of little use, but as the Young Pretender stepped carefully beyond that, he saw quickly with the eye of a man trained to hunt from childhood that there was one set of footprints that did not belong to them or the victims.

"As far as I know"—he beckoned Sorcha over and pointed to the line of footsteps—"geists do not leave trails."

A little smile tweaked the corner of her full lips. "Not usually—but I won't be disappointed if it is just a madman."

"We'd better be quick about it." Then Raed turned and fixed

the guards with a stern look—the look of disappointed royalty. "Protect your Prince's women—better than you have already done tonight." Could his own sister have been better protected? Could her guards have been a little too lax in their duty?

With those bitter thoughts, Raed spun on his heel and followed the trail. It was a blessing that careful gardeners had raked the gravel so precisely and regularly—possibly only a short time before the murders. The power of Princes was for once working for the Young Pretender.

"Keep behind me, if you please, Honored Deacons." He gave Merrick and Sorcha a little bow. "We shall use a little of my skill."

She rolled her eyes, and Merrick tilted his head, neither happy with this change of circumstances.

Together they pushed through the lush jungle foliage, following the disturbed path back to the buildings. The trail did not lead to the exit they had tumbled out of so recently—and Raed was grateful for that. The idea of a crazed murderer or a possessed innocent rampaging among the frightened women was not one the Young Pretender wished to contemplate.

Instead, the signs led them toward a door that was obviously meant to be barred. When Raed had snuck into the palace, it had been over the undulating roofs—someone else had taken a far more direct approach.

The three of them there stood there and gaped. The wrought iron gate lay with its thick lock askew and hanging off its hinges as if kicked by a great horse—except no creature on four legs, or indeed one on two, could possibly have twisted and destroyed it in such a way.

Raed turned and cocked an eyebrow at the remarkably silent Deacons. "Still think this is the work of a madman?"

"Point made, Your Majesty," Sorcha replied tightly.

They slipped into the corridor, and Raed managed not to make any further comment. Once beyond the loose white pebble paths, there was still a possibility of tracking the offender. The dry, soft mud walls and floor of the Hive City still held a faint impression that even the most careful foot could not avoid. It was a good thing they were not trying to do this in the Imperial Palace with its much-admired marble flooring.

Sorcha and Merrick followed behind him, and Raed was

pleased he was able to show some of his skills—he had witnessed theirs often enough.

Why the younger Deacon was unable to sense the flight of the murderer remained a mystery, but he looked none too pleased to be stripped of his powers. As Raed knelt and examined the signs at a corridor junction, he glanced over his shoulder at Merrick. "Anything?"

The younger Deacon pushed his hair out of his eyes, even as they dipped away from reality again. "It's like"—he waved his hand, searching for a word—"a shadow of something in here. Not a geist—something else."

It was easier by far to see the press of a foot and the brush of a cloak against the walls than to understand what Merrick was going on about.

With a gesture, Raed urged them to follow him. They were moving off the main corridors and into dustier rooms. These appeared to have been abandoned long ago. The shapes of sheet-covered furniture and stacked boxes were eerie in a palace so packed with people. What could have caused them to abandon perfectly habitable looking rooms?

A strange odor permeated the air; not just dust but something almost sweet, as if an incense bearer had just passed by. Raed's heart began to race at the air of menace in these rooms. Nothing warm or welcoming lingered here, and he found himself hurrying through them.

Apparently he was not the only one feeling it.

"I didn't realize the Hive City went so deep." Sorcha shot Merrick a look as if she expected him to say something, but her partner was fingering his Strop and completely distracted. Raed was glad he was not the only one with flesh rough with goose pimples.

Still, it gave him a chance to show off something else—his education. "Orinthal is called the Hive City because it is modeled after the red flame termite—the one that builds those red earth towers in the desert."

She blinked at him.

"I think you need to get out more," Raed chided as he paused to examine the floor leading to a set of stairs spiraling down. "Unfortunately, it won't be tonight—this person is going even deeper."

"I still can't feel anything human ahead of us." Merrick sounded both troubled and annoyed at the same time. "Insects, small mammals, but nothing larger."

Sorcha pulled her Gauntlets out of her belt. "Nice to know the Prince is not above having a vermin problem."

"Shall I try the Strop?" With shock Raed realized that the Deacon was asking him, not his partner. It was frightening how easily the three of them slipped into roles, just as they had beneath Vermillion. Something in the gaze of both Deacons told Raed that they also remembered their time together in the ossuary.

Raed cleared his throat. "We can't afford to let this person get away—stay here if you want." The empty place on his belt where his sword should have been suddenly felt even greater. Like every other person in the Hive City, he had been forced to surrender his weapon before entering—everyone, that was, except the Order.

Sorcha unhooked her sword and handed it, sheath and all, to him. "I am already armed enough." She put on the Gauntlets. The brown leather with the faint flicker of luminescence made her point.

Her tone was light, as if she didn't know the implications of lending her sword to someone not of the Order. It was this trusting gesture, a surrender of control, a placing of her reputation in his hands, that stopped Raed in his tracks.

He would not question her trust, however—to do so would be to sully it somehow. Instead, Raed buckled the sheath onto his own belt, then, taking a sputtering bare flame torch from the wall, he lead the way down the stairs.

The Hive City was naturally cool, thanks to its thick soil walls, but as they went deeper underground it actually became freezing. The thin clothing they all wore was inadequate—but no one was turning tail at this point.

"I sense running water." Merrick pointed down, his eyes slightly unfocused. "It is interfering with my Sight a little."

"Water—down here? I don't hear it." Sorcha stood between the two men, her voice an unintentional whisper.

"The Hive City only survives because it sits on a huge network of underground channels." Raed, though he didn't particularly feel like a history lesson, was glad to have something to add. The pressing atmosphere had nothing to do with the water supply and everything to do with the churning feeling in his chest—a sure sign that the Rossin was hovering on the edges of awareness.

Yet Merrick had said that there were no geists about. Raed repeated that to himself, trying not to think that Merrick was also not able to sense a person whose blatant trail they were following.

And then there was a noise. All three of them froze on the stairs. It was a dragging metallic sound—and not very far ahead.

Carefully, Raed led the Deacons forward, his hand locked tightly around the pommel of Sorcha's sword. They were now so deep that there was even faint moisture in the air, and the long, low corridor that they were in was becoming more and more like a tunnel.

"Still nothing!" Merrick now sounded really annoyed.

Sorcha, who had taken a place at Raed's shoulder, looked back. "Certainly there is *something* down here—I think you better try the Strop."

Her partner had just reached for his talisman when the tunnel began to shake. The sudden wild movement knocked Sorcha back against Raed, and he in turn actually came off his feet. The sound was now the angry roar of a disturbed beast. Small stones came loose and bounced off them even as the Young Pretender threw his arms around Sorcha, protecting her head.

Merrick, by some act of luck or grace, had managed to stay upright—at least until the floor abruptly gave way beneath him. Raed caught the distinct impression of his wide eyes and shocked face before he tumbled out of sight.

"Merrick!" Sorcha screamed and crawled on her hands and knees to the gaping hole, even though the edge looked anything but stable. The earth's shaking subsided as quickly as it had come, and now her calls were more desperate.

"He'll be all right." Raed grabbed her around the shoulder and peered down into the void. "It's one of the channels I told you about." When he thrust the torch in, he fully expected to see Merrick staring back, perhaps nursing some bruises, perhaps a little embarrassed. The drop was not a great one, and the running water below must have only been enough to cover his ankles.

And yet, once his eyes became used to the even greater

darkness, there was no sign of the young Deacon. Hanging on to the broken lip of the tunnel floor, Raed looked to either side of the channel, but there was nothing. Merrick would not have run off. He could not have been swept away, because the water was not nearly that deep or fast-moving.

"Where is he?" he said half to himself and half to Sorcha. Raed levered himself up and glanced across at her.

"I don't know," she whispered, her hands clenched uselessly on her lap. "I can't feel him."

The lonely, broken tone in her voice was not one that Raed was used to hearing. It sounded a lot like grief.

"Stay here." Hanging from his arms, he dropped easily down into the tunnel. Pieces of broken floor lay scattered in the chill, running water—there was no sign of the Deacon.

How is that possible? he wondered and stalked a little way up the channel on each side. "Merrick? Are you there, lad?"

If calling him "lad" didn't get a reply, then Raed didn't know what would. He felt so incredibly powerless. *The young Deacon had just been there, by the Blood!*

"He's gone." Sorcha leaned down and called to Raed; her face was as hard and calm as stone. "I felt something as he fell. You can stop looking—you won't find him."

Raed's stomach clenched, and somewhere deep down the Rossin flipped over. "Why?" he asked, afraid he already knew the answer.

"Because I felt the Otherside opening." She said the words matter-of-factly and then held out her hand to Raed. When he had heaved himself back into the tunnel proper, he didn't let go of her.

Sorcha's eyes were downcast as she stripped the Gauntlets off her hands. "I felt it—just for a moment—it opened. It opened, and it took him."

"What do we do to get him back?" Raed asked, and the blank, hopeless stare he received in return told him much.

Down there in the depths of the Hive City, Sorcha let him hold her tight as she told him the truth. "I don't know. I don't have a clue." And then she did something that frightened Raed. She cried.

FIFTEEN

Lost Loves

Merrick fell into stars, and for a long moment he had no idea if he was awake or sleeping. This did feel very like his dreams—but he would not be a Sensitive if he could not tell the difference between those two states.

No, he decided, he was not dreaming—and immediately after that he guessed what had happened. That tunnel under the Hive City was both incredibly distant and only a hairs-breadth away.

He was on the Otherside. The chill in his lungs could have told him that, if nothing else did. Once, not many months ago, he and Sorcha had ventured into the home of the geists, just in spirit. Sorcha had been lucky—the Otherside and its memories had been wiped away when she returned to the human world. Merrick had not been so fortunate. It was a nightmare he would never shake—his naked soul flayed by the winds of the geist world. Sorcha and he trapped in flames, tortured by geists that had been waiting for their chance to torment Deacons. His bones had burned, and everywhere the runes that they'd trained so hard with were used against them.

Now the Deacon stood in a great sea of stars, his body cold and very much present; his heart was racing like a galloping horse and his breath pumping in his lungs. It was far too close to the details of some of his recent dreams for his liking.

Merrick was completely baffled how this had happened. Sorcha could open the gateway to the Otherside with the rune Teisyat, but he would have felt her use the most feared of the runes carved on the Gauntlet. Her partner was absolutely sure she had not done that.

By the Bones, I am a fool, he thought angrily. *The Bond.*

Sorcha was gone. The absence hit him harder than the sudden chill in his body—harder even than finding himself in the Otherside. Panic flooded him. Deacons worked in pairs, always, always. Now here he was, a Sensitive out on his own, trapped in the Otherside—

But you are not alone. The voice whispered from among the stars. It was sharp and cruel and the one that had invaded his dreams. *Mongrel homeless child that you are, inside there is still greatness. The Body. The Beast. The Blood.*

It was the chant, the purpose that had brought Sorcha, Raed and him together. He had heard that chant before, spoken in the sanctuary of the Mother Abbey where it had been frightening and disturbing enough. When whispered by someone or something within the vast void of the Otherside, it made Merrick's blood, already icy, grow far colder. Nothing but the stars were around him, but the presence was close. He dared not stretch forth his Sight and attract the attention of geists.

"Be gone, this is not your realm." The voice was familiar, light, female, and suddenly the Otherside, the stars and the presence did not matter one little bit.

Merrick turned, spinning in space as if he were swimming, and there she was.

"Nynnia," he whispered, and tears immediately sprang to his eyes, even as a smile spread across his face.

She had died for him, died for the people of a world not her own—and he had never stopped missing her. Her dark hair and small frame were just as Merrick remembered, her eyes set in the sweetest face he had ever seen. The only difference was that she floated in the air, and he could see stars through her body. And he knew why that was—she had none.

"Darling Merrick." She moved closer, and he was so pleased to see she smiled just as much as he did. For an instant he was washed away by giddy elation. Everything had been gray since she had died, but now the world was bright again. Even if it was not Merrick's world.

Nynnia's expression, though, faded suddenly to terribly sad. "I am sorry I had to bring you here." Her voice was swallowed slightly by the great void that surrounded them.

"Don't be." He held out his arms to her. "Whatever the explanation—I don't care—really, I don't."

Her eyes flicked to his open embrace, and then when she moved forward, he began to understand her sorrow. Her gleaming form slipped through his with not a single sensation of warmth and contact reaching him. Merrick's stomach knotted with frustration, and his anger at her death flared anew.

As if sensing it, Nynnia pulled back and cupped her ethereal hand lightly and exactly around the line of his face—careful not to again break the illusion that she could touch him. "You cannot stay here long, my love." She pointed down, and Merrick followed her gesture.

Below, the Otherside was stretched out before him like a vision of nightmares. Everything of his spiritual journey here came racing back. The chaos of geists and human souls moved under him, a terrifying vista that spread from horizon to distant horizon. And it was not silent—there were screams, howls and panic below.

Yet he floated above it, safe in the painted panoply of stars. "You . . ." He cleared his throat. "You are holding me above all that?"

The smile on her face was slightly amused. "I couldn't let you down—not when I meant to save you." Her body shimmered, becoming nothing but silver light, wrapping itself around and through him.

And then Merrick flew. There was no feeling of air flowing over his body, but it was still an amazing thing. The stars blurred and the vast nightmare landscape passed beneath him. Despite the danger of being on the Otherside, he wanted to whoop and crow as he hadn't since before his father's death—since he had been a child.

A mountain loomed on the horizon before a golden sky. He could discern a stream of human shapes making their way toward it.

"If they get to the mountain"—Nynnia's voice was warm in his ear—"they are in our domain."

And he saw what she meant. A giant fortress was built into the rock, gleaming with that same golden light. Suddenly he was able to think beyond the joy of knowing Nynnia was not lost. The Deacon realized that he was seeing what so many scholars of the Order had theorized and argued about for hundreds of years. Some of their ideas on what lay on the Otherside were extreme and rather bizarre—but none of them could compare with this.

The warmth of Nynnia wrapped about him, and her voice whispered in his ear, "This is my home, Merrick. The place I left to go to your world. Does anything look familiar about it?"

Baffled, he attempted to orient his mind. He tried to look at the sprawling fortress and focus his logical senses on it. The long walls were carved with incredible friezes depicting all the life in Arkaym. The towers were topped with strange ornate cupolas that gleamed and reflected the light of the mad horizon. It was like nothing he had ever seen—except for the once.

He remembered as a child going with his parents to his grandfather's house. The young Merrick had followed them out into the garden, where a great head lay toppled and covered in ivy. When he had shrieked, his father had scooped him aloft and tossed him up, until his tears turned into giggles. Then the older man had carried him into the broken remains of the Ancients' temple—the place where his grandfather's castle had been built.

Even as a child Merrick had found the deeply and intricately carved ruins amazing. "No one knows much of the Ancients," his father had told him as he sat atop his shoulders, but the touch of reverence was strange in a man so proud of his aristocracy. "But look, Ales—what they did, what they built, is still unmatched after all these centuries."

And now, in the depths of the Otherside, Merrick saw the very same finesse and craft that his father had admired. He couldn't have been more shocked if Nynnia had hit him between the eyes.

For generations scholars had argued about what had happened to the Ancients and their wisdom. They had vanished, and all they built had been left lying empty. Other nations had gradually taken apart the buildings to use the fine stone for their own edifices. The Break, when the Otherside had finally spilled into Arkaym, had swallowed much knowledge.

"You see"—Nynnia's voice in his ear was so soft that for a minute he thought it might actually be inside his head—"you *know* what I am—what we are."

"The Ancients . . ."

Her laugh was so beautiful that he felt tears spring to his eyes. "No more ancient than you, dear, sweet Merrick—and when we walked the world, we had our own name for ourselves."

"But how . . ." He cleared his throat, watching the light run in rivulets over the beautiful white fortress. "How did you end up here, on the Otherside?"

A cool shiver ran over his skin, more an absence of warmth than any ethereal wind. "We had to go—or the world would have been wide-open to the Otherside."

"But . . ."

"There is no time," Nynnia said, just as prickles of hotness now ran up Merrick's spine. "This place was not made for living beings—you should remember that from last time. Even with the protection of your body, your time is short."

He opened his mouth, but the fire up his spine was now a burning that brought a gasp to his lips. Nynnia's presence undulated over him, relieving the pain for at least a moment.

Nynnia slipped away from him, her form resolving into the one achingly familiar to him from her time in his world. "I cannot protect your body, my love, but I can send you to a place where you can help your cause."

"Cause?"

"Your fight against the goddess." Her gaze tightened on him, until Merrick could actually feel it. Those eyes, now as back then, saw so much. "And the stars—the voices, my love."

He was not so foolish as to be blind to the meaning of the stars that had haunted his dreams. Even if Merrick had been just a normal citizen of the Empire, he would still have known the Circle of Stars was the symbol of the old Native Order. The one that had supposedly died out at least eighty years before his Emperor was summoned from across the water. "So they are not dead." He did not frame it as a question.

"Many were killed, but others were driven underground. The Order of the Circle of Stars is still very much alive."

Merrick clenched his jaw as fresh pain exploded through him. He was left gasping, reeling. Nynnia's image swam before his eyes, while his breath came in short, hard gasps.

She held out her hand to him, as if she still did not quite understand that they could not touch. "They are trying to reach this place, Merrick—trying to harness what was never meant to be harnessed. To stop them this time you must go back."

It was hard to concentrate on her words past the terrible slow pace of his heartbeat in his ears. Merrick didn't need her to tell him he was dying. "Back?" the words came grating out of his struggling throat.

Nynnia's voice by comparison was very light and very far away. "Time has little meaning to us here, Merrick. I will send you back to her. You must plant the seed."

Her? What did she mean?

He was now beyond speech, and the Otherside before his eyes was tearing apart—but he couldn't tell if it was his perception or reality—all he knew was that it hurt.

Nynnia. Despite the pain, he didn't want to leave her, but Merrick didn't have any way to hold on. He was falling, spinning like a leaf into a well of shadows. No air in his lungs meant he could not scream.

And then reality grabbed him hard, yanking back into the world he'd been born into. Now the pain was deep and real, in muscle and bone and sinew.

Merrick shook his head, finally realizing that he was lying on something hard and very much like stone. After a moment of contemplation, he was able to wrench his eyes open.

She had not left. Nynnia was leaning over him, but it was the real Nynnia. The smile on her face was confused rather than welcoming, but he didn't care. The weight of her hand on his chest and the gleam of late evening sun on her hair all told him instantly she was a living, breathing woman.

It didn't matter how it had been done. Merrick lurched upright against a wave of pain and clasped her to him. Her small form was as solid and warm as it had been cold and unmoving when last Merrick had felt it against him. "Oh love," he laughed, "by the Bones—you're here, you're all right!"

The hand around his throat was abrupt, sobering and tight. The words he had been meaning to whisper in her ear died in his windpipe. She was a small woman, and yet she was holding him as lightly as a feather above her head. It felt as though a giant had him just under the jaw.

Nynnia's eyes were as cold as steel. "Tell me who you are and why I should not break your neck for such impudence?"

Merrick's vision wavered, and he had no way of crying out—something that this confused and martial Nynnia had obviously not taken into account. The young Deacon would have found the whole situation amusing, but the stern gaze of his beloved did not offer any humor.

He had just seen her—but she had no body. Now a very real, physical Nynnia appeared not to recognize him at all. Merrick had been tossed around like a rag doll—and now it appeared his love would kill him. If it was his love. His fingers locked around hers, desperate to break her hold, but he might as well have been trying to bend the hand of a granite statue.

The world dimmed, colors drained away and shapes wavered. Whatever the reasoning for sending him here, Merrick was now sure this was not what his Nynnia meant to have happen.

It was the last thought in his head before blackness wrapped around him and sucked him down into another void—one in which no geists awaited.

SIXTEEN

Taking the Reins

Sorcha swallowed hard on the lump in her throat as the words of Rictun came back to her. *You really know how to go through those partners of yours.* At the time she'd thought it merely another attack by a man who had always despised her. Now, however, she was wondering if there wasn't a grain of truth to it.

Slowly, Sorcha got to her feet. Raed was waiting in the shadows of the corridor, waiting for her to speak, waiting for her to tell him just how bad things were. And she knew the huge question weighing on his mind.

"Ask it." Her voice was flat and distant, but she needed someone else to do it.

He rubbed his red gold beard, tilted his head and spoke under his breath. "Is Merrick dead?"

Unholy Bones, it hurt to hear it, though. Sorcha's hands tightened into fists, but she had to revert to her training and not let emotions overrule her. Considering, she leaned back against the cool wall of the tunnel and stared down into the blackness where they'd last seen Merrick.

This was not the first instance where Sorcha had lost a partner, and that alone was the only reason she was able to stave off panic. Her recollection of those times had been nothing but pain, the disconcerting loss of Center and finally the weighty sensation of severance. It had, in short, felt as though a part of herself had been amputated.

Sorcha was almost afraid to try, but she closed her eyes and felt out along the Bond, like someone who had been burned in the past and feared being scorched again.

It took her a moment to reach the place where Merrick should have been. It was empty, but not in the aching void way that was caused by death. Her partner was not there, but the Bond remained as it had been.

"I don't think he is dead," Sorcha murmured, hesitant to appear as if she had only wishful thinking in mind, "but he is not in this world."

"The Otherside? Surely he cannot survive there?" Raed reached out and took her hand.

The Young Pretender was definitely more aware of the nature of the Otherside than any other normal person in the Empire, but every child in the Empire knew that only spirits and geists could survive there. Flesh was not meant to exist in a place made of void and soul. Sorcha let out a long breath, fully tasting the bitter bile of helplessness.

She had to hold on to her belief in her partner. "You know Merrick as well as I do, Raed. He is a remarkable young man—and if anyone can survive—it is he." In the back of her mind there were two little nuggets that she did not share with her lover. The first was, as insane as it sounded, they had some allies on the Otherside. The second was the existence of some kind of wild talent in Merrick.

"And we do still have a murderer out there and your sister to find—let's concentrate on that. We can't do anything to help Merrick right now."

"You could open a doorway yourself . . ." Raed ventured.

She shook her head slowly. "It is not something to be done lightly—and even if I went through, without Merrick I would be blind."

Raed pressed his hand over his own eyes and rubbed them wearily.

"As you can imagine," Sorcha whispered, "a blinded Deacon in a world of angry, vengeful geists would not be very sensible. We should focus on what we can do." It sounded so

very sensible—very orderly—and almost like she was at peace
with the idea. It was very far from the truth.

"And what exactly can we do, Deacon Faris?" Raed looked
at her so sternly that she was reminded of Merrick.

Sorcha tucked her Gauntlets back into her belt. "I am getting the feeling that the Prince of Chioma wanted Merrick
and me to stay for some other reason than finding out about
the Emperor. I suggest we ask him what that is."

Raed's eyebrow shot up. "Interrogate the highest royal in
this kingdom? It's that easy, is it?"

"For Deacons . . . yes, it is." When Raed looked shocked,
Sorcha smiled. "We are tasked with hunting out the unliving
everywhere in the Empire—no exceptions."

The Young Pretender kissed her; it was gentle, soft and not
about passion. It was just what she needed.

Sorcha led the way back to the garden. None of the guards
noticed there were only two people now—too busy trying to
calm frightened women and keep them back from seeing the
dreadful mess. She jerked her head at them. "We lost him in
the tunnels."

The innate authority of the Order worked in her favor
again—no questions were asked, even in this distant principality. Drawing Raed over into the shadows, she pressed her hand
lightly and briefly against his chest. The weak part of her
wanted to fall into his arms, be kissed and looked after—but
Sorcha had never been one of those sorts of women. "I don't
think we dare risk taking you back into women's quarters.
Meet me tomorrow morning in the audience chamber atrium."

Back in her room, the dark was not friendly, lying warm
and heavy over her like an unwelcome blanket. She could not
stop thinking about Merrick when she knew she should have
been thinking about Raed and keeping him alive. The vision from
the spectyr still burned in her memory, but overlaid with it were
imagined images of what might be happening to her partner.

She was struck with the terrible and sudden thought that by
bringing her partner to Orinthal she might just have traded his
life for that of the Young Pretender.

Carefully Sorcha closed her eyes and tried to find that
calm Center that the Order had taught her so well. She had to
trust in Merrick. The young man was strong, disciplined and

intelligent enough to take care of himself. *He is not dead,* she repeated to herself. *I would feel it. I would.*

Her sleep was full of tumbled and broken dreams, where all her past failings found her. Their gnawing gave her very little rest.

The next morning she felt so drained that it was an effort to get up. The Bond ached deeply like a sore tooth, reminding her that partners shared more than just a mental connection. Some of Merrick's youthful energy usually leaked across to her and palliated the subtle twinges of her age. Without him there, they had come back full force. It was not that she was that ancient. The Order would have no plans to pull her from the field for many years, but the life of a Deacon was not an easy one. Old wounds ached, and broken bones remembered past outrages.

She sat up with a loud groan and found at the foot of her bed someone had laid out a beautifully embroidered turquoise silk robe—the design was birds of paradise and the symbol of Hatipai. Picking it up, Sorcha fingered the slippery fabric and considered what needed to be done. Without Merrick's help it would be hard for her to get behind the Prince's damned mask. She needed every weapon in her arsenal—and it was obvious that the Prince was partial to a pretty face.

Quickly Sorcha stripped and slipped into the robe. For a second she worried that she would have to leave her Gauntlets behind—something that she had never done since first earning them. Luckily, the robe contained pockets, so she was able to fold the thick leather over once and stuff them in there.

Feeling a little better knowing the seat of her power would remain close, she padded to the greatest luxury in all of Orinthal: cool, springwater showers. In a desert kingdom, water was more precious than gold or gems, so it was only fitting that the Prince provided his women with facilities that were the envy of all in Chioma.

The smell of running water, after so long in the arid heat, was enough to make Sorcha a little giddy and bring a smile to her unwilling lips. In Vermillion, a city that lived its life half on the turning tides of a lagoon, a place of bridges and canals, water was transportation—here it was life. The sound of it was by consequence magic.

The shower room was not huge—at most it could accommodate perhaps fifteen women—but it was spectacular. Thousands of lapis lazuli tiles coated the walls, while the water tumbled down from the ceiling and was guided into jets by gold spigots set just above head height. In the center was a dry raised area, where robes could be laid or women could sprawl—or both.

The mechanics alone of such a feat made Sorcha pause for breath. She was used to the austerity of the Order, where washing was considered a necessity—not something to be enjoyed. Dropping her robe in the center area, where she could keep an eagle eye on it, she stepped under the fall of water with something that distracted her mind for a few moments—anticipation.

She was not alone. Two groups of women were also taking advantage of the luxury of an early morning shower. The room's undulating walls meant that they all had the illusion of privacy.

A pair of young women, one dark as night and the other with the olive skin of the north, watched her as covertly as possible with the eyes of deer observing a wolf. The darker beauty was being washed by the other, her skin covered in soap that smelled of lilies. It looked like she had been enjoying her friend's ministrations right up until the moment she had seen the naked Deacon.

Sorcha wasn't about to take that too personally. Even without her cloak or her Gauntlets, she was obviously recognized. Still, she gave them a little nod and moved on to the farthest stream of water. She kept her back to the wall and her own eyes on her robe as she shuffled out of the line of sight of the two washing women and into earshot of an intriguing conversation.

". . . Japhne—it is always Japhne." The unseen female's voice was laced with such bitterness that Sorcha pressed herself closer to the fountain head so that she was less likely to be seen around the curve of the wall.

"Well, she is pregnant with his child," another, softer voice went on.

"A miracle," the other snapped. "An old baggage like her, full with his child? Surely the world is laughing at us—you know she usually walks the garden at night."

Sorcha glanced around, but none of the other women were close enough to overhear as she was—and they appeared not to be taking any notice of her anymore. In a closed world of women, where they were all vying for the attention of one man, intrigue, jealousy and backbiting were to be expected. Yet, with the murders in Orinthal, such events took on a new, sinister meaning.

"Hush," the quieter woman hissed. "Don't speak such things!"

"But it's true." Her companion gave a little harsh laugh. "Japhne walks in the courtyard just before bed every night— if she had last night, who is to say that it would not be her being buried in the ground—"

"Myel—if our Prince heard you say such things, you would be joining them!"

"It was not I, Emelie," the other replied. "But it would have been convenient for us if she had just . . ."

Such ill-wishing was far too much for the other woman, and Sorcha had to duck back as a thin blonde scuttled from the shower room. Carefully, the Deacon finished washing herself and thought.

Speaking in such a fashion, right out in the open, meant that the woman just beyond the curve of the wall was an idiot. And whoever was committing these murders was not. Nor had all the murders been conducted in the confines of the harem. It was highly unlikely that such a woman could have snuck out of the shelter of the woman's quarters, beyond trained guards whose lives depended on staying alert, and slain so many without notice.

Yet this Myel had revealed one thing to Sorcha—the Prince's consort, the one pregnant with a rare child, had been the real target. Whatever had caused her to break her usual habit had been a lucky chance.

Now there was Raed's problem to consider. Sorcha slid as nonchalantly around the wall of the room as she could. Three young women remained, all completely ignoring her. The Deacon pressed her lips together for a moment and wished Merrick was with her. She was certain her partner would have very much wanted to be there.

It had come to Sorcha's attention since getting her new

Sensitive that she was perhaps lacking in the social graces. Without him, now was the perfect time to try to find some.

"Lovely weather," she barked at the nearest blonde beauty.

The girl spun around like she'd been shot and stared at the naked Deacon in open hostility. Stripped of her Order's insignia and cloak, Sorcha realized she was also denied its inherent command. She could actually feel her cheeks begin to grow redder.

"Who are *you*?" A second woman, this one tall and dark-skinned, glared at her. Obviously women of the Prince's harem were not used to being addressed in such a tone.

"Too old to be a new arrival," the first said very matter-of-factly.

"Deacon Sorcha Faris, of the Order."

They blinked at her.

It was truly fortunate for them she did not have her Gauntlets. "Have you had any new arrivals in the last week to the harem?"

Her tone, if not her attire, must have convinced them, because the second woman slowly shook her head. "Not for the last two months." Then both of them made a hasty exit. If they believed she was a Deacon, then they had just insulted her, and if they thought she was lying, then she was clearly mad.

The Deacon's good mood went with them. Not only had she lost her partner, but she had nothing to report to Raed either.

Sorcha washed off, dried herself on the thick towels and, wrapping her robe about herself, hurried back to her room. She got dressed quickly, her mind buzzing.

Raed was there waiting in the antechamber, his face tight and drawn.

On his right was an older woman with a trim form and dark hair licked with gray. Despite everything, Sorcha felt a little flare of jealousy. On Raed's left stood the tall, handsome young man she had seen yesterday.

Raed gestured to the woman. "This is Captain Tangyre Greene, one of my old friends and protectors, and this is Isseriah, who managed to get us inside the palace."

The women nodded, but the man sketched a bow.

"Where is Aachon?" Sorcha asked. "Did something—"

"Oh no." Raed flinched. "I instructed him to remain with the *Dominion*. The crew could not all come with me. Nor would I want them to."

"Raed said you might be able to help us find some trace of Fraine." Tangyre tucked her hands behind her back. "Our trail has run cold in the palace."

Sorcha heard the stiffness in her own voice. "I will do my best, but I hardly think it is coincidence you were led here, and now there seems to be some kind of geist activity."

"They seek the royal blood again?" Raed's jaw tightened. "They could not get me—so they took her!"

"We don't know that." Sorcha didn't want him to do anything foolish, and she certainly didn't want the Rossin turning up to complicate things.

Their hushed conversation was interrupted by Bandele striding down the corridor toward them. His former jovial nature must have been lost somewhere in the night, for he bowed very slightly when he reached Sorcha. "Deacon, my Prince is calling for you."

He did not wait for a reply, instead spinning around and walking brusquely away. "Come on." Sorcha wrapped her fingers around Raed's forearm. "I want you with me."

Tangyre and Isseriah glanced at each other.

"He is under the protection of the Order," Sorcha snapped. "Raed will come to no harm with me." Then, before they could argue, she and the Young Pretender trotted to catch up with Bandele.

"If we can convince the Prince that he needs our assistance, we will have the run of Orinthal," she murmured, "and then we will have a much better chance of finding your sister."

Raed's fingers brushed hers, a little squeeze. "They are going to notice I am not Merrick, you know."

"Trust in the Order."

She was prepared for the seneschal's query, but everyone must have been in a dreadful mess after last night's panic, because he just ushered them in.

The sheer blind daring of bringing the Young Pretender into the presence of the Prince of Chioma satisfied some deep part of Sorcha. The only thing that would have been more so was bringing him into the presence of the Emperor himself.

For all the wealth and luxury of Chioma, its Prince kept a remarkably stark private room. The bright yellow light of the morning was filtering through the open window and illuminating the red earth walls. The Prince was sitting at the opposite end of the small room, robed in a similar shade, but still with the gleaming mask in place. Behind it there were only glimpses of dark skin, but it was impossible to tell anything else about the face beyond.

Sorcha sketched a bow of the appropriate depth. "Your Majesty."

"Deacon Faris." Without the echoing effect of the throne room, his voice was much softer but still melodious and deep. The Prince's head turned toward Raed. "But this is not your Sensitive!"

Sorcha straightened taller. "Indeed he is not. My partner Deacon Merrick Chambers is missing after the events of last night. This man is one of our trusted lay Brothers from the Mother Abbey. He will be assisting me to locate my Sensitive."

"This is dire news indeed." The Prince sat back farther into his chair.

Sorcha took a long, slow breath. "It is indeed, but that is why I am here, Your Majesty, to ask a few questions of the other murders and in the process get my partner back."

"I thought your intention was to protect the people, not to interrogate Princes—is that not why your Order exists? Or am I perhaps mistaken?" The outrageousness of this statement, even from royalty, was enough to stop Sorcha's breath in her throat.

Perhaps people did question the Deacons still, but they had proven their worth against the geists again and again since arriving with the Emperor. And it was Princes like this one who had asked—no, begged—both to come. If they had not, she and the rest of her fellow Deacons would not even be in Arkaym. It set her teeth on edge to hear such a questioning tone from one placed so high.

It was half in Sorcha's mind to bite back with a harsh question of her own. *And is it not the place first for a Prince to protect his people—especially in his own capital?*

"Many things have changed, Your Highness." Raed's voice held no deference but a chill command that he might regret later. "But someone is definitely stalking your Court."

"Then things are far worse than I feared." The Prince paused, but his tone was carefully controlled and revealed nothing. "Sit and ask your questions; I will answer as best I can."

It was perhaps not a ringing endorsement, but it would have to do for now. All three of them sat on the low stools that he indicated. As she folded herself into one, Sorcha surreptitiously opened her Center. It was not as powerful or as far-reaching as that of a Sensitive, but it would have to do.

It was not an illegal thing to do—for the power of the Order went beyond even the power of a mere Prince of the realm—but it was more than a little impolite. Sorcha kept her voice light as she leaned forward. "What can you tell me, Your Majesty, about the first murder that took place?"

The Prince shifted, the strange crystals hanging from his mask swaying slightly. It was so irritating that Sorcha had to restrain herself from leaping up and knocking the damn thing off his head. The political implications of doing that might be a little too tricky. Instead, her hands clenched on each other, and she dared spreading her Center as far as an Active could.

She could sense the guards outside, stern and resolute, and Raed next to her. While he might be outwardly calm, the swirl of his emotions was like looking into a thunderstorm. He was terrified of not finding his sister and yet resolutely trying to ignore that possibility. And there was more—a bright mote that gleamed through all that. A tiny seed of feeling for her that could easily grow into something bigger.

Sorcha jerked back in shock, utterly unsure what to do with that knowledge and utterly disarmed by it. Instead, she swung her Center toward the Prince and was almost as shocked. The scintillating display of the mask was the same in the ether as in the physical world. It spun, turned, and behind it she had trouble seeing anything about the Prince of Chioma—instantly she understood that the tiny stones that made up the strings were not just diamonds—they were tiny weirstones.

"I think you can find out the details of the other murders in the city from my Chief of the Guards." The Prince leaned back in his chair.

Focusing her Center on him was like bending light with a lens, but far less useful. Sorcha tried her best not to let her

frustration show in her voice. "You must have an opinion on
how or why these are happening, Your Majesty."

"The Prince of Chioma has always had a reputation for
insight." Raed folded his arms. "I am sure you must know
everything that goes on in your kingdom—let alone your own
palace."

It was a charming challenge, and Sorcha did not bother to
conceal her smile. The Prince tilted his head, sending the confusing strings of his mask swinging. A tantalizing glimpse of
a pair of full lips was all she got. The silence in the chamber
was tense, however, and she wondered if this interrogation
would end with them all thrown out into the corridor or maybe
the dungeon.

"The first murder," the Prince finally spoke, "was not the
first murder."

Sorcha reached into her pocket and fished out the piece of
paper that she had scribbled on the previous night. "Someone
was killed *before* Baroness Alian in the city?"

"No."

A trickle of fear down her spine made Sorcha sit straighter.
"So, Your Majesty—who was the first victim?"

The fine, dark hands clenched on the arms of his chair.
"My Chancellor, Devane."

Raed glanced at her. "I heard the rumor when we arrived;
he had died of old age in his room."

The Prince's laugh was dry. "Only if old age slits your
throat."

Sorcha leaned back and shot a look at Raed, whose shocked
expression she imagined was the mirror of her own. The
Chancellor of a kingdom was second only to the Prince—and
if he had been murdered, then that cast a very different light
on the whole situation.

Pressing her hands together, Sorcha cleared her throat. "I
think you need to tell us the whole story, and please, this time
no deceptions."

He was a Prince—so she had no way of forcing him to give
her that, but hopefully death on his doorstep would insure it.

→ SEVENTEEN →

Out of Time

Merrick knew he had to be dreaming. Yet, as he sat up, his headache was disturbingly real, pounding in the rear of his skull with a strength that he had never felt before.

Cautiously he looked around. Under his legs was a floor of white marble, smooth and cool. Disoriented as he was, for an instant he worried he was still strapped to the draining table in Ulrich. Blood, they had wanted his blood—but Nynnia had sent him here for a reason—and he trusted her.

Perhaps he had just been traumatized by the sudden departure from the Otherside. Perhaps he had not really seen what he had seen. A strange scraping rattle caught his attention, and the young Deacon lurched to his feet.

Not three yards away Nynnia was hard at work. He noted her back stiffen, so she was aware of his presence, but she did not turn to face him—too busy in her task. She was standing next to a machine that was about the size of a saddle but made of gleaming brass rather than leather. At the front it had a layer of spinning cutting wheels that were busy desecrating the carvings on the stone pillar. The Deacon looked around wildly and saw that all of the pillars, bar this one and one other, had already been given this terrible treatment.

Merrick was on his feet and lurching toward Nynnia without even thinking. "Stop!" For he recognized these pillars—though when he had seen them last they had been covered in dirt and moss, having been recently dug from the earth.

She spun to face him, and Merrick felt immediately the dissonance. This was Arkaym, yet it was not. Nynnia was herself, yet not. He stopped in his tracks.

She was older. Lines of silver in her long dark hair gleamed in the morning sun, and a tiny landscape of wrinkles caused by laughter and frowns decorated her face. It did nothing to hide her beauty. Merrick felt as though he were sitting on a shifting ice floe, unsure which direction was safe.

"'Stop'?" Her voice was the same. "What do you know about what I am doing? What do you care?" Behind her the machine continued its work, grinding its way up the pillar with amazing speed and efficiency—destroying as it went.

Merrick examined the towering, curved ceiling above them. It was similar to the Mother Abbey—but so much grander. Curls of carved words ran up the dozens of pillars—those that had not already been destroyed. Merrick's world reorientated itself, and though it was disturbing, at least now he could understand it.

His breath came faster as he walked to them. "I know that these pillars are priceless treasures. They contain so much knowledge." He held his hand out like that of a blind man looking to touch a face. The markings on the pillar were written in Ancient script, the one he had learned so easily while in the novitiate.

In the future. Merrick felt the whirling of the world about him; he was in fact in the spot his childish self would occupy hundreds of years hence.

"And that is why they must be destroyed," she replied.

He recalled the toppled pillars in his grandfather's garden and the strange scouring that had wiped away their meaning. If he could just stop this Nynnia from continuing—if just one pillar survived . . .

Then he thought of the consequences for his future and realized he would have to tread carefully. Merrick raised his hands in defeat. "You're right—if I stop you, then who knows what changes could be effected in my own time—it is impossible to predict if the future would be better or worse."

Her gaze was hard but not surprised. "Who are you?" she asked, stepping closer to him.

The words cut him, but he sketched a bow, as deep as he would have given to the Emperor himself. "Deacon Merrick Chambers—the man you will one day love."

If he had said those words to any other woman, she might have laughed and then walked away. However, this was Nynnia. Whatever she was, she was open to new possibilities.

The corner of her mouth twitched, as if it might break out into a smile. "Well then . . . that makes quite a bit of difference—but your title"—she cocked her head—"what does that mean?"

Those were words indeed to chill the heart of a man who had spent all his adult life in the care of the Order. Yet, as a student of history, he knew that the Ancients had vanished from the world before the Break and the Order's establishment.

The sheer magnitude of everything he knew—everything that had happened before being snatched away from Orinthal spun in Merrick's head. In the young Deacon's Sight Nynnia blazed. It was not the same as Raed's signature—in fact it was like nothing he had ever seen before. When he had first laid eyes on Nynnia, she had dazzled him with her beauty and her sweetness—but she had appeared nothing more than a normal human. Later events had proven that very wrong.

The second incarnation of Nynnia he had met on the Otherside had been beyond anything mortal. Now this one standing before him was human, but scintillating with a strange energy.

One thing at a time. He tried to frame some reply to her that wouldn't alter time or end up with him burned at the stake. The lecturers teaching in the novitiate had been remarkably silent on the rules of etiquette when thrust back into time. He was still framing the answer, when Nynnia spoke for him.

"So, you've traveled from some future, then," she said, folding her arms in front of her. "Our scholars have postulated such travel is possible, since the essential nature of the Otherside is beyond time." She gestured upward. "In fact, the router is just erasing that portion of the Grand Knowledge."

Merrick flinched, and his mind darted to the horror the librarians of the Mother Abbey would feel to see this scene. "Where . . . where am I, exactly? Or when?"

"Where—the Temple of the Ehtia. The when is harder to say—by our reckoning fourteen sixty-seven after the Fire was Lit."

Her dating convention made absolutely no sense to him; no calendar he had ever heard of or studied used anything like that. He put it aside for the moment. So many questions crowded the front of his mind that for a second they all jammed there.

"Tell me." Nynnia circled him, the nearness of her banishing all other concerns. "How do we meet, Deacon Chambers, in this future of yours?"

"I could have already given away too much."

"But you said I will love you?" Nynnia thankfully kept his pride intact by not dismissing the idea out of hand. Up close, he judged her age to be nearer fifty than forty, and he couldn't help but stare. This was how the woman he knew would have aged if she had ever had the chance.

"You do," he replied and clenched his fingers tight before they reached out for her. "Or rather you will . . ."

Nynnia stood scant inches from him, tilting her head up to look into his face. "I do not see how someone from a religious order can possibly help us . . ."

Merrick was about to correct her when the ground began to shake, rattling every bone in his body like a tuning fork. The Temple above them creaked and groaned, the stone joints shattered against one another, peppering the two people below with dust and pebbles. Instinctively, Merrick threw himself over Nynnia, wrapping his cloak around them both as they crouched on the ground like frightened children.

When the rumbling finally subsided, Nynnia jerked, her face twisted in anger—not fear. "It can't be much longer."

The images of the toppled pillars flashed in Merrick's mind, and he hoped he was not about to get a personal view to how they had ended up that way. The worst thing would be to perish and not to know the answer to the question that was tormenting him.

"What's happening?" he threw caution to the wind and

grasped Nynnia by the arms. "Who are the Ehtia, and why are you destroying this place?"

"You really don't know?" Her smile was wide, with a hint of mad delight in it Merrick did not like.

The Deacon took a long, slow breath. "In my time this place lies buried, broken and destroyed." He gave up wondering what effect his actions here might have for the future—it might never matter.

An aftershock rattled through their feet, sending the Temple once more to singing in complaint. Nynnia looked up. The infernal device she had called a router had finished its work. It ground to a halt, a gear shifted and then it slid from the top of the pillar to the bottom. "One last pillar to go. Help me with the router." She grabbed his arm.

It was entirely mad. This world wasn't his, and even so, it was falling apart. None of that mattered. The woman he'd fallen for was near him again. So Merrick leaned forward and kissed her.

Nynnia flinched, only a little, before returning the kiss with an ardor he recalled easily. Her lips were sweet, and with his eyes closed, Merrick could tell no difference between this Nynnia and his younger Nynnia.

When she pulled back, her hand cupped his face, stroking the line of his jaw in a sad, almost contemplative way. "We are the Ehtia—and this is all our fault." She led him over to the machine, and he was fascinated by the complexities of gears and drives that were revealed when she pulled it from the pillar.

"Your fault?" he asked, taking one side of the machine and heaving. Together they crab-walked it over to the only pillar in the deserted hall still with its carvings.

Nynnia adjusted the clamlike device, until it wrapped around the stone with a sharp snap. "There is a good reason we are destroying this place. We went too far."

The earth rumbled again, as if in counterpoint to her statement.

Merrick's mouth was dry. "What . . . what do you mean?"

"The Otherside is coming," Nynnia said, her fingers dancing over the complicated surface of controls embedded in the router. "We thought we knew better. We could go where we wished, harness all that power. We thought weirstones were harmless . . ."

The young Deacon took a step back, his fingers tightening into tight fists. "You mean the Ehtia brought this all about?"

She didn't notice—too busy with the machine. Her words were flung very casually over one shoulder. "To our shame—yes, but we will pay for it." She straightened and fixed him with a gaze full of an odd mixture of fear and pride. "The Ehtia will pay for it soon enough. You've arrived in time to see that. I am so very, very sorry."

"I have very little time." The Prince of Chioma paced to the window. "And if we take too long, people will begin to wonder."

Raed managed to hold in his sarcastic snort. The pressures of ruling were something he had been born to—yet never actually experienced. It was also something his sister had been meant for. That thought spurred him to action. Something was happening here in the Hive City, and Fraine could well be caught up in it. Finally, Raed had enough of this Prince's ducking and dodging.

"Too busy to take care of your own people's safety?" His voice echoed sharply in the bare chamber. It held not a hint of deference. It was the voice of a man meant to be Emperor who should have stood in Vermillion, moving Princes of this one's standing like pieces on a castle board.

Onika's head jerked around, the beads swaying dangerously until Raed could be fairly sure he had caught a good glimpse of the other's eyes. Yet, he did not react with anger. He did not flare up. He did nothing that Raed might have expected. Instead, he coolly returned to his carved chair and rested one elegant hand on the back.

"Nothing is more important to me than the well-being of Chioma and her people—but you must understand not everything is as it seems. I may be Prince here, but I am constantly watched."

"Watched?" Sorcha whipped about as if she had been shot.

The Prince's hand tightened on his chair. "I can trust very few in my Court—not even my own Deacons."

Raed shook his head. By the Blood, they were still in the

same situation. Conspiracy and corruption. He wondered why Sorcha looked so shocked—she should have seen it coming.

She swallowed, her pencil hovering above the small note-pad she'd pulled from her pocket. "What makes you think that, Your Majesty?"

"I don't think it—I know it." Onika's voice brooked no argument.

"Yet you think you can trust us?" Raed stroked his beard and not for the first time wondered what exactly was concealed behind that mask. He was beginning to understand some of his grandfather's irritation.

The Prince's attention flicked in the Young Pretender's direction, and though he could not see it, Raed had the distinct impression of a smile. "From what I have heard—yes."

Sorcha shifted, and her fingertips, just for an instant, brushed her Gauntlets. "We're flattered to have your confidence, but if you want us to stop these killings . . ."

"They were related to me," the Prince said smoothly. "And for you to understand the importance of that, I must tell you that I have very, very few relatives in this world."

"You mean someone is killing those you have—even your Chancellor?" Raed was reminded of his own father's conspiracy-laden Court.

The beads rattled as the Prince nodded. "I have doubled the guards on all in the city and the palace that have a portion of my blood in their veins—yet still they die. Only a handful remain."

Raed's grandfather had called the Prince of Chioma a snake, suspected him of treason, and been insulted by his insolence. Could the same faults exist in this, his descendant? It was impossible to judge behind that damned mask.

And then there was the question of the geist that had attacked him on the river. The gleam in the eyes of the woman as they tumbled into the water were burned into his mind. As much as he tried to avoid thinking of it, when he did, he knew instinctually that her attack on him had been very personal.

Sorcha stood up. "Then give us your leave to investigate. The Order is at the service of the Empire—not just the Emperor. And after last night, I am convinced there is some geist involvement." Like all Deacons, she lied well.

Raed waited—either for the Prince to agree or perhaps to reveal that he had recognized the Young Pretender. Instead, the interior door popped open, and the heavily pregnant woman they had seen in the audience chamber the day before appeared. She was older than might have been expected to be a mother, but very beautiful. Her brown eyes, like those of a doe, widened further.

"I am sorry, Majesty," she murmured, circling her hand protectively around her belly, and turning back as if to slip away.

"Japhne." For the first time, raw emotion crept into the Prince Onika's voice. "You do not need to go." He held out his hand, and the woman grasped it immediately. She was elegant even while so large. Raed did not have much experience with pregnant women, but he knew that had to be rare.

The love and tenderness the two shared was immediately obvious. That, Raed knew full well, was a rarity in aristocratic unions—especially royal ones. Seeing the way Japhne looked down at the masked Prince made the Young Pretender ache a little. He doubted he would ever be free enough to look at Sorcha in that way.

"This"—Onika reached out and rested his hand against Japhne's belly—"is the future—this is my son."

Certainly for a Prince there could be nothing more important than an heir, but there was some other note in Onika's voice—it was awe.

"I have had few other children in my life, honored Deacon, all of them girls—but this, this will be my very first son."

Japhne's smile at him was radiant.

"If they are in fact killing my blood," the Prince of Chioma went on, "this is what they will come for."

The look on Japhne's face was calm—so she must have already heard this. It was the confidence of love.

Sorcha got to her feet. "We will try our best, Your Majesty. My partner has been called away for a short time, but I will give this investigation all of my attention."

"Called away?" Japhne's attention abruptly broke free of the Prince. "Is everything all right?"

Sorcha's mind was already on the path of investigation, so she didn't see the stricken look on the other woman's face, but Raed did, and it didn't make sense.

"Yes," the Deacon said, already standing up. "He will be back." She sounded so certain.

"Then find the truth." The Prince held out a scrap of paper with his wax seal stamped on it. "This gives you freedom to roam anywhere in the palace."

They made their bows and were about to exit the privy chamber when Raed spun about. "Your Majesty, one final question. Have you had any recent additions to your harem of late . . . any blonde women?"

Onika frowned slightly but shook his head. "No, I have made it clear that there will be no more women added to my Court. Not until Japhne wishes it."

The Young Pretender's shoulders slumped, but he managed a "Thank you, Your Majesty," before following the Deacon from the audience chamber.

Raed caught Sorcha's arm and then, hidden by her cloak, squeezed her hand.

"I am sorry," she whispered to him. "We have both lost people we care for, and both of us will get them back." Raed nodded, fearing she might crack if he didn't agree. She threaded her fingers with his. "We will get Merrick back, find your sister and hunt down whatever is responsible for these deaths."

"Indeed," he replied with plenty of conviction. He was tired of being chased and always losing. With Sorcha at his side, Raed felt more optimistic. They had already done incredible things together—defeated a Murashev and gotten Raed out of an Imperial prison. After that, surely everything would be easy.

Sorcha glanced at him, and he wondered if that Bond she talked of so often let her see into his soul—or maybe read his mind. Then, in a daring gesture, she raised his hand quickly to her lips, depositing the lightest of kisses on his knuckles.

"On to the Chancellor's quarters, then," she said and waved the Prince's edict in one hand.

→ EIGHTEEN ←

Familiar Faces

The Ehtia. The name echoed and bounced in Merrick's head as he tried to keep up with Nynnia. The world was falling down around them, and yet he could not keep a foolish grin off his face.

He knew for fact things scholars of his own time would have killed to know—and he was with the woman he loved—the one who had died in his arms. But she wasn't dead. It was almost enough to make him start believing in the gods of his childhood again. If he had time to stop and consider such things.

Nynnia's hand was wrapped tightly around his, and she pulled him on as the rocks twisted under their feet. The smell of the loamy earth filled his nostrils, and they stumbled together a few times. Merrick smashed his knee into a jutting piece of rock, but the pain was a distant thing in the tumult of noise and fear. Blood poured down his shin, filling his boot, but there was certainly no time to stop and bandage it.

The Temple of Ehtia was tumbling in a roar of carved marble above them. As they scrambled down the hill, bits of it rolled and bounced past them. Merrick clutched Nynnia, yanking her back just as a piece of a carved column went flying past. The dust and rock pelted them, but they ran on.

Suddenly she grabbed him, wrapped her body around him, and rolled with him under an overhang as a rain of gravel poured down the side of the hill.

The roar of the earth beneath their feet filled their ears, yet all Merrick was aware of in that instant was her warm body pressed tightly against his. Her breath panted against his cheek, and despite the situation, it took a will of iron to stop him from kissing her then. It was not the rumble of the earth that stopped him—it was the knowledge that this might be Nynnia, but it was not the Nynnia who had fallen in love with him.

"We're nearly there," she said, her eyes dropping away from his. Still, she took his hand, and once more they were running. Merrick cold see no destination, because the foothills of the mountain looked much as they were in his time, barren and rock-strewn.

Something snapped behind them, and he managed a quick glance over his shoulder. Half the mountain had slumped away completely, and a wave of rolling rocks was thundering toward them. It was Nynnia who saved him.

Without so much as a look behind her, she dodged a tumbling stone with the kind of accuracy that could not belong to a normal human. Merrick, attached to her hand, followed after.

It was an impossible feat, and Merrick wondered if she was using some version of his own Sight to accomplish it. If he had tried to use the rune Masa, it would have taken so much focus he would have been squashed like a bug while concentrating. Just as he was contemplating that mystery, Nynnia came to a complete stop.

"Here it is," she panted, and for a moment he had no idea what she was talking about. Then a great chunk of the earth's surface slid away to reveal stairs going down. Merrick didn't need an invitation to follow her.

As soon as they were inside, the door closed behind them. It was suddenly very silent. By the strange green light Merrick could make out they were in a small chamber, and when he touched a wall, it was made of slick metal.

A deep frown etched itself between his eyes—he could not identify the metal.

He turned to Nynnia. "Are you some sort of Tinkers?"

A soft smile flitted across her lips. "If you mean do we create and build things, then yes, we started that way. Our ancestors were curious people, and soon we became our own separate tribe of seekers. The knowledge we've collected has been passed on through the generations."

"Until you were able to make this," Merrick whispered. He thought of that lost knowledge—the kind his people were only just rediscovering. He swallowed hard. "Will we be safe down here?" he gestured somewhat futilely up.

"For the moment." Nynnia let out a long sigh, tilted her head and then put her hand on his shoulder. "We must talk to Mestari—he will know what to do with you."

The light in the chamber was kind, softening the lines, and wiping away the gray, tired pallor of her face he had seen in the Temple. Under these conditions it was easy for Merrick to imagine that she was his Nynnia. The possibility that he might lose her again drove the Deacon to the point of recklessness. He clasped her by the arms. "Whatever your plan is, we have to hurry."

She opened her mouth to reply, paused, and then touched his face. "I see you are a good man, Merrick, and if you say I fall in love with you in the future, I believe you—but there is nothing to be done."

The resignation in her voice broke his heart. So her kissed her again.

She pressed her hand against the Deacon's chest. "I don't know what sort of religious orders they have in the future." She chuckled. "But I think I like them."

Merrick opened his mouth to tell her how the Order had transitioned from a religious community to something else after the arrival of the Otherside—but he stopped himself. Talking to someone from his past was rather confusing.

Nynnia was looking at him with the same piercing gaze she would level at him in the future. "You don't need to tell me anything—what we have to deal with right here and now is more than enough." She brushed a curl back from his face. "But I don't think you can help but give me hope. I must live to know you—now, mustn't I?" The smile she gave him was wicked and beautiful.

As always with her, Merrick was quite vulnerable, so caught unawares he fell back on the truth. "I don't know what is safe to tell you." And he shook is head. "And I don't know if the place I come from is worth saving."

"Don't fret," she replied softly, turning to the flat surface of the metal wall. "We have come to the end of our time. I do not expect the Ehtia can be saved by one man alone. It's too late for that."

Before he could answer, a rattle of gears announced something working out of sight. The wall slid aside; Nynnia took his hand and led him through the opening.

They went down a set of metallic stairs, which rang underfoot, and into a vast room of which there had been no sign aboveground. Merrick's mind was now whirling faster. Nynnia on the Otherside had said she was sending him back to learn something and to plant a seed—whatever that meant. If he could only stop to take notes on the marvelous etched walls they were passing, or at least to copy the towering cogged wheels, then perhaps all would be well.

Yet Nynnia was not slowing down. They passed a few other people who were of the same small stature as the woman at his side—but their skin coloring was as diverse as that in his own Empire.

So many questions were bubbling in Merrick's head, but he managed to hold his tongue. This was borrowed time. He shot Nynnia a look out of the corner of his eye—she seemed to be well aware of that.

They reached yet another door. This one was wooden and, as with everything in this place, etched and carved with symbols. Nynnia flung it open with great vigor. Tugged after her, Merrick found himself in what appeared to be a war room.

A long table ran the length of it, and seated around it were ten harried-looking individuals—well, at least nine harried-looking individuals. Merrick's Sensitive training helped him take in the gray faces, the lost looks, and the air of despair. However, his immediate focus was on the one person he recognized in the room.

Or rather he recognized the sparkling mask. Merrick stopped stock-still for a second drenched in a sudden chill, and then his logical brain caught up. The Prince of Chioma was indeed the only Prince who could be at such a meeting before the Break. It was one of the most powerful principalities in this time, so the man sitting before him must be Onika's ancestor.

Still, it was very eerie to be confronted with that strange swinging mask—the very one he had seen only a day earlier in the Hive City. The Deacon gave his head a little shake in an effort to clear it and turned to the person who Nynnia was introducing him to.

Though this man was short in stature, he had an aura of instant command around him. His long salt-and-pepper beard was neatly trimmed, but the eyes above were deeply shadowed, even if their icy blueness conveyed a determination as steely as the walls they were surrounded by.

"Mestari"—Nynnia gave a little bow—"this is Deacon Merrick Chambers." And then, horrifyingly, she added, "From the future."

The older man did not call her a liar or even laugh—he merely nodded his head and then held out his hand.

Merrick took it reflexively in a clasp of hands that even in this time must be a sign of friendship. Immediately his senses leapt, and the world blurred for a long, terrifying moment.

For a Sensitive to be blind was a terrible nightmare of an idea, but before the Deacon had a chance to cry out, the sensation passed. Now the man Nynnia had named as Mestari was looking at him differently.

"You have our blood in you, lad—but you have traveled so far to reach us. Truly amazing."

Rune Kebenar, Fourth of the Runes of Sight, allowed Sensitives to see the true nature of things—yet this man had done that without any visible sign of using it. Once again Merrick's curiosity was piqued, and it was particularly difficult to hold his tongue.

"The Otherside is capable of many things." The Chioma Prince broke the silence. "Even time has only a tenuous grip upon it—and now my mother uses it against us." The voice that came from behind the sparkling mask was smooth, powerful and—shockingly to the Deacon—familiar. Through his Center Merrick knew. This was no distant ancestor of the Prince he had met—it was the same man!

Now his tongue would not be still. Merrick spun about and pointed most rudely at the seated form of Onika. "That . . . that is impossible!" For a little bit all other words failed to come.

"Merrick!" Nynnia was horrified at her guest. "This is the Prince of Chioma, our greatest ally."

The rest of the table jerked to their feet. The more martial of the Ehtia grabbed their swords, worried no doubt that this newcomer was about to attack one of their number. Merrick was not moved to violence, even if the world had gone quite mad.

The Deacon reconsidered; he must have been mistaken. So he backtracked. "Forgive me, Majesty, it is just that in my time there is a Prince of Chioma, and he sounds exactly like you. Perhaps I should not tell you that one of your descendants—"

"I have no sons, nor can I ever have," the Prince replied and then he swept aside the curtain of beads.

Over the many decades the mystery of the ruler of Chioma had been whispered about, discussed by scholars and rumor-mongers alike—so the sudden exposure of reality stunned Merrick.

Onika, the Prince of Chioma, was a handsome man. His skin was smooth and dark, the color of the strong coffee of his kingdom. He had a powerful jaw and a narrow, tidy beard—what he also had were eyes that would suck out a person's soul.

Merrick forgot this mad situation. He lost the feeling of Nynnia's hand on his shoulder. Everything faded to insignificance. In the eyes of the Prince, none of those mattered.

He staggered, dropping to his knees, banging his shins on the table leg. Pain didn't matter either. Onika was a bright star drawing him down—whatever the Prince needed Merrick would have given to him. If he had asked for his arm, his heart—even Nynnia—he would have given those to him.

Then the Prince dropped his hand, and the shivering crystals fell back into place. The spell, or whatever it had been, also fell away. Merrick was left breathing heavily through his mouth, shaking and sweaty.

When the Deacon finally recovered himself and climbed

to his feet, his certainty in anything was rocked to its foundation. Nothing he had ever experienced, nothing he had ever read, explained what had just happened.

Mestari pulled the chair he had just gotten out of over toward the Deacon and guided him into it. "Knocks you about, doesn't it—no shame in it—everyone has the same reaction."

The Deacon struggled to find his Center, the one thing that he had been able to rely on. It took a long, terrible time for it to come back. Finally he was able to say in a shaky voice, "What . . . what, by the Bones, was that?"

Nynnia took an empty seat by him and reached across to cradle his hands in hers. "You've never felt a touch of the gods before?"

"Gods?" Merrick was far too shocked to hold his tongue any longer. "I have no truck with the little gods—they are the domain of the weak-willed and the desperate." He spat the words out without a thought.

Then he realized that everyone else looked as though he had slapped them in the face. "I mean . . . I don't know . . ."

"You've said enough," Mestari growled through a choked throat. "To know that we succeed—even if they destroy what we have made—it is enough."

"We should ask no more of him." The Prince of Chioma raised one perfectly manicured hand. "What he knows may affect how we act in these last days."

Nynnia squeezed the tips of Merrick's fingers, making him warm instantly. "How can it? We have so very few choices before us . . . only one, in fact. And we made that long ago."

The Deacon's insides clenched. He knew that the Ehtia ended up on the Otherside, but he was still not certain if they died or somehow managed to get there alive. Unbidden, he once more thought of his and Sorcha's experience there.

Most of the Ehtia in the room looked away, but one, a woman with a sharp bob cut, slammed her palm firmly down on the table with a clang. "Nynnia, may I remind you that this is our business alone. Even our allies"—she nodded to Onika—"cannot know all our secrets—let alone someone you have just met."

The Prince arose smoothly from his seat. "Then let me

take the young man aside—I am sure he has questions." He gave a little bow to the people. "We will leave you to make your arrangements."

Merrick kissed Nynnia lightly, without thinking about how it might seem to the others, and followed the elegant form of Onika out of the room. As a man alive in both times, the Deacon somehow felt he could trust the Prince—though he realized that this was perfectly ridiculous. The Prince would not know him for a thousand years—and he was not entirely human, either.

They exited into the throbbing, vibrating metal room, and now that Merrick had recovered his composure a little, he could see how many of the Ehtia were scurrying about. The Prince stood still and watched, his hands folded in the small of his back, and the Deacon had the impression that behind that damned mask he would be frowning—though he would not ask to see.

"Tell me what is happening." The Deacon stood to his full height.

"You don't know?"

"Much is lost in the future—I didn't even know the name of Nynnia's people. We simply called them the Ancients."

"How very imaginative." Onika chuckled, but there was a hint of bitterness in it. He walked over to another door and inclined his head. "Let me educate you a little." The sharp gesture caused the crystals to sway, and for a second he caught a glimpse of those riveting, horrific eyes.

The Deacon had to have the answers to all this—it was more than just his nature that demanded it—it was his training as a member of the Order that had to be satisfied.

The Prince spun a narrow iron wheel set in the door, then he tugged it open. It swung noiselessly on its hinges—or at least Merrick assumed it was noiseless, since he could hear nothing at all above the sudden banging and clattering that issued from the room. It was the kind of cacophony that shook the whole body and made thinking impossible. The only comparable sound had been the stamping presses in his father's mines. He'd only visited there once. That noise had also made quite the impression.

Onika led the way into the room, and even he had to clamp

his hands to his head. Apparently whatever he was, a pounding headache or a ruptured eardrum was still a risk. Merrick
found it hard to concentrate on what he was seeing in this
chamber with the ringing in his ears. The stink of oil here
added an extra layer of delight to the experience, clogging his
nostrils and making it difficult to breathe.

It was a machine, the kind that would make the Master
Tinkers of Vermillion weep with jealously. It filled the room,
which might have been small in circumference but was now
revealed to have massive height and depth. Merrick and the
Prince of Chioma stood on a metal walkway and looked over
the edge. The Deacon could not see the top or bottom, because
it was filled with a thick mass of spinning cogs, wheels and
driving pistons. The only thing he did recognize the purpose
of was a great weirstone set not three feet from his hand—the
largest he had ever seen in his life. If he stretched both his
arms wide, he could barely touch each side of it. The blue
surface was swirling madly, and the faint crackle of power in
the air made him nervous.

If only Sorcha was here with him, because even with the
delight of finding Nynnia and the wonder of this great
machine, he was beginning to feel the loss of his partner.
Although an Active would never admit it, they knew full well
that they were blind without their Sensitive. However, a Sensitive also needed his Active—Merrick was aware of that space
where Sorcha's power had resided, buoying him up. As well
he sorely missed her physical presence.

The Prince drew him on, and they passed through another
door on the far side that opened in the same way as the other.
Once beyond it, and with it secured at their backs, the sound
of the massive machine was thankfully diminished.

Merrick had thought the weirstone in the machine was
impressive, but now he realized they were in a room filled
with weirstones—many the same size as the one they had just
seen.

It was a magazine, much like the storage facilities on the
Imperial Navy ships, and he knew he was holding his breath
just as he would in those situations. Weirstones in the most
trained hands were unpredictable, but the Prince of Chioma
looked unconcerned and even leaned up against one very

casually. Merrick winced. Only a Deacon should have been able to touch a weirstone without consequence.

"You needn't worry," Onika said in a conversational tone. "The Ehtia are, among other things, masters of the weirstone. These are unkeyed. In point of fact, the Ehtia are the ones who made this for me." He gestured to the shimmering strings of crystal that hid his face.

"How could I not sense that?" Merrick blurted, aware of a faintly angry tone in his voice. "And I thought all weirstones are blue."

"Most are—but even those rules can be bent by the Ehtia." The Prince sighed. "And you could not sense them because they are too small to register in anything but True Sight."

Merrick frowned. The Prince must be speaking of some form of the Sight taught to Deacons—or rather that which *would be* taught to Deacons. He had indeed not opened his Center during the one interview with the Prince in his own time. He crossed his arms and stuck his hands under his cloak; the room was slightly chillier than the other Ehtia rooms. "And the machine? What does that do?"

"So very curious." The Prince's hand traced the surface of the weirstone he was almost reclining on. "You should take a care that you do not dig too deep. Even a time traveler can be caught out."

Merrick found being in this awkward position made him bold. "The machine," he repeated obstinately. "What is its purpose?"

Onika answered in an almost condescending fashion. "The machine is powering this transport, digging us through the ground in an attempt to escape her wrath."

The Deacon had been in some very strange situations and had used some advanced methods of travel in his short time with the Order—but a machine that burrowed underground like a mole was quite the concept. However, something else had caught his notice. "Her?" he asked, wondering why his throat was feeling dry and his heart was racing.

The Prince of Chioma's hand tightened, the sound of fingernails on the weirstone as pleasant as it would have been on a blackboard. "Yes, my mother."

The Deacon did not need to open his Center or call on any

of his runes to know that he wasn't going to like the answer to
his next question—but he drove on regardless. "And who, by
the Bones, is your mother?"

A long pause followed, where in the eerie silence of the
weirstone magazine, he could hear the Prince muttering
something under his breath. It sounded almost like a prayer.
When he spoke to the Deacon, his voice was resigned, heavy
with regret.

"She gave me these eyes but denied me everything I have
ever wanted." He swept back the curtain of bright weirstones,
so that once again Merrick dropped to his knees. Even so, he
heard what the great and magnificent Onika said next. "My
mother is the goddess Hatipai."

Suddenly everything made sense. Merrick fell to the floor
and wept with the joy of a believer who has found revelation
in the unlikeliest of places.

NINETEEN

Looking Deep

Sorcha opened her Center. Merrick had said something curious about the Young Pretender the first time they had met: *"He blazes."*

And he did. The whispers across the Bond, the ones he could not hear, gave her strength—helped her reorient in a world that felt like it was spiraling out of control.

Find his sister. Find Merrick. Find a killer.

As the door to the audience chamber swung shut behind them, the bang nearly made her jump. Raed was already moving, however. His companions Tangyre and Isseriah came to meet them.

"Take this." Raed thrust the Prince's seal to the older woman. "I want you to go into the Prince's harem and find if my sister is there. I suspect not, but I must be certain."

"We need that!" Sorcha blurted.

"Really?" Raed grinned in that disarming way he had. "We have your Order to rely on, and if I know my Courts, then the rumor of what the Prince has asked us to do is already well-known."

Holding her Center for so long was draining her, and she found she didn't have the strength to argue.

"I suppose so."

"Now, Isseriah." Raed took the young man by the elbow. "We discovered some tunnels last night. I want you to follow them and see where they lead. Take my crew with you, but be careful."

Sorcha listened while the Young Pretender gave instructions on how to find the tunnels where they had lost Merrick. She knew they would find no sign of her partner, but Raed was right; the attacker had used them last night, and they needed to know where they led.

When he was done, his two companions barely stopped themselves from saluting. For a brief second the Deacon wondered what sort of Emperor Raed would have made—then she yanked her thoughts away. Such musings were not only foolish but also treasonous.

"Let's find this Chancellor's chambers." Raed turned them in the direction of the western wing of the palace.

They hurried toward the part of the palace where all the bureaucrats labored. Raed's nearness was distracting her, making her Center even harder to hold. Sorcha knew she was avoiding labeling her feelings for the man deliberately, but she couldn't so easily ignore the strength of them. And it was quite typical of her life. Nothing was ever simple.

When they reached the stairs leading up to the rooms of the most important councilors and bureaucrats in Chioma, Raed leaned into her side. "Brace yourself; we are about to enter a world where there is very little air—except of the hot kind."

Managing to keep a straight face, Sorcha flashed the gold of her Order badge at the guards at the bottom of the stairs. The Young Pretender was right—it was enough—they were let through with a wave.

It was an effort of will not to race up the smooth, curving stairs to the Chancellor's room on the top floor. It had his name on it and a guard posted outside. This time Sorcha didn't even have to show her badge; the man outside unlocked the door and let them through with a bow.

"Don't say a thing!" she whispered to Raed in a mock growl.

Behind the cedar door Sorcha's enhanced senses picked up the tang that could only be the scent of not-so-old blood. She heard Raed's indrawn breath rasp over his teeth, and she reached back to place a hand in his.

The Rossin. She had not thought of the geistlord once since seeing the Young Pretender who was his earthly focus. Yet, as a Deacon, she could never forget that he was still there.

"Let's look around," Sorcha said more confidently than she felt and began examining the desk, piled with papers, pens and ledgers. "I may need your help identifying which of these is important."

Raed's lips twisted. "This is one aspect of rule that I am glad to have avoided." He took a place next to her and then looked down. "And I daresay this is where the poor old man was killed."

The carpet was soaked with dried blood, but it had also splattered the bookcase behind the desk, the wall and a globe of the world that stood next to the window.

"Quite the mess." Sorcha stared down at the evidence of slaughter.

"I would have thought the staff would have cleaned up in here." Raed pulled the chair gingerly over the stains and sat down to examine the papers.

"Often people are too afraid of the geists to clean up." Sorcha began to circle the room, her eyes half-lidded, her Center as open as any Active could manage.

Even without the smell of blood in her nostrils, she would still have been able to tell that murder had been done here. The ether was stained and rent; an ugly color burned her senses, and there was a tang in the air, like before a thunderstorm.

The Chancellor's death had not been quick nor easy. Strange, considering that with one cry he could have summoned guards—yet here he had fallen at the foot of his own desk and choked on his own blood. The sound of his last agonized breath lingered in the ether.

"I've found his journal with a list of appointments." Raed's voice snapped Sorcha back to this reality and this time. She joined him at the desk as they flicked to the date that the unfortunate Chancellor was killed.

"Such a busy man," she muttered, running a finger down the dates. "An appointment with the Prince's Chamberlain and another with the food taster. I hardly think they would have killed him . . ."

"You never know." Raed nudged her. "The royal bed linens and food are weighty subjects."

"And yet it could well be something as common as that." Sorcha stared down at the ruined floor. "It could be hidden in the mundane. Most killings are by someone the victim knows rather than some random violence—comforting as most people find the lie."

"The Chancellor was a eunuch—without wife or family—his entire life devoted to the Prince of Chioma. His work was all he had."

"Perhaps," she conceded.

Together they began to yank open the drawers in the desk and paw through them—giving up on any pretense of tidiness.

Raed pulled one drawer out and examined it particularly closely. "Seems a little short." When he shoved his arm into the space it had previously occupied, he grinned. "Never known a piece of bureaucratic furniture that didn't contain a hidey-hole or two." The rap he made on the back rang beautifully hollow.

He made a face, flexing his arm in the void, and then came a snap of something metal. Sorcha felt her heart begin to race a bit faster. Raed's hand withdrew, and he was holding a fold of vellum.

They exchanged a glance. Vellum was unusual and reserved for important documents—state documents. Raed spread it on the desk.

"This is a blood oath." Raed's jaw was tight. "A blood oath to Hatipai—probably half of Chioma has one tucked away somewhere."

The ether flared, a wind flicking through the drapes, bitterly cold, when outside everything was fiendishly hot. Sorcha wished that Merrick was here—his insight, his calm was sorely missed.

"Unfortunately, the Chancellor won't be easy to get answers out of." Sorcha sighed and slid on her Gauntlets. The feeling of leather against her skin, the faint prickle of the runes calmed her. She was not powerless. "This is going to be so much harder without Merrick . . ." Her voice trailed off even as her eyes fixed on Raed.

He did not flinch at the gaze. "What is it? If I can help, then take whatever you need."

It was less than ideal, yet the Bond still persisted, and through it she would have some chance of at least seeing what she was doing. He wouldn't have Merrick's same abilities, but Sorcha was used to working as a pair. Flying solo was not something she was prepared to do.

So she gestured the Young Pretender over to her, precisely in the middle of the dried mess that was what remained of the once-fine carpet. "They destroyed him, Raed—there is a good chance a shade is still here." She kept her voice level, because she knew he was wary of anything to do with a geist.

He looked at her—his hazel eyes steady, and he squeezed her hands.

"I sometimes see their point." The words tumbled out of her in a way she was not used to.

Raed tilted his head. "Who?"

"Those who believe in the little gods." In her pocket she fingered one of her cigars. "Sometimes there just seems to be too much coincidence—too much irony—in the world."

"Don't start falling apart on me now, Deacon Faris." Raed pulled her into a hug that she really did need.

They kissed, standing there on the blood-soaked carpet, and when they were done held each other tight for a second time.

"Now"—Raed pushed her back gently—"let's stay on the path. You find the shade and make him talk."

He didn't understand what he was asking for, but he was right. With a long, slow breath, Sorcha pulled out her knife from its sheath at her waist.

"We will need to bring him out."

The cut she made on her left finger was clean and not very deep—but it also hurt unreasonably compared to other far worse wounds she'd had in the name of the Order.

Unfortunately, there was nothing quite like the blood of a Deacon to bring geists from every corner. Bending, she drew a circle right on the blood that had been spilled—that had started everything off. Cantrips were not to her liking, but without one, they could be here for hours waiting for the shade to appear.

When she rose from her crouch, Raed handed her his very fine ivory-colored handkerchief—quite a strange thing for a fugitive to have on his person—but also quite charming. Wrapping it around her finger, she opened her Center as wide as she could.

The Bond was her spine in these dangerous moments—holding her to the world when runes and geists could well rip her away from it. Sorcha kept one hand in Raed's, while the ruby flames of Pyet flickered on her other Gauntlet—just in case.

Dark shadows danced along the line of the bookshelves as if reluctant. Sorcha frowned—this was curious. Most shades of the murdered were in a hurry to reveal themselves.

A whiff of something sweet—cinnamon or some other exotic spice—filled the room, and goose pimples ran along Sorcha's arms. It was so much easier when you just destroyed geists, she thought vaguely.

However, the shade that began to form in the circle was not the one either of them had been expecting. It was no wizened Chancellor. It was instead a young woman—no, a girl, on the cusp of womanhood. She had long, dark hair plastered to her face, which seemed pale, even though it was as dark as any other citizen of Chioma, and her outstretched hands showed deep wounds on both of her wrists. Her expression was confused and terrified—fairly usual for the shade of a recently murdered person.

Raed shifted behind her. "By the Blood, who is that?"

Sorcha would have warned him to stay quiet, but it was far too late. The shade fixed her eyes on the Young Pretender, and then she did something remarkable. She spoke.

"Where is it? Where is it?" Her voice was a bare whisper in the gentle breeze that had come with her. It was so plaintive that Sorcha felt her usually tightly controlled emotions swell into sorrow.

A shade that spoke was remarkable indeed. Most were confined to re-creating the actions of their everyday life or the moments leading up to their death. Conversing with a geist was a tricky business, but now unfortunately, it had locked onto Raed and not her.

"She can see you," Sorcha hissed under her breath, though there was no point. "You are the focus now—she won't acknowledge me or any other living being."

"Oh." Raed swallowed hard. "Sorry."

"Don't apologize. Ask her what it is—the thing she's looking for?"

The Young Pretender actually took a hesitant step toward her. "Where is what, sweetheart?"

The shade let out a long moan that rattled the pictures on the wall and shook the ranks of pens on the desk. "The money." She held out a bloodless hand. "They said I could have money . . . if I was pure of heart. Where is it? My little brother is very sick."

A virgin of either sex had a particular power, because standing on the edge of change was the most attractive place for a geist to strike. Attacks most often happened at sunset or sunrise. Beaches and marshes, the in-between places were the most dangerous. The moment between sleeping and waking was also a particular favorite for a poltern to take possession.

Raed turned to her, his face written with anger and rage in equal amounts. "What do I say? By the Blood—what did they do to her?"

"I don't think our Chancellor is dead at all—but he certainly used this poor girl for something . . . evil."

"But what do I tell her?"

It was terrible, but all they had to go on was what the girl had seen in her last moments. To tell her the truth of her state would destroy any chance they had of learning more.

When Sorcha whispered the words he needed to use into his ear, the Young Pretender looked at her with horror. After a moment he nodded firmly, understanding that if they lost this chance, his sister might be lost as well.

He sighed, cleared his throat and then looked directly at the poor girl. Sorcha was used to the forms a geist could take, but the shade was most difficult to get used to, being a reflection of a dead person.

"You may have your money and go home," Raed said, his

voice stern with command. "But first you must tell us about the people who brought you here."

The girl's empty eyes darted back and forth. "The guards brought me to the palace—I've never been here before. There was a lady, she was standing there." Her finger pointed to the spot by the window. "She was wearing a cloak of gold, so pretty."

The poor child of the slums must have been dazzled by a woman from the harem—the cloth of gold was the signature of one of the Prince's consorts.

"She said I was pleasing to the Lady—my purity was a blessing in her eyes."

"Always with the purity," Sorcha muttered under her breath, "right up until the moment that they sacrifice the innocent."

The curtains fluttered, just at the corner of her vision, and suddenly the temperature in the room plummeted. The two living humans' breath was now visible in front of them, a worse sign still.

"What about the lady do you remember?" Raed's words tumbled out. "Quickly, sweetheart. I'll give you that coin."

The girl's form flickered, the wind from the window buffeting the edges of the apparition. Sorcha strode to the window, and with some difficulty jerked the shutters closed.

The poor sacrificial shade's voice was down to a very faint whisper. "She was veiled—but she had the prettiest blue eyes."

Blue eyes in Chioma were certainly highly unusual. Sorcha, however, didn't have enough time to feel victorious, because suddenly her Center was overcome with darkness. She cried out, for a second completely blind.

Something raced toward them through the ether like a bull charging. Reflexively she pushed Raed back behind her. Even though nearly blinded, Deacon training told her there was only one type of geist that moved that aggressively. A ghast.

A gleaming set of ethereal fangs, the stench of sulphur, and a wave of nausea confirmed Sorcha's suspicions. Yet it was not the humans who were the target of the attack.

The shade screamed, screamed louder than she would have when she was killed. Her shadowy hands reached out toward Raed, the person who had promised her the one thing she wanted.

He started forward, as if she were a mortal creature, as if he could do anything to help. The Rossin within him was writhing—inflamed by the danger to his host.

Sorcha grabbed the collar of the Young Pretender's shirt and yanked him back; he could not be allowed to follow the shade. Her reaction was so swift that he stumbled and fell against the desk. Sorcha was already releasing him and letting the fire of Yevah flare from her Gauntlets. The shielding rune sprang up before them with a roar like a gout of flame.

The room distorted through it, but still enough to see the final howls of the girl's shade in it. The ghast was outlined in fire, the dark orb of its eye fixing on the Deacon, but then it faded back into the ether.

They stood there for a long moment, panting, Yevah enclosing them. Merrick, by the Bones, she missed Merrick.

Finally and with caution, Sorcha let the Rune fade from her Gauntlet. The gagging smell of rotten eggs and a faint burn mark on the carpet where there had once been blood was all that remained to say anything had happened.

The geist had only come to destroy the shade—not, it appeared, to take on one of the Order. Sorcha let out a ragged breath and turned to Raed.

"Are you all right?"

His face was pale, his jaw set, but he nodded tightly. "Yes, but by the Blood, I have not seen a geist so close without the Rossin"—he cleared his throat—"appearing."

Sorcha reached out along the Bond, twisting past the coil of Raed's fears and deeper into the Rossin. The geistlord was close to the surface, and she caught a glimpse of his great muzzle, yet he did not venture out.

It was not just unusual—it was against the very nature of the geistlord. The Rossin was designed to feast on both human and geist. It reveled in destruction, blood and pain. Now it was something odd indeed: cautious.

"He's afraid." Rossin's shoulders were tense. "Only the Murashev has ever made him feel like this. It . . . it can't be another one, can it?"

She would have loved to deny it—but she didn't have enough information to be sure. "I hope not. I am not much of a Sensitive, but I can tell this much—something was controlling that ghast." She touched the back of his hand lightly, just enough, she hoped. "I think it is about time we went back to the harem and find out how many blue-eyed women it has."

"I wish Merrick were here." It was good for him to say it—it meant Sorcha didn't have to. She merely nodded in reply.

As they stepped out into the corridor, they were almost knocked down by a flood of young bureaucrats racing down the hall. Raed put an arm across Sorcha and held her back against the wall as half a dozen footmen dashed in the other direction.

It was as if they had stepped into a completely different palace from the one they had entered. Something was most assuredly up.

Sorcha exchanged a glance with Raed, and together they grabbed a passing servant who was laden down with a stack of books.

"What's going on?" The Young Pretender inquired, managing to sound both commanding and kindly at the same time.

"The Grand Duchess," the boy gasped, struggling to keep his pile straight. "Word came from the port—she is making her way to the palace this very minute."

Sorcha closed her eyes for a second, trying to balance this new information, but like the boy, she was failing miserably. Zofiya—of all people!

"What is she coming here for?" Raed, who had only briefly met the Grand Duchess when he was saving her in Vermillion, could not possibly comprehend how much trouble the cursed woman was.

"No one knows," the boy squeaked, trying to tug his arm free and keep his pile from falling on the floor at the same time. "But nothing is prepared, and she may want to see the Kingdom's tax records."

"Thank you, lad." Raed released him, and the poor thing scampered off to join the melee. By the Blood, those papers better be in order!

"It can't be a coincidence," Sorcha hissed into her lover's ear. "Zofiya isn't the type of person prone to flights of fancy—and there was no word of her visiting here when I left Vermillion. She could have come with the Ambassador, and yet she didn't."

Raed closed his eyes for an instant. "The ossuary wasn't everything, then."

It wasn't a question, and Sorcha knew they had better hurry. The Grand Duchess meant not just panic for the palace, she also created a delicious target for whoever was manipulating geists in Orinthal. The mess had just gotten larger.

TWENTY

A Grand Arrival

Zofiya stepped off the dirigible to be immediately bathed in sweat. They had burned four weirstones to get here in three days, and two engineers had been injured replacing the last one. The curious mathematics of this did not matter. She was here as her goddess had commanded.

"Perhaps the Grand Duchess would like to change into Chiomese silks?" The minor official who Orinthal had managed to rustle up on short notice was bent in an appropriately low bow.

Zofiya took a long breath and let the warm air fill her lungs. The nights it had taken to get here had been sleepless, and she was fully aware that her mood was less than perfect.

Still, she had been born to royalty and managed to control the outward display of her emotions—occasionally. Luckily for the trembling official, this was one of those times. "That will not be necessary—I will, however, require transportation to the Temple of Hatipai."

The man's eyes flickered behind her, and Zofiya concealed a smile as he took in her pitifully small entourage: only half a dozen Imperial Guards. Even when she was traveling without her brother, Zofiya should have by rights been accompanied by ten times that number.

However, when your goddess calls, you do not linger to gather what is proper. She could sense that the official was dying to ask more, full of questions he could not quite work out how to get answers to. Let him squirm, she thought; there would be plenty more Chiomese who she was bound to unnerve.

"The Temple is not far, Imperial Highness, but we have to assemble the proper carriage and honor guard. It will take us an hour or two." He actually winced.

The image of her goddess' Temple burned in Zofiya's mind. "We shall walk then and enjoy the views of your fine city."

The man's eyes widened, but he dared not deny her. "If I may be so bold"—a trail of sweat that had nothing to do with the heat ran down the side of the man's face—"may I ask what has brought this great honor of your visit to Chioma? The Prince will be most . . . surprised and delighted."

The movements of the Emperor's sister were always of the greatest interest to everyone—not least the hornet's nest of quarreling Princes. Yet Chioma was the seat of the worship of her goddess and the Prince of the kingdom was known for his reclusive nature and iron will. Zofiya anticipated no problems with him.

She had an excuse ready for just such an inquiry. "I have come to meet the charming Princess suing to become my Imperial brother's Empress."

It was at least a half-truth. When she had stood before Kaleva, he had not believed it. They knew each other too well, and he was able to read the look in her eyes enough to know her trip was connected to Hatipai.

It was one of the few things the siblings argued over. He had never felt the righteous burn of the faith she had found so early in her life. Zofiya loved her brother more than anything in this world, but there remained someone she placed higher: Hatipai.

Unlike her father, who had been horrified and embarrassed at a showing of faith in his daughter, Kaleva was only saddened by it.

"Little Wolf"—a twin set of frown lines appeared on his handsome face—"I fear this addiction of yours will bring you nothing but ill."

Standing in the blanketlike heat of Orinthal, she recalled

with a smile his pet name for her and his easily given love. The Emperor was remarkably softhearted for one commanding such power.

"I think it is you who may be hurt," she had replied. "With no faith to protect from the world, Brother."

It was an argument that had spun on and on and round and round for years. So he had not questioned her plans while in Chioma, and Zofiya had not offered to tell him. Hatipai's summons was something even an Imperial Grand Duchess could not ignore.

"Which direction is the Temple?" she asked calmly so as not to betray herself.

His face brightened as if lit by a weirstone. "We had reports, Your Imperial Highness, of you following our Bright Lady. Truly it gladdens the hearts of all in Chioma to know—"

"I am sure it does." Zofiya held up her hand, cutting him off in mid-flow. "But it is many years since I have had the joy of worshipping in a Temple—I would like to partake of her presence immediately."

Now it appeared as if the lit weirstone was under his feet, because he spun about and gestured her to follow him. Her Imperial Guard of six closed about her.

"Imperial Highness," Ylo, her guardian since she had been only ten years old, whispered sharply in her ear, "is this wise? Into the streets with so few to protect you?"

He didn't understand either. Nothing could touch her here in the land of her goddess. So she held up her hand, and he at least knew that gesture. Immediately he snapped to attention and followed her without further comment.

This was the city and the country where her goddess was still worshipped. The only one where faith still had a place. Certainly there were still other gods worshipped in the Empire, but mostly in quiet rural areas by simple folk who kept their altars by the hearth and gave small offerings when they could.

As the procession walked through the exotically scented streets of the city, Zofiya's pace quickened until she was almost knocking on the heels of the official. He turned his head, surprised. "The Bright Lady is calling, is she, Imperial Highness?"

He couldn't possibly know it was actually true, but he meant well. So she smiled and nodded. "It is a very, very long time since I have stood in one of her temples—back in my father's dominion, in fact."

"Forgive me, Imperial Highness"—a flicker of genuine interest overwhelmed his almost comical deference—"but is the Bright Lady widely worshipped there?"

A passing caravan of camels was apparently no respecter of high rank, and for a few minutes Zofiya's guard had to push back at the stinking beasts. They traded insults and threats with the owner, until he realized who he was dealing with and urged his animals as best he could out of the Grand Duchess' way.

Finally, when they were past them, she replied, "Her temples are very few indeed." Those words stung.

She would not share with anybody the events of the day that had first driven her to the Bright One's Temple. The memory of her father's towering rage, when he had caught her practicing hand-to-hand combat with the guard for the third time was deeply ingrained on her psyche. He had wanted another princess to marry off and secure his kingdom—not one so committed to choosing her own path.

In the Temple of Hatipai, the young Zofiya had found the strength to follow her own heart. As it turned out, even the King of Delmaire had eventually given up on her, finally declaring he had a surplus of daughters—and that she should make herself useful and protect her brother on his ill-fated ascendancy to rule Arkaym.

All that good fortune she owed to Hatipai, and now that Kaleva was sitting more firmly on the throne, it was time to pay back that strength she had found at the feet of the goddess.

"There she is." The official swept his arm up, indicating the slight rise in the road toward the Temple, as if he himself had conjured the magnificent red building from thin air.

The facade of the Temple had been masterfully carved. Vast friezes of the daily life of Chioma paraded around the outside of the Temple. All the trade and riches of the kingdom were depicted there; the smallest merchant to the greatest aristocrat were part of the magnificence. Every one of them, however, was climbing penitently up the walls toward the crowning glory of the building. The goddess sprawled atop her Temple, taking up all of the peaked roof, lying on her side, one hand propping up her grand head. The span of her wings beneath her served as a roof for the building.

Zofiya had never seen anything so complex or detailed— even in Delmaire—and it quite literally made her stop and choke back a breath of surprise.

"Would you—" She paused and cleared her throat. "I am sorry, what was your name?"

"Deren." His eyes, which back at the waterfront had appeared so lifeless, were now full and gleaming.

"Deren"—Zofiya let out a breath—"is there any way that I may be able to pray alone?"

He gave a little bow. "I'll run ahead and arrange it with the priestess. I am sure she will be able to accommodate your request, Imperial Highness." And he scuttled off to do that.

The Grand Duchess stood in the shade, fanned herself, and tried to hold on to her frustration. Eventually Deren returned to them, his teeth flashing in his dark face with genuine pleasure. "The afternoon prayers have not yet begun, so the priestess has managed to clear the Temple for you, Imperial Highness."

They climbed the steps to the doors, and Zofiya had a moment of disorientation—it was just as the goddess had shown her. Sweat that had nothing to do with the heat broke out on the rest of her body, and her heart began to race in beneath her ribs. "Stay here, Ylo," she whispered over her shoulder.

"But, Highness." His voice was uncertain, but he still tried to do his duty—she wouldn't fault him for that.

"Not this time." Zofiya craned her neck, looking up at the Temple where the image of Hatipai stared down at her followers as if they were ants—which of course they were. "This," the Grand Duchess said, "is private." Then, knowing that for the first time in many, many years she would be alone in the Temple of her goddess, she walked reverently up the last few steps.

Inside, the heat was left behind, even though the light came in through the glassless windows and burned white on the red floor. Zofiya slipped off her shoes and felt the rough prickle of the fabulous carpets on her bare soles. To have such a place all to herself was one of the true joys of being royalty—maybe the only one, as far as she could see.

You are a child of Kings, but you do not enjoy the privileges that it brings, Hatipai's voice whispered, and Zofiya could not be sure if she was hearing it in her head or if the dimly seen lofty ceiling might contain a hidden angel.

You need to learn to take the reins of power. Be what your heritage commands you to be.

Despite her faith and her love of the goddess, that stung. Her nature rebelled against that. "I am the sister of the Emperor, Lady. I take care with his life. I counsel him as best I can."

And you never think that the royal blood he has also runs through your veins. Foolish girl—you are as born to rule as he. Only the ridiculous tradition of males on the throne of Arkaym prevents you from your real potential.

A lump formed in Zofiya's throat. Arkaym and Delmaire had that in common. While many of the principalities that made up the Empire had female rulers, no Empress had ever sat on the grand throne in Vermillion. Empresses were made by marriage—not by birth.

"My brother was asked to come—to become Emperor," she finally ventured, walking deeper into the Temple but with hesitation now in her stride. "I was never even considered. I could not possibly—"

And that is why you always remain in the shadows. The goddess' voice was now sharp and actually hurt Zofiya, as if she were being pummeled. As she winced and pulled back, the goddess' tone changed, becoming softer and gentler. *You have much to learn yet, child—now is not the time. Go to the font.*

The Grand Duchess' confidence had been shaken. Suddenly the Temple was not cool and mysterious—it was positively freezing and deep in shadows. The holy water font, which in the goddess' vision had seemed full of joy, was in fact rather menacing.

Do you not love your goddess? Hatipai's whisper echoed around the vaulted chamber. *You are a good child, covered in faith—do as I ask.*

Zofiya swallowed, closed her eyes and thought back to her first visit to the Temple in Delmaire. When she concentrated hard, she could recall that moment of utter acceptance, complete love and being part of something—when in her parents' eyes she was merely a spare. Clutching onto that memory, she was able to go forward into the shadows.

The Temple was very sparse, the focus being an unadorned bowl of silver buried in the floor. It was ten feet wide, and worshippers had floated fragrant flowers on its still surface. The scent was exhilarating and somehow steadied her.

She reached the stairs and climbed up to the altar—but in the proper way—on her knees. Finally she began to smile as the warmth of her faith began to wrap itself around her. With hesitation dissolving, Zofiya stretched out her hand and dipped it into the water. It was icy cold. She pressed her wet fingertips to her own mouth and let the water enter her.

Now go down into the dark—bring me back what I need.

Climbing to her feet, Zofiya did what all worshippers of Hatipai would have considered blasphemy—she stepped into the font itself. Now her body was given over to the goddess. Now she could do what was required of her.

For the longest moment it felt like nothing was going to happen, and then a loud groan filled the room, mechanical and deep, from somewhere below her. Water began to drain out of the font as a crack appeared around the rim. It was pouring into a hidden space, while the altar itself began to come apart. Dust and stale air billowed up from below, making Zofiya cough and splutter—very unflattering in the house of her goddess.

When it finally cleared, she could see a spiral staircase that was thick with dirt and could have been a thousand years old. For all she knew, it was. Dripping with holy water, Zofiya stepped out of the font and onto the stairs. They creaked under her weight, but the light, supple metal, apart from being dirty, felt strong. As she walked down deeper, she saw that the stairs were in fact hanging from silvery chains, yet she could see no sign of a mechanism.

None of this looked like the work of a goddess, and the faint carvings on the interior of the staircase walls were unfamiliar. Zofiya didn't quite understand what her goddess was asking of her, why she could not send someone else down here.

Finally the Grand Duchess reached the bottom. Lights flickered and then sprang to life, illuminating the room with a blue gleam that unnerved her a little. She had danced beneath the red glow of chandeliers in the palace of Vermillion and lived her life by the amber flicker of candles and lanterns—what she had never done was see any sort of blue light in her life.

The room smelled of linseed oil, and the air was sharp in her nostrils. The only experience she could compare it to was the time she had spent in Tinkers' Lane, watching the construction of the engines for her brother's newest airship. The heavily guarded mysteries of the Guild of Tinkers had fascinated her. Yet, merely by looking around, Zofiya knew that this place was far older than anything she had seen in Vermillion—except for the prison from which she'd helped the angel escape.

Then, warmth and her goddess' voice had carried her on, insulating her from the strangeness of that place. However, now she was alone, shivering in a room that was bone-achingly cold and strange. The wall was carved with numerals and figures and, under her fingertips, felt metallic. The light was coming from the eyes of the people depicted, each of them a piece of blue glass. Yet the pictures were similar to the ones in the palace. People crying out in terror as the Revelation of the Otherside began, the Season of Supplication—but this time there were no other gods represented—just Hatipai.

The people crying out this time were obviously citizens of Chioma, with their high headdresses and sumptuously draped clothes. The artisan who had made this was incredibly skilled at capturing the anguish in the people's faces and postures. Except for one.

Zofiya stood frowning for a moment. A central figure stood in the middle of the almost prostrate crowd—but where they were bent and knotted in fear, he was erect, proud, looking directly up at the representation of Hatipai.

Unconsciously, one of the Grand Duchess' hands stole to her throat, because two things disturbed her greatly. That man, carved with such drama and precision, was unfamiliar, but he wore something she had read of. The mysterious headdress of the Prince of Chioma had been widely reported. She had learned of this ruler who rarely traveled beyond his own borders and whose face was never seen.

In the frieze the artist had depicted the headdress in great detail and embellished it with the different colored clear glass so it fairly blazed in contrast to the other parts of the image.

The second detail that caused a deep frown in the forehead of the Grand Duchess was the depiction of her goddess. This was nothing like the images in the Temple above. This Hatipai was a nightmare, her hair flying wide like a nest of angry vipers, and long, predatory teeth visible in a mouth that was spread wide—yet she knew it was her goddess because of the symbol hanging about her.

Words were written beneath, obviously words, but not any that Zofiya—even with a royal education—could understand. A lost language; it had to be. It was terribly frustrating, and she made a decision that when she got aboveground, there would be scholars questioned rather vigorously.

As in Vermillion, she followed the frieze around to the end of the chamber. Here the image was stranger still. The Prince of Chioma was shown wrestling with the nightmare vision of Hatipai, and it looked as if he was pulling something off her. Zofiya leaned forward, until her breath was fogging the cold metal.

It looked as if the Prince was struggling to rip a cowl or perhaps the skin from her goddess. The people of Chioma were shown screaming, clapping their hands to their ears, their mouths in a terrible rictus of pain.

"What is that?" she muttered to herself as her fingertips hovered inches from the metal.

A loud clank echoed through the chamber, and Zofiya leapt back. It was a display of fear that she was glad none of her Imperial Guard had to witness.

The light in the chamber grew brighter, the eyes of the people beaming out at her, and things were shifting. Just beyond the light, the sound of metallic rattling made her wonder if some metal giant was stirring.

The whispering began: soft, insistent and growing louder by the moment. Zofiya took another step and looked around her but was unable to see where the sound was coming from. It could not be that there were people in the chamber with her, but perhaps it was the whispering of shades trapped in this awful place.

She was no Deacon, had no weaponry that would possibly harm a geist—but she had the faith of her goddess burning inside her, and her goddess had told her to come here. So Zofiya stood still in the middle of the chamber and waited for whatever was to come, to come.

Gradually the sound of the whispers began to resolve into languages that Zofiya knew. As well as Imperial she could make out at least ten familiar native tongues. Her heart was chilled by what they were saying.

Who are you?
Die in the dark if you have not the blood.
Who are you?
Identify!

Her spine straightened as the cold of the room began to change to an ominous warmth, and her hand clenched around her sword hilt. However, there was nothing to strike, no threat that she could identify—just a feeling of doom sweeping toward her out of the untapped darkness.

Throwing back her shoulders, she spoke as loudly and as firmly as she remembered her father speaking from his throne in distant Delmaire. "I am Grand Duchess Zofiya Nobylchuin. My father is King of Delmaire, my brother the crowned Emperor of Arkaym, and I am second in line to the throne of the Empire."

It was true. All of it. Yet she had never really considered that last part, until she had yelled it into the black. Zofiya stood there panting, for that moment forgetting her fear of this chamber and instead remembering her brother's strange looks, the murmured conversations in the Court when she passed by, and finally particular attention several of the Dukes had been paying her.

She and her brother were all that there was of a very shaky new dynasty on the throne. Both of them had to marry and produce heirs—immediately. For that same moment Hatipai, the strange room, and her mission evaporated. Her brother had been concealing something behind that ever-present smile. Had she been so busy protecting him that she had noticed nothing else? It was a terrible wounding thought that froze her in place.

Zofiya snapped back to her current concerns, because the

room was moving again. The eyes of blue glass now beamed narrow lights that flickered over her. The voices, the harsh whispers died away and were replaced by something just as ominous.

The sound of metal screeching against metal reverberated around the room with such vehemence that she had to slam her hands over her ears.

Finally it stopped and, breathing heavily, the Grand Duchess cautiously uncovered her ears.

The Emperor or his heir may enter.

The final frieze slid apart. Zofiya wondered how many of these Ancient places there were around the Empire, waiting to be discovered. The Rossins must have known about them, but unfortunately during their rather hasty exit from Vermillion had decided not to leave instructions for their successors.

The Rossin line was the enemy of Hatipai and all other deities, for they had allowed the population to turn away from the gods when the Otherside opened. Letting them diminish, become "the little gods."

Zofiya's heart was filled with certainty. Her brother might have plans for her—but she had plans for him too. The gods would be brought to power again, and her goddess would be placed above them all. She would bring faith back to Arkaym.

She stepped forward confidently into the darkness toward a gleaming pillar of light. That was when the device above the door attacked her. The long, articulated arm struck her shoulder with a needle the thickness of a lacemaker's instrument. The Grand Duchess barely had time to react before it was withdrawn. She stared at the device as it clicked and whirred. Nothing happened, so after a few moments she continued into the room and, strangely, into the sunlight. One glance up told her that somehow those Ancient craftsmen had worked a lens that funneled light from a distant point to here.

"Goddess be praised," Zofiya murmured under her breath. Her feet echoed on the floor, and her breath was coming in short, shallow gasps. Up on the pedestal was another device she could not name, but she was positive this was what Hatipai wanted her to retrieve.

It looked to be a sphere of gray metal. She might have faith, but the Grand Duchess was not stupid—she did not grab the object straightaway. Instead she studied it, head tilted, eyes narrowed. It was the same size and shape as the round balls children everywhere in the Empire played with. Two circles of flat gray metal encompassed the ends of the sphere, and between them the rest of the ball looked to be made of some kind of glass.

Zofiya's fingers hovered only an inch from the sphere. The glass was as fine and clear as any made for the Vermillion Palace, and through it she could make out that the sphere held some kind of liquid. In the light from above it appeared to gleam silver. Walking around the pedestal a little more, she observed that the discs at each end were not just flat—they too were etched and contained little wheels and cogs. They were tiny examples of the Tinker's art—the kind of work seen only in the clocks made for aristocrats or the Imperial Court.

Such things were recent inventions, and yet this place was unquestionably old. Faith did not stop Zofiya from being curious, either. The Ancient folk and their arts had been lost after the Break—this had to be an example of their craft. Yet, why her goddess would need something from them, she couldn't comprehend.

Maybe it was not her place to understand. Hatipai had only asked her to bring her this thing. She wiped her palms on her breeches before taking the sphere.

Perhaps it was her imagination, but something felt like it shifted within the orb. She paused, frozen in place, waiting for the terror to begin. It could explode in her hands like a mistimed weirstone, break into a myriad of shards, or maybe burn.

Yet after a few terrifying heartbeats, nothing happened. All was still in the chamber. Standing up, Zofiya wrapped the sphere in the red silk of her kerchief and tucked it into the lining of her cloak.

Cautiously, making sure her feet landed in the dusty footprints she had made coming in, she backed out of the room. Once she was beyond the huge metal frieze, it slid shut in front of her, scant inches from her nose.

The whispers began again, swelling around her, sounding angrier than before.

Now they spoke something else, something that chilled her heart.

Destroy it.
Break it, daughter of the blood.
Destroy it as we could not.

Zofiya's jaw tightened. She did not reply to their foolish demands. Her goddess had given her a command, and the Grand Duchess would not fail to obey it.

Turning, she began to climb back up the stairs, back to reality. Whoever or whatever this strange place was, she had what she'd come for. The whispers would just have to look after themselves.

TWENTY-ONE

Interview in a Library

Raed knew a palace in uproar when he experienced it. As they passed through the corridors and atriums, he was reminded of the Unsung's house in exile. His father always had a flair for the dramatic. He could send servants scuttling and his put-upon valet running about as if the Otherside was opening again.

They were lighting little cones of incense in sconces on the wall, and the scent was floral, thick, and though Raed knew it was supposed to be welcoming, he found it too cloying. It remained to be seen what the Grand Duchess Zofiya would think of it.

She was the second in line to the throne of Arkaym, and no one as close to the ultimate power in the Empire had been to Orinthal since his grandfather. It was a big event for Chioma.

"I wish they'd just get out of our damn way," Sorcha grumbled. He wanted to hold her hand again—but this time he restrained himself.

Fraine was out there, and Sorcha had managed to find a lead when everything Isseriah found had come to nothing. Yet they had to hurry. The shade of that girl had stirred every fear in his body. It could have been his sister.

Sorcha stopped and turned. Her blue eyes focused on him with that intensity he found both amazing and a little scary.

"We'll get her back, Raed." Then she leaned forward and whispered for his ears alone, "If we have to pull down every brick of the Hive City to do it."

In another's mouth that might have been a joke—but the Deacon was deadly serious. "Then let's start with the brick we know about," he replied.

She shot him a little smile, tight and slightly wicked, and then strode on toward the women's quarters. Outside the door stood one guard, a eunuch who must have been at least six and a half feet tall, with arms crossed. He appeared not nearly as impressed with the Deacon standing before him as he should.

"No entire man can enter," he rumbled.

"I stand surety for his behavior," Sorcha replied, crossing her own arms. "I and my Order."

The eunuch shifted slightly.

The Deacon took a step forward. "Or I could return to your Prince and tell him you have stood in the way of the investigation he charged us with . . ."

The mountain of a man glanced around as if he expected someone to relieve him, but finally even he gave way to Deacon Sorcha Faris. He unlocked the door and stood aside.

She was not done with him. "I want a full assembly of every blonde-haired, blue-eyed woman in the harem. How many will that be?"

The eunuch glanced her up and down, and after a moment gave her a little bow of his head. "The Prince chooses his women almost exclusively from Chioma—there are only three women who fit this description, my lady." It was not the proper honorific for one of her standing, but the guard undoubtedly didn't have much contact with the Deacons of the Order.

Raed observed Sorcha's tiny flinch, but she nodded. "Then we will need a room to interview them." The guard directed them a small antechamber just off the cloistered area, where a small library was housed so the harem would have something to do other than gossip and sew.

While he lumbered off to get the women, Raed looked askance at Sorcha. "So how are we to tell which of them are responsible for that girl's death?"

The Deacon pressed her lips together. "If Merrick were

here, it would be easy. But since he is not . . ." She paused, eyeing him in a calculating fashion that Raed did not appreciate. When she did that, the woman who entranced him was washed away, and he caught a glimpse of the Deacon the Order had made.

She shook her head. "I guess that method wasn't the best for the shade—we will just have to rely on my limited Sight and manipulating them into revealing themselves."

The eunuch had obviously taken her orders to heart, because he appeared with the three women and even knocked courteously on the door. The ladies smiled at Raed—but he didn't feel particularly flattered—after all, they saw very few men who still had their balls.

They were all indeed blonde, blue-eyed lovelies, and he couldn't help smiling back at them. However, a second afterward he felt Sorcha stiffen at his side. No matter how intelligent or disciplined the female of the species was, competition was a part of their makeup that they could never shake.

These women were a little different—they were used to sharing a man, and it was obvious that Onika of Chioma enjoyed the trappings of his rank to the utmost. Each of them was delightfully curvy, with varying shades of honey hair and blue eyes, and being in the harem, they dressed to emphasize these attributes.

"Ladies." He gave them a little bow, slightly more awkward than it might have been. "Thank you for your attendance." Part of him couldn't help wondering what Sorcha would look like dressed as these women were. The twitch in his pants at the thought was slightly distracting.

Two of them beamed at him, while the third and most beautiful looked far less impressed.

Sorcha tilted her head, looked at him askance, and raised one eyebrow as if to say, "I am interested to see where you are taking this." Yet she remained silent, her fingers resting on the Gauntlets at her waist.

"You pulled me away from a game of trange," the least amused one snapped. "I was about to win a pretty fortune from Lady Moyie."

Raed tried not to take offense. "I am sorry, Lady . . ."

The woman let the sentence dangle in the air for a second

before folding her arms over her chest and replying, "Lady Gezian."

"Well"—Raed pulled out a seat, and offered it to her— "Lady Gezian, my Deacon friend and I are terribly sorry to have taken you away from your game—but the Prince himself has sent us here on a mission."

"Really." One of the other two women beamed. "Lady Lisah and I would love to help."

"Speak for yourself, Jaskia." The other pouted. "I have never cared for Deacons."

"I know," Sorcha spoke up, her voice light while she directed her response with ruthless efficiency, "we are such a bother, what with protecting everyone from geist attack. Terribly dull of us, we know."

Lisah opened her pretty mouth, struggled to find something to say in response, but coming up with nothing, snapped it shut instead. She sat meekly on the chair next to Lady Gezian. Meanwhile, Lady Jaskia continued to beam at Raed.

He wasn't quite sure if she expected him to throw her on the table and have his way with her right away, but it was actually a little unnerving after a moment or two.

Luckily, Sorcha stepped in with her usual bluntness. "We are investigating the deaths that have been happening in the palace—and more specifically the Chancellor's."

"You know very little, then," Gezian interrupted. "The Chancellor died of old age . . . or boredom."

"Oh really." Sorcha pointedly pulled her Gauntlets from her belt and slapped them down on the table directly in front of the three other women. Jaskia gave out a little squeak and jumped. "That's not what your Prince thinks."

Suddenly all traces of amusement, lust and irritation were washed from the ladies. It had to be the conditioning of the harem to instantly take very seriously anything that fell from Onika of Chioma's lips.

"What did Father have to say?" Jaskia asked, and Raed, taken by surprise, turned on his heel to look at her. She certainly did not have the Prince's coloring, but it was naturally impossible to tell if they had the same features compared to him—thanks to that damned mask.

"You're the Prince's daughter?" Sorcha leaned forward,

resting her hands on the table and pressing the whole weight of her attention on the girl.

Jaskia blanched a little. "Just one of them in the harem—maybe ten or so. We remain here until we are married off."

No tone of bitterness lingered in her tone, giving the impression that she had no resentment over that. Something had sparked in Raed's mind—he recalled his grandfather's journal and the mention of the peculiar breeding habit of that Prince of Chioma.

"And the heirs? The male children—where are they kept?" he asked, pressing his hand against his beard.

Jaskia shrugged. "I don't know—obviously they are not kept in the harem—so I have never seen one."

Which sounded perfectly normal, except the words of his grandfather echoed in his head. *None have ever seen the heirs to the throne of Chioma.*

Sorcha cleared her throat. "Well, regardless, your *father* deputized us to get to the bottom of these murders—and as daughter and"—her gaze fell on the other two women as she obviously struggled to find the right term—"loyal citizens of Chioma, you will be glad to help, I am sure."

Lisah sat up straighter in her chair. "Naturally—no one wants a murderer loose in the palace. What do you need to know?"

"Where were you and what were you doing on the day of the Chancellor's death?" Sorcha said bluntly, and Raed inwardly winced. Active Deacons were taught a lot of things—cantrips, runes and history—however, what they were not taught was tact. He knew that mostly the Order turned up, fought geists and sent them packing. They dealt with the undead—not usually the living.

"You suspect us?" Lady Gazian slammed back her chair and rose to her feet while her face blazed bright red. "How dare you come in here and suggest that we have anything to do with these murders!"

Lady Lisah replied in a slightly calmer tone. "We are confined to the harem. How do you think we could have even gotten out of it to go and murder the Chancellor?"

"You could easily go outside if you had help from one of the eunuchs." Sorcha folded her arms. "I am sure that even

without the lure of sex, you ladies all still know how to wind
men around your little fingers."

"But how could we—" Jaskia held her hand up to her
mouth. "How could we do such terrible things? None of us
could possibly do that . . ."

Gazian rolled her eyes. "We were at the trange tournament, if you must know—it is held once a month, and all of us
were playing that day."

"I presume others of the harem can vouch for you being
there?" Raed sat on the table and smiled pleasantly at Gazian,
who had trouble not smiling back.

"Is my word not enough?"

They might be cosseted and locked away, but these women
were like Court females all over the Empire: they expected to
be treated with respect. They demanded it, in fact.

He had to be careful. Though the Prince wanted them to
find answers, Raed doubted he would appreciate his women
complaining. "Normally, yes—but this is serious, and my
partner here"—he gestured to Sorcha, who tilted her head—
"is the kind of woman who goes on hard facts."

It was the tactic used all over the Empire—from city
guards to politicians—one nice person, one angry one with
the stick. When faced with that, people always chose to turn
to the pleasanter person—well, at least those not used to the
technique.

Gazian glanced at the other two women. "Both Lady Jaskia
and Lisah were at the tournament—we can vouch for one
another."

Lisah gave out a little chuckle. "Yes—of course we can . . .
but"—she paused, a tiny frown bending her flawless forehead—
"but Jaskia wasn't there in the morning. She—"

What exact excuse the daughter of the Prince had given
was never to be found out. The room shook and rumbled as if
thunder was bearing down on them. That was impossible,
since thunder in Chioma was restricted to the rainy season.

The smell of spice and sweat filled the room as shadows
swallowed up its corners. Jaskia screamed, her mouth flying
far too wide for a human body to bear, and the sound that
came out of it was far too large for her tiny body. Then she
began to stretch upward, flesh pulled impossibly long. The

sound of it grated on the ear and turned the stomach. Sinews popped, and bones poked from her joints in unnatural angles. Something was coming through her.

Lisah and Gazian screamed as if their lives depended on it, bolting for the door, but Raed was rooted to the spot. He knew there was no point in him running. He had enough experience with geists that he recognized a powerful one when it loomed over him.

At his side he heard Sorcha shout something, but he couldn't take his eyes off the geist. It looked like a perverse hand puppet of the Lady Jaskia, stretched around something else—something that was pushing up through her.

The Deacon at his side summoned her blazing rune Shayst; green light licked her fingers as she held her Gauntleted hand toward the creature. It was the rune designed to pull power away from a geist, but her face by the light of it was twisted—not the usual calm mask. Without Merrick, Raed realized, she was still struggling.

Then fire ran up his spine, his vision blurred, and everything became irrelevant. Raed clutched his stomach, feeling panic consume him along with the pain. "Sorcha!" he yelled as his flesh turned against him. The Rossin would not stand for this. It was roaring its way up from inside him.

Please, no, please. Not here. Not with her. His mind called out hopeless prayers to the unforgiving Rossin.

He caught a glimpse of the Deacon turning toward him and felt a faint tug of the Bond between them like the end of hope—but it was far too late. The control slipped away from her—without Merrick in the Bond, she wasn't strong enough to hold the Rossin.

Raed managed one more strangled cry to Sorcha, and then he fell toward the Curse, hearing his own scream turn into the geistlord's cry for blood.

It was one of *her* creatures. The Rossin flew toward reality on wings of utter rage. *She* had tried to destroy *him*, first by direct attack and now by sending one of her minions, her lesser creatures, to take what was his—to break this flesh that he treasured.

Yet the Rossin had strength that Hatipai had not really explored properly at their last meeting. She hadn't taken full notice of the changes time could produce among humans—let alone known the power of the Deacons. Her lack of knowledge was the Rossin's advantage—one that he seized upon.

Since she had been contained, the various Orders of Deacons had come to power, and as he ruptured into the world, he felt it again—the rune-fed strength that flowed from the red-haired one. The Deacon's foolishly constructed Bond was still in place—it constrained him, but it was also a source of unexpected strength.

As he took over Raed's body, he drew on it with great satisfaction: fur rippled and broke through skin, jaws lengthened and grew teeth as sharp as razors, flesh twisted. The Rossin was once again breathing in the world of humans. He announced his coming with a roar that sent humans screaming in blind panic.

Unlike Hatipai, his enemy, he was confined to one person, his essence tied to a single bloodline, and he could not construct a body from scraps of flesh. It had advantages and disadvantages. As the great lion shape snarled his rage into the confines of the library, he felt the advantages particularly strongly.

Muscles stretched and popped, and he shook himself. Human females squealed and tried to run, but his bulk blocked the door. The Rossin did not bother to swipe at them but leapt at the ghast snapping in the corner of the library.

This creature was made of human flesh as well, but it was merely a meat puppet compared to a fully realized geistlord. The thing's curved, needlelike teeth shattered on the Beast's hide as it lunged forward. Its smell was something dried and moldy—an odor not to the Rossin's liking. The human trapped within the ghast screamed in pain as her flesh buckled in the ghast's control. Unlike the Young Pretender, she was feeling everything her inhabitant did.

It was almost mercy when the Rossin's jaws closed like a trap around its throat. He shook the ghast hard, like a cat with a particularly vile rat. The thin thread of human life was broken and the focus of the geist destroyed. It was sent howling back to the Otherside, and the flood of human blood in the Rossin's mouth was untainted.

It poured over his long, rough tongue and filled his throat with sweet, sharp flavor. Blood and power—they had always been tightly bound. This is what had brought him here to this world.

The Rossin spun on his paws, his great size making him awkward in the confines of the library. A shelf fell and smashed the window with a tremendously satisfying clatter that sent the humans into another massive screaming panic. It drew the Beast's attention to them.

The Deacon was nearby, standing still against the far wall. She had her Gauntlets on, but her hands were limp at her side—for there was no rune in their lexicon that could draw power from the Rossin. He was as grounded in this world as they were.

"Shut up," he heard her hiss, presumably to the terrified females sobbing in the corner, smelling of urine and sweat. They were jammed in between two tumbled shelves of books. "Stay very still," the contemptible Deacon instructed them, and the Rossin felt her trying to take hold again with the Bond. Yet she was weak. The Bond was weak. Somehow the foolish creature had lost her partner.

The Rossin's lip curled back and it inhaled. The other Deacon was not dead; that would have left this female completely exposed to him. No, the Otherside was close, and he had gone through there. Such a thing had not been attempted by a flesh human for generations. The Rossin was almost impressed.

However, should the male Deacon make a miraculous return, then the Bond would be restored to its strength—the Rossin had to move quickly.

The great cat snarled and lashed his tail, but he had no time to wreak havoc upon these quivering females. She was out there once again seeking to overcome him. All she had to do was find a body strong enough to contain her, locate the Ehtia device, and then even he would have trouble overcoming her.

When he roared at the female, all curving fangs and hot spittle, it was to show the Deacon that he would deal with her later. Soon she would feel his wrath. That quite unhinged the other two women, and they bolted from the fragile safety of the tumbled bookshelves toward the imagined safety of the door.

In reflex the Rossin lunged, his massive paw catching one

around the torso, ripping her open, spilling blood and gore over his fur and the floor. The other he snapped at, enjoying the tiny scream, and then the crunch of her backbone between his jaws. He enjoyed a few more satisfying chomps before dropping the broken thing to the ground.

The Deacon yelled, her Gauntlets now flaring bright red with a rune that could not touch him. If she was protected from the ravages of the geistlord, then he was just as protected from her. The fire flowed over and past him as if he were her, which in a way he was.

It must have cost her to do that—foolishly loving his host as she did. With great contempt the Rossin bunched his hind-quarters, leapt clear through the window, and landed on the roof of the lower palace. It was a feat no mortal creature could have performed.

Behind he could hear running and shouting—but such sounds were no longer his concern—all that mattered were those sounds of horror that lay ahead. His mouth was already watering as the prospect.

TWENTY-TWO

The Last Time

Merrick pulled himself to his feet, feeling the effects of Onika's presence pass. Barely had he finished his recovery, when the burrowing ship lurched, knocking him off them again. The Prince caught him by the elbow, and with an impressive display of catlike grace managed to wedge both of them against the wall while the ship continued to vibrate and strain. The weirstones in their cradles rolled like children's marbles, but thankfully none came loose.

Around them the metal groaned like a sick person, and for an instant Merrick had the image of it collapsing inward. He could almost taste the earth in his mouth, and he immediately reacted how he'd been taught—he flung his Center out. Instantly his senses were flooded with power—a power that he recognized.

"A geistlord!" he yelled, but Onika was not there to hear his pronouncements. He snatched up a weirstone and bolted back through the hatchway they had come through. All the way the ship shifted and bucked under them, but there was a definite direction—up.

Once in the main room, Merrick's ears were assaulted by the clanging of the machinery around him: gears spun and pistons pumped harder than could be good. The Ehtia were everywhere, scrambling to keep their ship from tearing itself apart, shouting orders at one another, and wide-eyed with near panic.

Merrick lost sight of Onika but spun about when Nynnia grabbed his arm. Her eyes were dark pits in the strange green light of the ship. "We're going to have to surface—she's found us!"

The young Deacon could guess what kind of "she" she meant. He might be out of his own time, but his training still held.

"We've surfaced!" someone yelled, and now they were all running for the exit. Merrick jerked away from Nynnia and joined those pounding through the corridors and hatchways. This was not panic—this was the organized pelt of warriors toward a battle. He had seen it before in Vermillion, and as a trained Deacon the battle was where he had to be—it didn't matter what time in history it was or that it was not his fight.

He burst through the final hatch, with a press of people at his back, and the sudden influx of light blinded him for an instant. A Sensitive without Sight, he stumbled forward. The Ehtia, with their strange dark clothing, spread out into the suddenly silent landscape. The weapons they carried were gleaming brass crossbows and long, curved sticks that he couldn't identify. At their head stood Onika, a weirstone clutched in one hand. The interior of the stone was swirling like a vortex, and it boded ill.

Merrick could smell the arrival of the geistlord. It was sweet and pungent, very like the thick perfumes found in the temples of the little gods. He flinched when Nynnia touched his shoulder. Her face was set in stern lines, and she flexed her fingers around one of the strange sticks. "Now you will get to see our folly, Merrick Chambers." She looked so sad that he wanted to offer some comfort, but he didn't know what would work. "The weirstone-craft we thought we were so clever to create"—Nynnia flicked him a bitter glance—"it brought their attention to us from the Otherside."

Merrick was about to answer, when the earth twisted under him. It was not much, but a shiver that foretold something more. He could feel all the animals fleeing from where he and the Ehtia stood; the earthworms dug deeper, the bugs that could fly caught the breeze as best they could, and the furred beasts scampered in among the rocks. He wished he could join them.

A woman appeared over the rise of the hill, though it was hard to see her shape or form, concealed as it was in darkness. Merrick drew in his breath and felt primitive fear clutch his stomach.

Few Deacons had seen a geistlord and lived to report back. The first Deacon sprang to Merrick's mind, the ancestor of Raed Rossin, and how he had made the first bargain with the geistlord. As the woman drew nearer, Merrick realized one thing—no one had spoken of their terrible beauty.

Her dark hair tumbled down flawless, naked skin. As his vision cleared he was entranced by the glimpses of her body beyond her curls. She was perfectly nude, and her soft feet landed on rock or moss without reaction—as if pain was for smaller beings. Shadows cascaded from her shoulders and circled her head. Thankfully he could not see into them fully . . . and he knew why.

"Shades," he whispered, his Center revealing the captured souls that followed her. He could not count the number of them—it had to be thousands. Suddenly the horror of the Rossin did not seem so great.

Geists fed on the souls of humans for the most part—but it was not all that could sustain them. Emotions like rage and love often drew them, so what greater sustenance could there be for a geistlord than adoration? These shades suggested this one had fed well.

"Mother," Onika spoke clearly to the advancing woman, "you are not welcome here."

Merrick shook his head—for a moment pulling the two difficult facts together. That Hatipai was a goddess, he was sure. But that was not all he saw when he looked at her. She was also a geist.

Though he was horrified, it made sense. Scholars had always just assumed that the population had turned away from the gods because they had been unable to protect them from the arrival of the Otherside—but if any of them had suspected they were in fact geistlords, then denying their deities was just retribution.

"Son," the woman spoke, and it was like sweet honey. A sound to make men weep with lust and women commit suicide in despair. "Come to me, and all will be forgiven—even trying to turn my faithful against me."

Onika straightened. "I could not do it."

"No." The goddess laughed. "Not for lack of trying, though. They would have none of it. Foolish boy."

Though there was no expression visible under the mask, the Prince's weight of sadness was reflected in the set of his shoulders. He certainly did not appear to enjoy his godhood.

She stepped closer, and even the Ehtia drew back as her presence threatened to wash over them. "I made you for a purpose, Onika: to protect my realm and all the people in it. So long as you live—and I made you to live forever, dearest—Chioma will endure."

Onika's laugh was low and bitter. "Yet what is the point of eternal life without love? And you made sure that there will never be love or an heir for me."

His voice was so sad that it instantly brought Merrick back to the moment where his mother was sitting next to him on the bed, smiling, with her hand resting on her full stomach. *I don't know how he heard of me,* she had said.

Suddenly the future opened up before him, and he heard Nynnia's words. *Plant the seed,* she had said. His mother had smiled and glowed with such happiness. It had been true love in her eyes, not the mad, hopeless faith of one trapped by the demigod beneath the mask, but real love, as unexpected, delicious and treasured as that could be. Merrick knew what Nynnia wanted and why she had sent him here.

He almost blurted it out, but then Hatipai was speaking. "You alone can hold Chioma—you must live."

Onika was her focus. The Order's training made this blatantly obvious. Just as the Rossin had invested in the Imperial family, Hatipai had made her own anchor to this world—similar but different ways of surviving the perils of the real world.

"Let these people pass," Onika growled.

"Your allies?" The shadows began to race counterclockwise around the face of the geistlord. "They practically invited us into this world, and now when they betray us, you would protect them?" The shades darted apart, and her face was revealed.

Merrick's senses betrayed him. He dimly heard the Ehtia around him also fall to their knees, but nothing mattered apart from the glory of Hatipai. None of them were worthy of it. When her gaze fell on him, he wanted to slit his own throat lest he insult her with his own pitiful nature. He rolled onto his back, his hands grasping desperately for his knife.

To his right, he caught a glimpse of the vile woman Nynnia fumbling with her stick. She did not seem to have quite as an appropriate reaction to the glory of Hatipai.

From the ground he also saw the heretic Onika raising the weirstone. His glory was nothing compared to his mother's. But somehow in his fitful delight, Merrick saw a parting of the shades, a gap in her armor of souls. And he reached deep for his training—throwing his mind into the puzzles and recitations he'd studied for years. In there he found a moment of respite.

"There." His voice cracked. "Onika, there!"

He had no Bond with the Prince as he had with Sorcha, but his voice was just loud enough to hear. Onika said a bright, hot word and threw the weirstone into the shadows and the gap that the Deacon had spotted.

Hatipai screamed, a sound that went deeper than bone, and the shadows flew high. Shades, those mindless, repetitive remains of souls, broke from her like a cloud of scattering crows. Merrick saw them escape the pull of the geistlord and was glad, though everything was mad and dead to him in that moment. Then the world was swallowed by darkness.

When consciousness found him again, his head was cradled in Nynnia's lap. Her fingers gently stroked his hair, calling him back to reality. It was a lovely moment, but eventually he found his feet.

Nothing dark remained on the blasted cliff top—only the Ehtia, their machine and Onika. "What happened?" The young Deacon turned to Nynnia, but it was the Prince who replied.

"She is gone . . . for now." His shoulders slumped. "I have bought you enough time to escape. The path is free for you to reach Mount Sytha, my friends." He sounded desperately alone. "She and I will continue our tussle once you are gone."

Nynnia grabbed him in a tight embrace. "You will find other allies, Onika. She is not as all-powerful as she thinks."

Then the Ehtia surrounded him, hugging him, whispering thanks in his ear—while Nynnia and Merrick stepped back.

The weight of sorrow pressed on the Deacon—especially as he knew how many lonely years Onika would have to endure. As the crew of the ship began to clamber back into the hatches, Merrick squeezed Nynnia's hand and went to speak to the Prince. "Thank you for what you are doing, Your Highness. The people of Chioma might not know what you sacrificed to keep them safe, but others do."

"I have to be a hero," Onika muttered, "or become like her."

"Then I hope you remember this—" Merrick paused, caught by the circular nature of this weird logic, before plunging on. "In the time of an Emperor called Kaleva, seek out a woman known as the flower of Da Nanth."

"Da Nanth?"

Naturally he wouldn't know of the principality—because it had not yet been created. It almost hurt his head to think about it, so he merely smiled. "Trust me, it is a place—though not yet."

The Prince frowned, but a spark of something that felt like hope lurked in his expression. "Thank you, my friend."

"Do not thank me"—Merrick clapped him on the shoulder—"thank Nynnia."

The Prince smiled uncertainly and embraced the woman. "Go safe into that place, old friend—part of me wishes I could come with you." He kissed the top of her head.

She laid her hands over his for an instant. "You have your people to take care of, Onika—and where we go, you cannot."

The Prince turned and sketched a little bow in Merrick's direction, the beaded mask swaying. Onika's voice was smooth, strong and just as it would be when next they encountered each other in throne room in the Hive City. "I find myself looking forward to meeting you again, Merrick Chambers."

As the Prince of Chioma left, the Deacon recalled his first meeting with the Prince. Looking back on it, he presumed Onika had recognized him. That damn mask always concealed so much—it was hardly a surprise that the ruler had developed a reputation as a mystery.

"Why can he not go with you?" Merrick found himself whispering to Nynnia.

She sighed and tapped him lightly on the arm, as if a teacher correcting a pupil who should have known better. "Think of it: a half human/half geist in that place. He would be torn apart by the geistlords shackled as he is with a mortal frame. They feed on the energy of their own kind there."

The Deacon shivered as he recalled the landscape of that dread place.

"Still, Onika made quite the impression on you, didn't he?" Nynnia's eyebrow crooked, and a slight smile lurked around her delectable lips.

"He certainly is . . . different." Merrick wrapped his arm around her waist. "Though my Emperor is a fine person, still some part of me is always surprised that anyone in power can be good—let alone the son of a 'goddess.'"

She nodded thoughtfully and then led him back into the tunneling machine. "I confess, we did not believe Onika when he first offered us his help. Many doubted that he would turn against his mother—but he proved himself." She took his hand and pulled him along a long corridor.

"Where are we going?" His stomach clenched as the machine began once again to descend—this time with no terrifying rolling.

"As Onika said"—Nynnia squeezed his fingers—"Mount Sytha. All of our people are gathering there to perform the ceremony."

The Nynnia on the Otherside had said there was a reason for her to send him here, and then she would bring him back to his own time. Merrick didn't want to go back—even if this world was falling apart. This was where Nynnia was still alive.

He knew that Sorcha was back in his own time, his mother too—and both Merrick knew were in deadly peril. The Deacon found himself torn between duty and happiness.

"And then what?" he asked, terribly afraid of the answer.

Nynnia stood poised with one hand on a door handle, her brow furrowed. "We have to atone for our crimes: swear off the use of weirstones and runes. Give up our bodies."

"You're leaving this world," Merrick whispered. "Traveling to the Otherside."

A muscle in her jaw twitched as she gave a sharp nod. "If we stay, Hatipai and the other geists will tear this world apart hunting us. We will go to the one place she dares not follow. Having anchored herself into this world with a focus, she can no longer go back to the Otherside—nor would she want to—the human meat here is so much sweeter. So, with our knowledge, we can build a place there—and maybe one day come home when it is safe."

Merrick pressed his lips together and closed his eyes—remembering the tales of that Dark Time. The suffering the people of this time were about to endure would be terrible. Yet from that maelstrom would arise the Order, the Rossin dynasty, and eventually the Empire. It would take hundreds of years, but they would conqueror the geistlords, even Hatipai, and learn to contain the lesser geists.

Nothing he could do would change that. Nor should it.

Nynnia pushed open the door, and he saw that it led into a small bedchamber with a reasonably sized bed bolted to the wall. A luxurious cerulean quilted blanket brightened what would otherwise have been rather bleak accommodations. He drew in his breath and shot the woman at his side a confused look. "Nynnia, I—"

She stopped his words most effectively by pulling his mouth down to hers. The kiss was long, desperate and sweet. When she finally let him go, her brown eyes were wide and her smile crooked. "When we leave this world, Merrick Chambers, we Ehtia will abandon our bodies—become part of the Otherside. I intend to give mine a proper send-off."

The Deacon's blood raced. Merrick wanted to grab what time there was that remained, but his gentlemanly sensibilities wouldn't let him take total advantage. "You hardly know me."

The pad of her thumb brushed his mouth. "But I know you love me, and sometime in the future, however that may happen, I will love you. When we next meet, I would have one of us remember these moments."

The Deacon's mind did another flip. It was all too complicated and painful.

"We will love each other," Merrick replied and let himself

be led into her bedroom. He said nothing of them losing each other again. That pain could wait.

Once the door was shut, nothing outside mattered. The Deacon did not care to think that this would be the one and only time for them—he pushed that realization as far back as he could. He would have her find nothing bitter in his mind.

Instead, Merrick took his time undressing Nynnia, even as she raced to strip him of his cloak, shirt and breeches.

"So young," she breathed, looking up at him. The comment was soft and almost sadly said.

Nynnia would in fact have taken a step back, but Merrick paused unbuttoning her blouse and captured her hand, pressing it firmly against his bare chest. "You will be young again someday—the very one we meet."

She frowned, shook her head, laughed and then leaned forward to kiss him. Perhaps there wasn't as much meaning for her as there was for him, yet it was still precious. Merrick delighted in her unashamed trust, when he released the last of her rather intricately tied trousers and she stepped back to allow him to look at her.

"You are beautiful, Nynnia," he said through a voice grown abruptly rough with desire. It was no lie; she was. However in the future she regained her youth, for right now, she had a lithe, muscular body, only slightly touched by age. He thought it ripe like a fruit brought to sugar and fullness.

Merrick ran his hand down her right arm and felt the ridges of five wide scars that streaked from shoulder to elbow. As he slid his palm around her, he was able to make out that they in fact took in half her back.

Nynnia looked at him so very earnestly. "Very few escape the geistlords without some sort of mark. I hope they don't put you off—"

When he bent and ran the sweep of his tongue against the ridges, she stopped mid-sentence and let out a low groan. Then Merrick pulled her with him as he flopped back on the bed. The sensation of the full length of their bodies pressed against each other with no unnatural hindrance was bliss.

Please let this go on forever. Merrick's head was spinning. The Nynnia he had met in his own time had loved him, but they had never been able to find a time to consummate those feelings. He had wanted to badly, and yet he'd been so wrapped up in being a Deacon, he'd missed the chance.

"Are you—" Nynnia's gaze narrowed, even as her breath began to come in shallow pants that were echoed by his own. "Are you a virgin?"

Sometimes telepathy was a double-edged sword—but Merrick had only become used to it between Sorcha and himself. Whatever gifts the Ehtia had meant that very few of his surface thoughts were sacrosanct.

Nynnia blushed. "I am sorry—you are broadcasting so loudly."

A chuckle rolled through his body. "Well, it is at the top of my concerns right now. I don't have much experience, but I am not quite a virgin. I just don't want to disappoint you."

Her teeth nibbled along the line of his neck, rising toward his ear, and suddenly those concerns melted away. Nynnia pulled back and licked her lips. "A handsome young man, travels back through time to find me, and beds me on my last day in this realm? How could you disappoint me?" Her voice was low, husky and laced with raw desire.

Warmth was stealing through Merrick, warmth that needed to be fulfilled, yet he couldn't help it. One tiny thought ran like a dark streak through this moment of utter bliss. "I want more. I want the woman I love forever."

She could have replied something trite. She could have leapt off him, offended. Instead, Nynnia only smiled sadly and kissed him.

Yes, Merrick realized, he might only have this moment with her, but only a few hours of his time before this, she had been dead. It would be churlish to diminish the delight of finding her alive and in his embrace. He would not sully this gift.

Deacon Chambers put aside all those nagging fears and doubts and plunged into the moment. Soon enough she would be gone. Soon enough they would all be gone.

The Rossin's roar faded even as Sorcha screamed after him—a sound that echoed the pain inside her—a confused mix of loss and anger. The geistlord was still as he had been when first she had encountered him, and even worse, she remembered how it had felt to *be* him.

As she ran to the window and watched the elegant, massive creature bound off the edge of the terrace, she nearly forgot to snuff out the rune burning on her Gauntlet.

The great lion was beautiful, terrifying, destructive, and it had just carried Raed away. Yet, for an instant she stood there, quite forgetting the mess that the geistlord had just made.

By the Bones, she thought to herself, I am *not* pining after the Rossin. Her hands clenched on the broken window, the glass crunching under her Gauntlet.

A burbling cry behind her made the Deacon spin on her heel. Lady Lisah was sobbing, spluttering, her eyes wide as blood trickled from her mouth—scarlet red against her pale skin. Unable to speak, her hand was spread and stretched toward Sorcha. Only minutes before they had been adversaries—now they were just people.

The Deacon dropped to her knees, stripped off her Gauntlets, and clenched the dying woman's hand tightly in her own fist; that which had been so beautiful, flawless and cosseted was torn and gaping. Too much was now outside that should be inside.

Sorcha didn't know how powerful the healers were here in Chioma—so perhaps there was still hope. Blood bubbled and ran through her fingers as Sorcha pressed down on the wound, trying to stop it from gushing. It was warm and sticky, but the worst of it was the desperate look in Lisah's eyes—as if the Deacon could save her.

Sorcha whispered to her—foolish, impossible things that were becoming more so. It had been a long time since she'd comforted the dying. That first year when the Emperor landed at Arkaym she had experienced it quite enough. And now, looking down at this beautiful woman whom she had so easily judged as vapid, Sorcha thought of those young Initiates they had lost. Certainly she had hoped to never be in this position again.

Desperately she pushed down harder. "Listen, Lisah. Help will be here soon—don't give up." The younger woman's mouth worked as her face grew paler. She was trying to say something, but there was no air in her lungs—only blood.

Then she spasmed, gouts of her life pumping over Sorcha's hand. Lisah's gaze went from full of life to glazed and empty in a split second—so quick that Sorcha could not have said when it was she had gone. Her beautiful bright blue eyes were now surround by scarlet drops she coughed up.

Unable to save the poor woman, Sorcha opened her Center and waited. She might have failed to protect the innocent women of the harem, but she watched as their shades gathered and made sure no geist took them on this side. Their souls swirled, confused by the abrupt severance from their bodies—and that was why most shades stayed in the human world. Sorcha would not let these women suffer that fate.

Slipping her Gauntlets over her blood-drenched hands, she pressed them down against the cooling flesh of Lisah. The rune-clad leather would not hold the blood, and without Merrick, the added presence of it would help make the connection easier.

"I'm sorry," Sorcha whispered as she opened Tryrei, the peephole to the Otherside. What they would find there she could not say, but it was the way souls had to pass for any chance of peace. The tiny gold light pierced reality, and the souls drifted toward it.

Maybe there were gods waiting for them as some said—she wished she could believe that. Maybe it was a place of trial before they could be reborn. It wasn't her place to say, but at least the slain women would not be condemned to walk the earth repeating the moments of their death.

Sorcha watched them go and then closed her fist around the rune. These were not the first people she had been unable to save—and would likely not be the last, either.

With a soft sigh the Deacon leaned over and closed Lisah's eyes, smearing blood on her face but at least giving her an illusion of peace.

It was at that moment that the eunuch guards shoved open the door. For a minute Sorcha stared at them as they took in the room. Books scattered around the room, shelves pushed over, three women's bodies dismembered, and there she was sitting in the middle of it all—covered in blood and gore.

Deacons were considered necessary—yet it was not unheard of for them to go suddenly and spectacularly mad. The hospital at the Mother Abbey had a whole ward devoted to the care and restriction of such poor creatures. In all the Empire there was no more dangerous madman than a Deacon.

Then Sorcha realized how it looked to these new arrivals. She had asked to see these women; she had demanded they be alone. The Chiomese guards might have respect for the Deacons of their own realm, but she was a stranger—a stranger wearing her gauntlets and bathed in the blood of the Prince's women.

The rifles in the guards' hands spun and were quickly raised to their shoulders. The tallest eunuch, the one who had brought in the women to see her, bared his teeth at her, his brow darkening like a thundercloud. These women were his charges, so she knew he was not going to stop and ask questions.

These men had been bearing the shame of deaths all around them for weeks—and now they had a very convenient target to blame. One dead Deacon would make a handy scapegoat to drag before their Prince. Dead would be preferable to alive.

Without a single word of protest, Sorcha sprang to her feet, leapt over Lisah's body, and ran toward the inner wall. Unlike the Rossin, she couldn't survive a jump through the window— but fleeing into the city was a very good idea. She was not about to take her chances with the guards or even the Prince— who surely, with the deaths of his women, would be considerably less gracious.

"Fire!" the chief eunuch bellowed, and the Deacon dived as bullets spat over the chaotic scene. Luckily, the opportunities for these guards to shoot at anything must have been few.

With her Gauntlet outspread and Voishem blazing on its palm before her, Sorcha leapt through the wall. It was a most inelegant use of her training.

The sound of bullets spitting against the hardened mud was the last thing she heard as she phased through the wall and tumbled onto the other side. In this situation she had no time to find somewhere to wash off the blood and think. Sorcha knew she had to keep using Voishem until she was beyond the palace and into the city.

The Deacon dared not stop running, knowing that soon enough the whole city would be in an uproar, looking for the stranger who had gone mad and slain women of the Prince's harem. Already she could faintly hear the palace alarm bell ringing. While in the grasp of Voishem, everything was dim and out of sync with her eyes. People were reduced to gray shadows, and the palace itself looked more like an artist's sketch than something real.

Sorcha knew she had to find the Rossin and stop his rampage at all costs—there simply was no one else who had a chance of controlling the Beast. So she dashed through the palace, hearing screams echo softly in her wake, and the rune she dared not release drained her strength. She was running blind without Merrick's power to help her and would have to take a gamble.

Wherever you are, Merrick—come back soon. I need you.

And with that final thought, Sorcha passed through the thick mud walls of the palace and out into the chaos of the city itself.

⇥ TWENTY-THREE ⇤

Freedom and Fight

The Rossin was running, and for once it had nothing to do with his need for the taste of blood. The women in the harem had given him his fill, and he was strong on it. Instead he was running toward something just as tasty: revenge.

His wide paws struck the sturdy mud roofs of the Hive City precisely and loudly. Flocks of shrieking birds fled from their nests as he thundered past them. Citizens below caught glimpses of the lion as he leapt between buildings, and their screams, which would have once satisfied him, now were as meaningless as the squawks of the birds.

For the first time in a very, very long time, the geistlord known as the Rossin had a mission, and his golden-flecked eyes were narrowed on the target.

Ahead, close to the curve of the river, was the Temple of Hatipai. Even thinking that name brought a snarl of hatred from the massive chest of the Beast.

In the thick jungles to the east of Chioma there were snakes that preyed upon other snakes; they were the most feared of the poisonous creatures that crawled in Arkaym. And now, one of those creatures, or at least the geist equivalent, had come home to her lair.

The Rossin stopped on a wide rooftop at the edge of the

city and rested for a moment. In a body of flesh, the geistlord enjoyed the heady rush of blood in his veins and the joy of a heart pounding in his chest. His tongue ran over the curve of white canine teeth and licked over his muzzle, drawing in the last few drops of blood that stained his fur. The Rossin contemplated the last small distance between him and his goal.

Ahead the palace complex finished and the long, well-guarded road to the port and markets of the city began. No more rooftops remained to provide him access.

He was not out of breath or frightened at the prospect of going down among the humans, but he was worried about alerting her that he was coming. The proud head of the Rossin turned to glare once more at the Temple. No Deacon of the Order could have scanned the horizon as well as he did—but if they had been able, they would have trembled.

Through unearthly eyes that saw better than any human and pierced deep into the reality of this world, he watched a great storm drawing in on the kingdom of Chioma and its Prince. The patterned fur on the Rossin's head rippled, and he raised his head and sniffed. The odor was of the tomb and lost hopes—the smell of the long dead—something that the Rossin despised but she loved. Hatipai's adoring followers had no rest, even when they were dead. The self-styled goddess had that much of a hold on them.

Nearly a thousand years before, it had been the family that bore his name that had, with his assistance, trapped her beneath Vermillion. His lip pulled back from his fangs at the memory of that bright and terrible battle. Now the tables had turned. She was in the ascendant, while the bloodline that had protected him was whittled down to two fragile twigs.

The great cat felt his ire rise and perhaps a little fear. Hatipai had destroyed many geists and geistlords, and the Rossin had only survived because he had not done as many of his kind had done—relied on faith and worship. It had not been easy to become part of a human bloodline, yet it had proved to be the smartest choice.

I survived. I triumphed, the Rossin thought, even as the unfamiliar edge of fear began to gnaw at him. Yet there was something else . . .

He looked east, feeling a tug in that direction and knowing

full well what it meant. Only one other possible home for him remained—the sister of this body, the young one, Fraine.

The Rossin knew very well that it was no coincidence that both Raed and Fraine were here now, so close and in the domain of Hatipai. She might not yet have a usable body, but his enemy had allies, human and otherwise. She always had.

His huge head swung back toward the distant yet looming Temple. If they found what was hidden there—

That thought decided the Rossin. Flinging back his head, he let out a thundering roar that bounced off the red mud buildings. It was his defiance and his warning to Hatipai. Her star had not yet risen so far that he could not knock it back down.

The Rossin sprang down from the building and landed right among a train of camels heading in the opposite direction. They brayed and danced and kicked to get away. Chaos as always followed in the Rossin's wake.

Men and beasts in the pack train panicked. Loads strapped to the camels' backs were flung loose as the animals bucked and spat and tried to get out of the lion's way.

For his part, the geistlord hissed, snarled and struck out. The smell of animal sweat and panic mingled with that of heady, iron-rich blood, and for a second he went mad with it. The Rossin bit down and ripped out the throat of a beast that got in his way. The spurt of life into his mouth was a brief joy, but he remembered his goal, whirled on his back paws and sprang up the road toward the Temple.

The road was busy, packed with merchants, guards and every kind of humanity in between. The Rossin plowed through them, scattering the travelers like chaff. He snapped and bit while he went but did not stop to enjoy the sensation of destruction. His concentration was focused on the road and the Temple ahead. He had to get there and make sure the unholy device of the Ehtia was secure.

At the gates to the town a squadron of Chiomese guards were able to throw together a defense. They could not have missed the rising screams and roars that marked his coming, and so the portcullis was being lowered behind them and riflemen were ranged on the battlements above.

These recent inventions were not to the Rossin's liking, and he bellowed his rage. They responded with a volley of rifle fire that filled the air with buzzing lead. When they struck the great lion's patterned hide they *hurt*. They made him snap and snarl, but the pain was fleeting, his body knitting and healing what humanity wounded. The Rossin had fought far more deadly foes than a group of mere guards.

As swordsmen rushed out bravely to confront him, the Beast leapt in among them, streaks of his own blood drying in his fur. The guards didn't stand a chance, but the Rossin appreciated their bravery even as he ripped and shredded them. He tore shields away and clawed through armor, yet many survived. Those who got knocked down or broke and ran, he left.

The Temple was not getting any closer. The Rossin charged the portcullis, hearing more guards running down from inside the tower. For creatures with such short life spans, they were in an awful hurry to waste themselves under his claws. However, he could not tarry to aid them in their destruction. The portcullis rattled and shook in its casing but was made of stern iron. The outraged guards were yelling and shooting. The noise drove the frustrated Rossin to the breaking point.

With a heave of his muscular shoulders the Beast flung his whole weight and might against the gate. The metal did not give at first, but his sharp ears heard the sound of the mud brick walls groaning under his assault. Again and again under the rattle of rifle fire the Rossin threw himself against the portcullis, roaring and snarling as he had not since the Break. Eventually the walls could take no more, and around the gate the bricks cracked like dropped eggs. Huge pieces of red earth fractured and flew away in thick shards.

And then with a massive shrieking groan, the gate toppled. The Rossin came with it as it slammed into the ground. The iron hadn't stopped ringing and the dust had not even settled before the lion was off and running. Soon he had left the rifle shots and the shouting guards behind.

The streets in the city were mercifully clear—so the great lion knew that alerts must have been sounded. He took the chance and bunched his muscular haunches under him and bounded through the streets, heading straight for the Temple.

Luckily, all the main roads led to her place. Hatipai was predictable in that way. All the geistlords who survived as she did had suffered the same arrogance—they began to believe what their worshippers told them. They began to believe they were indeed gods. This weakness made them much easier to find.

The Rossin leapt up stacked crates in the marketplace onto the red rooftops of the city. Below he could see streams of people running through the streets. They were singing and dancing, waving their hands about and laughing. As much as he wanted to be down there among them, tasting their blood, he knew that his great enemy was near. He could in fact hear her.

His lip pulled back from his long fangs, and a snarl rumbled in his chest. Her voice ran through the ether. *Come to me, my children. I have returned.* To her followers it would have been a beautiful balm, a siren song; to the Rossin it was an irritating buzz that set his fur to standing on end.

So he would save his rage for her and not the foolish humans. The great cat's claws clenched on the mud brick, and then he leapt across to the next rooftop, following the direction of the crowd below.

The Temple stood in a square and reeked of faith and desperation—her stock in trade. The large carved representation of her lay sprawled on the roof, and the Rossin could not be sure that she wasn't smiling. Yet he could not smell her nearby.

The great Beast roared again. A group of more guards, only half a dozen, were clad in red and standing by the Temple doorway. The Rossin recognized them as Imperial, and his stride faltered. Was he too late?

The one advantage faith did bring to Hatipai was that she had had and most assuredly still did have plenty of unquestioning followers to do her bidding. She didn't need to be corporeal or even the littlest bit present at this moment to have her will carried out.

However, there was still a chance. He bounded up the stairs, sailing over the heads of the astonished guards in a leap that carried him to the doorway. That was when he saw the woman standing in the shadows, waiting.

The Rossin snarled and brought himself up short before reaching her, because she held in her hand the one thing that he had feared. The foolish Ehtia might have gone, but they had left behind plenty of dangerous devices. Things that even a geistlord might find of use.

The Ehtia device was a sphere of glass filled with that strange silvery substance—the very one he had helped Onika of Chioma rip from his mother centuries before. They had been uncomfortable allies back then, but both of them were aware that Hatipai would destroy the world eventually. The Rossin had never wanted the world to end. He liked the blood, the flesh and the freedom here. Why Onika had turned against his mother the geistlord did not ask nor care to ask.

Yet the Prince was not here.

The dark-haired woman holding the Ehtia sphere had that glazed look in her eyes, the look that the Rossin had not forgotten after all this time. Hatipai might not yet have form, but she had presence in this woman. She held the sphere aloft and smiled at him. It was not a human smile.

"Too late, old friend," she whispered, and the voice came from no human lungs—instead it was coming from a very long way off.

The cat's head flicked up, looking for the light that would signal she was nearby, but there was none. Hatipai was taking the safer option and remaining incorporeal.

It was too late; the Rossin realized that. Now the only option was too flee and protect the body and bloodline he had. Swinging around on his haunches, he changed the flesh to his avian form. Wide wings sprouted from his back, and his feline head shifted to that of a massive eagle, but the rest of his body remained that of the lion. The Rossin leapt to the sky, knowing his escape would be a momentary reprieve. If his enemy succeeded, then running would become his only chance. He would find the female Deacon—she might fill the gap left by the now-weak Prince.

Hatipai had been nothing if not relentless in all the time he had known her. She had shown no mercy for their kind, perhaps even less than what little she showed the humans.

However, the geistlord was wrong. Immediately and suddenly wrong. This was not the beginning of his flight—this was the end.

The sky darkened in a moment, and the clouds that caused it were nothing natural. It was her followers. Every soul who had worshipped Hatipai filled with an intense hatred of the geistlords. The Rossin's newly formed wings had only lofted him to the height of the buildings around him when the swarm of spectyrs descended.

Like diving eagles they shot through him, leaving no physical mark but ripping through the geistlord and taking away a little of his power. It would take more than one to bring down the Rossin—but this was a cloud of them, thicker and more deadly than a thunderstorm. They flew through the geistlord with their anger and their pain and their loss.

Each one pierced him. He screamed and howled and batted his wings, trying to rise above them, to flee into the open sky. Yet they kept coming.

The Rossin roared and fell, tumbling back to earth with the cry of a frustrated eagle. Nothing remained to save himself, as he smashed into the ground only a few feet from the steps on which the woman stood.

The spectyrs were remorseless. Each one was ripping away at his strength, and he was given no choice. He had to flee back deeper inside his host or be lost entirely.

As the Rossin released control, he heard the woman approach, her boots rapping on the cobble street, and he smelled death wrapping around him. She bent down and whispered into his ear, "You see, old friend, it is as I promised—you will pay for what you did to me."

What she meant to do, the Rossin had a very good idea. He didn't want to, but he did the only thing now possible. Taking hold of the Deacon Bond, he called to the female. Now she was his only hope. She would save him in the name of his host. She had to.

Voishem was an exhausting rune to hold up by herself, so by the time Sorcha was free of the palace, she was staggering.

Emerging through the outermost palace wall, she took a ragged, gasping breath. It felt like it was the first she had taken since before the ghast appeared. Her heart thundered in her chest, and her whole body shook. Everything was spinning and out of focus so that she thought she might throw up her breakfast.

If any Chiomese guards came upon the Deacon now, there wasn't a thing she could do about it. They could have sliced her into a million tiny pieces, and Sorcha would not be able to raise a hand to stop them. Even breathing was an effort. Only the firmness of the wall at her back kept her sitting up, which was ironic, after running through so many.

She pushed her hair back out of her eyes and with numb fingers tried to tuck the loose strands back into the braid. This simple habit gave her a moment to recover herself. When she was done, Sorcha looked about to see where she'd come out.

By sheer happenstance she'd not directly appeared near any main road. Instead she was in the shade of a guard tower. Perhaps this was not the luckiest place, but when she'd run it had been completely blind, so she was lucky she'd not dropped into a cesspit or materialized over a cliff.

Cautiously Sorcha flicked her cloak out, and on hands and knees, not yet daring her feet, she crawled to the outer edge of the tower to peer around it. Perhaps it was a kind of arrogance to imagine that all of the palace's attention was directed at finding her, because what she saw before her implied that the Rossin had also made quite the impression.

The Beast had cut a wide swath through the guards and citizens of the Hive City. Bodies were still lying about, as if a very angry small child had cast them right and left while leaving a very large nursery. Except there was blood—lots and lots of blood. As a Deacon, Sorcha had seen plenty of such atrocities. What concerned her more was Raed. He had mentioned that he only remembered flashes of what the Rossin did while in possession of his body—but they were enough to weigh him with guilt and revulsion.

Sorcha sat back and leaned against the wall for the moment. Losing both men was unacceptable. Though she had no idea where her partner was, she could feel the tug of the Rossin inside her. The rampant delight in blood and chaos was such a heady mix that she had to pull back or be lost in it.

"Unholy Bones," Sorcha whispered and slumped back on her heels to slide her head into her hands. Passing through so many walls and using Voishem more than she ever had before had taken every ounce of her strength. She was unsure how much more she had to give. Without Merrick she was risking her life and her sanity drawing on the runes.

Though Raed was out there, if she made any move toward

him, she was bound to get caught by the guards. Sorcha clenched her jaw tight, feeling a very odd sensation—a mixture of panic and desperation. Yet driving it was something even stranger—loneliness.

"What do I do?" she said to absolutely no one.

Ever since she could remember she had been surrounded by Deacons: teachers, fellow Initiates and her partners. Even before she had mastered the runes she had felt part of something greater and had known that whatever she did, they would be there to catch her.

No, Sorcha thought, I am not going to cry. To do so would have been weak and pointless.

Taking a deep breath, Sorcha pulled out a cigar from her pocket and lit it as a way of trying to find her focus. Pulling the thick smoke into her mouth, she held it there, letting it tingle on her tongue as she thought as logically as she could.

She could go to the Abbey in the city to throw herself on the mercy of her fellow Deacons, yet there was Hatipai hanging over that option like a dark cloud. The Prince himself had said he could not trust his Deacons—so there had to be some corruption there that the Mother Abbey was not aware of. It would not be the first time, she thought with a wry twist of her mouth. The Order she had once thought of as a towering megalith of protection for the common folk had lately been proven full of cracks.

Since the goings on in Ulrich, she was disabused of her former certainty in the sanctity of the Order. The Deacons, which Sorcha loved and believed in, had been compromised in both Ulrich and the capital of Vermillion. The Chiomese outposts were very different from any she'd ever seen—but the attachment to Hatipai made every one of her instincts prickle. Lately she had been forced to rely on her instincts more and more, but comfort she had once had in the Order she really did miss. Especially at moments like this.

However, throwing herself on the mercy of the Prince was just as dangerous. Looking down, Sorcha realized both her shirt and her arms were caked in blood, some of it dry and some of it still damp and sticky. If she was to do anything other than cower in this place, she had to fix that.

Burying her fingers in the sand, Sorcha used a handful to

scrub as best she could. It got rid of most of the blood but dirtied her in equal measure. Her cloak was easy enough to turn around. The strange thought that popped into her head that the last time she had done this was at the funeral procession for Arch Abbot Hastler. Shortly after that, she and Merrick had broken the Young Pretender out of prison.

Raed . . . She swallowed. This was another mess for them—another one that meant more running and less time to be together. Even so, it wasn't as if they could ever be an actual couple—a Pretender to the throne she had sworn to protect. Yet apparently her emotions knew none of that. She'd run through all the possibilities—and only he remained.

Propping her cigar on her boot, Sorcha closed her eyes and pushed out. The Bond, which she had made with so little thought, connected them and made it impossible for him to be lost as long as he was in the same world.

Something was wrong. Sorcha's head began to hurt as she concentrated. Pain flared suddenly along every nerve ending she had, and the cause was the Bond. The Deacon pressed harder even as the agony continued. The Rossin was there, wrapped around Raed, but somehow shrinking and sliding away. The smell of sweat and panic filled her nostrils right up until the moment she could take no more.

With a shuddering breath she had to let go of the Bond. With the second round of the shakes setting in, Sorcha picked up her cigar and sucked a mouthful of smoke. It helped distract her from the echoes of pain still running through her body—since it felt like every muscle was spasming to its own rhythm. So she sat very still until it passed, focusing on the fact that, whatever else may be happening, Raed was still alive. What she did hold on to very tightly was that he was still alive.

Once Sorcha had finished, she stubbed out the cigar, brushed off her clothing as best she could, then with a little twinge of guilt, turned her cloak inside out and tucked the badge of the Eye and the Fist into her pocket. If the Order wasn't going to look after her, then she would have to look after herself.

Merrick, she thought as she set off toward the Temple: *Come back soon, because, by the Bones—I need your help.*

TWENTY-FOUR

Return to Reality

Merrick could not recall having fallen into sleep—yet he must have. His last memory was the smoothness of Nynnia's skin, the warmth of lovemaking and the feeling of completeness. Unfortunately these were not sensations that could last.

I had to have this. He heard her in his dreams, her voice ringing like a crystal bell far off in the distance. *I had to have this moment with you. I had to not just because it happened but for us. When I saw you that first time I had not forgotten your touch, your love. It was because of you I chose to be born back into the world.*

The light of the Ehtia building on the Otherside burned against his eyelids, but he would not look. He didn't want to see the Nynnia who lived there; he didn't want the cold, bodiless image of her to overtake the one he had been holding just minutes before. She lived beyond his reach, and there was no comfort in that fact.

Instead, Merrick waited until the light receded and he could not hear her voice in his head anymore. He was empty. Only then did Deacon Chambers open his eyes.

He was lying in a pile of straw while a set of beautiful brown eyes were watching him. They were, however, not the ones he had fallen to sleep beneath. A very curious camel was breathing heavily on him—and her breath was not sweet. In fact, it might have been the worst thing he had ever smelled had he not been dealing with geists for a long time.

Levering himself upright, Merrick found himself dressed when he most assuredly had been naked when last he lay down. More of Nynnia's magic.

The young Deacon got to his feet and picked hay out of his cloak, while the offended camel jigged sideways, snorting and shaking its head on its long, shaggy neck. Thankfully she did not spit.

Looking around, the red mud buildings told him that he was once more in the Hive City, but when in time that might be exactly was another question. It came back to him with a rush. The Bond. The connection. Merrick's vision blurred, and he was immediately relieved; Sorcha was nearby.

And if she was here, then Nynnia had managed to drop him back in the right place and time. The Ehtia were indeed powerful. Some part of him wished that he'd taken more notes, asked more questions—perhaps have brought back some of that power for the Deacons. Another part altogether wasn't sorry for an instant of the time that he had managed to snatch with Nynnia.

Merrick walked in a somewhat tentative fashion from the yard and peered out onto the street, trying to orient himself. Turning his head to the left, he felt that was where Sorcha was. Her mood was easy to read: dark and despairing. Even in the madness under Vermillion, she had not felt like this.

Reaching along the Bond, he alerted her to his presence. Her reaction was an almost overwhelming surge of relief and delight. They had come a long way from that first awkward pairing that the Arch Abbot Hastler had thrust them into.

We are a good team. Her voice in his head was clear as a matins bell. Many partners in the Order would have been jealous of Merrick and Sorcha's powerful Bond—if they had dared reveal it.

Raed! Sorcha directed Merrick's attention to the other part of the Bond: the Young Pretender. Immediately he flinched back as pain burst through the connection.

Merrick groaned and doubled up, his hand going against

the smooth mud wall to stop himself from falling. What exactly had happened while he'd been gone?

Find me. Sorcha's call was her usually abrupt tone but mitigated by her genuine fear. *Things are happening.*

Like a needle seeking magnetic north, Merrick turned and strode toward her. After a moment he broke into a jog. He was not the only one running. It didn't take a Sensitive to notice that everything was wrong in the city. Where before there had been organized chaos, with the streets full of merchants and citizens, now there was no one in the streets except for the occasional person darting for their house. Until Merrick turned onto one of the main streets—and then he discovered just where nearly everyone was.

The main street of Orinthal was choked with its citizens, and every single one of them was wearing the mustard yellow of Hatipai, either cloaks or merely torn strips of cloth bound around their arms. Merrick stepped back and hugged the wall. Maybe it was some local festival.

He opened his Center wider, tasting the air like a dog sniffing the breeze. A crowd, any crowd, could be a frightening thing; but this one full of religious fervor frightened him down to his bones.

And there was more. A sensation akin to turning his back on a lurking danger. Every hair on his neck was standing up, and every muscle was twitching. As he spun around, he wouldn't have been surprised to find someone coming at him with an upraised knife.

Taking a chance, Merrick peered out onto the street again. The people were moving silently and smiling, but he spotted disturbances at the edge. Some of the citizens of Orinthal were not entirely happy with this display of religious zealotry. Unbelievers were being beaten and kicked in the side streets. The crowd ignored all that, moving like a sluggish beast but not toward the palace.

Wait, he projected to Sorcha. He couldn't walk away from this situation—he had to see more. With dread knotting his heart, he found a building with soft stone steps leading up to a flat roof. Until he reached the top of them, Merrick kept his eyes cast on the ground. Before he raised them, he opened his Center wide, flinging open everything that he had as a Sensitive. The sun was beginning to fall toward the horizon, sending beams of scarlet and umber light darting over the buildings and making them glow. It would have been a beautiful sight, but for Merrick it was a bloody vision, punctuated with shadows and dire portents.

The spectyrs were no longer content with occupying the distant mountains; like the humans, they were heading east into the desert. The sky was thick and dark in his vision—though none of the citizens seemed aware of it as they trooped off under its shadow.

Merrick's fear rattled through the Bond, and he could feel Sorcha's response, like an echo on a taut string. With a wrench Merrick closed his Center and staggered back into the real world.

I'm coming, he called along the Bond to Sorcha. As he leapt down the steps back to the road, he saw her in a nearby alley. She was wearing the cloak of the Order but turned wrong way around, the blue of the Active hidden by the black. It reminded him starkly of Hastler's funeral and the long ranks of the Deacons mourning that liar. Sorcha's face then had been calmer than the one he saw under the hood now. He had never seen her paler or with wider eyes, and she smelled of blood. She was running too—like they were two parts of something broken that needed mending.

Merrick darted forward, and they threw themselves into each other's arms. It was not the embrace of lovers, but it still contained love. The Bond wrapped around them until for a brief heartbeat there was nothing but the two of them. It was an echo of the time under Vermillion—the time when they had in fact been one.

Finally Sorcha tugged him off the street into a darker part of the humid alleyway. "By the Bones," she whispered, not letting go of his forearm, "it is good to see you, Merrick."

His partner had a lovely way of repeating emotions that their Bond already told him, but this was not the time to chide her. This close, his Deacon senses told him that she was indeed soaked in blood and sweat under the cloak.

"What happened?" he asked, his eyes already darting into

the shadows, though he could not sense Raed anywhere. In fact . . .

"He's gone," Sorcha snapped. "I couldn't stop the Rossin without you, and he transformed right in the palace. People died, and they're hunting me, thinking I did it."

She delivered a hint of an accusation to go with his sliver of sudden guilt. Yet that was foolish—Nynnia had shown him things, taken him places he needed to be. Instead, Merrick clasped her arm right back, completing the link. "Then that is what we need to do—find Raed and sort this out."

As Merrick turned to go back out onto the street, his partner stopped him. "Where *were* you, Merrick?" The crack in her voice was something that he had not expected.

He wasn't ready yet. The tumble of time and death was something that he needed to sort into words. But he knew Sorcha would not let him get away without some form of explanation. "Nynnia saved me," he said simply, surprised at the steadiness in his own voice.

Those blue eyes widened, and then a frown creased her forehead. "Nynnia is dead, Merrick." She was afraid for his sanity.

"I am not crazy—you would feel it if I was." He smiled. "And yes, Nynnia is dead . . . but also alive."

Sorcha sighed, her lips twisted into a knot of frustration. "You Sensitives are hard to understand at the best of times. What do you mean?"

"I will tell you all soon." Merrick found he was rather enjoying flummoxing his partner. He clamped his hand around her arm, giving it a firm squeeze when she looked ready to demand more. "They have taken Raed, and we need to get him back quickly."

Sorcha's gaze unfocused slightly, her head lifting and turning east where the spectyrs had disappeared. "Yes." Her voice was soft, concerned, not the usual from his sometimes prickly partner. It remained unspoken how many cruel and evil things the blood of his ancient line could be used for.

"What do we do?" Merrick couldn't be sure, but that could have been the first time Sorcha had turned to him for advice so completely. She was older, more experienced and far more confident than he was. Usually.

He thought back on what had happened during his trip into the past: the determined, dark face of the Ehtia and the great crushing despair in the divine face of Onika. They were in a strange city, unable to trust their own Brothers and Sisters of the Order, and far from the protection of the Arch Abbey. Only one person remained who knew the way of things here.

Merrick straightened. "We go to the Prince and lay the case before him."

His partner jerked upright. "Remember when I said people died? One of them was his daughter. I think going back there would be a quick trip to the gallows or maybe a rapid introduction to a bullet."

"I think, with me standing at your side, we should be all right."

"I don't care what the Bond says—I think you have gone raving mad!" Sorcha snapped, her voice reclaiming some of her usual bravado.

"We'll be fine." Merrick pressed the flat of his hand against her back, guiding her toward the palace. "Onika owes me a favor."

She batted his hand away and glared at him. "You better explain yourself before we get there. I hate mysteries."

Despite the situation and what he had lost, Merrick couldn't help but laugh. By the time they reached the palace, he just knew she would be convinced of his madness.

Raed felt the world claim him again, and it was not a pretty thing. His muscles ached right down to his bones, so he knew that the Rossin had taken a lot from his body. The taste of blood in his mouth confirmed it.

His eyes were glued shut, and he wasn't sure for a moment if he had enough strength to lever them open. So the Young Pretender lay still, trying to take in his surroundings.

As the aching subsided, he was able to perceive that he was lying on something that was swaying, so it had to be a carriage or cart. No, a carriage, because under his left cheek he could feel the softness of some kind of brocade.

Outside, wheels were turning, but it did not sound as though it were on gravel or cobblestones. Instead, he could hear the hiss of something far softer than any of those surfaces. His mind made the connection only slowly; the wheels were running over compacted sand.

And if they were doing that, then they were no longer in the Hive City. Raed struggled to control his breathing as he flicked through the images of what had happened before the Rossin took him.

Something had attacked them in the library. He'd been standing next to Sorcha and had felt the geist only for a second before the Rossin inside had reacted as he always did.

The Young Pretender inhaled sharply though his nose, because there was another familiar sensation he suddenly recognized: the pull of blood dried onto his skin. Was it Sorcha's? Had he killed the one woman he had dared to have feelings for just as he had his own mother?

"You did take life, Raed Syndar Rossin." The voice was just across from him, low, accented and somehow familiar—he just had to sort through memories to get to it. But everything was too sluggish, just as it always was after awaking from possession by the Rossin.

So he yanked his eyelids apart, and Grand Duchess Zofiya looked back at him. If Raed could have picked anyone to be sitting opposite him in the fine carriage, it would never have been her. His one and only contact with the sister of the Emperor had been back in Vermillion when he had taken a bullet for her.

In that split second she had looked grateful—even if her brother had later thrown Raed into prison. Now her beautiful dark eyes were leveled on him with far less grace, and more than that. If he hadn't known better, he might have thought she was growing cataracts. Yet she didn't appear to have any trouble seeing him.

In the impossible heat she was wearing a sheer white garment that only barely concealed her admirable curves. Again, the last time he had seen the Grand Duchess she had been wearing the Imperial Guard red uniform—and from what he had heard, that was all she ever wore—even to state events. Another strangeness.

Raed pushed with his hands, levering himself off the carriage seat, but quickly found that they were bound, and it was not with anything he had ever encountered before, but he knew what they were immediately.

"Weirstones." He held up his hands before him, swaying slightly and still a little muzzy. The string of tiny stones gleamed like diamonds in front of his slowly focusing eyes. "Really—you shouldn't have."

Zofiya laughed, but it was a short sound with no real amusement behind it. "But if I did not, then your passenger would become very troublesome."

Raed twisted so that he was sitting a little more comfortably on the seat, though it still felt precarious. His feet were bound in the same fashion. "It takes very little to restrain the Rossin." He measured how far it was across to the Grand Duchess, but at this moment he remained curious rather than angry.

She leaned back, some of the baking Chiomese sun filtering in through the curtains and outlining her form even more in the thin white dress. Raed was aware, if not entirely immune, to her tactics. Zofiya was a beautiful woman, and the dress not only showed off her womanly curves but also the lines of honed muscles years of military training had given her. He began to reconsider how great his chances of overcoming her physically really were.

"It is not merely the weirstones that restrain the Rossin," Zofiya replied, "but the fact that he was soundly beaten."

Raed had dreamed most of his life of hearing someone saying that to him—telling him they had a way to defeat the great geistlord that haunted his life. Sorcha, Merrick and the Bond had given him some comfort, but he had never thought that there could be any more.

Raed was not comforted—not when her smile did not reach her strange eyes. Raed knew about possession better than most, and there were many small signs of it on Grand Duchess Zofiya: a tiny twitch under her right eye, unusual fashion choices, and a complete lack of sweat on her body.

"What are you," he asked through dry lips, "to sit there talking so calmly about beating the Rossin, when most people don't even want to say his name?"

She gestured down her body. "I dare because I am protected." When she shifted, Raed saw something that his

blurry eyes had not noticed before. Sitting on the seat next to
her was a mahogany box, large enough to hold a man's head.
He wondered if that was what was in it. "My goddess Hatipai
has cast her cloak over me, and even your passenger carries no
dread for me."

"A goddess?" Raed couldn't help letting out a little snort of
disbelief. "You are relying on the protection of a little god
against the Rossin?"

She moved so fast that all he felt on his skin was the sting
of her slap. She had enough strength behind her attack to rock
him back in the seat, and something else—a brush of power
that tasted familiar. It was gone too quickly for him to identify, but the Young Pretender was left staring at the Grand
Duchess with a new appreciation.

"Don't you dare talk about things you have no idea of," she
whispered to him over bared teeth. "You may call them
little—but Hatipai is a living goddess—my living goddess!"

Raed rubbed his cheek somewhat awkwardly and smiled
in what he planned on being a charming manner. "A gentle-
man doesn't like to bring up debts in front of a lady, but this
seems hardly fair, considering I saved your life only a season
ago."

She tilted her head, her luminous dark eyes full of regal
pride. "And a Grand Duchess does not acknowledge what is
hers by right. Every citizen of Arkaym does his duty when he
protects the royal family."

Now, that pinched his pride. "I have never sworn an oath to
you or your upstart brother—I owe you nothing!" Raed hoped
to enrage her to the point where he might be able to overcome
her—perhaps get the tight length of weirstones around her
fine neck.

Idly Zofiya drew her long knife and began to clean her
nails with its shining length. "Perhaps *you* do not . . ." The
way she said it so archly implied something that chilled Raed.

The Rossin. It always came down to the Rossin. If it was
not enough trouble to be the Pretender to a throne with a
bounty on his head, he also carried a geistlord inside him that
apparently had even more enemies.

"What do you want with him?"

Now Zofiya leaned back in her seat, a beautiful woman

with something dark lodged in her. The Young Pretender knew a lot about that. He also knew this was not the Duchess he had taken a bullet for back in Vermillion.

Her smile was devastating and knowing. "She wants him. She must have her revenge."

Raed let his head drop back on the seat with a slight groan. "Hatipai, you mean. This is what it is all about?"

"Maybe, maybe not." And that was all she was going to say.

"Where are we going?" the Young Pretender asked, hating to sound so helpless, but peering out from the carriage still only revealed more sand and a group of Imperial Guard.

The Grand Duchess did not respond at first, so Raed tried to weigh his options. Without the Rossin there were very few. He couldn't be sure of overpowering Zofiya, who was a fine warrior in her own right. If she carried any sort of geist, which he suspected was the case, then the chances went down even further.

He couldn't for the life of him find the Bond that Merrick and Sorcha talked about. Raed was ready to roll from the carriage and see what happened, but just as he was gearing up to do that, Zofiya spoke again.

"We are going where you wanted to go all this time, Raed Syndar Rossin—we are going to meet your sister." Her voice was soft and precise.

The Young Pretender only just managed to stop himself from leaping on her. "Fraine? You took Fraine?"

She bared her teeth in a smile that would give him nightmares. " 'Took' is such a strong word."

Raed clenched his teeth, sucked in his self-control, then gave her a curt nod. "For now you live, Grand Duchess Zofiya. Until I see her."

She did not reply, and he did not try to engage her any further in conversation. In this manner they traveled on into the darkness and the desert: the second in line to the Imperial throne and the man who had been born to it.

TWENTY-FIVE

The Eye and the Fist

Sorcha let Merrick lead the way mainly so she could keep an eye on her young partner. They had to avoid the main thoroughfares, which made getting back to the palace a rather laborious process. Everyone not on the streets was slamming shut their doors—barricading them if they could.

"The pull of the geistlord"—Merrick shot a glance over his shoulder—"is only felt by those true believers."

Sorcha's laugh was so sharp it could have cut. "I always knew faith was a bad habit."

"It may be that all gods are not geists." The alleyways were strung with washing lines so that Merrick had to push through someone's dirty linens merely to make headway.

Just how her partner could say such a thing with such confidence was a mystery. He had returned with more secrets than was right. She was just about to demand some sort of explanation when Merrick flicked two sheets aside and saw a scene that neither of them could walk away from—even if they wanted to.

Abbot Yohari was the last person Sorcha would have expected to see in the back alleys of Orinthal, especially bleeding on the ground holding up the blue fire shield of Aydien while being attacked by his own Deacons.

Merrick stood there for a moment, horrified by the sight of those attackers Delie and Jey. The older partner saw Sorcha and smiled—a smile that sank reality into the Vermillion Deacon's heart. She was not wearing her Gauntlets—the other Active most certainly was.

It was not the first time she had faced off against one of the Order, so she moved a little faster than Merrick. Grabbing him by the back of his robe, she yanked him hard, sending them both tumbling, just as the lightning of Chityre filled the alleyway. It danced over the Abbot's waning shield before flicking and spitting up the mud walls. Seldom had Sorcha had the opportunity to experience the rune from the other side of the Gauntlet—it really was most impressive.

Still, finally she had a target for her rage. Sorcha had her Gauntlets on in a heartbeat, rolled to her feet and wrapped her own Aydien around them. No Chiomese turncoat Deacon was going to best her. Even the idiot Arch Abbot Rictun had never brought into question her own talent or power. Her shield pulsed brighter, moved faster and enveloped Abbot Yohari before his could drop away. Together Merrick and Sorcha went to his side.

She could not, however, spare a glance down; it was not that holding Aydien up was hard, but she watched Delie carefully as she dropped Chityre. The older woman whispered a word to her Sensitive, who looked as calm as a rabbit before a polecat.

At her side Sorcha heard Merrick tending to the Abbot, though her partner's Center still remained open and shared with her. *He will live.* Merrick's voice in her head was hot with outrage.

"You've attacked your own Abbot—a cardinal offense whichever way you cut it." Sorcha cocked her head and addressed the two rogue Deacons through the flickering blue of Aydien. "As representative of the Mother Abbey, I demand you surrender your Strop and Gauntlets to me and prepare to be escorted to Vermillion for trial."

Delie's lip curled while her hands flexed—Sorcha already knew the answer before it came. "Never! The Order is a hollow nothing now that the Bright One has returned."

The idea that anyone would place the Order of the Eye and

the Fist below a little god made Sorcha bark out a laugh. "You break your oath to the people of this land for a childish imagining? I did not know fools were so easily let into the Chiomese Order!"

"Perhaps not the best reply—" Merrick's warning was cut short as Delie shoved Jey out of the way and raised her Gauntlets. The green light of Shayst flickered on the Chiomese Deacon's Gauntlets, and Sorcha felt her rage flare at the same time. She had to let it out.

If these Deacons thought that they could drain power from her with the very same rune they used on geists, they were about to be disabused of the notion.

"Take out that damn Sensitive!" she snarled at Merrick while calling Seym to her. A giddy rush and then the Rune of Flesh filled her muscles with strength, giving her the power of one possessed.

Kill her? Merrick's question made her head ring with his horror.

Not unless you have to. Reaching the older Active, she sprang upon her with vengeful glee. Delie's eyes widened as she realized that Shayst was not taking power away from Sorcha nearly quickly enough. The depth of the triple Bond was unique, but the Deacon from Vermillion did not give Delie time to ponder it long.

Gauntlets were seldom used as a weapon of physical attack—but that did not mean they could not be put to that purpose. Sorcha delivered a strong left hook into the other Active's stomach, knocking her back and leaving her gasping for breath.

However, she too could draw on Shayst, and when she did, she came at Sorcha with as much rage as the Vermillion Deacon. They had no time to spar or take each other's measure; the runes could not be held indefinitely, and this was no competitive boxing match.

Merrick and Jey were fighting nearby, their strikes fast and more accurate than those of the Active. Yet none of them were drawing swords. Despite falling on one another like brawling children, not one of the Deacons would draw their blades on another.

Though she might be angry, somewhere in the back of Sorcha's mind lurked the suspicion that Hatipai had done something to her fellow Deacons. Unlike the traitors in Ulrich, these two had a bemused air about them, as if they were not quite all there.

Still, they could do plenty of damage. Sorcha took a good uppercut blow from Delie and reeled back. The Rune of Flesh dulled pain and swelled muscles, but she would feel the damage all the same when she let go of it. The next blow the Chiomese Deacon hammered down at her, Sorcha caught fast with her left hand. Pivoting on one foot, she caught Delie in a wristlock behind her back.

"Give up," she hissed in the other's ear. "Remember your training and your loyalty."

Her opponent struggled. "My first loyalty was always to the Bright One—there can be no greater calling than to obey her will."

Sorcha dared a glance at Merrick. His eyes were shadowed with pain, even as he kicked out and knocked Jey from her feet. It was not surprising that he took no pleasure from attacking a fellow Deacon and a woman. The female Sensitive looked up at Merrick and for a second there appeared some clarity in her vision.

"Delie," she gasped, "please—let's just go."

Her partner struggled briefly and then sagged in Sorcha's grasp. She was wise enough to know she was outmatched. Sorcha pushed her away hard, using her arm as leverage. When Delie turned about, her eyes were hard and bitter. Whatever force had the Chiomese, it had sunk its claws deeper into her than Jey.

Logically, Sorcha should have drawn her sword and dispatched the two of them, because they would undoubtedly bring back reinforcements to finish the job—but she hesitated.

Her training had taught her sympathy and care for those possessed—and though Sorcha had never seen anything like this kind, she knew it was something similar. Though her hand caressed the pommel of her sword, she did not draw it.

"Come, Jey," Delie snarled, yanking her Sensitive to her feet. Tears looked ready to spring to the young Deacon's eyes as she followed her Active away down the alleyway.

That was when lightning struck out of the clear blue sky. It smashed the three-story wall above the Chiomese Deacons with a deafening boom of thunder that filled the tiny space and knocked Sorcha and Merrick off their feet. For a moment everything was white.

When it finally cleared enough for her to see again, she turned to see Abbot Yohari propped up on the street behind them, his Gauntleted hand raised with the remains of Chityre still dancing on it. His dark, handsome face was twisted in pain and rage for a heartbeat before it was quickly smoothed away in a wash of trained discipline.

One glance back to where the tumbled remains of the building stood told Sorcha that no one was climbing out of that wreckage. Still, she looked to Merrick. His shake of the head was the final confirmation.

Standing over the Abbot, she released her breath slowly before pointing out to him, "They were retreating."

His expression would have suited a statue. "They strayed from the path," was his only reply.

Sorcha couldn't decide what to make of this implacability. The Order had plenty of rules that she was sure she didn't care to know about.

Yohari stripped off his gloves, tucked them under his belt and then imperiously held out a hand to Sorcha. Their gazes locked, and for the longest moment Sorcha didn't move. Finally it was Merrick, faithful, dependable Merrick, who darted forward and helped the injured Abbot to his feet.

Every muscle that Sorcha owned, as if on cue, began to ache—but it was highly unlikely that she would have time for a soak in a hot bath. Not for a very long time. Despite the pain, she did not remove her Gauntlets.

"Take me to the Prince." The Abbot leaned against Merrick and glared at Sorcha. "We must get to the Prince."

She would have loved an excuse to leave Yohari—but somehow the Bonds of loyalty still held her to the path of the Order—and she couldn't let Merrick shoulder all of this burden. Taking her place under the Abbot's right arm, smelling the tang of blood and incense, Sorcha found herself agreeing with him.

"To the Prince, then—and by the Bones, it had better be a short, uneventful walk."

* * *

They reached their destination in the sullen cold of the evening. Raed had long ago given up trying to outlast Zofiya and had dropped back to sleep in the swaying carriage. If life on the run had taught him anything, it was that you were always best to take rest where you could.

So when the carriage rumbled to a stop, he jerked awake and reached automatically for his sword. The sheath was empty at his side, and his hands remained tied firmly with the weirstones.

Zofiya, on the opposite seat, smiled at him almost coyly, then, leaning forward, she yanked on the cord that bound him. For a second Raed contemplated putting up a fight but then decided his energy was best preserved. If the Grand Duchess got her thrills leading him around like a tame animal, then he would let her grow accustomed to that illusion.

"I hope we haven't kept everyone waiting," he muttered as he stepped out of the carriage.

Zofiya's laugh was low and delighted. "They would wait for you, Raed Syndar Rossin, because *you* are the guest of honor."

It was not exactly a cheery comment, so Raed decided to ignore it.

They were still out in the sand—hardly surprising, since they had been traveling with the setting sun on their left, which meant only more desert. The heat had long dissipated; instead, a freezing cold wind was blowing off the dunes. Raed shivered and looked about him. A long row of flaming torches led somewhere in the dark, though he could make out a hump of some kind on the horizon—it blocked out the stars. It could be just another sand dune, but some deeper awareness, something from the Rossin, most likely, said it was not.

"I do hope this isn't another 'we need royal blood' ritual." He sighed in mock boredom. "Because I already went through one of those recently."

"The Murashev in Vermillion?" Zofiya's voice was tiny in the vast desert. "That was a geist—this is for our Bright One."

"It's not royal blood they want, Brother"—a second female voice came out of the dark—"else they could have had some of mine."

For a long beat of his heart Raed remained frozen, certain that somehow his mother's spectyr had found her way here. It was her voice, light and sweet but still full of the command of a royal lady. Tears leapt to his eyes in an instant as the last image he had of her flashed before him—her beautiful face twisted in agony, just before the Rossin took her life.

The Young Pretender spun around. A form, tall and shapely, stood by the closest torch. It was hooded, but as he watched, delicate hands pushed aside the cowl. Curls of bright gold hair tumbled down her back but were held away from her face by a string of gleaming pearls, and Raed took a step away in shock. His sister was the living image of their mother.

"Fraine?"

His sister stood by the torch and made not a move toward him. It had been nearly ten years since he had seen her, but her face held not one ounce of joy. Nor was she bound; however, as he looked closer, there was something missing in her eyes—they were as blank as a blyweed user.

Raed shot a glance back at Zofiya, who merely smiled. "Fraine"—Raed ventured cautiously forward, his eyes darting into the darkness—"what have they done to you?"

"That isn't the right question you know, Brother. You should be asking what *I* have done to you." Her voice was strangely flat.

Raed felt his spine run with ice water as a terrible sensation of unreality crept over him. This couldn't be Fraine! It had to be some cruel illusion of his beloved sister. He couldn't have traveled all this way to find this.

"Fraine?"

"Do stop using my name!" she hissed, finally moving forward. Dimly, Raed realized that his sister was as tall as he. "Don't tell me you honestly thought I had been kidnapped?"

Everything was still. Even the wind off the dunes had died down. Raed's mouth was dry. He did not know what to say.

"But Tang said . . ." He was grasping at anything—any facts.

"I am not as blinded by old loyalties as I once was." Tangyre Greene walked into the light to stand next to Fraine.

This was like some sort of grotesque stage play. Raed had always prided himself on his quick wits, and yet, though everything was making a kind of cruel sense, he still couldn't bear to accept it. He shook his head. "What would make my family do this to me?" It was whispered under his breath, but the two women heard him well enough.

Tangyre glanced at her Princess but saw that for the moment she had the floor. At least Captain Greene had enough loyalty to look guilty. "It's not about you, my Prince—but about what you have failed to do."

Raed managed to find some dull anger. He glared at her. "And what is that?"

"Protect your family." Her jaw clenched. "You have been happy to leave your father and sister to rot on that stinking island."

"I had no choice." He turned to Fraine, pushing aside the shade of their mother that hung between them. "You have to know that."

The corner of her lips twitched. Her reply, when it came, was finally full of some kind of emotion—it was just a pity that it was real anger. "I'm still young, Raed—and that place is filled with the old and broken. You just left me there."

That was when the Pretender knew and understood why his sister had turned on her own kin. He knew, because he was responsible. He knew, because he had chosen to leave the *Dominion* and take the chance, since they were close, to reunite with his family. They rarely visited the mainland, but a loyal lord, who lived on a remote peninsular, invited them to celebrate the harvest with him. The risks were very low—at least from their enemies.

Back then the Rossin Curse had been merely a quaint legend—something that they chuckled about over family dinners. It was sheer chance that he had spent his youth from the age of ten aboard a ship, learning to lead and to fight and surrounded by the open water that geists could not traverse.

When the Rossin took him, right during just such a meal, there had been no more laughter. Raed remembered the tearing sensation deep in his flesh, hearing the baying of the Beast and the screams of those around him. He even recalled the feeling of the bullet's strike as the more quick-witted of his father's guards tried to stop him. The worst memory, however, was of the jaws of the Rossin closing around his mother, the scent of her fear and the taste of her blood.

Raed clenched his teeth, ravaged again by those sensations, as if they had occurred only yesterday. He had awoken
aching, screaming and covered in the lifeblood of the one who
bore him. His father had been destroyed, but out of some kind
of guilt of his own had sent his only son out onto the world's
oceans. They had all learned that day the true sting of myth.

And now here was Fraine, looking at him with the same
rage but untempered by any remorse. Raed could have spoken
in his defense, said something about the Curse or the Beast or
how he had no choice. Instead he remained silent, his jaw
locked around any reply.

"You robbed me of my mother," Fraine said, as Tangyre
squeezed her shoulder. "And then you abandoned me. I
wanted a life, but instead I was trapped with Father."

At five there would be only flashes of memory for his sister, but he suddenly could see through her eyes: an island full
of the elderly and damaged. Zofiya was silent, swaying slightly,
and barely taking any notice of the little family drama being
played out.

"You were safe there," he finally croaked out. "And we
thought it was better you were safe than—"

"What I had there was not worth saving." Her hand went to
her sword hilt, and abruptly Raed realized she was dressed for
war. So mesmerized had he been that he had not noticed her
Imperial dress. The dress of purple and dark blue of their
family, including the Rising Star Crest of the Rossin heir.

"This is insanity, Fraine! Why are you wearing that?"
Raed lurched forward, only to have his feet knocked out from
under him by Zofiya.

But it was Tang who replied, "As heir to the Rossin name,
Fraine will have excellent marriage prospects. Especially
once the Empress stands on the throne. She will cancel the
price on her head."

The thing behind Zofiya's eyes shifted, and Raed felt himself plunge deeper into madness. "Empress?"

The smile on her face was stretched. "With your sister's
backing, the rebel Princes will fall into line. I will rule, and in
return my Bright Lady will help your sister by taking care of
the Rossin. Once the faithful have gathered tomorrow, you
will die; he will die with you and not be passed on to her."

Raed pressed his lips together lest a cry escape him. When suicide had tempted him, it was the thought that Fraine would suffer the Rossin if he did, which stopped him. Apparently none of this mattered to her—he was simply the man who had killed her mother and any chance of a happy life.

"I want to watch you suffer first. I want you to know real loss." Fraine got up, brushed off her pants and gestured to the guards waiting in the darkness. Raed managed to struggle to his knees just as his crew was dragged through the sand dunes; all were bound, and many looked as though they had put up a fierce fight.

Abruptly he knew what their fate was. "No!" Pulling his feet under him, he charged at the guard nearest him holding the silent and bruised Snook. The Young Pretender never reached them.

Other guards sprang from the shadows. Raed fought back with forehead and shoulder, but they knocked him down quickly, and with rifle butts and fists kept him down. The Young Pretender swore, snarled and wished for the Rossin to take him, but nothing happened. He had the wind knocked out of him, and when they were done, he was left staring at the stars.

"Get him up." Fraine's voice reached him like he was underwater. It should have come as no surprise to him that it was Isseriah who tugged Raed back up onto his knees. Under the rule of a new Rossin Emperor it was certain that the rebel had been promised his earldom back. Raed had no more venom, but he spat at the traitor's feet.

Bruised and heartsick, the Young Pretender looked at his five crew members: Snook, Laython, Balis, Nyre and the young blade Iyle. They looked back at him with clenched jaws, dark eyes and resignation. They knew as well as he what was coming.

"It has been a pleasure to sail the waters with you, my Prince." Snook tilted her head up, the light washing over her narrow, sweet face. She had never used his title as Aachon was wont to do. That she did so now poured cold horror through him.

"Long live Prince Raed," she cried, and the other four crew members repeated her call as if their lives depended on it—but it made not one jot of difference.

"It's been my honor," Raed choked out.

He was held tightly as, in one practiced move, all five guards slit all five throats. Not one of them cried for mercy. The gushing of blood flooded over the sand, and then they let the bodies drop. Like that, they were no longer human, just bundles of meat he had once known, loved and sailed with.

Raed bellowed, reaching for the rage of the Rossin, not caring what happened after—but all he found was emptiness. This was his crew. They had followed him for years, and he'd taken them to their deaths far from the oceans they loved. Like everything else, it was his fault.

"I see now, Brother"—Raed glanced up as his sister's words fell on him like rough stones—"that you do in fact have a heart. That is, until they cut it out of you."

What could he say to his sister? No matter how many times Raed told himself that it was the Curse, the Beast, the Rossin that had torn their mother to shreds, he could not shake the guilt that it had been him in some way.

For Fraine, the Young Pretender could find no words. She was not the little sister he had carried on his shoulders, but neither was he that carefree lad anymore. The Rossin had killed both of them along with their mother.

Fraine and Tangyre looked down at him for a second. Raed wanted them to stop looking at him, wanted it to be over with. Every bone and muscle ached in his body, but it was not as terrible as the pain in his soul—if he had a soul.

His sister looked across at Zofiya. "Will it be painful?"

The Grand Duchess hummed a little tune under her breath, her eyes on the looming mound that blackened the horizon. "They will all be gathered tomorrow, and the Bright One will descend."

Zofiya's laugh cracked halfway through, and even in his pain Raed could hear there was less and less of herself in her voice. He knew all about being eaten up from the inside. "Oh, it will hurt. The Bright One will devour his heart and brain and through them the Beast inside."

In the firelight Fraine swallowed hard, for a moment looking pale, but she regained her composure and nodded. "Good . . . I want him to suffer just as our mother did. I want him to know pain and fear before he dies."

"That you can be guaranteed." The Grand Duchess sketched a little mocking bow. "Now, get you to the north and rouse the Princes there to our cause."

Then the two women who had brought him to this fate turned on their heels, and quickly the darkness took them.

Raed shook himself, feeling the blood of his crew beginning to pool around his knees. He knew he had to stop Zofiya—she would tear the Empire apart. Even if she did manage to claim the throne, it would mean death and war for years—maybe generations.

"Zofiya," he said, twisting around, "what are you thinking? You will have to kill your brother to take the crown. Everything I have seen says you love him dearly!"

Her eyes, when they looked at him, were confused, as if the spirit of the Grand Duchess was down there somehow, swimming desperately toward comprehension but unable to find it.

Sensing a chance, Raed tried to throw her a lifeline. "You swore to protect Kaleva! He is your brother—your blood."

A flicker of horror passed over her finely carved face, the look of a sister who did still love her sibling. Yet even as hope surged in Raed, the expression passed, and she was once more a statue of calm. "The Emperor has always despised religion. He will never accept the Bright One as I have. I will show them the proper path."

"You will bring about chaos!" Raed tried to surge to his feet but was held down by three guards.

Zofiya's mouth formed a smile that was not her own. "And that will serve my mistress well." She turned and faced the darkness on the horizon, the place where no stars burned. "Bring him—we go to make ready for her."

Raed struggled weakly, but it was now only a primitive survival instinct. He had never felt more beaten and broken. It was almost enough to make him yearn for the next day. Almost.

TWENTY-SIX

The Unseen Prince

Dragging a bleeding Abbot through the almost empty corridors of the palace was not how Sorcha had imagined this visit to Orinthal ending up. Yet that was exactly what they were going to do.

They had stopped briefly to bind Yohari's wounds, and Merrick had pronounced it a clean through-and-through stab wound. The Abbot must have flinched away from Delie's strike with her sword at just the right moment. Still, it bled plenty, and the Abbot, hardly used to a life of stabbings, was not the best patient. If anyone thought Deacons were stalwart, they would have been surprised at his wincing and grumbling.

Still, Merrick was proficient in the art of field medicine, as Sensitives often had to be, and the palace would have much better facilities.

They finally reached it by scrambling through every alley and backyard in Orinthal—at least that was how it felt to Sorcha. The gate was devoid of any guards and even hung slightly ajar.

Sorcha ached to stop and light a cigar—at the very least a cigarillo. It was her usual reaction to stress and the impending feeling of doom.

"It must be quite the party if even the palace guards have given up their posts," she commented, hitching the Abbot a little higher. His arm was over her shoulder, and his badge of the Order was digging into her neck. Such little discomforts at time like this shouldn't have mattered—but they did.

The older man winced and clutched his side. "The number of Hatipai's devotees is no less in the palace."

"Well then," she said jauntily, "let us hope they have all gone off for the event, or we shall make most unwelcome visitors."

Merrick in his rather travel-stained green cloak, shared his Center with Sorcha, and she was able to breathe a little easier; there were many people still in the palace, but not so many that it appeared to be an ambush.

Pushing open the gates, they staggered in. Whatever had happened here was very similar to what had happened in the town. It looked as though some kind of wild party had taken place: pictures hung askew, amphoras of water lay broken on the floor, and there was the distinct odor of sweat in the air. It was entirely different from the palace that Sorcha had been in only a few hours before.

"We must find the Prince." Abbot Yohari wheezed. "We must make sure he is alive."

All traces of the joviality that the Chiomese Abbot had exhibited on their first meeting were gone. As they worked their way closer to the throne room, the damage got worse; now it was more like a riot than student pranks. In one doorway they passed there were several bodies.

"Looks like some guards tried to make a stand," Merrick whispered, though the corpses were far past caring. About ten guards blocked a corridor along with bodies of petitioners, servants and bureaucrats. Like all battlegrounds, it smelled rank, but the Sensitive stopped to look with his Center. "No shades or spectyrs."

"By the Bones, that would be all we need." Though Sorcha knew that by day's end there would be plenty to clean up in Chioma, she had other more pressing issues.

After they skirted the pile of corpses, they made it to the throne room. Rather unsurprisingly, it was barred. "He's inside." Before she could stop him, Merrick strode forward and banged on the huge doors. The brass rang like a bell, and Sorcha flinched. If there were any enemies around, it might just sound like a dinner bell.

Her partner was well educated and talented—yet the one thing he lacked was real-world experience.

"They better let us in now," Sorcha muttered to the Abbot, and he grimaced across at her.

"Indeed."

All it took was a whispered conversation through the viewing port, and the mechanism on the other side of the door sprang into life. The lock snapped free, the cogs whirred, and the doors swung open. Sorcha had not noted the lock on the doors before—probably because it was used very rarely. Not many throne rooms had locks, since it was the object of the room to let people in.

Once again the Prince of Chioma had proved to be rather forward thinking. Either that or justifiably paranoid.

The three Deacons found themselves ushered into the throne room. If they needed proof that a battle had indeed been fought, then it was here in the heart of the Prince's kingdom. The room was full of civilians nursing wounds: women of the harem with wide eyes, clerks tending one another's injuries, and old women from the kitchen sitting shaking in the seats once occupied by the cream of Chiomese society. A couple of guards manned the door, and a handful of civil servants clustered around Onika at the far end of the room.

Nothing about this group said they were capable of holding off a riot, so Sorcha was a little confused. Even the huge brass door and its workings could not have resisted a decent attack. Yet here they were, the survivors of a wave of madness.

Abbot Yohari, who must have been conserving his energy for this moment, pulled loose of Merrick and Sorcha and tottered his way toward the Prince. The little huddle around Onika gave way before him, some even remembering to bow. The Prince spun about as Yohari stood swaying before him.

"Abbot?" His voice was calm but with the underlying edge of stress. "Where are your Deacons? We are counting on them to stem this tide of violence!"

Yohari sketched a bow and almost toppled. The Prince caught his wrist and guided him over to the steps of the dais as if he was leading his grandfather. "Your Highness"—the Abbot shook his head—"they are all gone. All gone—to *her*."

A ripple of gasps and sobs ran through the little crowd. Soon the survivors were whispering and clutching one another. Sorcha didn't need Merrick's aid to see despair taking hold.

Even the Prince took a step back and sank down next to the Abbot.

This could quickly get out of hand. Sorcha had dealt with plenty of groups beset with geists; those who lost hope and the will to fight never lasted long. It might not be the right time, but it was the only time. She pushed her hair back out of her face and flicked a look at Merrick.

Yohari was too injured and too defeated to lead anything. They had to take charge, so Sorcha cleared her throat and spoke. "Your Highness, I think the time for pretense is over."

Onika's shoulders pressed back, the only discernible sign that he had even heard the Deacon. After a long moment, in which Sorcha decided which rune she might need if those around them pulled out knives, the Prince's head suddenly flicked around like a viper's and stared at her.

"Everyone, leave me to talk with the Deacons." The tone was deep, powerful and suggested imminent pain if it was disobeyed. The courtiers and the guards recognized that too—scattering to the rear of the chamber.

"Your Highness," Yohari began, "I do not think that these Vermillion Deacons can quite understand the uniqueness of our position—"

"Enough!" Onika held up one hand and cut the Abbot off. "I charged you with watching your Deacons just as I charged all your predecessors. You failed me, Abbot Yohari."

Sorcha's brow furrowed. Just how old was the Prince? Along the Bond, Merrick was unsurprised. The feeling that her younger partner knew something she did not was rather frustrating.

"As for you," Onika began, and Sorcha's hands clenched on each other, "I expected you to find the killer in our midst—and instead one of my daughters is murdered. Explain yourself."

His tone now was so flat and dreadful that even though he

did not have the resources he once had, Sorcha was sure
Onika could still find a way to make her dead. She would have
defended herself, tried to find the best words to say, but Merrick stepped between them.

"You should take my word on this, Onika—Sorcha did not
kill your child." That was the way of Sensitives—they saw so
clearly that they could dance around the truth so much more
easily. Sorcha knew she might not have killed Jaskia, but she
had contributed to the situation that had led to it. Deacons
often did.

The word of a member of the Order, least of all one so
young, should not have had any sway with this imperious and
mysterious monarch, yet he let out a breath that suggested
beyond the shimmering veil he might actually be crying.
"Merrick—you don't know what else has happened." Even
without seeing his face, Sorcha observed the set of his shoulders, the weariness in every muscle—it was as if a great
weight was pressing down on him.

"Onika?" Merrick took a step forward and actually grasped
the Prince's elbow. Such a breach of protocol could have
resulted in a challenge to a duel or at least a reprimand, but the
monarch did not move. Sorcha grew more confused by the minute, especially when the next words came out of the Prince's
mouth.

"It is your mother." There was no mistaking the tone; there
was grief in his voice. "They have taken her."

Her partner's face went white, and a surge of fear suddenly
rose above the other emotions muddled in the Bond. Sorcha
could no longer stand still and let these strange events unroll
around her.

"Mother?" Her eyes widened. "By the Bones—who is he
talking about, Merrick?"

When he turned around, his eyes were wide but his jaw set.
He looked younger than his twenty and five years—almost
like a frightened child stepping toward anger. His voice was
flat as he told her, "You've already met her—she's pregnant
with his child."

She recalled the woman, beautiful and heavy with pregnancy and curiously devoted to the Prince. Suddenly the simi-
larity between her and Merrick smacked his partner between

the eyes. She almost laughed—there were plenty of good reasons she had never been considered as a Sensitive.

Sorcha hadn't heard much from Merrick about his family—but then neither had she told him anything about hers. Most of the Deacons were trained from childhood, many orphaned or sent into the Order by impoverished parents. It was so common that it was taken as the rule. But Sorcha knew from what she had heard in the harem that the royal concubines and wives were no commoners. They were proud of it.

So, if the woman she had seen was Merrick's mother, then that meant by consequence that he was no common orphan picked up off the street.

"We have no secrets from each other," Onika stated, "and she was so happy to find you."

Sorcha, please. Through their connection she could taste Merrick's panic. Her partner. He was her partner, and he, unlike her, had family. That had to mean something.

When this situation is sorted out, she replied, *we will talk about this.*

Just help me find her. It was the voice of a son, traced through with love and fear. Some part of her yearned to have that loving connection with kin and was jealous that she did not.

Sorcha, who had never known her own mother, had however loved the Presbyter of the Young deeply. Merrick was her partner now, and his family was her family. "Where was she last seen this . . ."

"Japhne," Onika broke in. "Her name is Japhne, and she was in her bed. The baby was tiring her, so she went to her room early this afternoon to rest. This was before Hatipai's madness infiltrated the palace."

"Perhaps she is simply hiding from the rioters?" Sorcha glanced across at Merrick.

He was opening his Center, spreading it farther than she had ever felt him do before—the effort traveled through his body like a vibration and humming along the Bond.

"Nothing," he gasped and reached for the Strop. Only the last two runes of Sight required the Strop, and she knew he meant to use the sixth one, Mennyt. Without questioning him, she drew her Gauntlets out from her belt and slipped their comforting weight over her hands.

Mennyt meant looking into the Otherside, and sometimes the Otherside could look back. She would protect her Sensitive. "Stand back, please, Your Highness." The beaded curtain swayed before Onika, but he took several steps until he was against the wall of the audience chamber.

Merrick strapped the wide leather around his head, hiding his brown eyes behind the Runes of Sight carved into the Strop. Then he slid the round of obsidian, with his own personal sigil hammered into it, up on its brass loop to sit in a spot between his eyebrows. Sorcha was not sure if the Third Eye that it was meant to be covering was just some strange Sensitive myth, but she knew when it was brought into play, things were serious.

In the Bond everything went still as Merrick's concentration sharpened to knifelike intensity, and his partner was once again reminded how powerful the young Deacon was. The brightest star of the novitiate. Despite a rocky start to their partnership, she was proud of him and the strength of what they had.

Still, looking into the Otherside was nothing to be taken lightly. *Careful, Merrick, don't look too deep.*

The image of his mother, young, beautiful and laughing, bending down to kiss the top of his head, flashed through the Bond along with a surge of powerful emotion.

I have to know if she is there.

Merrick opened his Sight to the Otherside. The winds raged, and Sorcha swallowed panic. The view of the palace was different when seen through Mennyt; it was a wild place of dark shadows and whispering voices from unseen people.

Every building that had ever housed humans bore some echo of them after they were gone, but in places like palaces, where great and dreadful events played out, a geist could snatch away a human soul and leave the shattered remains to wander. Those who had been murdered were especially easy targets for the unliving—and this was what Merrick was looking for.

Now his Sight spread through the palace, looking for a familiar shape and yet terrified to find it. Some isolated survivors lingered in distant rooms, and some broken souls ripped from bodies still floated through the corridors.

Yet Merrick still cast about, delving deeper. Shadows grew darker, and the distance between the human world and the Otherside grew thinner, like someone rubbing at a painting with a piece of cloth. Now he was boring down until his blood called to her blood. Deep in the tunnels a few tiny drops called to him.

Merrick—that's enough! Sorcha stretched out across the Bond to him. She knew all about going too far, having done it herself in front of the gates of the palace at Vermillion.

Eventually her partner heard her and pulled back. Looking deeply could draw the attention of things that were best left lying. With shaking hands, Merrick slid the sigil back on the Strop and undid the belt of leather from around his head.

"She's not dead." He turned to the Prince of Chioma. "By the Bones, she is not dead, but there is blood . . . just a little."

"Then where can she be?" Onika sank down on the dais where his empty throne stood. None of the Deacons answered.

Blood was powerful magic when used with runes or cantrips even, and royal blood more powerful than that. And there were indeed terrible dark things that could be done to a pregnant woman and her child to summon geists. Sorcha sometimes hated the knowledge of a Deacon; it made dreaming or imagining a stained thing, and she was cursed with an active, powerful imagination.

"I wonder what they are planning." Despite the horror of it, she found herself pondering what their unknown assailants would want with Merrick's mother. He was doing the very same, though with considerably more pain and bleakness.

So drawn in by these dark thoughts was Sorcha, that for a minute she didn't register the Prince's movement—his raised hand to the swaying mask of beads.

"They are planning to make me pay." His deep voice was edged with resignation and fury, and then he ripped the mask from his face.

Nothing else mattered. Sorcha dropped to her knees as if poleaxed, as the glory that was Onika filled her. He filled her with beauty and adoration, so much so that tears spilled from her eyes even as she raised her hands to him in supplication. Sorcha felt the true dawning of faith, and it cut more deeply than she had ever imagined.

He was everything, and life before had no meaning. It had been gray and hollow until this moment.

As if through a mist she heard Merrick cry out, his voice cracking, "Onika, please!" It sounded half a prayer, half an admonishment. Sorcha turned, her chest full of sudden anger. This was their god—how dare the young fool question him? She was going to tear his heathen eyes from his head.

Onika, with a sigh from his perfect mouth, bent, scooped up the mask and threw it around his head once more.

It was like plucking the sun from the sky. Sorcha sank back on her knees, a dreadful grief welling up to take the place of faith. It was hard to shake, but eventually, after wiping away her tears, she levered herself back to her feet. Merrick had recovered far more quickly and helped her.

Sorcha had read widely on the subject of the little gods; how they were foolish, and those that followed them were even more so. She had even as part of her training studied the reckless religion of the Wyketel tribesmen in the forests of the West Highlands, and how even now they could not be persuaded to give it up. Having had a taste of faith, having seen a god on earth, she was a little more forgiving.

"A god . . ." She shook her head.

"No." Onika's voice was firm but still angry. "Not a god— merely the son of a geistlord, Hatipai—one that has been pretending to be a god since before the Break."

Her reaction was primitive and instant; Sorcha drew her sword, the ring of it sounding loud in the silent audience chamber. She should kill him now and save his people.

It was Merrick who brushed aside the point of her blade. "Onika abandoned his mother; he fought with the Ancients against her. He is not the threat here, Sorcha."

"How do you know?" The prick of humiliation had her now, and she would not back down. She could feel the eyes of the Court on her, the held breaths, the aimed rifles.

"Because I *saw*." His fingers clenched on the tip of her blade. "Nynnia took me there, before the coming of the geists."

Sorcha frowned. The sword wavered slightly in her hand.

"I was one of those who imprisoned my mother, along with the Rossin family and their geistlord." Onika's hands disappeared behind the mask, holding his head or crying, it was impossible to tell. "And this is her revenge. I was never able to have any sons of my body—until Japhne came into my life."

He looked up at Merrick. "I remembered what you had told me, and I found love and acceptance as I never had in a thousand years. Even when I was not wearing the mask, somehow she still was able to love me as a man."

Sorcha made up her mind, sheathed her sword in one smooth gesture and realized foolishly that she still had her Gauntlets on. "Then we have to get her back."

"I am the only one with any hope of stopping my mother."

All three of them paused, ragged and torn.

"Then I will make it my mission to find *my* mother," Merrick said, his hand resting on his own sword hilt. "I will follow those tunnels, and I will find her. You must both go after Raed and stop Hatipai."

"But—" the Prince made to disagree.

"No, Your Highness," Merrick snapped. "This is how it has to be."

For a long moment the two men stood toe-to-toe, and Sorcha merely watched. For once she would let her partner tell her what to do. She owed him that.

Onika laughed shortly. "It has all come down to mothers, then—because if I do not stop Hatipai, then she will make a graveyard of Chioma. Starting with the Rossin."

Sorcha flinched. "Raed?"

It was Merrick who answered, "No, the Beast. Remember, there is no hungrier creature than a geistlord. They dine on one another."

"And my mother has a terrible hatred for the Rossin—since his family helped me restrain her." Onika strode to the window and pointed east. "I closed her primary Temple—the one in the desert. That is where she will go to make herself a new body and devour the Beast."

Sorcha clenched her teeth, her throat tight, for a moment stopping any words. The Bond, which had been their greatest strength, was now stretching her in opposite directions. Raed was her lover, possibly even more, and Merrick was her partner. She didn't want to have to choose.

Merrick took her arm, pulling her out of the circles her mind was running in. "I need you to go with Onika and help him. Hatipai is far more powerful than any bunch of kidnappers."

"I can't." Sorcha paused, shook her head. "I can't just leave you—" He was her Sensitive, and she'd only just gotten him back. He was her responsibility. Everything that she had ever learned in the Order told her not to leave his side—least of all when the world was exploding around them. Her mind flashed to Kolya and when he had been attacked right in front of her.

"Sorcha." Merrick squeezed her arm hard. Sometimes she still forgot his strength—too used to thinking of Sensitives as weak. Her partner, she had learned quickly, was anything but that. "I'll take some palace guards, and we will be fine. You have to stop Hatipai and save Raed. I will be with you—our Bond is strong."

Sorcha felt his strength surge around her. It was funny how she had never truly appreciated it as much as she did in this moment. Their Bond, which she had forged so carelessly, was now an essential part of her life—as much as her affection for Raed.

I am inside you. My Sight is yours, no matter where I am. Such a thing was impossible—at least as she had been taught—but she and Merrick had already broken so many rules. She looked into his steady brown eyes, and she believed him. He had never lied to her. For once in her life, she believed. While this spread through the Bond, she nodded slowly.

And with a final squeeze of her hand, Merrick turned on his heel and strode out the door. Like every Active, Sorcha had always assumed that she was the dominant in their partnership. If they survived this, she realized, she would have to reassess.

I will find you soon, were the final words he shot across the Bond before sealing it shut, cutting off communication though not the strength. Sorcha was not one to weep and wail over a man, even if that man was bound to her as tightly as Merrick.

Onika called the remaining members of his guard, told them to follow after the Deacon, and treat him as they would their Prince. They were all well trained and obeyed without question.

The doors were shut, and without turning, she listened to

Onika's footsteps walking on the polished stone toward her. She was not without allies, even if she still didn't have the full measure of them.

Sorcha contemplated the Prince of Chioma, hidden behind his swaying mask. "So, how difficult is it going to be getting into this Temple?"

"I think you have seen I am not without my own resources." His voice was hard, distant and worthy of a god. "It was how I stopped the mob getting into the throne room, after all. The trouble will be getting to the desert Temple in time. Unfortunately, I do not have wings."

It was hard to tell if he was attempting some kind of joke—certainly Sorcha was not about to ask him to remove the mask, and besides she did have an idea.

"Tell me, Your Highness—have you ever traveled by Imperial Dirigible? It is quite the way to fly."

His low chuckle was the most cheery noise Deacon Sorcha Faris has heard in many, many hours.

TWENTY-SEVEN

A Son's Love

Walking away from Sorcha was hard, and Merrick was afraid to do it. Everything that he had ever been taught told him to stay with her—but a child's love for his mother went deeper even than that. It was certainly not a situation he had ever envisaged, but if they found Japhne quickly enough, then he should be able to get back to his partner before she faced the goddess.

The palace was not making Merrick feel confident about his goals, though. He kept his Center open, but all he captured was the feeling of panic and terror.

"Sir." One of the guards, by his insignia a sergeant, glanced around the corner of the corridor. "If you don't mind me saying, don't you Deacons always travel in pairs?"

Merrick could smell the fear coming off the man; these guards were trained to deal with assassins, rabble-rousers, and maybe a catfight between the Prince's women. "What's your name, soldier?"

"Dael." His eyes flickered uncertainly to Merrick.

"Well, Dael"—Merrick led them around the corridor brusquely, communicating certainty he didn't feel—"while members of my Order do indeed customarily travel together— we are also trained to look after ourselves." He left out the bit about the strange Bond and the power it gave him and Sorcha over and above a normal Deacon.

They reached the harem to find the doors swinging open and a dead eunuch in the garden, but it was another direction that interested Merrick. There in the disturbed gravel of the once immaculate path he found what he was looking for—a single tiny drop of blood.

He bent and held his open hand over it. It was hers, and Merrick would not permit himself to think about the circumstances in which it might have landed there; the thing that mattered was it was just one tiny drop. This was no murder scene. Aiemm, the Second Rune of Sight, flared in his mind, and he looked back in time to his mother's terror.

Running, she was running, and someone pursued her. The cut in her hand was tiny, one slip of the knife she'd used to defend herself. She held it tightly, the pain inconsequential in her panic. Her pursuers were cloaked, even in the heat of the garden, and her stride was awkward this late in her pregnancy.

Merrick opened his eyes. She hadn't seen; they weren't just chasing her—they were *herding her.*

"Quickly." He stood up. "There is still time."

It was down into the tunnels once again—that was where they had harried his mother to, like so many sheepdogs. Except he suspected these dogs would bite.

Merrick's mind raced, and not just with the unnaturalness of this situation; he was thinking of a time when he had lost another parent.

The taste of remembered fear filled his mouth, and suddenly he was that little boy hiding behind a tapestry and watching his father being ripped apart by something from the Otherside. He hadn't cried, hadn't uttered a word, but he recalled the anguish. His mother's sobs had seemed to have no end, all through his childhood. And finally he summoned up the image of Japhne of a few nights before, sitting on the end of the bed, smiling with genuine happiness. He had never thought to see that look on her face again. He had thought *she* would never see his face again.

He swallowed hard on the knot of fear in his throat.

Remaining calm was the only course now—if not, his mother would be lost.

"Down here," he barked as they turned the final corner of the final staircase and reached the tunnel from which Nynnia had taken him. Something had reached out to grab him then, and she had pulled him through time and space to save him. Merrick could only hope she would understand why he was now stepping right into the jaws of that trap.

The guards waited patiently as he stared down into the broken maw of the storm-water pipe that had collapsed under his feet what felt like an age ago now. His Center was wide and open, so he easily found another splatter of blood—this one larger. Japhne had placed her hand right there and somehow lowered herself down into the tunnel. It was quite a feat for a woman seven months into her pregnancy—but there was nothing like being pursued to provide motivation.

His mother might have been a noble lady, but she had never been one to stick to needlepoint—it was one of the reasons she had been such trouble for her brother to marry off. When Merrick's father had been alive and in his own senses, she had ridden often to the hunt with him. Still, running for her life in the dark tunnels under Orinthal while heavily pregnant was something no one trained for.

"Light your lanterns," Merrick instructed the guards over one shoulder. As a Deacon he didn't need light to see, but the others would. Three of the ten guards at his back took hooded lanterns from the walls of the corridor, while others nervously waited for his next instruction.

When Merrick gave it, he knew that they wouldn't like it. "Follow me." And then he swung down into the pipe. He had never actually hit the bottom before; Nynnia had been very accurate when she snatched him away.

It was pitch-black, but with his Center open he could feel so many more details than mere human sight could give him. When the guards dropped down behind him, he barely registered their arrival.

The tunnel was old, more ancient than even the palace above, and had been made with great care. The whispers of the makers, even after centuries, still clung to the curved brick walls. The water at the bottom was only an ankle-deep trickle, and thankfully this was not part of the smaller sewage systems that burrowed above this grand pipe.

"This carries flash flood waters away from the palace," one of the guards muttered. "I pray there is nothing happening in the mountains while we are down here."

Despite the serious situation, Merrick's lips twitched in a faint smile. With the kingdom gone to chaos above them, the guard was worried about the weather? If rain came, then it would wash all of them away before they had time to care.

No sign of his mother or any other human was on the ether, but there were plenty of rats and crawling creatures in the pipe to keep them company. Merrick pushed harder with his Center, burrowing into their mercurial brains in which thoughts ran like water, but the most important ones were for survival.

It was possible for some people and geists to erase their passing in the ether—not common but possible. However, everything that walked or scurried on the earth had a memory, even if it was a small one, and that was far harder to erase.

The Deacon inhaled slightly, closed his physical eyes, and drew in his mind the outline of the First Rune of Sight, Sielu. Using it to look through human eyes could drain his strength, but he was not using it on them in this instance. Instead, he spread his net far wider and far lower.

In the tiny brains of the rats that lived here there was a flickering memory. A large shape, slipping and sliding in the dark had disturbed them. She had screamed and sent the rodents squeaking in annoyance. Then more shapes. The rats did not like the smell of these ones—they reeked of danger and the sharp tang of the Otherside. Not that rats really knew what that place was, but their natural instincts were well attuned to survival—like all living creatures, except Deacons, they fled it.

Merrick could make out no details of the pursuers that had disturbed the rodents, since what they had seen was in a very limited range—boots, and trailing cloth—however, Merrick was able to tell they had traveled up the pipe to the west.

It was the opposite direction than everyone else in Orinthal was taking, so it was not that his mother had been enthralled by Hatipai. "What lies west of here?" he asked the guards.

The lead one, whose burly frame nearly filled the storm-water pipe, shrugged. "The valley the palace is built on runs out and becomes nothing but desert."

"And this pipe?" Merrick pressed.

Another, shorter guard seemed glad to offer what he knew. "It flows into the irrigation ditches, I think."

Merrick didn't want to tromp through fig and date plantations as night drew in, but they had no other choice; that was the way his mother and her mysterious pursuers had gone.

Holding Sielu in his mind gave him a disconcerting fractured vision through the rats' perspective, but it also meant there was no way anyone would shake him off. Merrick steadied himself for just a moment on the wall of the pipe and then led the way deeper and west.

The guards followed silently, their concern a dim impression on the Deacon's senses. Holding the rune while keeping his Center open was tricky and not something recommended by the tutors at the Mother Abbey. It was akin to rubbing your stomach and patting your head while walking—but Merrick did not want them to run into the pursuers without warning. He had a feeling that would be a very bad idea.

The pipe began to flare wider, and other tunnels began to join onto this main one, though the smell was damp and tinged with the odor of rot. The guards' footsteps echoed and splashed. Suddenly every one of them irritated Merrick.

He turned and hissed over his shoulder, "Gentlemen, please . . . a little stealth if you can!"

The guards grouped together and by going single file managed not to splash in the overflow quite as badly. It wasn't their fault that they were used to guarding doorways rather than engaging in covert pursuits.

"Thank you," Merrick managed. His mother had always taught him politeness in any situation—and it seemed particularly appropriate in this one.

Together they traversed another few feet, until an unexpected warm breeze wafted over Merrick's face. He jerked to a halt. The pipe suddenly had a branch, but this was different from the others they had already passed.

The rune Sielu was no longer needed, for there were absolutely no rats here. Dropping it, the Deacon checked with his

Center; it wasn't just rodents, there were no animals at all in the area around this new opening.

As the guards waited at his back, Merrick examined this new pipe. The breeze coming out of it was indeed warm—not cold like the other junctions. The brickwork too was different. Unlike the ancient bricks they had been traveling past, these were bright red and very, very fresh.

"Someone has been doing a few renovations," the Deacon commented, running his hand lightly over them. These were different from the original bricks in another way; he could feel no hint of a maker's impression on them. They were wiped clean as effectively as a clever murderer would clean a knife. Yet here again was the handprint of his mother, just a few more specks of her blood. Maybe it was a son's imagination, but he could almost smell Japhne's fear.

"Keep your rifles primed," he whispered to the guards, "and your blade loose in its sheath." If Hatipai was heading to her Temple, then someone else must be pursuing his mother, and few of the unliving ever bothered to hide their tracks like this. Only humans were this crafty.

Merrick Chambers had not forgotten his dreams nor the whispers in them. They had not tried to hide themselves. They wanted him to make the connection. The circle of five stars was an echo from an Order supposedly many generations dead—the Native Order.

He could not shake the feeling that it was not just his mother who was being led.

This new direction was not one any sensible person would take. He knew it. The guards knew it. It mattered little; they still had to go forward. After taking a long breath, one a diver might suck down before heading for the deep, Merrick led them into this new tunnel.

Immediately he knew the tunnel was more than it had appeared to be. His Center, which he had kept open, twisted, and for a terrifying moment everything went black. Panic washed over Merrick—he was being suffocated, scrambling for life and tumbling through space.

Then just as quickly it was over. The Deacon spun around, but all of the guards were still behind him; their eyes were wide and terrified in the lamplight, as Merrick knew his own to be.

The opening to the main pipe was right behind them, but Merrick's Center could travel no farther than the doorway. They were now a very, very long way from the tunnel beneath the palace—certainly more than a few strides.

Dael licked his lips before he dared use his voice. "Honored Deacon, what just happened?"

Merrick closed his eyes for a second, orienting himself in the world again, feeling his place in it. What he found made no sense; they had not only moved hundreds of miles, they had moved hours—well into the belly of night. It was something that might have been achieved by cantrips and weirstones, but he had seen none at the entrance to this tunnel.

Letting his guardsmen know how this surprised him would do them no good. "We are no longer in Chioma—we have moved." The men shifted, but in a testament to their character and training, did not break for the doorway, which did seem only inches off. "This means nothing—we are still going after the Lady Japhne."

"Yes, sir!" Dael spoke up, and the Deacon was so grateful he could have shaken the man's hand right then.

Instead, Merrick merely nodded and took the lead into the darkness. What had felt like warm air when they'd been in Chioma was now freezing. The change had to be a result of the power used to create the gateway.

What was more disturbing was how little his Center was bringing him. Merrick did not mention it, but the darkness was just as deep around his senses as it was around the guards.

Merrick was as shocked as the guards when the void suddenly came alive, but he had no way of telling with what, because the first men to go down were those three carrying the lanterns. Around him he heard something moving; to his confused ears it sounded like wet laundry flapping on the line. The guards screamed only a few feet away; the sound echoed in the pipe before it was cut off with a choked gurgle. His first thought was to draw his sword, but he dared not strike without knowing where their attacker was. In the confusion they could all kill one another.

Apparently the guards had not considered that. They raised their rifles and fired about, punctuating the darkness with bright flares that burned Merrick's eyes, now used to semidarkness. He strained his ears to hear past the sound of angry, frightened men and the reports of gunfire. Merrick spun around, aware that other guards had their steel drawn and were laying about them in the pitch black. The ice-cold tunnel now smelled of blood, gunpowder and panic.

He had to drop to the rock-strewn ground several times or be cut to pieces by his own terrified companions. Rolling to the side out of their way, Merrick drew his own weapon and came to his feet. In his mind he also drew something far more useful, the Fourth Rune of Sight, Kebenar, so that he might see the truth of what was happening around him.

It did no good. Another guard went down howling, his blood pumping from a torn throat, while his colleagues lashed about them hoping to hit something—anything! But whatever moved in the dark was either too fast or had no physical body.

Merrick called out to them. "Dael, the rest of you, come here! By the Bones, keep calm!"

Yet he was asking them to go against the most primitive human fears: the thing in the dark that had a taste for blood. One of the final two guards struck his compatriot in the neck by complete accident, and he went down like a felled tree. Then the monster in the dark took the last of the men.

Now there was only the Deacon, the darkness and whatever fell creature inhabited it. He stood there in a crouch, holding his sword before him, and waited for death to come.

Sorcha and the Prince of Chioma reached the Imperial Dirigible Station with little incident in the darkest part of the night—mainly because there was no one left to challenge them. Those few unbelievers of Hatipai had made themselves scarce, while the rest of the town happily marched out into the desert. She wondered if the call of the false goddess allowed the poor wretches to gather water before they did so; if not, there would be terrible casualties—especially among the children and the elderly. Sorcha doubted it would trouble the "goddess" much.

The Prince was staring at the two dirigibles outlined by the blue glow of weirstone torches with undisguised awe.

"Have you never seen the Emperor's creations?" Sorcha asked, a tiny note of smugness creeping into her voice.

"Never," Onika replied, as his contingent of half a dozen guards clustered closer.

"Well, if any of you smoke—I would suggest not to," the Deacon went on, even though her fingers were twitching to be holding a cigar. "There is a reason they only use weirstones to propel the ship."

When they looked at her questioningly, she mimed an explosion that made them blanch.

Luckily, Captain Revele appeared from out of the station buildings and trotted over to Sorcha. Though she cast a curious glance at the strangely masked figure at the Deacon's side, she saluted Sorcha. "Deacon Faris . . ." The slight slumping her shoulders was only perceptible to a trained Deacon. Sorcha knew full well it was because there was no Merrick at her side.

"Captain Revele"—Sorcha turned and looked toward the two moored dirigibles—"have you had any trouble here?" The last thing she wanted to get onto was a damaged vessel.

"There were a few locals who took exception to our presence"—Vyra's lips jerked at the corners—"but we fired a few volleys over their heads, and they quickly decided there were softer targets."

"The pull of the goddess is powerful," Onika muttered under his breath, but he did not introduce himself.

Sorcha decided that it was the best policy to keep things that way. "Who is the captain of the other vessel?"

"Captain Poetion." She turned, gestured to the rank of seamen standing watch over the guide ropes, and a tall, thin man strode over to meet them.

He snapped a salute to Sorcha. "Captain Poetion of the *Winter Falcon*, at your service, Honored Deacon."

"Good, because service is what we need." Sorcha pointed to his vessel, which looked to be the sister of the *Summer Hawk*. "We must make all haste into the desert after the citizens of Orinthal."

Poetion's face flickered with a moment of indecision that she really didn't need to deal with right now.

"Speak up, man," she snapped.

He cleared his throat. "The *Falcon* is currently at the service of the Grand Duchess Zofiya."

Sorcha pressed her lips together; in the confusion she had completely forgotten about the Emperor's sister. So there were only two options: she was either hiding, or she was lying in a pool of blood in the backstreets of Orinthal. If she said either of those things to Poetion, he would demand they start searching, and by then Hatipai would have the kingdom of Chioma in the palm of her hand.

So Sorcha did the only thing she could do at this vital moment; she lied. "The Grand Duchess is who we are following—I don't see any conflict in your orders there, Captain."

Immediately Poetion's face relaxed. He was happy to have someone else taking responsibility. He stepped back and saluted. "Then the *Winter Falcon* is at your service. Please come aboard."

"Deacon Faris," Captain Revele broke in. "What are your orders for me and the *Summer Hawk*?" What she really meant was: "What about Deacon Chambers?"

Sorcha smiled slightly. "My partner will follow us as soon as he has concluded his business. I want you to bring him as fast as that contraption of yours can go to the Temple in the desert. It's in the east, and apparently you can't miss the damned thing."

"Yes, ma'am." She grinned broadly.

Sorcha found herself strangely satisfied that at least someone was happy in this crazy situation. "Just take care of him," she said over her shoulder, and the words felt curiously final.

Onika and his handful of guards climbed aboard the *Winter Falcon* with the kind of trepidation that reminded Sorcha of Raed. The slight swaying and creaking of the dirigible had also alarmed him, but his anxiety had disappeared when they had lain together in the swinging bed. This trip would be considerably shorter and nowhere as enjoyable.

The crew leapt to their positions quickly, and Captain Poetion strode past his newest guests to take control of his ship. The *Falcon* took her name very seriously. She soared into the air toward the dark clouds highlighted by the moon. It was a surreal and beautiful moment, and Sorcha was determined to enjoy the spectacle, because she certainly wasn't allowed to smoke.

At her side Onika's hands gripped the railing. "Such things are not right."

"Not right?" Sorcha looked down as the Hive City slid past under them. From up here, the little fires looked pretty, though they signaled chaos.

"Such things were why the Ehtia left this world," the Prince muttered.

"The Ehtia?"

"Never mind." Onika slid his hand beneath his mask and rubbed wearily at that magnificent face his mother had given him.

The Prince's facade, hidden as it might be, was starting to crack. He sounded almost human under there. "Very well, Your Highness, perhaps we can talk about what we will face when we reach this Temple."

He sighed heavily. "My mother will create a new body so she can have a grip on this world. It was what we took from her last time—but we could not banish her spirit, and that is what we imprisoned under Vermillion. Only a Prince and a person of faith could free her—it was the best lock we could make."

"I wish Vermillion wasn't such a popular place to dump problems." The Deacon drummed her fingers on the railing as she digested this. She knew there were no true acolytes of the little gods in the capital—except one very famous one: the Grand Duchess Zofiya. She swallowed. The Emperor's sister, who lived in the palace and was well-known for her strange adherence to a curious religion. Still, no one in Vermillion would have questioned Zofiya. Doing so would be detrimental to their health.

The Deacon began to wonder if she might have to kill the Emperor's sister rather soon, and then she began to consider what her Arch Abbot would think of that.

"I hope your partner has found Japhne," Onika said, his voice so low that it was almost drowned out by the hum of the weirstone engine.

"She's his mother, so I think he has plenty of motivation, and Merrick is the most determined person I know."

Onika nodded and became silent as they flew on. Sorcha stepped away and helped the guardsmen find places to sleep. They, like she, would certainly need rest. A lifetime of the thin mattresses in the Abbey helped her sleep pretty much anywhere, and it had been a long, long day.

Sorcha curled up in the empty hold with a mat of straw under her and caught a few vital hours of sleep. What the Prince of Chioma did was his own business. The smooth progress of the *Winter Falcon* lulled her off to sleep, where dark shadows waited to chase her.

What woke her up, however, were a lurch and the sound of feet pounding on the deck. Grabbing her Gauntlets, Sorcha leapt up and ran outside to find what fresh trouble had them.

It was a staggering progress, though, as the dirigible was bucking and shaking itself like a maddened bull. The clouds, which had been distant, were churning around them with lightning rumbling in their bellies. The *Falcon* shook and creaked, throwing around her occupants, so that even the crew had to hang on to the rigging.

Sorcha proceeded forward in a sort of monkey scramble, more swinging than walking. She found the Chiomese guards clustered around Onika—all of them were wet and panicked. The Prince's mask was shaking and trembling, and this meant that every few heartbeats his face was revealed. His poor guardsmen were alternatively terrified and struck dumb with his glory.

Sorcha averted her eyes and tried instead to make out what was happening to the *Falcon*. Sharp rain stung her face, and howling winds pulled her hair loose from its pins. She'd been on dirigibles during storms before, and usually the captains took their vessels above the clouds—yet she couldn't feel any change in the *Falcon*'s altitude.

"Stay here," she yelled over the sound of wind and then half crawled toward the cabin. The dirigible bucked and hummed as if she were in pain, and the Deacon had to latch on to the rigging as best she could while working her way forward.

She had only just reached the flight cabin when the door flung open, and Captain Poetion appeared. His face said it all, though as a trained officer in the Imperial Air Fleet, he tried to hide his look of terror beneath a mask of professionalism. Yet it was there.

"We have reached the Temple," he yelled over the cacophony, while clenching onto the frame of the door. "But we can't get above this storm. It's like nothing I've ever seen."

"That is to be expected." Onika appeared at Sorcha's shoulder. "Captain, if you want your vessel to survive this, you must let us off. Immediately."

Poetion glanced back into the flight cabin where the wheelman struggled with the controls of the *Falcon*. The dials danced as if possessed, while another member of the crew tried to hold the levers steady.

The captain leaned into the wind and shouted at Onika and Sorcha, "We can't control the altitude at all. If you want to get off, we are going to have to use the swings."

The Deacon's stomach lurched, and it didn't have anything to do with the mad bucking of the dirigible. Nobody could be sure how high they were, but Sorcha was sure the Prince knew what he was doing.

As quickly as possible, Poetion led them to the rigging on the starboard side. The swings, which Sorcha had used once before, were unhitched by crew who looked glad to be rid of their passengers. In the rain and the wind, Sorcha's fingers were numb as she struggled to get into the harness. She couldn't see much, and her heart was racing. The firm wood placed under her bottom did indeed resemble a swing, though there was a small comfort in the fact that she and Onika were buckled into it.

The guards were arguing with Poetion, demanding to go down ahead of their Prince, but it was Onika who cut in.

"The sooner I am on solid ground, the better for all of you," he said, and that was that. The tiny glimpses of his compelling face made sure that no one disagreed. He and Sorcha poised on the edge of the railing, their feet dangling out into space. The Deacon took a long, deep breath, trying to keep herself from breaking out into full-fledged panic. A crew member stood ready on the each of their winches, waiting for the signal.

Poetion looked to the Deacon, and she realized that even in this moment of madness it was up to her to say the word.

Clenching her hands around the swing's chains, she pushed with her feet. The arm of the device swiveled out, and now she was hanging over nothing. Below, all she could see was mist and rain—no sight of the ground at all.

"I wonder how many people have wanted to drop a Deacon like this," she muttered before waving to the grinder on the end of the winch. "Ready to go."

And then there they were, descending into the darkness. Her hair was blasted free of its ties, so she was almost blinded by it. The rain picked up, each droplet sharp on her skin, while the rumble of thunder deafened her. It didn't seem that the storm was abating—in fact, it was intensifying. She wondered if this was how a worm on a fishhook felt.

The swing was certainly living up to its name, but unlike a childhood pleasure, this jarred her stomach and robbed the breath from her body. Sorcha couldn't even see Onika, though he was surely only six feet from her.

Pushing her hair out of her face, Sorcha looked up with her Center. She immediately wished she hadn't. The clouds above danced with lightning, but this only served to illuminate the darkness that was deeper in the throbbing mass. It looked exactly like a clawed hand reaching down. Sorcha tried to work out what sort of geist could do that, but it was hard to think clearly when those talons were obviously wrapping about the *Winter Falcon*.

The swing jerked, spun her around, and began tipping backwards. A scream escaped Sorcha and was swallowed by the storm. Falling had always been her greatest fear, and hours of Deacon training had only blunted its edge. A terrified glance down told her nothing at all, because the storm wrapped around everything. They could be five feet from safety or a hundred.

Lightning flashed and thunder boomed immediately after. Sorcha's head rang, and she was blinded for a second. Some primal survival instinct made her look up again, and there it was; the hand clenched around the dirigible flashed with lightning. If no one was allowed to smoke on the Imperial ships, they were certainly not allowed to throw lightning into them either.

"Onika!" Sorcha screamed, uncertain where he was. The

envelope of the *Winter Falcon* caught fire with an ear-ringing roar. The heat was so intense that the Deacon threw her arms around her head, fearing her hair would catch alight. The dirigible burned bright blue, and flames licked up the skin as if caressing it. It would have been beautiful if it wasn't also everyone's death.

The Deacon knew there was nothing to be done now. The *Falcon* was bending in half, falling toward them, and they only had one chance. Everything slowed.

To her right she could at least now see Onika. "Cut the harness! Cut the harness now!" Sorcha screamed to him, unsure if in the panic he would hear her. Then she pulled her knife from her belt and did as she hoped he would.

Free of the swing, she didn't want to let go for a split second. Her mind screamed denials, but the device was a false safety—they would be tangled with the doomed *Falcon* and burn with it.

Sorcha took a deep breath, wiggled free and then with a cry dropped into the darkness. All she could hope for was sand or a quick death.

TWENTY-EIGHT

Despair and Delight

They dragged Raed into the Temple and locked him a room about the size of a cupboard, but his surroundings mattered little. The Young Pretender lay there waiting for the hurt to stop. It didn't. Eventually blessed unconsciousness wrapped itself around him.

The next morning his eyelids flicked open, revealing the world and its ugly realities. His hands were numb and still bound with the weirstones. Raed licked his lips, trying to focus his eyes. The only light in here was from the narrow crack under the door. The cupboard was tiny, like a hot box found in a prison.

As a thin line of sweat ran down Raed's forehead, he tried to come to terms with the fact that last night had been real. He had found his sister—and she hated him. His crew had died for him. All these things were true.

These were merely another long line of bitter facts that he'd been facing all his life. Raed would not give up. Fraine, poor damaged Fraine, had gone. However, if he could get away from this mad situation, he still could catch up to her, make her see the error of what she was doing. As painful as it was to think about, it had to have been Tangyre that had twisted Fraine's mind. Raed had thought Captain Greene was his friend, but he was now positive he didn't know half the things that had gone on in his absence. She must have been feeding Fraine venom for years, venom that now threatened to engulf them all.

So Raed struggled to his knees and assessed what his chances were. His body ached with the various kicks and punches he had taken last night, the kind of deep bruising that would take a while to heal. Still, he had taken notice of what the charming women had said last night and wondered if he would even get a chance to heal. He just had to go on as though he would.

Somewhere out there was a wild card, one that Zofiya, Tang or his sister didn't count on—Deacon Sorcha Faris. He'd put his trust in her before, and she hadn't failed him. Getting to his feet, Raed pressed his ear to the door of the cupboard. An ominous chanting, soft and low and from many throats, was all he heard. It didn't matter if it was for gods or geists, chanting was never a good sign. Yet there was no handle for him to try, nothing else in the cupboard he could use as a weapon and the walls were of sturdy stone.

Just as he was contemplating trying his shoulder against the door, two Chiomese guards yanked it open and pulled him out into the light. Now Raed was able to take in the beauty and terror of the Temple of Hatipai. It did nothing to cheer him.

She, according to the nature of her kind, dominated it. No other decoration detracted from the huge carving of her that slithered its way around the walls of the Temple. Her stretched body resembled nothing so much as a snake eating its own tail. Her undulating neck carried the depiction of her head up the stairs so that its distorted face rested at the top. Her open mouth was like a void, and a freezing breeze poured from it. Raed was no expert, but he had always imagined that in a Temple the object of adoration should be lovely, offering comfort or inspiring awe. This looked like something out of a mad dream.

The citizens of Orinthal didn't appear to feel the same. They were crowded into the building with barely an inch between them. Parents had their children on their shoulders so they could see the scene. Raed wasn't so lucky. All he experienced was the shoves and jeers of the mob. A few managed to

get punches in, so that by the time he was dragged to the foot
of the stairs he had all new aches and pains.

One of the cuts on his head had been reopened, so when he
looked up it was through a veil of blood. Zofiya and an old
man waited for him at the top of the stairs, and behind them
was a device that gleamed in the torchlight. In his childhood
Raed had found one of his playmates cutting a rabbit to pieces
in the orchard. The boy had nailed each of the poor creature's
feet into the ground and was slicing into it with the care of a
surgeon. Yet the creature was still conscious.

Now, looking up at the metallic X-shaped device studded
with weirstones, Raed recalled vividly the white, panicked
eyes of the rabbit and heard again that strange scream it had
made. He wondered if he would make the same sound when
they got him up there and began their vivisection. Zofiya had
promised Fraine it would hurt. It looked like she would keep
her word.

Death didn't find him. Merrick stood panting in the dark and
tried to gather his calm about him.

The guardsmen were dead at his feet, but he still had his
mission to find his mother. Taking a few deep, slow breaths,
Merrick bent and felt around under his fingers, feeling for a
guard's abandoned rifle. Standing upright, armed with gun
and blade, he slowly opened his Center. He could still feel
nothing of the attacker in the dark. It could not be geist or
human, as he would have detected it—so then what could it
be? His mind whirred.

If he could not find the attacker nor see it, then he had to
move on or remain frozen in fear while terrible things happened to his mother. His Center flowed out from him, seeking
his kin. She was there . . . in the shadows, not far away now—
but also other presences. Human. Powerful. Near to her.

Merrick's eyes flickered open as he realized they were as
aware of him as he was of them. He grasped his saber's hilt
and ran forward into the dark. He couldn't see a thing and was
led only by his Deacon-trained senses. The tunnel echoed
with the rapid slap of his feet on the damp ground and was
accompanied by the sound of his own heartbeat in his ears.

When light spilled from ahead of him, even though it had only been moments since he'd last had it, Merrick's eyes still watered. It was no geist that stood before him—it was four robed figures—three men and a woman.

For a heartbeat Merrick was back in the Mother Abbey, in front of his peers. A habitual smile almost made it to his lips at the familiar cloak of his Order.

And then he noticed the differences. The cloaks were not green or blue but brown. The light they had summoned gleamed on the brooches pinned to their shoulders, and he was not surprised to see the circle of five stars.

Another shape, another Deacon, for want of a better word, stepped out of the shadows, and he was dragging Japhne. Merrick started forward in rage.

"Now, now, Deacon Chambers." One of the older men, tall and with a hawklike nose, held up his bare hand. "Do not be hasty. Young man, this is the meeting on which your future turns."

Merrick paused a moment to gain a foothold on this new reality. "It is rather hard to think clearly with a knife at a pregnant woman's back." He couldn't see it from here, but his Center was still open and was becoming useful again. By telling them about the knife, he was telling them he was not quite as helpless as they might think.

Still, everyone could see he was a Sensitive without his Active.

Their leader, if that was what he was, tilted his head, and a disturbing smile spread on his face. Yet he gestured to his cohort, who then dropped the tip of the blade from close proximity to his mother. "You must know she is the key to controlling Hatipai, and I am sure you're clever enough to realize how important that is."

Merrick swallowed hard. "I presume you mean to use her unborn child to do that."

The man shrugged as if they were talking about the price of milk. "The blood she left behind is her focus. That is why she wanted to get rid of it. Instead, we will use it with runes and cantrips to put a leash on 'the goddess.'"

As he spoke, the young Deacon tried to judge how many of them he could shoot before they did anything to his mother.

He was good with a blade, but it had been some time since he'd fired a rifle. "And who are you to do that?"

The man gave his name easily. And then grinned as if it were nothing.

The look in Japhne's eyes was terrified, and she wrapped her hands about her belly, trying to provide some protection to her second son.

"But you're consorting with Hatipai." Merrick shuffled forward a little. "The murderer stalking Chioma was no crazed killer—you called that Beast for her, for the geist who will have Chioma again."

The old man smiled, an expression that chilled Merrick to the core. "We use what instruments we need—even geistlords can sometimes have their uses." His eyes flicked down to Japhne. "Once Hatipai's son is dead, she will take Chioma and bring down chaos."

His mother was looking at him, her eyes swimming with tears but also something else: the mad determination for her children to live. At her side her fingertips brushed her dress, pulling it away a little, revealing the fact that tucked in tightly against her wrist, nestled in the palm of her hand, was a knife. It was stained with her blood and must have been what she had defended herself with before. It was not much, but the set of her jaw told her son that she would not let her children die without a struggle.

Merrick swallowed hard. "But why would you want that? Your Order fights the geists too."

"We did once," the female Deacon broke in, "until we realized we could do so much more. We could use them. We could be the ones in control of the whole Empire."

Her superior shot her a look that instantly silenced her, but he seemed happy to finish the conversation. "You stopped the Murashev, Deacon Chambers. So we had to find other ways. We are not so foolish as to make the same mistake we did last century."

Merrick thought of the book back at the Chiomese Abbey. "The people rose against you. They would not tolerate you using the geists."

"Be on the winning side, Merrick." The man's gray eyes were harder than stone, his voice smooth and alluring. This man had charisma and power; he was used to being obeyed. "You became a Deacon to make a difference—with us you can change the world for the better."

"You are the only one of those fools we have offered to join us." The female Deacon had spoken. Her voice held a strange accent that Merrick, despite all his training, could not quite place. Her hair was pure white, though her face looked no more than twenty.

Merrick was now only ten feet from them, looking far more confident that he felt. If he chose the wrong words, his mother, his unborn half brother and he would die in this place.

He cleared his throat. "No offense, but the Native Order has been dead for at least a generation—what could you offer me that my current Order does not?"

"We know the true path of things." The older man's hand appeared from under his cloak, and he was clutching a weirstone. This one was not blue but instead burned white.

Merrick glimpsed a face, misty and terrified, pressed into it. It was a shade, a person trapped within.

"We have learned the art of using geist and weirstone together in ways that not even the Ancients could have imagined." The lead Deacon was very pleased with himself, though such a thing was the worst abomination that Merrick could imagine.

He was totally unable to contain his reaction. "But you trap souls—human souls—in order to do it!"

"Not just human," the woman said softly, "but geists too."

This was why the population had turned against the Native Order. This was why the Rossin family had set about destroying them. And these Deacons thought they saw something in him. "You would set yourselves up as tyrants!" he barked, hand clenching tightly on his sword hilt, even though he knew it was useless.

Yet, by the Bones, he did have another weapon: the wild talent. He'd spent months trying to avoid thinking of it. The shameful thing that had welled out of him on the street in Vermillion. Merrick had never spoken of it, even with Sorcha. Any sign of such a talent would result in ejection from the Order and then most probably imprisonment.

It was not his nature to kill, so he gave them one final

chance. "But you can still turn back." He held out his hand.
"Give me the woman and let me set Chioma to rights."

The native Deacon grinned. "What is she to you, Deacon
Chambers? Another slut of a corrupt Prince. We can offer you
the world."

The slur was enough to set Japhne off. With a shriek of
outrage, she plunged her blade down into the foot of the man
holding her. The knife was small but obviously very sharp.
Her captor bellowed in agony as it skewered him to the floor.

Displaying incredible athleticism, Merrick's mother came
off the floor and raced toward him. Yet she was clever, keeping to the side of the tunnel in order to give him a clean line of
sight. The heretic Deacons were throwing back their cloaks
and reaching for their weirstones, but he was faster. Merrick
fired off a shot that clipped the younger man in the shoulder
and then cocked the weapon and fired again. The woman went
down with an inch-wide hole blasted in her head—it looked
like a masterly shot, but Merrick had been aiming for the
hawk-nosed man.

It wasn't enough—he was still just a Sensitive—and they
would reach for runes or something even direr. So, in desperation, Deacon Chambers reached deep within himself and
tried to find the hidden spark.

It was like grasping a fish in murky water. He thought of
the moment it had welled up inside him. He thought of Nynnia
and her own mysterious powers. And finally he thought of his
mother dying down here in the dark when she had so much to
live for after so long without.

And then he felt it, waves of power bubbling up from some
unexplored place within himself. The Deacons before him
were full of arrogance, confidence in their own power and the
situation they had him in.

It was so easy to turn that confidence into crippling fear,
like flipping a coin from heads to tails—even though what he
was really doing was close to scrambling their brains. Merrick realized he should have been horrified both at what he
was doing and its ease—but they had threatened his family—
nothing was off limits.

Suddenly the centered Deacons were anything but. They
were twisted, sobbing, terrified at the dark they had created.

Merrick had no way of telling if they could fight back against his wild talent, but he was taking no chances. "Mother." He ran forward and grabbed her hand. He had no idea how long what he had done would last.

The darkness was so complete that only the barest hint of the tunnel they were in revealed itself to Merrick's Sight, and worse there was no end to it.

"We should be back to the main pipe by now," he muttered under his breath. "I don't understand it."

"We're not in Chioma." Japhne wheezed at his side. How his mother would have such an idea Merrick could not afford to stop and ask. Yet he feared she was right. Weirstones and even runes could be used for such things.

Screams rang out from behind them, the sounds of the Deacons but higher-pitched—the sound of pain and death rather than just fear. Whatever shackles they had put on their Beast had obviously required concentration.

Merrick was not sorry for them. Any who chose the path of consorting with the Otherside deserved their fate. However, he knew the creature would pursue them now that it was done with its tormentors.

He slipped his arm around his mother. "Then we have to find the entrance—it must go both ways for them to come and go into the palace."

She nodded against his shoulder, but her breath was coming in ragged gasps. Merrick had little experience, but he was fairly sure that heavily pregnant women should not be running for their lives in the dark.

And then the sound he had feared and half expected came; the high-pitched whine of a geist on the hunt. It was like claws on glass—but several types of geist had similar sorts of calls.

His mother stumbled and would have gone to her knees without Merrick catching her. The ground underfoot was now getting slippery, and she cursed. "If only I was younger; if only I could see!" It took a lot to get his mother upset, but she was obviously at the end of her tether.

"It's not much farther," Merrick lied. His Center was only giving him details of the cave walls a mere five feet in front of them.

Japhne tripped again, and the sound drew closer, along with

a wave of cold so intense it might have come from the heart of winter. For the first time in his life Merrick regretted being a Sensitive. If Sorcha was here alone with the heavily pregnant woman, she would have at least been able to protect her.

"Leave me." Japhne tugged on his cloak, and he didn't need to see her face to know it would be racked with pain. As a mother she wanted to protect her unborn child, but she also wanted him to protect himself. It was a decision no mother should have to make. "Run."

It was an idea that Merrick did not entertain for a moment. If one person was going to survive this, it was his mother. The geist was upon them. He shoved Japhne, something that as a good son he would have never have done until this desperate moment. She stumbled and fell against the wall, while Merrick stood alone between her and the creature.

"Go!" he bellowed, pulling his sword, though it was a totally pointless gesture. The geist loomed out of the darkness, or maybe more precisely gathered itself from within the darkness, because he finally recognized it: a ghast. The dense knot of shades was held together by cantrips and weirstones, a snarling, snapping creature composed of twenty or so tormented human souls and their lost hopes.

Racked with so much pain, a ghast was a maw of destruction that would enter a human body and pull it apart from inside, creating another shade to add to its conglomeration. They had created more pain and destruction than any other kind of geist and had been the priority for the Order of the Eye and the Fist when they had made landfall on Arkaym with the Emperor years before.

Merrick remained calm, though he knew the odds; he was a Sensitive adrift without his Active and had nothing to offer up except his body.

Flicking around, he screamed at Japhne, who had not gone much farther than he had shoved her. "Mother! Save yourself, save the child!" The howl came out raw, and he knew it would be the last thing he said.

She clutched the rock wall with spread fingers, tears streaming down her face and unable to chose a path. They would all die here then in this lonely corridor, not even knowing where they were.

Merrick turned and became Active. No Deacon except the Arch Abbot ever held both the Gauntlets and the Strop, but every one of them had the seed of both specialities in them. Merrick did not have the Gauntlets that would provide protection from the backlash of the runes, and he didn't have the training to control them, but at this moment he was out of all other options. The one thing he did have was knowledge.

In his mind's eye he drew Pyet, the cleansing flame. The long, looping line of the rune, bisected by the horizontal straight line leapt into existence, carving itself into the flesh of his palm.

The fire cut to his core. Never having done it, Merrick nevertheless imagined it felt the same as shoving his hand into a burning hearth. But he couldn't afford the time and energy to scream. If he lost control of the rune now, they would all be consumed by it. Trained to see through pain, he managed to hold out his hands.

Red fire coursed from the rune, flowing over his hands—thankfully not melting his flesh yet—and enveloped the ghast as it gathered itself to leap from the shadows.

The conflagration filled the tunnel, and Merrick wondered, even as the pain chewed at his concentration, how he had managed such a display. His Active side was latent only, and he had at best been hoping for a mere distraction so that his mother could escape.

The smell of charred brick and dirt filled his nostrils, even as the power filled him. It was heady and terrifying. The Active talent heightened every sense, until he was choking, sobbing, overwhelmed—yet still Merrick held on.

Pyet was more than a physical flame. It had to be to have any effect on a geist. As the intense flame poured from the mark on Merrick's hand, the ghast writhed.

Its screams were filled with the pain of dozens of souls trapped and feeling death again. But it was a little pain compared to the agony of holding the rune. Merrick knew it was burning far too brightly and far too long. The ghast was gone, a candle held in a blast furnace, but the Deacon could not stop the destruction gushing out of him.

Now the smell was that of his own mortal form; the hairs on his arm burst alight, and he could feel real physical flames reaching out to consume skin and flesh.

He had saved his mother and unborn brother, but now it was he who would be the candle. Merrick prepared himself to be taken, until the moment Japhne laid cool hands on him. He jerked away, trying to shake her loose, but she was surprisingly strong. Forcing her fingers around his wrists, she pulled him to her, and Pyet and the flames were suddenly gone.

Merrick stood there for a long moment, feeling his mother's arms now go around him. She was soft and cool comfort. And he was alive.

When the Deacon pulled back, she still held on to his hands, cradling them in her own. He looked down, fearing what he would see. They were not blackened lumps as he might have guessed, but they were bright red and blistered. It was going to be painful, but he might keep his hands.

"How did you—" he began.

Japhne smiled, leaned forward and kissed his cheek. "The Ancient blood flows in your veins—but not from your father's family."

"The Ehtia," he whispered in return, wondering how much of the wild talent that his Order was so afraid of came from them. "So you—"

"It is a little talent." His mother stroked his hair back from his face. "I can calm magic from time to time. It turned out to be a very useful skill when I fell in love with Onika."

Despite the situation, Merrick blushed—he had wondered if the Prince kept his mask on in private—but if Japhne was unaffected, then it all made sense. He quickly changed the topic of conversation, which was unseemly and awkward for him as both a son and as a Deacon.

"Come on." He put his arm around his mother. "We have to get you back to the palace, and then I must try to catch up with Sorcha and Onika. They have gone to stop the goddess Hatipai gaining a body in this world. I fear I know how I was able to channel an Active rune."

Holding each other up, they made it back to the junction with the pipe under the palace. Now, with the darkness lifted, Merrick could make out a circle of weirstones embedded in the brickwork—it was a masterfully done job.

"But your hands," his mother murmured as they stepped out of one pipe and back into Chioma.

Once there, Merrick could feel the Bond singing in his head. The buzz was not a comforting noise. Somewhere not far off, he feared he had left his partner significantly diminished. He glanced down at his palms. "I'll bind them. Perhaps if I take the fastest horse, I can still catch them."

Japhne frowned, undoubtedly thinking of her own lover in danger. "What use can you be, my son? Surely what is done is already done?"

"Not where Sorcha is concerned, Mother."

"Then go to the dirigible station." Now she was tugging him along. "There are two vessels in port, and if they burn weirstones, you may just get there in time."

Merrick's heart welled with admiration and love for Japhne. He had saved her, and then she had saved him. The young Deacon could only hope that he would get to his partner in time to bring her the same hope.

TWENTY-NINE

Prodigal Son

Sorcha woke in a cradle of sand. It had blown over her, cushioned her, but was now trying to swallow her. She jerked erect, the broken swing tangled on top of her, her mouth dry and her pulse racing. Turning her head to the left, she saw the still-smoldering remains of the *Winter Falcon* spread over the dunes.

The brave Chiomese and the Imperial sailors had died together because of Hatipai—Sorcha had no doubt of that. It was up to her to stop the false goddess from taking any more victims.

After she pushed herself free of the remains of the swing, she dragged herself to her feet and examined her body carefully. She felt as though she'd been given a damn good beating, and even without pulling aside her clothes, Sorcha could tell there would be plenty of bruises. Though she had no way of knowing how far she'd fallen, nothing felt broken. Next she tried to orient herself under the blazing sun.

"It's over there." Onika's voice at her back made her jump like a green Initiate. The Prince of Chioma could have been a statue revealed by blowing sand—he certainly didn't look as though he had fallen any great distance either. He looked no more ruffled than if he'd been standing in his own Court.

He didn't point, but then he didn't need to. The Temple of Hatipai was the only structure in a blinding ocean of sand. It stood out, red like a blister among the gold of the dunes.

"You don't have to go." She tottered over to stand at his shoulder. "I have sworn an Order Oath; I have to go down there, but you—"

"I too swore an oath." The Prince raised his hand and tore off the shining mask. He flung it into the sand as if it were something vile, but he didn't turn around. "The people of Chioma are mine to protect—they always have been."

Sorcha averted her eyes. "How can you protect them if you are dead? What about your son waiting to be born?"

His voice was calm. "I cannot think of that now. Even as much as I love Japhne and him to come, I cannot put them above my people. I trust Merrick will take care of his mother."

The Deacon heard his cloak slide through the sand as he moved forward, but she still dared not look. She could almost feel the heat of his charisma beating on her head like the sun. "A child should always have its parent."

"Not everything that can birth a child can be called a parent." Onika touched her hair. "Some parents do better to leave this world before they can teach a child to fear. How could I have a son who cannot even look at my face?"

Sorcha had never known her own parents, so could not argue with him. His open hand appeared in her peripheral vision.

"Please, Deacon Chambers, I need someone to look at me."

His voice cracked with melancholy and fear. Sorcha looked up and opened her Center. While her humanity was stunned by the immortal god, her Deacon training helped her see behind it to the man he was.

"Why?" she stammered through numb lips and burning eyes. "Why are you going down there straight into her hands?"

The Prince smiled and jerked aside his cloak. Underneath, hanging from his belt was a long, curved dagger with a weirstone gleaming on its hilt. "Not long ago I found a secret book of prophecy. It can only be done by me, with this blade, in her Temple, as she becomes mortal. Just before she does, there will be a moment of weakness." His hand touched Sorcha's head lightly. "I am the only one who can strike."

As a Deacon, Sorcha was sure she didn't believe in prophecies or fate, but in the gleaming light of his charisma, she trusted him.

"But I have something for you, if this should fail." From one of the pouches at his belt Onika pulled a strange sphere. It was about the size of his fist with a miniature crank in its clear side. When he turned it, a high-pitched whir sounded, while around the Prince the air shifted. His face flickered with momentary pain as a silvery gray liquid filled the sphere, but from where it came, Sorcha could not tell.

"Hold out your hand, Deacon Faris." Sorcha offered her palm, and he placed the strange device into it. "This is one of my mother's gifts, a protection for the body. For a human with no trace of geist it should not last long, but it will help you if things go wrong in the Temple." Onika spun the crank in the opposite direction. The gleaming liquid now began to drop away in the sphere, until there was no liquid apparent. Instead, Sorcha felt warmth spread over her.

For a second her skin gleamed like it was covered in a thin film of oil, but then that too vanished. "You've made me immortal?"

Onika laughed again. "Temporarily your body is protected—that is all, Deacon Faris. Do not get arrogant, for it will wear off in a few days. You are not born of a geistlord as I am."

"And you?"

"If I survive this, I want to grow old with Japhne." He glanced back toward Orinthal. "I want my son to rule in Chioma, so it is no loss to me."

Giving up this was a sign of faith Sorcha could not understand, but she wouldn't argue with it. The look in his eyes said this was no sudden decision.

"Then let us unshackle your people," she said, slipping on her Gauntlets and facing the Temple.

"Thank you." His fingers tightened on hers, apparently immune to the sting of the runes, and then together they walked down toward the Temple. With every step, as long as she didn't glance at him, Sorcha felt her equilibrium recover.

As they got closer to the Temple, she couldn't help it, she began to chuckle. "Oh, your mother is quite modest."

Onika's laugh was loud and unexpected as he got her point.

The Temple was shaped like a beautiful woman lying on her side, one hand propping up her head, the steps leading to the interior literally burrowed into her belly button. It was the bright red of the city of Orinthal but not nearly as charming.

"That has to be the crassest thing I have ever seen." Sorcha giggled. "And I grew up in Delmaire!"

"I think you should mention that when you meet her!" The Prince's laugh was long and genuine.

A mass of people were clustered around the Temple door. This was indeed where Orinthal had migrated to. Onika untangled his hand with hers so now he stood alone. "Follow me."

The people turned and then, like a wave breaking on the shore, dropped to their knees, abasing themselves before the Prince. It was not because he was their ruler. It was because he was unmasked. Hatipai had them in her control right up until the moment her son appeared. It was one thing to have belief in a goddess, but when a god walked among them in the flesh, it overrode all that.

A hot wind was coming off the desert and straight into Sorcha's face, flinging bits of sand into her eyes and mouth, but while she held her hand up and swore, Onika only kept moving forward.

"She's not far now." His voice was soft as he stepped carefully over and past the prostrate bodies. Sorcha followed in his wake as they climbed the stairs and into the Temple of Hatipai.

"I will go in first," Onika said, and with his godhood, false or otherwise, about him, Sorcha could not deny him.

Inside, the heat was the first thing the Deacon noted. Most Chiomese buildings were deliciously cool—but obviously the geistlord cared little for human comforts. As Sorcha looked around, she realized that in fact humanity cared little for those comforts, either. They were packed in here tighter than pickled herrings. It made it hard for them, but still the people of Orinthal managed to squeeze back a little, allowing their Prince farther into the Temple.

Above the crowd, there was a dais. Sorcha was pushed to and fro and had to stop and crane her head to see what was up there. Desperate to see, she was angry with the crowd, the foolish damn people. Finally, she saw.

It was a shadow of gold, hanging together like a faint mist that was trying to hold on to human form. A suggestion of wings flared out, twining and sparkling, and when she opened her Center, the shadow burned in her Sight—much as the Rossin did. A geistlord indeed, then.

Among the crowd she caught sight of the mustard yellow robes of the Chiomese Deacons, and yet they were just as smitten. Every face around her wore the same idiotic look; all logic, all reasoning washed away in fanaticism.

And the humans were not the only observers in the Temple. Through her Center the Deacon saw the shadows that filled every corner of the Temple: the shades of Hatipai's followers. Even after death, the so-called goddess kept her hold on them.

Sorcha struggled to keep her feet as the crowd surged forward, and she realized with horror that she was no longer in Onika's wake. The people had closed around her, and he had moved on. She pushed, shoved and swore, but it was as effective as a piece of flotsam fighting against the sea.

She was being pushed toward the far wall even as Onika walked up the stairs toward the remains of his mother. Then with a cry, she saw Raed. Her throat clenched, because if there was a better picture of sacrifice waiting to happen, she'd never seen it. He was bound upright on an X-shaped device that looked like an unholy melding of the torturer and the Tinker's art. Two long articulated armatures sprouted from the frame and hovered ready over Raed's naked body.

At the side of this device stood a gray-bearded man wearing elaborate robes, with the symbol of Hatipai over the broad sash of a royal Chancellor. He looked remarkably well for a man that should have died back in the palace.

Sorcha wished Raed would turn and look, but his eyes were cast down. Only the training and discipline of a Deacon kept her from raising her Gauntlets right then. Instead, she lowered her head and began shoving and twisting her way toward the dais. She didn't care how many toes she trod on or whose ribs got bruised in the process.

From her nearing vantage point Sorcha could now see the Grand Duchess Zofiya, but it took her a moment to recognize her. She was not in her usual dress uniform. Instead, she wore a thin white robe that left little to the imagination. In her hands, held stiffly out before her, was a sphere like the one the Prince had used. This one was larger but full of the same silver liquid. Zofiya's face was as expressionless as a statue— very unlike her usual restless nature. *This is where faith gets you,* Sorcha thought.

Ahead, the golden, ethereal form was bending toward Onika, and her words were loud and echoed off the walls of her Temple. "So, you have returned, my wayward son, returned to take your place with me?"

Onika threw off his cloak, and his voice too was impossibly loud. "I've come to finish what I should have generations ago, Mother." And then he swung down with the blade into the swirling mass of golden light.

Sorcha was now six rows of people away from reaching the theater of events, but she was blind without Merrick. The moment hung impossibly. Some of the people in the Temple began to wail and surge forward, carrying her with them. And then Hatipai's laughter boomed over everything.

It was not the sound Sorcha or Onika had been expecting, and now the Deacon's stomach clenched into a tight, painful knot. The crowd around her caught their goddess' mood and began to laugh too. It didn't make them any easier to get past.

Onika sank to his knees, his shoulders slumped.

"You really should not believe everything you read, my son." The golden mist solidified, an echo of a grinning woman's face.

The treacherous Chancellor laughed; his voice cracked like he'd been left too long in the desert heat. "We made the book, the prophecy, and you swallowed it down."

Onika's head sank to his chest as Hatipai enjoyed her moment. "You were always my backup plan, dear boy. The carrier of my flesh, should I lose it."

"Mother." His voice was angry, frustrated, lost. "Let her live . . . let my boy live."

"Never!" Hatipai's wings flew wide. "Every one of my flesh must die or be sacrificed—there will be no god or goddess but Hatipai!"

What else could he do? Sorcha felt herself on the edge of angry tears. The Prince was a pawn in this game but a good man despite everything. She threw herself toward them desperately. Now she was only two ranks of people away from breaking free, but this close, people were less likely to give way.

Hatipai looked at her son with a fierce look that hovered between rage and sorrow. "I knew you'd read the prophecy, and I knew you'd forget . . . a mother can always take back what she has given—if she has the will."

The goddess moved, but the Prince made no move to try to escape—there was, after all, nowhere to go. Unlike a geist, a geistlord could indeed hurt. That beautiful face was ripped from him with a terrible sound that all could hear, and then blood poured down the steps. He stayed on his knees for a while as the mist drained him, and then his body toppled. It slid down the steps slowly and then to one side with an audible thump.

Finally Sorcha broke free of the crowd. Hatipai was spinning, a cloud that was now red and gold; she was forming a body from what she had taken from her own son. The Deacon knew that she only had a few moments before the geistlord turned to Raed to take the remainder of what she needed from the him and the Rossin. It was the nature of geistlords to devour one another. Then she would take the sphere, which looked like the one her son had given Sorcha, and become impossible to stop.

So the Deacon tightened the lacings on her Gauntlets, then dashed up the stairs and threw herself into the maelstrom. The gold light enveloped her, and everything else ceased to matter. Her Center was blinded and useless. All there was was Hatipai. The Bright One.

The geistlord tore at Sorcha with her forming hands, and the pain was exquisite. The Deacon screamed as the geistlord wrapped around her and inside her. Yet Onika's gift held her body against the onslaught.

Sorcha tried to think past the pain. Though her body could not be destroyed, her mind and soul could be, so she had to work quickly. Desperately she called runes from her Gauntlets; Chityre and Pyet. Lightning flickered and danced through the red and gold of Hatipai, while flame bloomed around them. It could not touch the geistlord though.

Her face in the flames was now smiling and beautiful. "You cannot hurt me, Deacon. I do not yet have a body."

"But you can't destroy me either," Sorcha panted, her muscles screaming, "thanks to your son's gift. I will hold you here forever if necessary." She hoped her opponent could not read the lie from her mind. Sorcha had no idea how temporary her immunity was.

Dropping Chityre, she instead demanded the rune Yevah from her Gauntlets. The snap of the shield around them might offer some protection to the humans.

"Perhaps so." Hatipai caressed the Deacon's cheek, a line of fire following. "But I will eventually burn out your mind and then have my way."

By the Bones, she was right. The image of the broken members of her Order had always haunted Sorcha. She was an idiot to think she could hold out indefinitely.

"So many fears, so many doubts." The geistlord cooed into her ear. "We all have our secrets, don't we, little human, and I know the dirty secret of your existence . . ."

Sorcha didn't know what the damned creature was talking about, too busy holding up multiple runes while drowning in pain. Through the flickering of the shield she could finally see Raed. Now he was looking at her, his face a mask of horror and frustration as he strained against his bonds. They seemed to always be getting their timing wrong, and now there would be no chance for more. She regretted that.

The followers. The voice in her head was not Merrick, not even Raed; it was the Rossin. Trapped and angry, the Beast reached out to her. *The undead foci, they still follow her. Why? Why, you foolish mortal? Think!*

The foci of any geist were a strength and a weakness. Sorcha's streaming eyes flickered to those coalescing shades, and it was then she suddenly realized that most of them were spectyrs.

Yes, you see it. You finally see it. Vengeance.

Hatipai had lied to them, and they were not here at her bidding—they were here for her! They were out for vengeance, and it was the Deacon's place to give it to them.

Dropping the runes she held, Sorcha called on another, Tryrei, the rune that created a tiny peephole to the Otherside.

Hatipai roared with laughter. "You cannot drag me back home with that."

Sorcha, holding the rune, felt her strength begin to wane, but she would not let go. "The spectyrs can't see you very well. I'm giving them a torch," was all she managed to gasp out.

They had gathered together here to find answers to their ancient deaths. They knew they had been tricked by a geistlord and their faith had been misplaced.

The tiny hole to the Otherside got their attention, buried as it was in midst of Hatipai, the one who had fooled them. A terrible scream filled the Temple, the sound of a thousand souls in pain. They had lost everything to the geistlord: love, family, hope and life itself. The spectyrs flew at her like an angry cloud of ravens. Sorcha bit her lip, clenched her muscles and concentrated on the rune as they tore away at Hatipai. She had to hold it for them.

She was drawing too much—she could feel power draining out of her like a broken dam. Without Merrick's strength, she only had her own, and it didn't seem enough. She could see nothing, only hang on blindly. Awareness of her own body broke away, and she became a feather in a screaming storm. Something broke in her—she could actually hear it like a sinew snapping. What it was she could not tell, but Sorcha was overwhelmed.

The ground appeared from somewhere, smashing into her, but there was no pain. However, Deacon Faris still held the rune tight, though her Gauntlet was trapped and spread wide.

When the spectyrs took Hatipai's godhood, they vanished into the Otherside, filled with their own satisfaction. The goddess was no longer a lovely, golden creature but a snarling, snapping monster with the long snout of a wolf and baleful, red eyes. It loomed over the fallen Deacon, but she could only see it from one eye. Her head wouldn't move to give her a better view of her oncoming killer. Unable to control any part of her body, she was restricted to what she could see from her place on the floor.

Sorcha heard the crowd scream, their voices mingling into

a tangled web of horror and shock, and then the sound of running feet made the Temple ring.

The Deacon's eyes flicked in the other direction, catching sight of the Grand Duchess. Zofiya, her face showing her own distress, but still she somehow managed to see what needed to be done. With her white robe streaming behind her, she ran to Raed. She'd just seen her goddess stripped of illusion—and the Grand Duchess saw their only chance. In Vermillion she had seen the Beast—she knew its power. So she yanked the string of weirstones from around Raed's wrists, freeing him from the dreadful machine, and then staggered back.

It was a good thing she did, because the Young Pretender was not there for long. His flesh bloomed with the Curse, and the great lion was born, enraged and ready for revenge. He sprang up, snarling, and broke his remaining bonds in an instant.

Despite what he was, the Deacon lying on the floor could not deny the beauty of the Beast. The scene wavered before Sorcha, but she held on. She wanted to see the end. The rune finally faded from her Gauntlet, but her eyes still let her see the moment when the Rossin fell on Hatipai and with evident satisfaction tore her apart.

Somehow it was done, but Sorcha had no time to celebrate. She was so tired, so alone, and nothing moved when she commanded it to. Raed was alive, Hatipai fed into the maw of the Rossin, and soon, very soon, Merrick would come for her. Now if only her body would move . . . everything would be all right. She should have been afraid but found she was not.

Deacon Sorcha Faris abandoned herself. It felt like the best thing to do.

→ THIRTY →

Birthing Sorrow

Merrick didn't wait for Captain Revele to moor her vessel. He scrambled to the swing device and had himself cranked swiftly down to the desert. The Bond told him Sorcha was alive but also that something was terribly wrong. His throat was tight and his breathing echoed in his head as he ran toward the Temple.

People were streaming out of the building, sobbing and wailing. Many ran wild off into the desert, tearing their hair, while others looked stunned and simply knelt in the sand with faces stripped of any emotion.

Merrick knew immediately nothing would ever be the same in Chioma again. His mind whirled and his Center flickered lightly across the heaving mass of people, searching for his own people in the crowd. He found Raed, Sorcha and the fiery spark of Zofiya—which he recognized—but he couldn't find Onika anywhere.

Merrick stopped for a second and wondered how he would tell his mother. It wasn't unexpected, but it wouldn't be any easier because of that. The Deacon had studied the political struggles of Arkaym, but how they would affect her and his unborn half brother was impossible to tell. The young Deacon's head was full of so many whirling possibilities that it was hard to nail down any fact in those terrifying moments.

The crowd was lost, struggling—not the mob they had been in the city—and thankfully that made it easier for him to reach the Temple steps. Merrick had just put his foot on the first one when Raed appeared at the top. At his side was the Grand Duchess Zofiya—though looking like he had ever seen her; she was out of uniform, her dark hair wild and tangled, and most shocking of all, she was sobbing.

Yet even this sight could not hold him for long, because something even more horrifying filled his vision. In Raed's arms was Sorcha, her Gauntlets still on, but held awkwardly before her so they did not touch the Young Pretender. He need not have bothered—one glance said the runes were burned out and the leather destroyed. However, she was alive; her partner knew that instantly. As he darted up the remaining stairs to her, he fully grasped the damage. Guilt and grief washed over him.

"She won't answer me," Raed whispered. The other clue that something had gone terribly awry was the fact that he was wearing Sorcha's cloak and was completely naked under it.

As Merrick pushed his partner's hair out of her face and directed his Center upon her, he muttered, "How many died in there?"

The Young Pretender swallowed. "Under the Rossin's claws, just Hatipai—but . . ." His gaze drifted out to the sand. "More may follow."

That comment passed over and through Merrick as his fears were realized, and the full impact of his lie to his partner was now revealed. "I'm sorry, Sorcha." And he was—more deeply than he could ever say. In all his years in training, he could never have imagined having to choose between his mother and his Active. Merrick felt guilt begin to settle on him. The younger Deacon pressed his teeth together so tightly his jaw ached.

"What is wrong with Deacon Faris?" Zofiya asked, seeming to gather up some of her control while brushing tears from her cheeks.

"She went too far," Merrick replied, his tone as heavy as the reality he conveyed. He'd seen Deacons who had lost partners, read the reports, as well as spent a year as an Initiate caring for those in the infirmary. "Without me she could not tell when to stop, where to strike, which rune to use." He paused, swallowed and, not daring to look up at the Grand Duchess or the Young Pretender, instead he muttered, "I must get her back to the Mother Abbey as quickly as possible. They have the best chance to bring her back."

"Why weren't you there to help her?" Raed roared, his rage sudden, violent and uncharacteristic.

The Deacon was so full of guilt that it easily turned to anger. Defenses were up, and Merrick for once was not backing down. He was done being the diplomat—the quiet one who always took the abuse. He might have failed Sorcha—but they were only in Chioma in the first place because of Raed. They could be safely back in Vermillion right now; bored, perhaps, but safe. Sorcha had risked everything both of them had to save this man.

"Give her to me," the Deacon shouted back, his face only inches from the Young Pretender's. "Give her to me if you have any feelings for her at all. Only the Order can save her now. You've done enough!"

Raed's fingers tightened around Sorcha, his lips pressed together in a white line. For a second Merrick thought that he might try to run into the desert with her or drop her entirely and lash out.

"By the Blood, you better save her!" Raed spat and then handed her into her partner's arms.

A dozen Imperial marines had disembarked from the *Summer Hawk* and now pounded up the steps. They paused on seeing their commander in chief in such flimsy attire but snapped to attention.

"Take the Honored Deacon to the dirigible," she ordered as sharply as if she were in uniform. "We're returning to Vermillion immediately."

They gently took Sorcha from Merrick and followed after the Grand Duchess as she made her halting way toward the vessel. Her gait was painful but still proud.

Seeing the pain in Raed's eyes as he watched Sorcha going away from him, Merrick felt a stab of sympathy. This was a terrible situation for all of them. If he paused to make a list of all the terrible things that had happened, Merrick felt he might not make it back to the airship.

"Come with us." He touched the Prince's shoulder. "I know Vermillion is dangerous, but we have the Grand Duchess to vouch for you, and . . ."

"I cannot." The Young Pretender's face closed, his eyes hard as green agate. It was not an expression that Merrick was used to seeing on the face of the usually jovial Raed. He felt along the Bond, but all he found was a deep pit of pain past which nothing else could be discerned. The Rossin, who had fed deeper than he ever had on the power of Hatipai, was hidden and hibernating. This pain then belonged entirely to his host.

Merrick was suddenly embarrassed that he had raged at Raed. Something had happened to him in the desert, something he would not share. The young Deacon tried to make amends. "Sorcha cares about you—you must know that, Raed. She came all this way for you. Would you not see her well again? I know your presence would help her."

Raed swallowed hard, and his voice came out tight and low. "We only seem to ever meet in danger, Merrick; brief moments we snatch out of the mouth of peril. It isn't real, and my life is far too tangled for it to ever be. I would have her be well, but I cannot come with you. I have . . . business to attend to."

"Business?" Something tasted wrong in that statement. The Deacon could feel this old and painful thing turning within the other man, eating him up with grief, guilt and loss.

Yet he would not share it. His hand now fell on Merrick's shoulder. "I cannot tell you some things. Our three lives are too different for that. But if she—" Raed caught himself, and went on more strongly. "When she gets better, tell her what I have said. Tell her to forget me."

By the Bones, Raed Rossin, the Young Pretender, really was falling in love with Sorcha. The Bond told the young Deacon as much, but not why he would deny it.

Merrick, despite everything, smiled slightly. It was so wildly improbable. But then he thought of Nynnia, and how even in the dark there was always hope. If he could find her across time and death, then perhaps there was a chance for Sorcha and Raed.

"I will tell her you sent her to safety." He embraced the Young Pretender. The other man stiffened in the brief hug. "If you want to say hurtful things to her, then you'll just have to say them to her face." He pushed back and gave Raed a wry look. "And if you can do that, then you are a braver man than I. Look after yourself, Raed. I hope your 'business' is finished to your satisfaction."

A flicker of pain passed over Raed's face, and he ducked his head. "So do I."

As Merrick walked back to the *Summer Hawk*, he wondered what that meant. Yet, as bound as they were to one another, he and Sorcha were Deacons, and Raed would always be a threat to the throne they served.

He climbed back onto the dirigible and saw Sorcha's limp form being carried into one of the cabins. Merrick would have followed, but he remembered his other duty.

It seemed he was too late. Zofiya was talking to his mother in the shadow of the cabin. This was not how he would have had her told about Onika's death. The grieving woman's lips were pressed together in a tight, white line, her eyes crowded with tears, and her hands around her full belly. Her son could only imagine what fears and pains were going through her at this moment. The Grand Duchess, though, did have an arm around the other woman's shoulders. It was a touch of compassion Merrick would never have expected from her.

When they faced him, he realized how alike they were: beautiful women of power, used to being in control, able to stand firm against the winds of fate. He was proud to call one of them Mother. She had survived the gruesome death of his father—she would survive this.

"Your mother is returning with us to Vermillion." Zofiya had regained her Imperial tone.

"I wanted to have the baby in Chioma," Japhne said in a low voice that threatened to break, "but the Grand Duchess has pointed out that she and these troops cannot guarantee the little one's safety." She raised her head and looked at Merrick steadily. "I will have the boy in Vermillion, but then we will return immediately to secure his place as ruler of Chioma."

What could he say? He was a Deacon, and these women were stronger and more powerful in matters of state than he could ever dream of being. So he took Japhne's hands. "I just want you to be safe, Mother."

She brushed tears out of her eyes and stared at him bleakly. "Where are we ever safe in this world? Safety is just an illusion."

Mother and son stood still for a long moment. Beneath their feet the *Summer Hawk* shifted, lifting into the skies, the sailors around them running to their stations. It was Zofiya who broke the silence. "What is not an illusion, Lady Japhne, is the power of my brother. We will ensure your unborn son's future with a strong Imperial hand. Never fear."

"And what of the people of Chioma?" Merrick straightened, no longer afraid in the presence of the Grand Duchess. "Until your strong Imperial hand descends to bring order, what will they do?"

Zofiya's face betrayed nothing, but her voice was flat and grim. "They will have to make do as best they can. They did, after all, bring much of this chaos down on themselves."

He did not need to be a Sensitive to know there was no point arguing with her. Zofiya looked as set as a statue, and despite everything Merrick had seen, he felt sorry for her. "And what of you, Grand Duchess?"

Her eyes dropped away, but her voice was strong and clear. "It has all changed for me, Deacon. And I see, finally, the truth of many things—including myself."

Her eyes met his, and they were not sad. A Sensitive's peculiar talents told Merrick she had spent a long time looking after her brother, and yet only now did she understand her own value. What the Grand Duchess Zofiya would do with that knowledge was another question altogether.

Before the Deacon could see further into her, she turned on her heel and strode aft toward her troops.

Merrick watched her go but wrapped his arms around his mother. She hugged him tightly, her breathing unsteady but the tears still held back. He kissed the top of her head. "It'll be all right, Mother—I'll make it all right."

People always thought his partner was the most determined one—however, he would show them all. Merrick would take his mother to Vermillion and see his new brother born. Then he would get Sorcha well, so that she could once again bless him with her certain prickly charm. He needed that in his life.

Merrick decided that as long as he made those things

happen, then everything else could take care of itself. The Empire and the world owed Deacons Faris and Chambers that much. It was time to rest for a while and regain strength in the arms of the Order—then once more they could both begin setting the world to rights. Merrick was sure Sorcha wouldn't have it any other way.

ABOUT THE AUTHOR

Born in New Zealand, **Philippa Ballantine** has always had her head in a book. A corporate librarian for thirteen years, she has a bachelor of arts in English and a bachelor of applied science in library and information science. She is New Zealand's first podcast novelist, and she has produced four podiobooks. Many of these have been short-listed for the Parsec Award, and she has won a Sir Julius Vogel Award. She is also the coauthor of the Ministry of Peculiar Occurrences novels with Tee Morris. Philippa is currently in the United States, where her two Siberian cats, Sebastian and Viola, make sure she stays out of trouble. Visit her website at www.pjballantine.com.